B

A short, thick guy with a scar traversing his cheek steps into the doorway, his hand ominously held behind his back so I can't see its contents. He eyes me critically, but my boyish grin and hands on hips disarm caution. He shoves something in the belt at his back; then he goes for the box of chicken. I could take him as he passes, but the Mac is still within reach of Mama, and by the casual way she was holding it as intimately as she might one of her children, I'm afraid she knows how to use it. I sure as hell don't want bullets spraying around a room full of *muchachos*.

As suspected, shoved in his belt at the small of his back is a heavy long-barreled Ruger Blackhawk, probably a .44.

With my right hand, I reach under my loose coat and slip my shiny new .45 out of the belt holster at the small of my back, at the same time, without taking my eyes off Sancho, stepping over and grabbing up the Mac with my left, and shoving it under the couch.

In two steps I'm at Sancho's back and grab his Blackhawk the same time as I shove the muzzle of the .45 against the back of his head.

BOOK YOUR PLACE ON OUR WEBSITE AND MAKE THE READING CONNECTION!

We've created a customized website just for our very special readers, where you can get the inside scoop on everything that's going on with Zebra, Pinnacle and Kensington books.

When you come online, you'll have the exciting opportunity to:

- View covers of upcoming books
- Read sample chapters
- Learn about our future publishing schedule (listed by publication month *and author*)
- Find out when your favorite authors will be visiting a city near you
- Search for and order backlist books from our online catalog
- Check out author bios and background information
- Send e-mail to your favorite authors
- Meet the Kensington staff online
- Join us in weekly chats with authors, readers and other guests
- Get writing guidelines
- AND MUCH MORE!

Visit our website at
http://www.kensingtonbooks.com

BULLET BLUES

BOB BURTON

PINNACLE BOOKS
Kensington Publishing Corp.
http://www.kensingtonbooks.com

PINNACLE BOOKS are published by

Kensington Publishing Corp.
850 Third Avenue
New York, NY 10022

Copyright © 2004 by Bob Burton and Larry J. Martin

All rights reserved. No part of this book may be reproduced in any form or by any means without the prior written consent of the Publisher, excepting brief quotes used in reviews.

If you purchased this book without a cover, you should be aware that this book is stolen property. It was reported as "unsold and destroyed" to the Publisher and neither the Author nor the Publisher has received any payment for this "stripped book."

This novel is a work of fiction. Names, characters, places, and incidents are either the product of the author's imagination, or used fictitiously. Any resemblance to actual persons, living or dead, or events is entirely coincidental.

All Kensington Titles, Imprints, and Distributed Lines are available at special quantity discounts for bulk purchases for sales promotions, premiums, fund-raising, and educational or institutional use. Special book excerpts or customized printings can also be created to fit specific needs. For details, write or phone the office of the Kensington special sales manager: Kensington Publishing Corp., 850 Third Avenue, New York, NY 10022, attn: Special Sales Department, Phone: 1-800-221-2647.

Pinnacle and the P logo Reg. U.S. Pat. & TM Off.

First Pinnacle Printing: November 2004

10 9 8 7 6 5 4 3 2 1

Printed in the United States of America

Prologue

She's a big woman who obviously uses real lard in her beans and tortillas. I'd guess she's originally from somewhere in Central America as she's got that dusky black-brown skin that says mestizo, says part Spanish and native, part black.

Cuddled in her left arm suckling her right breast—a pendulous affair that would appear able to feed quintuplets with no strain—is a chubby-cheeked gurgling infant with eyes black as a raven's wing.

That's the good news. The bad is the Mac-10 fully automatic pistol hanging loosely in her right hand. She has stepped a half dozen paces back from the door after peering through the peephole, unlocking it, and yelling, "Come in."

The breast, I notice demurely as it's only partially covered with a diaper draped over her shoulder, has been strained with not only its own weight, but the load of a quart of mother's milk many times before, as it's striated with stretch marks. These merit badges of motherhood testify that the rest of the kids clamoring around a little living room scattered with trash and toys are surely hers.

Dirty diapers are piled on a hamper in a corner, and the odor of them does not add to the cheerful domesticity of the scene.

She's using the Mac to point with, which is a little disconcerting, to say the least.

Of course, who would shoot a guy wearing a chicken hat with bubble eyes and a silly plastic beak hanging over his forehead, his arms loaded with a pizza box topped with a smaller box of a dozen pieces of Smiling Sam the Chicken Man's crispy best? My sparkling white coat with red epaulets is emblazoned with an embroidered smiling rooster. Hat and coat set me back twenty bucks when one of the harbor bums who hangs near where I live in Santa Barbara Harbor was canned from Smiling Sam's.

"Hey, I'm just delivering here," I say, with my best worried but still boyish grin.

"So, I didn't order no pizza," she says, looking puzzled. This woman looks as if she might be intellectually stumped by "good morning," but the Mac makes her considerably more imposing.

There's rap music emanating from the bedroom, and the rest of the kids are gathered in a semicircle on the floor, glued to Spanish-language cartoons on a little TV, the thing turned up to a *SpongeBob SquarePants* shrill. So we're both having to talk a little loudly.

"Got chicken too," I say, then the smile fades to a worried frown. "You always come to the door with a cannon in your hand?"

"*Sí*, tough neighborhood," she mumbles, then ignores me and yells over her shoulder. "Hey, *vato*. Hey, Sunny, you order a pizza and some chicken? I ain't paying for this." She glances back at me hopefully. "You guys take food stamps?"

There's no answer from Sunny, only the sound of rap thumping with a wall-shaking cadence from the bedroom. As I've done my homework, I know that Sancho Tovar is called Sunny, and Sunny has skipped a twenty-five-thousand-dollar bail bond. He's a failure to appear, an FTA for the third time, and worth five grand to your friendly bail enforcement officer, me, if delivered to the local lockup. It costs the bondsman a little more to have me go after a known felon, a two-time loser, and into this kind of neighborhood, where housewives go armed like a marine-recon force team.

"No, ma'am. Sorry. We're not equipped to take food stamps. You're making the chicken man real nervous with that firearm. Could you put it away, please?"

She laughs, steps back, and drops the Mac on a gold crushed velvet couch that sags in the middle, a little like its owner. A sad-eyed Jesus on black velvet over the couch does not look kindly upon the scene. But she's a thoughtful mom, and yells at the kids, "*Mi hijos,* don't touch the *pistola.*"

"I'll tell you what, ma'am," I say with a serious glance at the kids. "Your babies look like they could use a treat. Somebody probably pulled a fast one on me." I laugh. "Kids like to order stuff from take-out places, then try to knock over the truck while you're inside a building like this looking for some bullshit apartment number." I set the pizza and chicken on a coffee table littered with Spanish magazines. "How about I just give you guys these eats?"

She grins wide enough that I almost feel guilty for running down her old man, who has boosted a half dozen cars since he was bailed. He's Santa Ana's most wanted man, if you happen to be a Toyota Camry owner—this year's favorite among car boosters. She quickly sets the baby in a stroller and goes for the chicken, trying to beat the four other kids to the best parts.

She slaps the hand of the oldest one, an angelic seven or so. "Maria, you *cerdo poqueto,* don't touch that thigh. Sunny gets the thigh."

A short thick guy with a scar traversing his cheek steps into the doorway, his hand ominously held behind his back so I can't see its contents. He eyes me critically, but my boyish grin and hands on hips disarms caution. He shoves something in the belt at his back, then he goes for the box of chicken. I could take him as he passes, but the Mac is still within reach of Mama, and by the casual way she was holding it as intimately as she might one of her children, I'm afraid she knows how to use it. I sure as hell don't want bullets spraying around a roomful of *muchachos*.

As suspected, shoved in his belt at the small of his back is a heavy long-barreled Ruger Blackhawk, probably a .44. The weapon of choice for Dirty Harry, and I guess now for Dirty Juan, Dirty Paco, and for sure for Dirty Sancho.

With my right hand, I reach under my loose coat and slip my shiny new .45 out of the belt holster at the small of my back, at the same time, without taking my eyes off Sancho, stepping over and grabbing up the Mac with my left and shoving it under the couch.

Sunny and Mama are so engrossed with the chicken and pizza, they don't even notice. In two steps I'm at Sancho's back and grab his Blackhawk the same time as I shove the muzzle of the .45 against the back of his head, just as he crunches down on a fat chicken thigh. He stops in midbite.

"You're under arrest, Sunny," I say in a soothing tone. Don't want to upset the kiddies.

"Motherfucker," he mumbles, his mouth full.

Mama begins to scream obscenities at the top of her lungs, her eyes searching for the Mac, which has disappeared.

"On your face, Sunny," I say. I'm shoving the muzzle so hard into the back of his head, he has no trouble going forward to his knees, then to his face. "Hands behind you," I command, but I'm watching the woman. I put a booted foot on the back of his thick neck, my gun leveled in the small of his back, as I speak to the woman. "You take the kids into the bedroom and close the door. Don't open it again for fifteen minutes. Do you understand?"

"*Comprendo*," she says, but it's through a curled lip, and I don't trust her. She does snatch up the baby and herds the others into the bedroom, slamming the door with a force that reverberates through the room.

I can see Sunny's eyes working the room, even flat on his belly with my heel grinding into his neck, and discourage him. "Sunny, you make a move and I'll blow your spine in half and you'll be crapping in a bag the rest of your life, if you live. A little jail time's better . . . ."

Stepping back, I fish the cuffs out of their leather holder and in short order have him hooked up and on his feet. I shove him face-first into a corner, commanding him in my limited *español*, "*No movimiento*," not to move. Then I go back and reach under the couch and retrieve the Mac to add to my collection.

In moments I've got him loaded into the backseat of my oatmeal Chevy and blow the horn; in seconds Iver, my black compadre, has joined up. He was waiting at the bottom of a fire escape in the alley behind the building, just in case Sunny didn't buy the Sam the Chicken Man bit and tried to slip out as I was banging on the front door.

Iver loads up beside Sunny in the back, and we're off on our way to the Santa Ana lockup.

We've only gone a few blocks, when I hear Iver's deep laugh.

"What?" I ask.

"You gonna scratch and peck your way into the jailhouse, chicken man?"

"Chicken shit, not chicken man," Sunny mumbles as I snatch the silly beaked hat off my head.

But he's easily ignored as I'm a happy camper—the rent and phone bills are paid for another month, and there's enough left over for a couple of martinis at Lucky's.

Another day, another hard-earned buck.

Chapter One

Grief is a funny thing.
And that, of course, is a bit oxymoronic, much like jumbo shrimp, resident alien, passive aggressive, act naturally; or in my business, found missing.

True grief manifests itself, early on in most of us, by our enwrapping ourselves in our arms, bending double, and splattering the floor with teardrops. In the case of the more demonstrable you might add wailing to the mix.

Not, however, in my old friend Mason Fredrich.

Mason, for the first couple of months, maintained his smile and gregarious manner with slaps on the back and encouragement that, yes, June would show up. Not June the month, but June his wife of a dozen years. A marriage so apparently happy it made others uncomfortable as the two of them clung inseparable and giggled like schoolkids, their smiles only fading when momentarily apart.

In Mason, grief was insipid. It descended upon him slowly, like a tapeworm, until if you pierced his formerly tan and healthy hide, which over the past year had gone placid, you felt as if you'd be sprayed with pus before the lack of it revealed a palled pulsating worm silently feasting on now feckless flesh. A vital outgoing human slowly subsiding to a cloistral chrysalis where a man had been. Previously looking ten years younger than his fifty, he now appeared twenty years older.

I'd never seen such a change in a person.

When he came to me on my boat, directly from being bailed from the Santa Barbara County Jail, it was apparent he'd lost thirty or more pounds. His Armani suit hung on his frame almost as if it graced a coatrack in the hall, his eyes, formerly flashing with intermittent bursts of joy, stared jaundiced, hollow, and slaked with remorse. I read in yesterday's *Santa Barbara News-Press* about his arrest the day before that, and, at the time, had to smile, if tightly, at the ludicrousness of that action by the Santa Barbara County District Attorney. Another oxymoron, an amusing arrest. But Mason was the last guy on earth whom I'd picture killing his wife.

Not withstanding the fact he is an old friend, how could I say no to a request from someone so blatantly pitiful? I couldn't, and didn't.

I will find her, if she's to be found. Alive, if the good Lord wills it.

Being in the bail enforcement business brings you all sorts of opportunities, mostly recoveries of other sorts, and at the moment, besides a list of Failures-to-Appear, I am retained to recover a bichon frise. That sounds very impressive, as if it were a rare piece of art, but in fact, that's a dog, if you can call a slavering puffball a dog. A bit of living, breathing fluff, but still chattel, which the court ordered to remain with the male side of a rather nasty divorce . . . it doesn't take a Sherlock to figure who might be the dirty dognapper. Futa, my ten-pound Siamese, yowled with utter prejudicial disdain when I accepted that particular assignment—I had thought better of him.

My second current non-FTA assignment is the recovery of a Benetti. Now, this is a piece of art, albeit an eighty-eight-foot one. An Italian-made yacht with transatlantic range, which was purloined from a gentleman who divides his time between Santa Barbara's neighboring Montecito, Palm Beach, and Costa Rica.

Why a lapdog might be worth a ten-grand recovery fee is a little beyond my ken—even though his master's divorce settlement was several million—but it's easy to deduce why an eighty-eight-foot, twin-diesel Italian masterpiece might be worth a cool hundred thou to the party who recovered her. And I plan that party to be Dev Shannon, my father's best-looking and, of course, only son. Even though I suspect it was stolen by some friends—no, acquaintances—whom I know from harbor nightlife.

Mason and I didn't talk money, and unless helping him means I incur a lot of out-of-pocket expense, we won't . . . if I have anything to say about it.

For June also was, and I hope still is, a friend of mine.

In normal circumstance, the above would constitute a full plate, and would consume my total attention and effort; however, there is one other small item that's distracting.

Someone's trying to kill me.

There's nothing like an early morning jog, but not through a minefield.

The Santa Barbara coast runs east and west, and Leadbetter Beach, where I usually jog, is just west of the marina, where I live. If I jog up to Shoreline Drive—Cabrillo changes to Shoreline just at the marina—I can also run through a great city park with some of those beautiful mature trees for which the city is so famous. But this morning I decided to jump the low wall at the Santa Barbara Yacht Club, the closest harbor complex building to the open sea, which gets me right to the sand.

I'm feeling fairly clever about my choice of hometowns. Where else could you jog on the beach in your swim trunks, a T-shirt, and tennis shoes in November?

I only run a quarter mile, with the gentle breaking waves to my left and the Santa Barbara City College athletic field off to my right across Shoreline Drive, when I feel the slap of a very close bullet. There's nothing quite like a bullet traveling at Mach 5 or so very close to your face. The realization that you are inches, maybe millimeters, from sure death doesn't take long to register, in fact milliseconds. I stay as low as possible, still moving as quickly as possible, until I am in the cover of a pile of sand. Lying on my back watching the big California gulls sweep overhead would normally be relaxing. Of course having to cross fifty yards of sand before I reach the first real cover chills that feeling somewhat. My heart's pounding so hard I can feel it in my temples, and it's not from the sprint to cover or the jog. I lie quiet for a long time, but it's hard to enjoy the silence when every muscle in your body is tensed as if ligaments are about to rip loose from bone. I wait a long while before I sprint the fifty yards to the next cover, and then have to try and disappear behind palm trees spaced fifty feet apart. I feel as if I were on Iwo Jima as I make my way back to the harbor.

It takes me a while to collect myself after I reach my boat, *Aces n' Eights*. I call the SB police, as it would be odd not to report the shot, and they send a covey of officers right over—three squad cars show up in the marina parking area, including a plainclothes car with a pair of detectives. I have to meet them at the entrance to the marina as the gate precludes easy access, and take a quick ride with the dicks to the spot. They, of course, think I'm a little nuts as another group of officers did when I reported the first shot, but I've done my civic duty.

As no one else reported a gunshot, I think they're beginning to think I'm a headline seeker.

I'm a little pissed when I return to the boat, but I know how to relax.

My adrenaline's still banging around in my bloodstream, and I'm pleased to be belowdecks—out of the line of fire. But I won't let some asshole stop my life.

You wouldn't think that an old boy who hauls skips to jail for a living would be domestic by nature, but I do enjoy cooking. With my being single and loving to eat, it's a natural transgression, and a survival tactic, to learn some culinary arts. It relaxes me, and God knows I need relaxing at the moment. Cooking has served me well for twenty of my thirty-five years. It's a common notion that the way to a man's heart is through his stomach, but the fact is, it's not a gender thing. The way to a woman's heart, and upon some occasion other equally intimate spots, is via the same route. Almost as important as a compliment or six, or a cocktail or six, or both, is a fine meal, lovingly prepared, beautifully presented, and delicious. Food and drink is next to breathing as a necessity, and is sensuous to the max.

And cooking truly relaxes me, particularly after being shot at with a high-powered rifle for the second time in as many weeks.

At the moment, tonight's menu, at least the *Aces n' Eights* portion, is limited. Pug, my old man, has elected to have his birthday dinner at our favorite harbor joint, Brophy's. I'm merely baking a birthday cake, not for a beautiful female, which would be more the norm, but for my father. What beautiful and intelligent woman would favor banana cake with orange frosting? Pug is sixty-two today, and as such is at the moment at the Social Security office to begin receiving his due from the federal government. If he wants a weirdo cake, he gets one from this loving son. He's received a retirement check from the city of Santa Barbara for the last seven years, having retired as a detective from that police force, which adversely affects the amount he'll receive from his Uncle Sam. But still, it's worth the trip.

My mom's been gone for almost ten years. At sixty-two, my old man was beyond surprising me, I had thought. I was wrong. I was more than surprised when I called to invite him to dinner, at a place of his choice. One of those choices being home-cooked using his favorite recipes aboard *Aces n' Eights,* my fifty-five-foot fishing trawler converted to yacht. The surprise was not that he chose Brophy's over my cooking one of his old favorites, but rather that he announced he was bringing a date—maybe enjoying Mom's old recipes with a new woman would give him indigestion. He enjoyed keeping me guessing as to who she might be. I hadn't known him to be interested in any other female since my mother passed. I was thinking about my mother when I called him, as she always made a big thing of birthdays, and more so because I was just looking at her beautiful handwriting as it was her handwritten recipe I followed—my father has never picked up a spatula in his life and her recipe box was about the only thing of hers I purloined after she passed, the only remembrance of her he would turn loose.

This evening should be interesting. A new woman. It makes me chuckle and cry at the same time.

There will be five of us for cake tonight, unless my fickle and beautiful private detective friend, occasional business associate, and even less occasional lover, joins us. Cynthia Proffer and I care for each other, in varying amounts at varying times. For the past month she's been among the missing, at least from making an appearance on *Aces n' Eights*. I called her office and left word about the dinner and post–Brophy's party on the boat. She might come, as the old man was always a favorite of hers; then again, she might not. She might be working, as both her job and mine require toil during the wee witching hours. If she comes, she might spend the night; most likely not. She's as unpredictable as the Santa Barbara weather is predictable—and right now the November-tenth afternoon is sixty-eight degrees and clear, as usual.

It should be a sin even living in Santa Barbara, and may be—but it's a longtime belief of mine that one should try never to be out of sight of palm trees, oceans, and martinis. I hope I'll have to wait five score or more to find out what St. Peter thinks of such easy living.

I'm pulling three cake pans out of the oven and setting them on a cooling rack, when I feel the telltale, if ever-so-slight, rock of a boarder. Futa, my ten-pound seal-point Siamese, has been directing the cake effort, and he, too, turns his attention to the gentle indicator of someone boarding. He cuts his dark ears and blue eyes toward the main salon. Even as heavy as *Aces n' Eights* is, I've learned to discern the slightest out-of-sync rock, and Futa's discerner works much better than mine.

Bail enforcement agents are sometimes not the most popular of a city's residents, so I'm always a little on the spooked side, even though I don't mess my own nest—I only work outside of Santa Barbara County. But, since I've had two sniper-style long-range shots taken at me while jogging the beach, I'm even more cautious than usual. Somehow the sound of a bullet cutting the air near one's head makes one a little more attuned to other strange noises. I palm my .38 Special and shove it into the tight waistband of my bathing suit, at the small of my back, before stepping out of the galley into the main salon.

The lady peering down the ladder at me is no one I know, but someone whose acquaintance I'm sure I'd like to make. I'm fickle that way, and have always had a soft spot—or maybe I should say a hard spot—for tall redheads with big brown eyes.

"Dev Shannon?"

"Yes, ma'am. And you're . . . ?"

"Sandra Bartlett . . . my friends call me Sandy."

I'm still a little on edge, but she certainly doesn't look like an assassin. She looks like a model out of the *Sports Illustrated* swimsuit edition. I should be more cautious under the circumstance, but find myself thinking with the little head. "Come on down, Sandy. Welcome aboard." As she does I study her. No telltale lumps or bumps say firearm.

She moves down the ladder facing me, with some confidence and dexterity, like an old salt, and climbs up on a stool at the chart table that doubles as desk. She's not in a bathing suit, but the tight white blouse is knotted just below generous breasts, and the red short shorts are just that. It's obvious to a trained eye like mine that she spends some time in the sun. Her skin is tan and flawless, except for a few freckles on nose and cheeks and a tiny rose tattooed on her left ankle, just above the line of her gleaming white running shoes and tasseled cutaway sock. And the single mole I can't help but notice as it's cuddled in abundant cleavage. Futa approves, as he strides over and leaps up on the chart table so she can scratch his ears.

"Great cat . . . yours?"

"I'm his would be a better statement. Dogs have owners, cats have staff."

She's got a great laugh.

"So, Sandy, what brings you to *Aces n' Eights*?"

"I heard you're the man in bail enforcement?"

"I am that Dev Shannon. Jump bail, I'm on your tail."

She closes the distance between us and sticks out her hand. The handshake is firm and confident. "Then I'm in the right place. I just took a National Institute of Bail Enforcement course, last weekend in Vegas, and I'm looking for a position."

A number of positions race through my mind as I ponder this circumstance. One of my hard and fast rules is not to mess with the help; of course that's been easy as I've never had female help other than my occasional associate, Cynthia, and she would be highly offended to be considered an "employee." I can't help but smile at the thought of "positions," and Sandy misunderstands the smirk.

Her brow furrows. "You find that funny?"

"No, no. I know some great women in the biz. You want a beer?"

"Glass of wine maybe."

"How did you get through the gate?" The master walkway into the marina has a card-activated lock.

"If I couldn't figure out how to get in a simple locked gate, you don't need me as help."

"True." And it's my turn to laugh.

I walk to the little under-counter fridge and pull out a pair of long-neck Coronas and pop the caps. "No wine aboard at the moment. I imagine you're the lime-in-the-Corona type?"

She sees the .38 jammed into the back of my suit. "You always carry a big gun in your bathing suit?"

I eye her, and she realizes what she's said. I laugh again. "Some things just can't be helped." Then ask again, "Lime?"

"Nope. No lime, no glass. The long neck fits the hand."

And a fine manicured hand it is. I liked her immediately from the brazen way she boarded the boat and stuck her hand out, and now I like her even better. I slip the .38 police special and flip it onto the counter behind me, out of her reach but easily within mine, smiling at her.

"You're not here to hold up the joint, so I guess I don't need this?"

"Hardly. Not that I couldn't use a little dough."

"I have no full-time employees," I caution, handing her the bottle.

She upends it and takes long swig as my phone goes off.

I check the caller ID and it's a call I've got to take. Sol

Greenberg is my biggest client, a bail bondsman from Van Nuys.

"Dev, my boy."

"What's shaking, Sol?"

"I've got a check kiter on the run. Sheila Chastine, out on twenty-five-grand bail. She's a pussycat, and I'd do it myself, but my grandson's bar mitzvah . . ."

"So, ten percent."

"I hate to bother you with such a piddling amount."

"Sol, for you . . ."

"You're a good boy, Devlin. I'll fax you the paperwork."

"I've got a full plate, Sol, but never too full for you." We hang up.

"So, anyway, I can work when there's work," she says, having the right answer.

"Mine is not a weekly paycheck kind of gig. This is not security-are-us. However, I get a lot of calls like that one. That's twenty-five hundred if I can pull it off."

"I've got a little put back. I can hang until something pops that takes a lady's touch."

Again, my thoughts are not pure, but I maintain, and instead of expressing the cheap sexual innuendo I'm thinking, I sigh. "Actually, I can't imagine hiring a woman to do the kind of rough-and-tumble I get tangled up with from time to time." At least that's what I say, but the fact is I'm just playing hard to get; 40 percent of all bonding agents are women. "I'm an old-fashioned kind of guy, and I hate to see women hurt."

She smiles, takes a sip, and gives me the once-over, over the neck of the Corona. She backhands away a bit of foam, then laughs. "I don't imagine you've gained the reputation you've got by using *nothing* but brawn . . . not that I can't hold my own in that department. I'll meet you on the shooting range any time you say, and . . ." She puts the beer down. In the narrow confines of my main salon, she steps forward, does a back bend, placing both hands flat on the floor behind her, then kicks over and lands softly on her feet. Although I'm sure the demo was to demonstrate limberness and dexterity, not sexuality, it worked overtime on the latter. Of course, her just sitting on the stool also did. She's sexy, and would be so in coveralls. She continues, without taking a heavy breath. "And I'm as tough as I am limber. Have you even considered that I can get information where you might get nothing but spit in your eye . . . and that I can walk into some places you can't, a lot of places, like a ladies' room? Do you have any idea what a woman can learn just while having her nails done? A beauty parlor is information central. Hell, man, you're only half a cupful without having a woman on your team."

I snicker, a little taken aback, my masculinity slightly challenged. "I do just fine."

"Half fine. I can add a lot. I know how women think." Then she gets a knowing twinkle in her eyes. "And can confuse the thinking of most men."

"Bull," I say, but I have no doubt she's right.

"No bull, big boy. I worked dispatch up in Sacramento for the sheriff, then worked the streets for a while. I did undercover for the narc unit and for sex crimes. Caught some interesting johns . . . an assemblyman and a judge . . . not that anything came of either one. I've paid my dues with ninety miles of bad road."

"So, what happened to that gig?"

She smiles and then the smile fades and the eyes cut away. She spins around a couple of times on the stool, and I can see the mind working like she's trying to decide. Then she zeroes those big eyes on me again and the sparkle has returned. "The State of California Commissioner of Insurance . . . a big dog in that town . . . wanted me fired."

"You too big a risk?" I ask, trying an insurance pun,

but don't let her answer and motion her to follow. "My cake is cool," I say, and head for the galley.

"Cool, as in neat? Cake?"

"Cake. Come on down while I lather her up."

She follows me and stands in the hatchway watching while I apply orange goo. There's not room for two in the galley.

"No frilly apron?" she asks, giving me a coy smile.

"I have a fine hand, thanks. Like the song, you want a man with a fine hand."

"That's a man with a slow hand."

"Oh, anyway, no apron required when there's no mess. Never a glitch with the butter knife."

She laughs, then continues the explanation. "Actually, it was the commissioner's wife who insisted I get the ax. Sac's a political town, and even the wives hold sway."

"Because you were getting something she thought belonged to her?"

The coy smile again. "That would be my business."

"You're the one applying for the position," I say. "Your business is my business if we team up." I top her coy smile with a knowing one.

"Live and learn." She shrugs. "No more married men in my life. I was on a special detail guarding him after he got some threats . . . insurance rates were going up. He wanted to make the special detail extra special, and did for a few months. He was a really good guy . . . at least I thought so for a while. That's when I decided to take up bail enforcement, and beat a trail out of Sac. You know Frank Flannigan?"

"In Sacramento?"

"That's the one and only Fatal Frank. You can call him and check me out. I helped Frank when I was in uniform . . . more than once. He offered me a spot there, but I wanted to get out of town."

I'm weakening. The good news is I do know and admire Frank. In fact, I was the one gave him the nickname Fatal Frank. The bad is if I let this lady team up with us, she's off the potential sack-time hit list if she's a coworker. I hate that part.

"I'll give Fatal a call. But that doesn't mean a thing. I got a group of guys I work with. I'm not saying you've got a Chinaman's chance to join up with us, but you do have a chance to join us for dinner. And for a piece of this ugly cake my old man loves after some good sea creatures at Brophy's."

"I don't do raw."

That breaks my heart. But she means fish. The phone rings, and it's Cedric, my computer guru who's working on my current three projects for me, working cyberspace to see what the computer turns up.

"Got some stuff on the Benetti and on the wayward pooch," he says.

"You're coming to dinner for the old man?" I ask.

"Wouldn't miss it. A comestible occasion is to my liking." Cedric never misses a chance to dazzle others with his vocabulary. I have no idea what comestible means, so I ignore it.

"Then let's talk there."

"The hound is probably basking in the Idaho sun, or I guess shivering in the snow this time of year," he says, always anxious to show off his deft use of the computer.

Sandy rises and holds up a finger. "You're busy. What time?" she asks.

"Hold on, Ced," I say, then cover the phone. "Seven, unless you want another beer before dinner."

"Wine, remember?"

She nods, spins on her heel, and I hear her escaping up the ladder. She's a woman of few words. When the business is done she's on about her business. I like that.

"Can't we do this at Brophy's?" To use a Cedric, he's overly loquacious, and my cake is languoring.

"You're busy scratching Futa's ears?" he asks.

"I was busy, but you've screwed that up. See you at supper."

"Hmmph," he says, but hangs up.

As soon as he does, the fax rings and begins chugging out the info on Sheila Chastine.

"You're a busy boy. That's a good thing," Sandy says, and continues up the ladder.

I watch her ascend the ladder and wish the journey was longer as it's a pleasant sight, and yell after her, "Seven."

She waves over her shoulder and is gone.

We'll see how Pug, Iver, and Cedric like her. I hope she wears long pants and a loose top, so they're not hypnotized like I've been the last few minutes.

I check out her booking information and photos. I can't seem to get Sol to use the e-mail and attach photos, and always have to rely on faxed poor-quality ones until a mail package arrives from him. He's archaic, like the old man. It seems Sheila is from Lancaster, California, northeast of L.A. And her next of kin, her mother, still lives there. I pick up the phone and call Harley Pinter. The bail enforcement biz is all contacts, and my Rolodex is my right arm. Many times I make a fee with merely a phone call, and would not be surprised if this is one of those times.

Harley answers and we agree on five hundred bucks if he picks her up and delivers her to the L.A. County Jail. It's good to have business chums . . . particularly those who weigh 280 pounds and would go after a grizzly bear with a switch. And Harley has a brain too, and won't get us into a civil suit.

Chapter Two

I'm early, in slacks and a Hawaiian shirt, seated at the bar sipping a Jack Daniels neat, but the old man's not far behind. He always did like a party.

I came early for a reason, a work reason, and have picked the bartender's brain about a number of the harbor types who've been missing from the scene, coincidentally for the same amount of time as has been the *Orion*, the yacht I've been retained to find. He fills me in on what he knows about Skip Hanson and his cohorts, which seems to be very little. Skip is an appropriate name under the potential circumstance. The most interesting thing I learn is harbor gossip about my client, Darwin Winston-Gray, and it's not complimentary. It would be nice if one only worked for good guys, but I've learned quickly that good guys are not the only ones willing to pay the big money. Winston-Gray is renowned as, to quote Tony, "a pure asshole who treats his employees like scum off the harbor bottom." I didn't exactly take a shine to the guy when I met him, but he could have been a lot worse, and of course he was trying to sell me on finding his prize possession. He's not loved by harbor employees, merchants, or vendors, and particularly not by bartenders . . . or so says Tony. I'll get some backup opinions, not that they will make any difference, so long as he pays up for yacht recovery. The only important thing is to determine that he's not a deadbeat.

"So, what's up with getting shot at again?" Pug asks, taking the stool next to me without even bothering with a hello. The old man is a half head shorter than my six-two, and built like a fireplug. And not long ago, was as solid as one. His hair is lighter than mine, I got Mom's Italian olive skin, but Pug's blue eyes.

"How'd you know?"

"I still got friends in the department. Maggie, the dispatcher, is an old bud of mine."

"Wish I knew," I say with a shrug. "I was jogging on Ledbetter Beach again, just after dawn. The beach was almost empty, and I felt the wind as a slug cut the air somewhere too damn close—"

"Sure it wasn't a bumblebee?"

I don't grace that with a reply, only a glare. "Then heard the report. He must have been firing from several hundred yards. Up the hill somewhere. I hauled ass to a mound of sand and hid out like a sand crab for several minutes, then sprinted over to Shoreline Drive and did the tree-to-tree, palm-to-palm, for a half mile . . . but this guy was too smart to shoot twice and give me a chance to peg his location. The good news is he's a lousy shot. The bad news is commuters look at you real strange as you're making your way down the road, scrambling from tree to tree."

"Or he was just trying to scare the hell out of you. Did you call the department?"

"Yes, I talked with a pair of dicks for a few minutes."

"And?"

"And they looked at me like I was nuts."

"Which detectives?"

"A couple of guys I don't know. I was pissed and purposely forgot their names. I would have pressed it, but then I'd have to spend several hours waiting for some guy while he's answering the phone and doodling when he should be taking notes. A guy who doesn't give a damn about anything except where the next donut's coming from."

"Jesus, what soured you this morning? They aren't that bad."

"Says you. You've been out of there for years. It's a new breed. The MTV generation in uniform."

"Now, that's an accurate statement. You'll find out how new in a few minutes."

I let that slide as he's looking way too smug. "I like your buddies in blue just fine, and even those who've graduated to cheap polyester suits. I'll get around to wising them up, but I had a cake to bake. Banana and orange frosting for the birthday boy."

He smiles. "Mom's recipe?"

"To a tee, or maybe better said, to a teaspoon."

But his smile again morphs to worry. "Who's got a hard-on for you this time?"

"Half the civilized world and most the uncivilized."

"Seriously?"

"Don't know; I've given it a lot of thought but don't have a clue."

"Dev, you can put off the first shot to somebody in a fit of anger . . . a condition that seems to affect most who've met you—"

"Ha, ha."

"But the second time someone tries to nail you . . . it seems like they're on a mission, and I'd be more than a little concerned."

I give him my best "no shit, Sherlock" look, but am interrupted before I can say it.

"What's up, Pug?" Tony, the bartender, asks.

"Not my income. Hell, you can't make but a few bucks more from outside sources if you draw your Social Security at sixty-two. They won't give you your own damn money back . . . got to wait to sixty-five."

Tony laughs. "Good, maybe they won't take so much

out of my next check to support you old codgers. You want a scotch?"

"Very funny." The old man gives him a hard look. "O'Doules," he growls, "and at that I'm celebrating."

"You got it." Tony moves away. He knows full well that the old man's a long-standing member of AA, and I don't think it's real funny him tempting the old man that way. I'll have a chat with him later. He was a little smart-ass when I questioned him about Skip Hanson, so he may have his hackles up about something. I plan to find out what, and put a stubby finger in his chest for hard-assing the old man. I'd wander down the bar and do it right now, but my cell phone is running over.

It's Harley Pinter. "The easiest five hundred I've made in weeks," he says.

"You got her cuffed?"

"In the backseat."

"Good man."

"I can't transport her to L.A., Dev," he says, and that's a bummer as I had presumed he would when I cut the deal with him.

"Take her to the local substation."

"Can't, I promised she'd go downtown."

"Then you'll have to settle for four hundred. I'll have to come over or send someone."

"If that's the way it has to be."

"Fair's fair."

"Okay, I'll hold on to her as long as I can. I told her she can stick with me, which she's agreed to do on her own, and I had her sign a statement to that effect, or I'll turn her in locally and they'll hold her for ten days before transporting her."

"Why didn't you turn her into the lockup right away?"

"She came to me, after hearing I was looking for her, but only with my promise that I'd transport her to sheriff headquarters. Seems she thinks she has enemies here with the local boys. She said she'd stick with me until one of you guys come and get her."

"Okay. Unusual, but it'll work."

"Call me again."

The easiest two grand I've made in weeks. I tell him we'll be over tomorrow to pick her up and transport her to L.A. and that I'll send his check as soon as I get mine, and business is done for the day.

The bar only has three patrons when I walk in, but it's filling quickly. Brophy's, my favorite seafood joint and one of the closer saloons to my slip, is one of a dozen or more businesses at Santa Barbara's five-hundred slip marina. It enjoys a great location on the second floor, with the bar facing windows that open onto a view of fishing boats, work boats, and a slew of fine pleasure craft. It's surrounded by a narrow deck on two sides, and the deck tables are normally full as the weather is normally wonderful. Santa Barbara's coastline faces south, an anomaly on the California coast and the reason it was picked as a harbor and mission location—her shoreline faces out of the weather.

Only one hundred of us privileged are granted immunity to live aboard harbor craft. In my case a privilege granted by slipping the former tenant a fat handful of Franklins. I'm tied at an end slip next to the channel. I like the remote location; there's little foot traffic and I can see damn near every boat entering and leaving the harbor for close inspection, if I'm interested.

"So," Pug asks, not wanting to drop the subject, "what are we gonna do about this shooter?"

"Maybe set him up. I jog, you and the guys are spotted along Shoreline so you can maybe peg where he's set up and shooting from?"

"Great idea, Einstein. That Desert Storm syndrome fried your brain. You do the shooting gallery duck bit, hoping the third time is not the charm?"

"All I got in Iraq was a snoot full of sand and my drawers full of sand fleas. Of course the heat might have fried my melon. I'm open to ideas."

"Bull. You didn't get those medals for killing sand fleas. Let's figure out who this guy is and why he wants to send you to Valhalla, without you painting a target on your sweatshirt."

"I was planning to jog in my running outfit with my Kevlar on underneath."

"That doesn't do much against a head shot, and that big head of yours would naturally be his best target."

"Very funny."

"Whassup?" Iver asks, having slipped up behind us, which at Iver's size takes some doing. Cedric is with him, but is staring off into space as usual, I'm sure contemplating some cyberspace computer problem. Iver and Cedric work for the old man aboard his fishing boat, the *Copper Glee*, a dive boat the old man bought after Mom died. He had another boat early on while he was still on the force, when I was in high school, but Mom made him sell it. She didn't like me diving, and liked less both of us being gone so much. I learned to dive aboard her, and went on to work for a commercial diving company, after a stint in Desert Storm as a recon force marine. After I was out, an accident while commercial diving that trapped me for twenty minutes while welding at two hundred feet got me a severe case of the bends, far-longer-lasting claustrophobia, and out of the diving biz. Which is fine, as I'm making as much dough in bail enforcement, and the sharks are closer to my size.

Iver is big, black, and granite hard. In fact, he looks like a Rodin sculpture. He's knotted with muscles, and not the Gold's Gym kind. His were come by honestly with hard work. Cedric is tall, blond, wiry, and tough enough in his stylish way—on first impression he comes across as the village idiot, or at least geek. But then you begin to realize he never forgets anything, has a photographic memory, and not being happy even with that, uses a computer as if he'd graduated from M.I.T., and in fact he didn't graduate from high school. His skills as a martial artist were demonstrated to me in a walnut orchard while face-to-face with some very bad boys, and I came to prize them. Both of these guys are smart as hell. Iver is street smart and worldly wise but so quiet you'd never know it, and so tough he'd fight a buzz saw and give it ten revolutions. Cedric's constantly talking enough for both of them. Google has come to be the bail enforcer's best friend, so Cedric's chatter is well worth putting up with. They and the old man, thirty years an investigator, make up my primary team when I need backup. It keeps us out of the bars during work time, except when often there on business, if not out of trouble.

My wannabe bail enforcement agent, redhead Sandy Bartlett, enters from the south door, spots me, and elbows her way down the bar, just as a beautiful brunette, an Oriental girl with skin as smooth as glass, enters from the north door, looks my way, and waves. My cup runeth over. But I don't recognize the second lady. I do manage to take my eyes off Sandy long enough to give the Oriental a curious smile.

As we're closer to the north, the beautiful brunette arrives first, extends her arms like she's gonna give me a big squeeze, then brushes by me and hugs the old man as if he were Daddy Warbucks. I hear her whisper, "Happy birthday, handsome."

"Jesus," I manage, just as Sandy arrives and extends a well-manicured hand. I shake, feeling a little slighted only getting a handshake, then she offers the hand to Iver.

"Hi, I'm Sandy," she says with a brilliant smile. Iver nods in his usual perfunctory manner.

"Evenin'," he manages. "Iver Jefferson."

She does the same to Cedric. "I'm Sandy."

"I'm just plain old dirty," he says with a slightly evil smirk. He never misses the chance to be a smart-ass.

"Okay, I'm Sandra," she says, with a laugh.

"Then I'm Cedric," he says.

"Okay, Dirty Cedric." She laughs again, turning to the old man, who sits on the stool with an arm encircling the beautiful Oriental, who I realize has eyes as lovely and sparkling and penetrating and jet-black as any I've ever seen. Could this be his date? I'm astonished, and envious.

"Sandy," she says again, extending her hand to Pug.

The old man, to his credit, rises and accepts the handshake. "Patrick Shannon, but my friends call me Pug."

"Pug then. Shannon? Any relation to this Shannon?" She winks at me.

"Don't claim him." He gives the brunette a squeeze, whom he still holds in an arm-around-the-shoulders iron grip. "This is Betty Ann Benson, everybody. *Detective* Betty Benson, to those of you who might be thinkin' of getting out of line."

It's my turn now to stand, and I do so and offer my name at the same time as both Iver and Cedric.

"Hold on," she says. "Iver, Cedrack—"

"Cedric," he corrects quickly. "My friends call me handsome, rich, and a gentleman who loves to be handcuffed."

"Well," Betty Ann says, not missing a beat, "I'd go for handsome, that's obvious."

"Don't go for rich, because that's a lie."

She laughs. She's a real politician and should go far in the department. Cedric is much less than handsome, with blond thinning hair, a crooked grin, and teeth that look as if he's been kicked by a mule.

"And you are?" she continues, extending a fine long-fingered hand, with perfect, appropriate, Chinese-red nails matching the lipstick.

"Devlin Shannon, my father's most handsome son."

"And only son," the old man adds. "And I'm not sure the mailman didn't visit while I was slaving away at work," and the table laughs.

Sandy takes the seat from which I rose, after I wave her there. She eyes Betty Ann. "How are you, Babs?"

"Great, Sandy."

Obviously they know each other. And I should have guessed the "Babs" with Betty Ann Benson being her handle, although I'd have guessed Betty Ann Lee or something far more exotic. I eye her closer and realize she's probably Eurasian: Oriental and European or American. Whatever the mix, it works.

"Let's eat," the old man says.

We sit, as the table's ready, we get the girls a drink, and Cedric rises.

"I want to offer a toast."

We all raise our glasses.

He clears his throat. "Just remember, if the world didn't suck, we'd all fall off." That gets a laugh, so he continues. "Now that we're about to eat, remember, brain cells come and brain cells go, but fat cells live forever."

"Boo," both girls say.

But he's undaunted. "Okay, okay, to Pug, who to all our great surprise has yet to be shot by a jealous husband."

"Sit down, Ced," I command, rising myself, and he does so, to my surprise. "To my old man, who's always had a lot on the ball, but is now too tired to bounce it."

"My ball equipment works fine, thank you, junior," he says, and I'm a little taken aback as I've seldom heard even a slightly off-color remark from my old man, particularly in front of the ladies.

Pug's crack draws a chuckle, and I quickly add, "If it weren't sentimental bunk, we'd all tell you how much we love you, but you'd probably try and arrest us."

I actually think for a nanosecond that he's going to tear

up; instead he gives us a snarling "right." And upends the O'Doule's bottle.

The evening is long and wet and the food is as wonderful as the conversation. By the time we make our way down the wharf to *Aces n' Eights*, I've learned that Pop and Babs are merely friends after she came to him checking on an old case, and that Sandy has applied to the Santa Barbara PD, who's not hiring at the moment. That makes Dev Shannon, manhunter, second choice, but that's okay, as I long ago learned that one can rise to the top.

It seems the two girls met at a criminology seminar somewhere, liked each other, and kept up the acquaintance. Babs is the reason Sandy came to Santa Barbara, and it was Pop who told Babs to tell Sandy to come see me. The world turns.

Cedric and I walk together back to the boat, and he fills me in on his day with Google, several questionable penetrations of other people's computers and cyberspace. I learn what he's gleaned: that the purloined pooch is probably in Coeur d' Alene, Idaho with Mama, who has gotten a house there, as part of her divorce settlement. That should be an easy snatch and grab for an obscene amount of money. I ask him to book me a cheap flight there. Pug overhears us and tells me he's got a good friend in the area, a retired Oxnard cop who's a member of the Renegade Pigs, and tells me to call him and he'll give me the guy's number so I can have him do a drive-by before I make the trip. As we're climbing onto the boat, Cedric clues me that the Benetti was last seen in Ensenada, Mexico, but has left and he's working on tracking her south. I'm sure the boat was out of the country before Darwin Winston-Gray knew she was missing.

I don't know why I always get involved in these out-of-the-country snatches, as it's dangerous as hell as other countries thumb their noses, and rightfully so, at our laws, as we do at theirs. One could find oneself hanging by one's thumbs, or worse, one thumb, in a foreign dungeon.

Futa, my seal-point Siamese, is perched on a deck-top ventilator surveying the harbor like Horatio Hornblower glassing for the French and greets us with a long yowl, piping us aboard. I'm happy to say, after going below for a quick inspection before my guests are aghast, he hasn't run his rough tongue over the cake, at least if he did he was clever enough not to leave tracks. I'm not sure I'm complimented that he disdained to do so.

I'm only a day away from beginning to investigate the matter of June Fredrich's disappearance and her husband's arrest, which is at the top of my list. I haven't mentioned it this evening, so I'm a little surprised when Detective Babs follows me down to stand in the opening to the galley and broaches the subject while I'm making coffee and cutting the banana orange concoction.

"I hear you're working with Mason Fredrich?" she says, a little too coyly and offhand.

"News travels fast," I say, not volunteering anything more.

"Then it's true?" she asks, her tone more serious.

I focus on those black eyes, now flat and centered on me like a pair of lasers. "True. So what?"

"So, he did it."

I smile. "Judge and jury, eh? I've known Mason a long time, Betty Ann."

"Babs, if you prefer. I would."

"Babs then. The last guy I'd suspect of murder is Mason, and the last woman I'd expect he'd kill is June. Besides, why the hell would he hire me to find her if he knows she'll be found dead?"

"Maybe he's convinced you won't find her, and hiring you is a good smokescreen. I'm telling you, he did it. I've known him a long time. Probably longer than you. He was a passionate but sometimes heinous man under all that smiling and slathering over her, and even more jealous than passionate . . . fanatical in his jealously, and even though those outside his house never saw it, incendiary in temper."

I choose to shine her rhetoric. "They only moved here five years ago. I knew them in Santa Monica."

"And I knew him long before that in La Jolla. He did it, Dev."

"You sound a lot like some dick that works for the PD and is as pigheaded and one-way as a train . . . . So, what's got you so convinced? And why are you so adamant?"

I guess I came on a little hard, as she flushes to a darker shade before she mutters, "June is . . . was . . . my sister."

Chapter Three

That revelation sets me back. I'm sure I'm looking a little confused.

"Yeah, I know. I'm Oriental and she's not. June is older, my half sister. Same dad, different moms."

I'm still a little astounded. "How come I never knew you?"

"We weren't close, in fact hadn't talked in years. Her old man, and mine, treated my mother badly. In fact, treated us all badly, and June worse than me. He was a pure unadulterated bastard. June stuck by the perverted prick. That's part of the reason June acted as badly as she did—"

"I liked June . . . like June. She never acted badly around me."

"You were a friend of Mason's first?"

"I was. But June—"

"For all he was, June respected Mason and would never insult him by coming on to you. June had problems you couldn't even guess about. You wanna have lunch tomorrow and talk about it? Maybe you'll give up on that prick and help me burn him, not that I'm gonna need much help."

"It's your case?"

"No. In fact I've been told to keep the hell out of it. I'm too close, of course, or so the chief says. But I'm not about to let it drop. I'll let the job drop first."

What do I have to lose? Knowing more about the SBPD's case will be to my advantage. Besides, I'm fascinated. "Okay, lunch ... on one condition, I won't show you mine unless you show me yours?"

"You wanna know what we've got on him, come to the arraignment."

I shrug. "So, no lunch?"

She hesitates for a long moment, weighing options. "Look, I'll tell you everything I can without getting my ... something in a wringer. How's that?"

"Okay, fair enough. But don't count on me giving up on Mason ... but sure. Name the place."

"You like the harbor. How about the Harbor Restaurant on the pier?" The Harbor has a nice second-story deck overlooking the marina. And good food.

"I'll be there at noon."

"Good, now let's have some cake and talk about something else. I don't want to darken your dad's day with downer stuff."

I don't agree with her about Mason, but I can't help but like her.

I notice that Sandy's worked the room. I told her she'd have to be accepted by "my team" and she's taken it to heart, spending time charming, and I'm sure impressing, Iver, Cedric, and Pug. I'm really attracted to this woman, and secretly hope she'll get on with the Santa Barbara PD and thus become fair game.

She and Babs leave together, but not until Sandy gives me a phone number and instructions to call her in the morning, so I decide to settle the matter then and there. "Hey, guys, I guess you got the drift that Sandy wants to come aboard in more ways than just having cake."

"So," Cedric says, "we could use someone with a modicum of charm. God knows, as she so aptly pointed out, she can go where we might fear to tread, and sure as hell might be unwelcome."

"Iver?" I ask.

"Seems like a good lady to me, and one who could hold up her end."

"Pug?"

He shrugs, but his brow, above ice-blue eyes, is furrowed deeply in a manner that always makes me think of train tracks. His thinking process is going somewhere. "She's smart, she's fit, which may be a distraction to you."

"Not if she's on the team," I say adamantly, but can see he's not convinced. I don't know if it's a father or cop thing, but Pug enjoys presuming I'm guilty.

"But she's a woman. You've dragged us through some deep ka-ka. You sure you want to do that to a lady like Sandy? She could end up with scars makeup won't cover, or even worse."

Cedric gets his pound of flesh before I can respond. "It's true, Devlin. Your concupiscence could interfere—"

"That means?"

"Urge to merge." He laughs.

I ignore him and direct my response to Pug. "I pointed out to her that she could get in trouble, and that trouble is our middle name. She shrugged it off. She's been a cop, she's worked narc and sex crimes. She's had to have seen it all and been at risk. And she and Cedric . . . Cedric upon occasion . . . make good sense: she can go places we can't. Besides, she'll probably go with SBPD as soon as they have a spot, and we can use another friend there." I eye them each in turn. "So, who's in favor?"

Cedric and Iver both give her the thumbs-up, but the old man doesn't. And I eye him with raised eyebrows.

"She's a beautiful young woman. She ought to be having babies and fixing her old man dinner. Of course, I've been called archaic. . . ."

Cedric points at him. "Pleistocene, maybe even earlier."

"The bilge does need a good swabbing," Pug threatens with a snarl, but then smiles. "It's true, I'm an old fart, and even older this very day. And I'm beginning to feel it. You guys do whatever you think. I'm gonna go home and hit the sack."

So, she's in. And I've got a job for her tomorrow. It's a starter job, transporting a woman a few miles. I never did like putting the handcuffs on a woman, not because I don't know full well that they're the deadlier of the species—and I have scars to prove it—but merely because they're women.

I've handcuffed some women and put them in compromising positions, but only when they begged to have it done. The fact is a woman is a good fit for the team. Besides, I've got a plateful, and acting like a chauffer is not my most productive role.

Sandy *will* be an excellent fit.

Now we'll see how she takes to the menial and mundane labor of the less exciting aspects of bail enforcement.

I made an appointment with Mason for early this morning when I agreed to help him, informing him I had to clean up some matters before I could launch into his problem. I didn't mention that the matters I had to clean up were birthday cake pots and pans, and other chores.

I pass the run on the beach, as I'm watching my weight and don't want to come back from exercising weighing even a portion of an ounce more, particularly if that portion is the weight of the lead that I seem to attract while running.

Before I can leave, I have to give Sandy a call and see if she's serious about the bail enforcement biz. She jumps at the chance to do the transport and agrees to meet me at the nearby Sambo's Pancake House so I can fix her up with the paperwork. She's already informed me she has joined the National Enforcement Agency and has ID and a badge, so she's ready to go as soon as I check her out on procedure, and the van.

Then I remember I have another call to make. The Renegade Pig boys in Spokane that Pug put me on to. There's no sense making a trip to Coeur d'Alene if the dog is not in residence. Poker Jack Doolin answers on the first ring. Pop has told me he's retired ATF, and a tough old bird. I like him right off, and he agrees to do a fifty-buck drive-by and make sure dog and master are at home. He talks about my old man for twenty minutes before I can get off the line.

Being a little late, I climb on my Schwinn and peddle to Max's Boatyard, only a hundred yards behind Brophy's. Max is kind enough to rent me space to park not only my van, which is mostly used to transport skips, but also my oatmeal-colored 1990 four-door Chevy, which is meant to be plain, except under the hood, where she's ported, balanced, blown, and screams like a turpentined cat. All of which is hardly noticeable until you put the pedal to the metal. It's a great day, so I decide to take my only sexy transportation, the third and last of my vehicles, and by far the most entertaining, my Harley Davidson Sportster. It's a good day to have the wind in your hair. I have on my leather jacket over one of my favorite T-shirts emblazoned with *When the chips are down, the buffalo is empty*, boots, and Levis just for that reason.

Mason lives in Montecito, one of the great places in this great land. The community borders Santa Barbara on the south, and is home to the rich and famous, and the even more rich who want to stay unfamous and out of the pages of the *Star* or *National Enquirer*, in fact out of the phone book. There are an abundant number of forty-million-dollar estates in Montecito. Mason's estate is probably a modest six or seven million, ten acres between

Hot Springs Road and the mountains. The property is oak and chaparral covered and cannot be seen from the road. Mason is an engineer who specialized in medical apparatus, and whatever he invented continues to pay well.

After receiving a number of scowls from Porches, BMWs, Mercedeses, and at least one Rolls, I wheel into Mason's driveway, a couple of hundred yards through the oaks on slate pavers, to the house. She's gray board-and-batt with sparkling white trim, those little paned windows with white shutters, and would seem to be more at home on the Maine coastline; but she's two hundred feet across the front, not counting the four-car garage, and her size is more impressive than her style.

Mason is puttering in the flower beds, awaiting my arrival. He totters over, seeming a lot older than his fifty or so, brushes off his hands and four-fingers his hair to try and make it lie down, then gives me what passes now for a smile and a mackerel-limp handshake.

"Dev. Glad you could make it. Go on in and make yourself a drink. I'm going in the back, don't want to soil the carpet."

"It's eight o'clock in the morning, Mason. I try and stay off the sauce until at least ten."

I get a tight smile. "There's juice in the fridge."

He walks away and I find my way inside. I've been in the Fredrichs' home before at a social function or two. It was always immaculate. Now there are magazines and newspapers cluttered about the living room, covering a white carpet and scattered oriental rugs, and litter that I would guess are some very expensive antiques. A few empty glasses, cans, and coffee cups are scattered about. He has an excellent sound system, and some seventies music—sounds like Diana Ross—is playing loud enough that you could hear it in the driveway. Hearing her makes me smile, as even Diana could have been an FTA, had she not fessed up on her DUI. It would have hurt to hook her up if she'd jumped bail.

Walking on through the entry, I spot the dining room, and a swinging door that I presume leads to the kitchen. I'm right, but only after you pass through a butler's pantry with its own little sink and dishwasher. The kitchen is even more cluttered than the living room, with dirty pans and dishes added to the mix. I do manage to find some orange juice in a wide double-door refrigerator with stainless steel doors and am pouring myself a tall one, when Mason enters.

"You found it, good."

He takes the bottle from me, pours himself one only half-full, then reaches into a kitchen cabinet and plucks out a bottle of vodka and tops the glass off.

"Helps me get through the day," he mumbles without meeting my eyes. "Let's go in the den. Cleaning lady's due tomorrow; pardon the mess."

He leads me out and into a small room that would be the den in most houses, but is the music room here. Moving to the wall of stereo equipment, he turns the music down. There are bookshelves here too, but these are full of old 78s, 45s, and old long-play albums. A number of album covers are framed and on the wall. I recall that June played a clarinet that normally sat on a little stand in the center of the bookshelves. It's not there, the stand looking rather forlorn.

"I thought you were the blues fanatic?"

"Actually, that was June. I have more eclectic taste."

"June's clarinet?"

He looks puzzled for a moment, staring at the empty rack. "I hadn't noticed it missing."

I nod, and shrug, but don't mean it. It's a piece of hard evidence, the missing instrument that she loved. My first impression would be that she left of her own accord.

"Any other of her personal things gone?"

"A few, Dev, but her luggage is still here, and all of her clothes, if that's what you're insinuating."

That confuses me somewhat.

He leads me to a dark-paneled den with bookshelves stuffed with leather-bounds lining two walls; a third is an ego wall full of citations and diplomas. A billiard table big enough to host a game of badminton centers the room, and a desk faces away from wide windows that look out onto the pool. There's a See's candy box on the corner of the pool table, open, a number of chocolates gone. A few remain, and a couple have the top bitten off them.

"Have a chocolate," he says.

"Seems you have mice," I say, and he laughs.

"June always got mad when I checked to see what the filling was. I hate coconut."

I pass on the worked-over treats.

Mason takes a high-backed dark green leather chair behind the desk, and I take one of a pair of matching ones across from him.

"So," he begins, "have you found out anything?"

"Mason, remember I told you I had a full plate yesterday. After we chat awhile, I'll get to work on finding June, but I need some information from you first."

He shakes his head, looking as forlorn as an old horse facing the glue factory. "Christ, I'm tired of answering questions. Those damn detectives went at me in shifts before my attorney got there. . . ."

"Still, I need some help if I'm going to help you. Help like, where would she have gone taking her clarinet?"

He sighs deeply and stares out the window, then turns back with the semblance of a smile on his face. "Hey, Dev, you remember when we all used to show up at Café del Sol? Those were great times."

I shine his lack of an answer and press forward. "More

to the point, Mason, when was the last time you saw June and under what circumstance?"

His face falls, but he sighs again and resigns himself and begins to talk. I'm there an hour before he completely runs out of steam and I can see I'm getting no more out of him. Most of what he's relayed to me is in regards to old times, happier times, and I've had to continually bring him back to the subject at hand. Who did June know, what where her habits, and where do I start? I'm strangely unsatisfied with his answers, but put this off to the doubts I couldn't help but develop after Detective Babs worked me over. It all comes down to the fact she "drove away late in the morning and never came back." He informs me her car was found in the public parking lot near the marina. He has no idea what she would have been doing there. I rise, as I'm not out of questions but it seems he's out of answers. I walk to the ego wall and notice a few spaces where nails reside but framed items have been removed.

"You take some things down?"

"Pictures. I can't stand to have her everywhere, all the time, reminding me that she's gone."

"Fact is I need a picture, a recent one if you have it."

He disappears down the hall and returns with an eight-by-ten, obviously taken by a professional. While he's gone, I've noticed a picture of Mason on a hunting trip with a couple of other guys. And he's holding a rifle and wearing a revolver at his waist.

"I didn't know you were a hunter," I comment.

"I used to be, but gave it up. I can afford store-bought meat."

"You still have the sidearm?"

"Why?"

"Curious. Do you?"

"Nope, it was stolen years ago. I sold my rifle."

"What was the revolver?"

"Hell, I don't remember. A .357, I think." He hands me the picture. "Will this do?"

"Sure. If you come up with some more casual ones, I'd like them also. I'll get this back to you."

"Don't bother."

Don't bother. That sets me back a little.

As he walks me out to the Harley, I ask him about his sister-in-law. "I met your sister-in-law last night. Have you asked her for help?"

He stops short. "Betty Ann, that bitch."

I don't think I've ever heard Mason swear.

Chapter Four

"You don't get along with Betty Ann? I'd think she would be in a position that could be a lot of help finding June."

"June hated her. I hate her. She caused no end of trouble for Harry."

"Harry?"

"June's dad. Betty Ann is younger than June, from Harry's second wife. She was always jealous of June and what we have, and jealous of June's wonderful relationship with me and more so with Harry. She even got her mother hating the old man, until Harry finally divorced her too."

"So we can expect little help from Betty Ann?"

"How the hell did you meet that venomous bitch?"

"Socially. I was surprised to hear June had a sister."

"I'm not surprised June never mentioned her. June put both her and Betty Ann's mother out of her mind."

"Okay, I guess I won't be asking her for help."

"Don't." His face softens. "Dev, I have a dozen of those photos. That one was June's favorite of herself and she used it for reunions and newspaper press releases for the charity work she did . . . things like that. That's the only reason I don't need it back."

I nod. He must have noticed the look on my face when he said he didn't want it back. I fire up the Harley, drop it in gear, wave over my shoulder, and am gone. I'm out of there, but a long way from out of questions.

But I have other business. I've got to meet Sandy at Sambo's, the pancake house on Cabrillo across from the harbor, and get her set up to pick up the rubber-check writer in Lancaster.

I'm happy to see Sandy is dressed in black jeans and a practical long-sleeve black shirt. Her red hair's pulled tightly back on her head and bunned under a black bill cap. She's wearing ankle-high hiking boots, but molded ones more like a sports shoe. She's not wearing, but carrying a black nylon blazer with *Bail Enforcement* stenciled on the back in big letters and the front in small. And she's carrying her ID and badge holder, and a butt pack that she informs me is holding her .38 police special. She's ready to rock and roll. And looking good. Of course, the woman would look good in sackcloth. And she smells even better.

I buy her a short-stack and fill her in with what I've received from Sol, trade cell phone numbers with her, and give her one of my cards with the combination to Max's gate written on the back as he'll likely be closed by the time she returns, pay the check, and agree to meet her at Max's Boatyard, only a half mile away.

I wheel the bike over to Max's office as I want to have a talk with him before I leave, wave at him through the window, dismount, and climb into the passenger seat of her little Honda, and we move back to where the van and Chevy are parked. We pass a couple of Max's yard hands perched fifteen feet up off the ground working on the deck of a Mason sloop on davits in the yard. Max is busy, as the yard is full. I wave at them, and make a mental note to stop on the way out and pick their brains over Skip Hanson also, as I know he worked for Max for a short time.

When we pull up behind my vehicles, she reaches over and rests a hand on my forearm and centers those warm browns on me. "Hey, Dev. I really appreciate the work, and won't let you down."

"I don't expect you will. This should be an easy hundred and a half for you. If the old man hadn't taken the *Copper Glee* out today, I'd send Cedric or Iver with you—"

"Hey, I've handled some ugly old boys twice my size, I can handle some wimp female forger."

"No question." I hand her the keys to the van. "You pull the van out and I'll put your Honda in the space and you can trade them back tonight."

"Okay. Then I'm off. You want me to stop by the boat when I get back?"

"Why not? I should be there unless something comes up."

"Try and get some decent Chardonnay for a girl who's been on the pavement all day."

"I'll give it a whirl."

She's out and in the van before I can find the door handle on the passenger side. I walk around the back of the Honda as I hear her engage the starter.

Just as I reach the rear, shock knocks me head over heels, the van explodes in a ball of flame and a bellow of smoke, and I get the sense that it's airborne as I'm blown tumbling among the flying rubble back across the driveway chased by a caldron of searing heat and a tornado of billowing flame. I end up under the prow of a power boat, gasping for air. I'm on my back, trying to catch my breath as the wind's been knocked out of me, and watching the big boat above sway back and forth. I'm thinking it's coming down to crush me and can't do a thing about it, but it settles just as I'm able to raise myself up. And wish I hadn't as the portion of a leg just below the knee, still sporting a black molded sports boot, lands with a sickening splat ten feet from me, remnants of black cloth smoldering, the flesh scorched and torn except where a recognizable small rose is tattooed.

On hands and knees, I upchuck my breakfast. The acrid taste of vomit, cordite, and fear flood my mouth.

So long as I live, I'm sure I'll get flashbacks of that leg, a leg that had been so lovely, flopping to the driveway in front of my horrified eyes.

Flames lick ten feet in the air, a roaring inferno, from the hulk of the burning van. A thirty-foot sloop to the left of the van has been knocked off its davits to the ground and is smoldering—I get a weird sensation as I try and rise when I notice her name, in pseudo flaming letters on her transom, *Hot Stuff* . . . illustrative of actual flames at the moment. I struggle to my feet and charge across the driveway, hope against all plausibility that she's still alive, at least above the knee, just as the van's gas tank explodes and I'm flat on my back again, scalding air scorching my windpipe. Everything smells of cordite, spent powder, smoke, and smoldering skin.

Again I struggle to my feet and start forward, but strong hands have me and are dragging me back. It's Max. He's carrying a fire extinguisher in one hand, and hauling me back out of the heat with the other.

"Sit down, Dev," he commands, in a voice far too calm for the situation.

"She's . . . in there!" I plead.

"You can't do anything. Nobody can. Sit down. You're hurt, no telling how bad."

Dazed and my head swimming, I obey, and flop down on my butt, trying to keep my gaze off that shattered leg. I realize then that I've got a face full of glass, and begin picking shards out of my face and neck as Max moves as close as he can and goes after the fire with the extinguisher. His two yard hands run up dragging a fire hose, and bring its strong spray to bear on the van. Steam roils, joining the smoke in a swivel-hipped dance upward.

In moments, it's nothing but a blown-out, burnt-out, smoldering hulk. I try to get to my feet, but end up with my hands on my knees, barfing up what bile is left in my gut, and realize I'm in shock, as well as horrified, and lie back down.

Less than ten minutes from the time of the blast I can hear sirens, then the screech of brakes as the big red truck slides to a stop and Santa Barbara's finest boys in yellow take over.

I sit up again, then try to stand, but this time it's an EMT who's got a strong hand on my shoulder, keeping me on the ground. "Sit tight, we'll transport you to the hospital in a minute." His voice is calm and reassuring.

"Sandy," I mumble, but it's not a question, it's a lamentation.

"Sandy?" he replies.

"The . . . girl, in the . . . van."

"Don't think about her now—"

"The dirty . . . son of a bitch," I say, through clenched teeth, and broken by gasps.

"The girl?" he asks, surprise in his tone.

"No, not . . . the girl. The bastard . . . who did this."

"Oh. Don't think about it now. There'll be plenty of time for that."

I lie back down, but I can't help but think of the bastard, and take some solace, but very little, from what I'm going to do to him.

"I'm going to give you something," the calm voice says, and I feel him pushing up my shirtsleeve. Then things grow hazy, but in the background I can still see flames licking and smoke pouring up into Santa Barbara's clear blue sky. I close my eyes and can hear my heart beating like a kettledrum, seeming as if it's trying to rip its way out of my chest, a plangent drumming for a beautiful redheaded girl with a radiant smile.

The flames continue to roar.
Lucifer at work.

As if I'm looking through gauze, I remember being toted from X-ray to lab to CAT scan, then finally rolled off a gurney into a bed.

After being in and out of awareness several times during the day, I awake with a spectacular sunset out the window, alert and where I've been too often in my life, a place I hate. An IV is poking me in the arm. I listen for the *beep-beep* of a monitor, and not hearing it, know I'm not hurt badly or I'd be in the ICU. Hospitals always make me think of death, and what looks like clean, well-scrubbed walls and floor, and fresh sheets, appears to me to be places from which the blood was just scrubbed.

It's the smell that gets me more than anything; no matter what they do it seems the coppery odor of blood lingers. I don't know why, but clean in hospital parlance means the smell of a gallant, but failing, effort.

Not a good attitude toward those who try so hard, like the nurse with gray hair, half glasses, and a concerned look, who's by my bed fussing with the IV. Pug, Iver, and Cedric stand at the foot.

"You're back," the nurse says, barely glancing at me.

I pat my head, feeling for why it hurts, and realize my hands are bandaged as is my forehead. I turn to her. "When do I get out of here?"

She laughs. "Usually I get 'can I have a drink of water?' before 'when can I go home?' "

"Okay, a drink of water. But when can I go?"

"Jesus, relax," Pug commands. "The doc said they want to keep you overnight. They need to evaluate how much fire and smoke you sucked up." He looks at his watch. "With luck, you'll be out of here in twelve hours or less."

"Good. Sandy?"

Pug shakes his head. "A rough one, son. The good thing is she never knew what hit her. There must have been a pound of something new and powerful under your van."

"God, Pop, I should have been more careful."

"Maybe, but you know how picky Max is about who wanders around his place. The van was in a locked yard with eight-foot fences, and, besides . . . who'd've thought a shooter would become a bomber?"

"Still, I should—"

"Spilt milk. We're working on it. An FBI bomb squad is at Max's, being as interested in bombs as they are these days. Those boys leave no leaf unturned. There's an FBI type and an SB uniform outside, but I told them all no questions until tomorrow. You've got your own bodyguard, as they're beginning to get the hint that somebody wants to snuff your young butt. They and the SBPD will be in to talk to you tomorrow. Dowty just left here."

"Who?"

"Paul Dowty. You remember him, I partnered with him for a short time when he first came on board. Redheaded kid . . . like Sandy."

I try to ignore the comparison. "Yeah, he's okay." I get my drink, and realize my throat is terribly sore, then manage to croak, "I'm hungry."

"They feed you in a few minutes," Pug says. "It's obvious you're not hurt bad, worrying about your stomach already."

"Bull to hospital chow. I want a bowl of chowder from Brophy's . . . or better yet, one of those bomber martinis from Lucky's."

"This ain't no short-order house. Tomorrow, junior. Tonight, it's hospital cuisine." He smiles and pats me on the leg. "And be happy you're getting it. You could be eating dirt being shoveled by a man in black. That was a close one . . . really close."

"What does the doc say?"

"You got some burns in your lungs maybe. You're carrying more glass than Harry's Bar, and you're bruised up a little bit. Doc couldn't believe you didn't have some broken bones, but couldn't find a damn thing. Just bruises and lacerations. You were thirty feet or so from the bomb, and got tossed twenty if we got it figured right, so the distance away from the blast helped. And for one time that damned motorcycle helped."

"How so?" I'd left the bike parked back at the office.

"Not the bike itself, but the gear. Your leather jacket, boots, and Levis offered some protection."

I think back about what happened. "I was walking around behind the Honda, or you'd be picking up my pieces. Her car . . . Sandy's car, saved me."

"God's will."

There's a long moment of silence, and I feel a little choked up as my throat's burning like hell, but that must be the seared esophagus. "I really screwed up, Pop."

"Everybody screws up, boy."

"Maybe, but this one will be hard to live with. She was a really nice woman. A girl, really. Her life ahead of her . . ."

"But you will live with it. One of the good things about growing old is that all of us eventually get a clear conscience, which is usually the sign of a failing memory." He smiles at me, trying to cheer me up.

"Sounds good when you say it fast. She got family?"

"Her old man's a retired cop up in the Bay Area. I talked to him on the phone this afternoon. He's on his way down."

"Let's find this low-life prick. That'll help me, and I'm sure her family, more than anything."

"That's a promise, Dev, me boy. A promise. You rest now."

It was a long time after they left, and after I had my supper, before I fell asleep. And I suspected it would be a long time before I would fall asleep easily again. Of course they awakened me a half dozen times in the night, I guess to make sure I was sleeping well.

I awake pissed, and having to. The nurse walks in just as the morning light is filtering into the window. This is a different nurse from last night, a lot more prissy-looking with a narrow face that looks as if she spends a lot of time sucking lemons. "You had three visitors last night, but you were sleeping."

"Any idea who?"

"A gentleman in work clothes . . . Max, I believe he said. A lovely redheaded girl. Cindy? And a lady reporter from the *News-Press*. The guard outside your door questioned them and turned them away."

"Cynthia?"

"That's right. Both asked that we mention they were here."

"Thanks. What's this IV all about?" I ask.

"Hydration. The doctor wants to make sure you're getting enough fluids."

"I'm drinking every damn thing you bring me," I say, and pull the tape off and slip out the needle.

"Don't you dare do that," she says, blowing up like a spiny puffer fish, and charging over like she's going to replace it.

"And I'm full of water." I get up, face her down, and head for a door, which I presume is to the john.

"I can bring you a bed pan," she snaps.

"You can bring me my clothes," I say, "unless you want me to walk out of here buck," and note her glance at another door, which I presume is to a small closet. She makes no move toward it. I take care of the bathroom business, find a washcloth, and take a long time washing my face, only wetting half the cloth so I don't soak the bandages on my hands and being careful not to wet the bandages on my forehead. The nurse yells through the door, "I'm getting the doctor, and you're getting back in bed."

I don't answer.

"I'll call security."

"I am security," I say, and laugh loud enough that she can hear me.

When I exit, a stern-looking doctor is waiting, and the prissy nurse stands smugly next to him, as if she's led a black-hooded executioner in to confront me. It loses something in the translation as I'm a full head taller than he is, and lifting his stethoscope would seem the extent of his exercise regimen. I head straight for the closet and find my clothes, stay behind the door, and am happy to shed the light green gown with the rear air-conditioning.

"I'm Dr. Jorgenson," he says, his look going from stern to exasperated. I give him a nod. "I have a respiratory test scheduled for you this afternoon. You need to get back in bed."

"Thanks, Doc, but I'm breathing fine. My throat's a little sore, but otherwise—"

"Back in bed, please."

"I'm out of here, Doc; get used to it. If you need to write me a prescription, I've got a pen." I dig one out of my leather jacket.

"I do, but I'd much prefer you stay. The hospital has liability—"

"Report that I left on my own cognition, Doc, and I'll back you up, 'cause that's exactly what I'm going to do. Grinelda here will testify too."

He sighs deeply and throws up his arms. "I'm going to the nurses' station. Stop by there and pick up your prescriptions. Take your temperature a half dozen times a day for the next few days. You could get pneumonia and things could go sour for you quickly."

"Thanks, Doc, I'll watch it."

"If it even moves up a degree, you get back here, understand?"

He's relented, so I give him a smile. "Scout's honor and cross my heart."

He nods, happy that I've finally bowed at the altar, and turns and leaves. The nurse is still huffing and puffing.

"What's your name?" I ask, giving Grinelda my most winning smile.

She doesn't answer, merely points at her name tag, which is half under her collar.

"Well, Miss . . . Snavely . . . is it? I'm sorry if I hurt your feelings. You gave me good care and I appreciate it."

She spins on her heel and stomps out, obviously unimpressed at my attempted reconciliation, or the apparently not-so-winning smile. Oh well, can't please 'em all.

My cell phone's in the jacket pocket, so I call the old man.

Obviously I awaken him. "Hey," I say, "the early bird gets the worm."

"Yeah, but the early worm gets eaten by the bird and, worse, the early bird has to eat worms. You up already?"

"This is a hospital, Pop, I've been up a dozen times. Come get me."

"Okay. You're officially sprung?"

"You bet." I lie easily, under the circumstance. Parents need to be lied to on occasion, and this is one of those.

"What about the guard?"

"He can follow along if he wants."

"Be out front and bring me a coffee."

"Hospital coffee?"

"Right, the mind's not clear yet. We'll stop somewhere."

I finish dressing, have a short talk with a very frustrated uniform cop, who gets on his radio, and pick up my prescriptions on the way out. The FBI is nowhere to be seen. I guess they found some real work for the agent. The nurses treat me like a pariah, but that's okay. I have health insurance, and pay my bills, and have been a model patient, except for jerking out their needle and fleeing the coop, of course.

While I'm waiting, with the uniform standing nearby, I call Iver, who's got a room in the back of some sweet old lady's California bungalow near the harbor. "Somebody's still got to transport the bad check girl from Lancaster to L.A."

"That would be me?"

"If you're not doing something else? It's worth a bill and a half to me."

"Then that would be me."

"Good. Call Sol and tell him what happened and get him to send you duplicate paperwork. Sandy had it on her.... And while you're on the boat, feed Futa before he decimates the bird population."

"Don't sweat it. I'll handle."

And I know he will.

The uniform SBPD guy walks over as soon as I'm off the phone and informs me that his boss says he can lay off, if it's my old man picking me up. I guess they still think highly of old Pug Shannon.

To the old man's credit, he's there in ten minutes, unshaven and red-eyed, driving his big Ford 250 pickup, not the most practical vehicle for city streets, but it tweaks his testosterone.

I realize how muscle sore I am when I climb up, take the passenger seat, and belt up. The explosion hit me like a Mack truck. I'm sore in places I didn't know I had.

"We're picking up Sandy's old man at nine at the airport, we'll eat something out there."

I take a long deep breath. "Not my favorite way to top off a good breakfast."

"I should mention, he's pissed."

Why am I not surprised?

Chapter Five

While we're having breakfast in the upstairs café above the waiting room at Santa Barbara's tidy little airport, Pop mentions that he heard I was traveling to Coeur d'Alene to locate the pup. Since I'm in a healing mode for a while and grounded, he goes into detail about the group of guys he mentioned before, the Renegade Pigs. I remember him chuckling about them at the party, but I figured they were some misfit motorcycle gang. I get an even bigger chuckle when I learn they are mostly retired cops with some firemen, FBI, ATF, and God knows what else thrown in, and they're Harley riders. They could do the recovery for me. The impressive part is they're twelve thousand strong all over the country—a real resource for a resourceful bounty hunter. He reminds me that he knows a couple of the guys who now live in Coeur d'Alene or close by, were with the Oxnard PD, and says he'll look some addresses and phone numbers up for me so I can have them do a drive-by and check out the purloined pooch. If there wasn't so much dough at stake, I'd have them pick the pup up and ship him, but I've got an inkling it won't be quite that easy. Big money usually means big problems.

Sandra's father's plane touches down and my stomach does flip-flops as if *I* were aboard for the bounce. I hate death and all its aspects, particularly involving grieving spouses or parents, and even more particularly parents or partners who might think I'm at fault. There's no way to defend yourself from a grieving parent, particularly when you feel guilty already.

The old man meets him at the gate, just to make sure he's not a raving maniac waving a police revolver, but he seems fine. Pug has a hand on his shoulder, as they come across the grass to the coffee shop where Pop and I have had breakfast and killed time sipping coffee.

I stick out a bandaged hand when they walk over. Pug introduces me to Andrew Bartlett, retired San Francisco detective. Pop's already calling him Andy, but he looks at *me* as if were what's been offered for breakfast, a cow chip nestled in a sponge cake.

"I'll pass the handshake," he says, and I hope it's because of the bandages. "You got burns?"

"Yes, sir."

"You look like hammered dog shit," he says. He's as tall as I, heavier but some of it's hanging over his belt, gray hair trimmed marine close but well cut, with eyes that assess me like an ATM scanning camera. He's still wearing PD-detective-cheap suits—Sears is the working dicks best friend—but it's dark gray and well tailored, the white shirt's well pressed, and the black-patterned tie's without soup stains. He's classy, like a rock star's bodyguard.

As he's lost his daughter, I ignore the insult. The fact is I do look like hell. "Did you get something to eat, Mr. Bartlett?" I ask.

His look softens as he takes a seat. "No, but this thing's got me off my feed. Coffee will do. Now, tell me what happened."

We spend an hour going over the circumstances leading up to his daughter's death.

Finally, he rises. "If somebody was trying to whack you, Shannon . . . you should have been more careful."

"I wish I could argue with you, and wish I had it to do over. I wish—"

But he doesn't much give a damn what I wish, nor does he want maudlin, and I don't blame him. He interrupts. "I'd like to see the scene."

As we walk out to Pug's truck, Benson asks, "How soon will they release the body . . . Sandy . . . so I can arrange to transport her north?"

Pug shrugs.

"They're gonna do an autopsy, right?" He has a rather sick look on his face, but he knows the grim realities of homicide. Thankfully he's addressed his question to Pug.

"Probably already have. I've got to tell you, Andy, it was a hell of an explosion. If it's any consolation, she never knew what hit her. We don't get much of this kind of thing in Santa Barbara. It's . . . it's going to be a closed casket."

"And when you did, it had to be my daughter." It's the first condemning thing he's said to match the looks I've been getting.

I finish my former thought. "I wish it had been me," I say, as I walk on over to the extended-cab Ford. I've heard that said before, and always thought it sounded cheap, but being in the circumstance, I now know that it's something you just have to say.

"Easily said, young man. Easily said. God knows, I too wish it had been you. No offense, Pug." I have no answer for that, nor does Pug.

As we're walking out to the truck, I get an unpleasant surprise. Skip Hanson is walking in. I know him slightly, and stop him with a friendly "Hey, Skip."

"How ya doing?" he asks, and I wonder if he remembers my name, then he ads, "How's the bounty biz, Dev?"

"Great. You haven't been around the harbor?"

"Working for the Chevron guy here at the airport. It's a steady thing."

I laugh. "You know the *Orion*?"

"The big Benetti. Sure."

"She's missing. I know you had a thing with Winston-Gray, and for a moment thought maybe you and the Benetti were on your way to the South Seas."

He smiles a little tightly. "I hate that prick, but not enough to go to jail for dicking him. Now, I don't know about Toke...."

"Toke?"

"Butterworth. He hates the old boy even more than I do, and I haven't seen Toke around lately."

"Interesting notion," I say. I know Toke about as well as I know Skip, having seen him around the harbor only a few times.

Skip eyes me carefully, then asks, "Is there a finder's fee, if I get some real information?"

"It would be worth a grand to me, if it put me onto the boat and I get her back here."

"I'll keep it in mind. Toke never was a friend of mine. I thought he was, one time, but he's a lowlife."

"Give me a call, you get something."

I catch up with the old man. There's one good lead gone down the drain.

We spend over an hour at the scene, which requires my old man convincing the FBI bomb squad that we have business there. I notice some ATF windbreakers. The feds are out in force. Out of deference to their hard work as they're now meticulously sifting the ground outside the paved area for the tiniest scraps that might lead us to the bomber, Pug suggests that only Andy Bartlett be allowed inside the crime tape, which encompasses a half acre. I've been there, and am not eager to return for a while. I wander back over to Max's office where my Sportster is still parked.

He's at his desk and looks up when I enter. Max is one of those short guys like my old man, somewhere between our ages, but with cul-de-sacs in thinning black hair that almost reach the crown of his head, leaving a patch of black curly hair right in front. He's built like a fifty-five-gallon steel barrel and is as tough as one full of cured concrete. He looks up with a day's growth of beard shading his heavy cheeks as he walks around the desk. He gives me an uncharacteristic hug. "Glad you're in one piece."

"Me too," I say.

"I came to see you in that morgue they call a hospital, but the cops ran me off."

"You are a suspicious-looking character. They told me and I appreciate it. You got a moment?"

"Sure, let me grab you a cup of coffee. If you can hold it with those King Tut mummy hands."

He goes over to his pot and pours me a cup and I plop in a chair across the desk. I'm sure I ask him the same questions as has the FBI and the SBPD, but he's patient. I'm still at it, when there's a rap on his open door.

"Hi," the lady says, "I'm Alice Townsend." She's built a little like Max, has salt-and-pepper hair that had once been blond, now askew from the ocean breeze. She is dressed something like a well-practiced frump in a slightly out-of-shape black skirt, a black-and-pink-striped blouse, practical flat-soled shoes, and a limp-brimmed black felt porkpie hat, but she's got a smile and a clever, inquisitive look to the eyes that offsets the rest. She's carrying a beach-bag-size purse. Even frumpy she looks like someone you'd want to know.

Max invites her in and introduces me.

"What can I do for you, Alice?" he asks.

"Actually, it's Mr. Shannon I need to talk to so long as he's here. I've been to the hospital and his boat twice this morning." Everybody seems to get through the gate. "I'm with the *Santa Barbara News-Press*."

She hands me a business card. I sigh. Pop has told me

that the place was crawling with TV transmission trucks, reporters, and cameramen when he brought the *Copper Glee* back in, and that was how he found out about the trouble.

I walk outside with her, agree to her little handheld tape recorder, and tell her as little as possible—which is about as much as I know. I pass on her wanting to take a photograph, discovering that's the reason for the big purse. It doubles as a camera bag, holding a Nikon. She's kind, for a reporter, and doesn't press me to exasperation, but does caution me as she gets ready to leave. "I'm going to work this dog until it doesn't hunt any more, Mr. Shannon. You'll see me again soon."

I couldn't help but smile. "Then you might as well call me Dev."

"Dev, then. I'm Alice. See you soon."

The old man comes back by the office and tells me he's taking Andy Bartlett to McDermott Crockett Mortuary, friends of his, to arrange to have Sandy transported home. He knows they'll give him a break, as Andy's a friend of Pug's, and a cop. I assure him Sandy could not be in better hands, and get only a snort in reply.

Pop instructs me, as if I was still fifteen, not to leave the harbor unless I call him and get him to go along.

It appears that he's promised the FBI and the SBPD to bodyguard little Dev. The hell of it is, I would have trouble holding on to my brand-new S&W model 625-10 ACP .45 revolver. Even as light as it is.

When I get back to the boat, there're a dozen phone messages from reporters, a half dozen from harbor buddies, including Tony the bartender, two from Detective Paul Dowty of the SBPD, one from the FBI wanting to know when they can interview me, and one from Sol. I return Sol's call and assure him the transport is being taken care of, and refuse his offer to come up. He says he's personally bringing me a quart of matzo ball soup, which cures all ills, and I laugh and tell him I'll get my infusion from the deli downtown, and that I'll see him soon. It's good to have friends, particularly ones who make you a hundred grand a year or so. But it's come to be more than that with Max over the last few years. He spotted me a cool hundred grand when I needed to get out of Paris last year. A little matter of a pile of Mercedes Benzes I left behind, the Spanish Mafia being close on my tail, and a bond I had to put up before being allowed to leave the country.

I hit the sack a couple of hours earlier than usual, thinking I'll have trouble falling asleep, but obviously don't as the next thing I know it's the middle of the night. The harbor is eerily quiet, with only the persistent lapping of the water against the hull and the slap of halyards as boats gently rock. I wish I was as quiescent as the sea. I'm in a cold sweat, having repeatedly watched that formerly lovely leg flop to the gravel in front of me. I promise Sandy that I'll find the scum that ended her life, and only then fall back asleep.

As I'm making coffee, I feel someone step aboard, then hear Cynthia call out, "Dev."

"Come aboard, I'm just casting off for Tahiti. Just you and me."

She walks in with a spring bouquet cradled in her arm and carrying a vase and her shoes in one hand. High heels are a little hard on a wood deck, and she's a thoughtful lady.

I haven't seen her for almost a month, but somehow she looks even better than I remember. "You look luscious," I murmur. I look her up and down in an obvious manner. True auburn redheads normally have the most delicious tan complexion, and Cynthia's no exception—in fact, she sets the standard. And that's just the frosting on an already well-put-together delight. One that's certainly good enough to eat.

"Where do you want them?" she asks. The green eyes sparkle, and she laughs. "You look harmless, already wrapped up for Christmas with nothing lacking but the bow."

"Don't let looks fool you," I say. "Put them on the chart table, and thanks, by the way. I don't believe I've ever received flowers from a beautiful lady."

She's dressed like she just came from Nordstrom's, in a tailored skirt and blouse of green silk. Class, which is normal for Cynthia. She walks down to the galley, gets herself a Diet Coke out of the little fridge, and yells over her shapely shoulder, "You want something?"

"Yeah . . . but you may have to be on top." I get a twinge of guilt, as all the living do when they try to go on with that sometimes difficult task. But it will help me forget. . . .

She returns, taking a sip, the smile and sparkle still there. "You're incorrigible, and you fresh out of the hospital. Besides, I'm going steady, and unlike yourself, I'm true blue. Besides, the urge to procreate always follows a close step behind damn near dying. Where's Futa?"

I sigh. "I never cheated on you. And he's roaming. He's fine. He's probably getting laid, like a healthy animal who wants to maintain his sanity. Did you come here to check on the cat or me?"

"Good that he's fine. Okay, okay, let's not hoe another hard row . . . the cheating thing. There's no way I'm getting pawed by something out of the *Return of the Mummy*. Tell me the details about what happened to get you in the gauze."

"For the one thousand nine hundred and eighty-sixth time, I didn't cheat on you. And, yes, I'll fill you in. First tell me who the lucky man is."

"I love it when you're jealous! Same guy, Tom Demarco. He's relentless, and I like it."

"And you get most your work from Ogilvie and Mathers. You should be ashamed. One should not procreate where one eats, so to speak."

"Don't start."

"Good sex?"

"None of your . . . It's breathtaking, okay?" she says.

But she smiles too quickly, and I know she's exaggerating. At least I hope she's exaggerating.

I have nothing to say in response, so she continues. "So now will you leave it alone?"

That does take some of the wind out of my sails, which she's smart enough to do at will. So I get in one more dig. "What do sperm and lawyers have in common?"

"Okay, I don't know."

"One in three million will become human."

She rolls her eyes. "Enough, okay?"

"Almost. You know what you've got when you have a dozen attorneys buried up to their neck in sand?"

"Not enough sand, okay?"

I'm disappointed she knows my punch line, but then it's an old joke.

Relenting, I spend twenty minutes relating what came down with the shooter and the van while she sits quietly and sips the Coke. When I'm done, she rises. "I'm going to see what I can find out. That poor girl . . . ."

"A nice girl, a beautiful charming girl, you'd have liked her."

"You look devastated. Sounds like you already liked her a lot."

"A hell of a lot. And I love it when *you're* jealous. Hell, I only met her the day before when she came looking for work."

She's moving toward the ladder. "I've heard tell you've moved a lot faster than that at times. You certainly tried with me." She looks pensive for a moment. "Jesus, did she ever sign aboard the wrong vessel!"

I stare out a porthole for a moment before responding. "Can't argue, and I don't need reminding." I eye her again, and give her a tight smile. "Anything you turn up I'd appreciate. I don't imagine this guy is gonna give up."

"You gonna need anything?" Cynthia asks.

"Nothing we haven't already discussed, and that you've shined like we weren't old bosom buddies."

"You're worse than incorrigible. But I still love you, even if I can't abide you."

"Come back," I suggest. She disappears out the hatch. As usual, I watch her until she's out of sight and enjoy every moment. And I know she will come back because she said she's going to look into it, and Cynthia is one of the best private investigators I've ever known, and unlike many folks I've known, always does what she says she'll do. This guy with the dynamite or C4 or whatever has made a bad error, getting Cynthia, Pug, the Santa Barbara PD, the FBI, and probably the ATF on his case . . . not to speak of a very, very angry, very large, ex-SFPD dick. Hell, even the harbor patrol is pissed.

I just hope no one finds him before I do, because I want him to live, live to hurt, hurt a long agonizing time, before I shove my .38 in his ear and clear up his thinking. Or worse for him, turn him over to retired detective Andy Bartlett. That, I'm sure, would be a rodeo to watch.

I walk up on deck, hoping for one more glance at a disappearing Cynthia, and I'm pleasantly surprised to get a last glance of her leaving, and again to see another beauty arriving. They pass on the dock, nodding to each other, and eyeing each other up and down in that appraising way women mastered eons ago.

Babs, the local detective who's *not* on the case, so I guess this must be a social call.

Chapter Six

My enjoyment watching one beautiful woman depart and another approach is interrupted by my phone.

Darwin Winston-Gray, who has retained me to find his yacht.

"I thought you'd be heading south?" he asks, his tone somewhat condescending.

"And I may, as soon as I determine her exact whereabouts. South is a big place," I say, a little impatiently as I can feel Babs ever so slightly rock the boat as she steps aboard.

"You can determine her whereabouts by going after her. You won't find her by lying around that tub of yours." His tone worsens, and I feel the creeping of heat begin to ease up my backbone.

"Like I said, Darwin, when I know *where* she is, I'll go after her."

There's a long silence. I don't know if he doesn't like what I've said, or merely the fact I've been presumptuous enough to call him by his first name.

"Mr. Shannon," he replies, "I'm not paying you—"

"Mr. Winston-Gray," I interrupt, and can almost feel the heat from his anger jolting through the phone line but it meets my own head-on, "you're right, you're not paying me. I'm not an employee of yours, I'm a retainee. A retainee who doesn't get paid if he doesn't perform."

Babs has filled the hatchway leading down into the

main saloon with a shapely silhouette. If you can call that lithe backlighted body "filling." There's something enticing about an Oriental woman, particularly one who's breathtakingly beautiful, even in a rather straightforward brown suit, black bag, and practical low heels. It's the eyes, almost mystic, hiding some treasure that it would probably be immense fun to discover.

Again there's a long silence on the line, but I don't mind, I'm enjoying the view.

He finally continues. "You don't need to be snappish. Then you won't mind if I employ others to perform the same task."

He thinks that's a threat, I think it's amusing. After all, there's no listing in the Yellow Pages for stolen yacht recovery. "As I said, Darwin, I'm not an employee. If you still want me to work on your *tub*," and I put emphasis on the latter, "then I will. You can retain an *employee* or the United States Marine Corps if you have that kind of political clout or whoever else suits you. Just have the money ready when this ex-marine brings in the *Orion*."

I can hear an audible sigh. His tone changes. "I heard you had an accident."

"Hardly an accident."

"Are you going to be able to work?"

"You didn't read about me in the obits, Darwin. Yes, I'm working right now." A little lie never hurt. Babs is standing in my doorway, looking serious. Work serious, not man-woman serious, I'm sorry to say. Maybe I am working, and only think I'm busy making time.

"If you turn anything up, call me."

"I don't do a lot of reporting in, Darwin . . . but I'll keep in touch."

"Do that." He hangs up without a good-bye. Max the bartender may have had a good read on my new chum, Darwin.

"Who *was* that?" Babs asks.

"A client."

"You have a wonderful manner with your employers," she says, an ironic smile on her face.

"I'll tell you the same thing I told him. I'm not his employee, I'm not a bit interested in having someone hire me for my expertise, then try and tell me how to do my job, which most novitiates try to do."

"Novitiate?"

"Novice. Sorry, Cedric's getting to me with the ten-dollar words when a two-dollar one will do."

She climbs up on the stool across the chart table from me. "So, how you doing?"

"Better than I look."

"When do the bandages come off?"

"I didn't ask. When I get sick of them, I guess."

"Bad burns?"

"Not really. Mostly glass cuts and bruises. I was shot-gunned with glass shards from the car windows, and maybe the van's, I guess. You want a cup of coffee?"

"I'm working."

I give her a questioning look.

"Coffee makes me nuts. How about a Diet Coke, or 7-Up?"

I give her my most appealing shy-boyish-charm grin. "And I thought this was a social call, and we were going to have a quiet cup of coffee on the deck."

"Nope, I didn't get my sister's case, but I was the lucky sap to draw the case of the exploding van. This is a work call."

So much for boyish charm. "Just you?"

"Nope, me and a couple of others. Seems the mayor and the chief frown on even the smallest of bombs going off near the harbor. Hard on tourism, or something to that effect. And the chief takes particular umbrage on an applicant to the PD being killed in his backyard. Not like she was an SB cop, but she was trying to be. But I'll take a Coke."

I walk down to the galley and pop her a can of Coke and grab myself a small plastic bottle of orange juice, then return. "So, what can I do for Babs, SBPD homicide detective?"

"Meeting this afternoon downtown. You, me, Paul Dowty from our department, the FBI boys, the ATF, and whoever else has an interest. Can you make it?"

"Why the FBI and ATF?"

"Well, first off, we invited them because of their superior lab, and second, they jump on bombings since nine-eleven. You're lucky we're not swarming with the rest of Homeland Security."

"Okay. That's probably a good thing. Meeting, sure, what time?"

"Three."

I eye her for a moment. "You could have called about this. Not that I don't appreciate the visit."

She jumps off the stool and heads for the hatchway ladder, taking the can of Coke with her. "I could have," she says over her shoulder, "but I wanted to see how you were doing. Get some vitamin E to rub on those wounds as soon as they begin to heal. Otherwise, you'll look like you had smallpox."

An old joke about smallpox, or more correctly small cocks, flashes through my mind, but it's not one to tell a lady. "Right. See you this afternoon."

She glances back over her shoulder and winks. A wink is good.

The *Copper Glee* has been out to the islands doing some diving, but the old man is back and at my boat by two.

"I'm going to this meeting with you," he informs me without bothering with a hello.

"You invited?" I ask, just digging him as I wouldn't

mind a bit his attending. He knows the FBI and ATF act much better than I, having been on a number of interdepartmental agency gigs with them.

"Nope, going anyway."

"Fishing must be lousy?"

"Diving today, but Cedric is scheduled to head up to some Buddhist retreat in the morning to hum for a couple of days and has to pack this afternoon and get someone to take care of his dog, which I refuse to do, and Iver is coming down with a touch of something. Good time to hang up the tanks."

"I appreciate your coming along."

SBPD has a conference room big enough for two dozen, and there's only a dozen there when we arrive promptly at three. Sandoval, the chief of police, is in attendance, but he sits off to the side, observing.

Paul Dowty is at the head of the table, Babs at his right and another SBPD dick I don't know to his left. Beyond Babs sit a pair of Fibbies and across from them a pair of ATF types. I recognize none of them. Near my end of the table, where Pug and I sit, is Howard Petri, the head of the local branch of the Harbor Patrol. A nice guy, whom I know well.

Dowty makes the introductions, and immediately upon his completing them an FBI agent, who's been introduced as Agent O'Mally, zeros his eyes on Pug.

"And what's Patrick Shannon's status here?" he asks.

Dowty answers, "He's a retired SBPD detective and Dev Shannon's father, been acting as an unofficial bodyguard with the FBI's approval, I might add, and I invited him."

It's only a small lie, as Pug took it upon himself to attend, but he and Dowty are old running mates.

"Hmmm," is the agent's response.

But Dowty cuts him off. "So, what have the bomb guys turned up?"

The agent next to O'Mally, who's been introduced as Agent LaPointe, rises, as if he were speaking to a college class. "A pretty sophisticated device. Plastique, probably a pound or maybe a little less of what at first analysis appears to be C4 or C5 . . . we'll know more after a spectrometer. Detonator was activated with a part from one of those radio-controlled toys, from a toy car or boat or airplane. We found evidence of the device."

I'm an admirer of the patience and dedication of these bomb investigators. They must have sifted through several hundred pounds of soil from the flower beds and sweepings from the pavement, examining all tiny fragment with a loop all of them carried on a lanyard around their neck. I'm surprised to hear that someone manually activated the bomb.

The ATF guys nod in agreement. Then all eyes turn to me as O'Mally asks, without rising and as LaPointe flops back to his chair, "So, Mr. Shannon, who wants you dead?"

"In a minute. First, you're telling me that someone manually set off this bomb. It wasn't the starter being engaged, or the key being turned, or the pressure on the seat?"

LaPointe starts to speak, but O'Mally lays a hand on his forearm and he stops immediately.

O'Mally clears his throat. "We'll have time to answer your questions, or Dowty will, later. We've got a heavy caseload, and need you to answer questions, not ask them—"

I rise, as does Pug, shutting him up, and the old man gives me the same gesture, laying a hand on my shoulder, knowing I'm about to go off on the FBI guy.

"Mr. O'Mally," Pug says before I have a chance to vent, "we're here voluntarily, at Paul Dowty's invitation. You FBI guys are not particularly good at give-and-take, never have been. We want this thing solved as much as you do . . . probably a lot more. We're also experienced in investigative techniques. I've probably handled as many bomb cases as you have, or more, unless you came up out of your bomb squad. You're not dealing with dorks off the street here. Relax."

Pug returns to his seat, and motions me down. And I sit. Paternal respect, because I'm a little irritable and O'Mally is already chaffing my bad side. I'm reminded of something Pug told me long ago: FBI, the acronym for Famous-But-Incompetent.

O'Mally shrugs. "Your son's a bounty hunter type, is he not?"

"He is," Pug snaps. "And I guarantee you, even though he's younger than you and me by a few years, he's hauled more bad guys to the slammer than all of us at this table. Now please answer his question."

O'Mally reddens. He obviously doesn't have much respect for bail enforcement agents, but he doesn't seem to want to debate the old man's assertion. I think it's probably an exaggeration; then again, I have seven or eight hundred arrests under my belt, and that might be more than many cops have in a career.

O'Mally again clears his throat. "We believe the perp was somewhere nearby. Probably within a hundred yards, where he could clearly see what was happening around your vehicles."

"Thank you," Pug responds politely. Then something dawns on him. "You know the tan rather nondescript Chevy parked next to the van also belongs to Dev. Did you check it out for another device?"

Chapter Seven

"Jesus," O'Mally says, embarrassment shading his face, then gives a head motion to LaPointe and he's on his feet and out of there.

"I hope nobody messes with it," Pug says, and O'Mally looks a little sheepish.

He mumbles, "Nobody mentioned—"

"Nobody asked," Pug says, but his expression is flat, not smug in any way. He turns to me. "How many guys want to snuff you?"

"Plenty, and a few women as well."

I go through cases for a couple of years back while O'Mally and Babs and one of the ATF guys take notes. This takes over an hour of my talking and answering detailed questions. Just as I'm done, LaPointe strides back into the room.

"Mr. Shannon was right. Another device, under the Chevy, just below the driver's seat. We have a perfect duplicate device. I have people on it."

O'Mally turns his attention to me. "So, there's no one in particular you can pick out as the most likely perp?"

"Hey, there's a dozen guys who might have a woody for me . . . pardon me, Detective Benson. A dozen if they're off on me because of getting hauled in as FTAs. A couple who I went after for personal reasons, wanted guys, but my motivation wasn't necessarily the dough . . .

but as far as I know, they're all serving time. There's also a couple of disgruntled clients . . . but nobody who might be this disgruntled, or is the type to—"

"You a profiler?" O'Mally asks, in his smug manner.

"No, I'm no profiler. I am a fair judge of character, and you have to be a bit of a psychologist to track skips down." I stand and stretch. "You've got it all, and I'm beat up and ready to put my feet up. You've all got my cell number." I rise and head for the door, taking Pug by surprise.

He's on his feet following, talking as he comes. "We appreciate it if you'd keep us up to speed on things."

"Sure," O'Mally says, but it's obvious he's just stringing us along. He shakes his head disgustedly while looking at Dowty, waiting for him to do something.

When we're settled in Pug's Ford pickup, he starts her up, and laughs. "Every time I turn the damn key on, I flinch."

"And I snap a piece of your upholstery up. What do you think?"

"Of?"

"Of the meeting?"

"Hell, getting anything out of the FBI guys or the ATF is about as effective as shoveling smoke. We'll have to keep up to speed relying on friends at SBPD. And the Fibbies will only tell them what they want them to know. But they *are* the best bomb guys in the world."

"Of course, you brought them a perfect duplicate device."

"A light went on, luckily. A senior moment, on the good side for a change. Let's get you back to the boat."

"I was bullshiting about feeling bad. I'm fine. I just wanted out of there as we were beginning to go in circles. Let's go see if we can figure out where this asshole was watching from."

We get back to the harbor and figure out a couple of

likely places where our boy may have been lurking when Sandy and I came back to the van, ask a few questions of folks who might have been in the area at that time of day, but strike out. I head back to the boat to do some thinking. Some of my best cogitating time is with Futa purring in my lap and me watching the boats go by. I'm wondering, *If the prick saw Sandy get in the driver's seat, why set off the device?* The only reason could be he thought the blast big enough to take me out too. And it almost did, had I not rounded the back of her Honda, and had it between me and the van when it detonated.

I've been thinking hard about who might be the culprit in this sophisticated attempt to snuff me. Shooters are one thing—almost anyone can pick up a rifle and pop off a shot at someone—a complicated bomb is another. I can probably narrow it down to a dozen possibles, but no fewer, depending upon how patient this guy is, which means how long ago he developed this horrendous grudge. The FBI is good, and maybe they will be successful tracing the explosive or in some other way. Yes, the bad news is the FBI is anal, and, yes, the good news is the FBI is anal. If something can be found out by tracing a single molecule, then the FBI can do it.

I'm not in my deck chair for more than ten minutes, looking forward to a beautiful sunset, when my phone chatters at me from deep in the bowel of the boat. I should have brought the wireless handset up on deck with me, but that would have required some forethought and I don't seem to be so good at that of late.

It's the fourth ring before I get there and I have to wait for the answering device to cycle. "Hey, I'm here," I yell over my voice on the machine. It finishes, and Cynthia's sexy voice asks, "How you feeling?"

"Good. Gonna ditch the bandages tomorrow or maybe the day after."

"No rush."

"Easy for you to say. I'm already tired of sponge baths."

"I've got a couple of possibles for you."

"Already. You're a whiz kid."

"I'm a sexy adult full-grown woman child, is what I am."

"No argument. What do you have, or who? is a better question."

"Last year you farmed out a pile for each of us, remember?"

I laugh a little wryly. "How could I forget?"

"And the good Dr. Hashim got hauled in for child pornography. And got a change of venue and left our life. Now, guess who just got a month's suspension without pay?"

Cynthia likes to tease with guess-whos and guess-whats. "For God's sake, Cynthia, what did you dig up?"

"Alverez and Thompson, the two detectives who helped you and Pug and busted Hashim, on an unpaid month's suspension. Entrapment. The good doctor is free and somewhere in San Francisco. It seems he produced a long dissertation on child pornography that he claimed to have been working on for many years, and all that crap on his computer was 'research.' "

"And I tried to put him out of my mind."

"And one of those guys you busted over in Kern County, Orozco—"

"Simon Orozco, who killed my buddy."

"One and the same. Last week, he climbed into a bread truck at the California Correctional Institution at Tehachapi . . . Tehachapi Prison, cold-conked the driver, and drove out in a Country Squire Bread Company uniform. He slit the driver's throat, who he had tied up in the back of the truck, before he left him and the truck in a field outside Bakersfield."

I chew on that for a moment. "I truly wanted to kill the son of a bitch when I had my .38 in his ugly mouth, but the old man talked me out of it. Now I'm sorry I didn't." I sigh deeply, wondering how many kids this innocent truck driver left behind.

But I have other fish to fry at the moment. "I'm not sure either of those guys is the bomber type. Simon is not smart enough and would much prefer a shiv, up close and personal, and the good doctor . . . poison was his game, from a long, long ways away. It seems, by the way, that our bomber was nearby, with the activator in hand, wanting to watch."

It's her turn to be quiet for a moment, then she says, "I don't know. Hashim was a real crazy—"

"Yeah, bring me another client like him sometime."

"A real crazy, who might just want to watch you get blown all to hell."

"And I was shot at with a high-powered rifle. I just can't figure Hashim for that kind of gig."

"Okay, I'll keep digging."

"Hey, don't think I don't appreciate it. And you may be right. I'll cogitate on it."

"I'll keep digging. Tell Pug and Cedric that you all can expect a visit from one of the assistant chiefs. The DA's office has decided not to pursue the matter with you civilians, but they are a little pissed that you set a good citizen up and exposed them to an entrapment charge. They've been contacted by some San Fran scum-ball attorney regarding a settlement with the gentle loving doctor."

"Gentle? Loving?"

"The rag-head son of a bitch, how's that?"

I laugh. "And you're the one always chiding me about political correctness."

"It's not his ethnicity, it's the son-of-a-bitch part that counts. . . . I've got to go try and make some money. Keep me up to date."

"You got it."

As soon as I hang up, I call Pug, then Iver, and clue them in on the potential ass-chewing by SBPD, then Cedric, my computer right arm, and invite him to meet me at Lucky's for a cocktail.

I say cocktail, rather than beer or to bend an elbow, as Lucky's is a high-class joint in one of the more high-class areas in the country. It sits right next to the Montecito Inn, in the town of the same name. Nine thousand three hundred of God's chosen. While at the bar, you're liable to turn to your left and see Dennis Miller trading barbs with the barkeep—and winning flat, hands down, no contest—and to your right to see Oprah sipping a Diet Coke. All served by Matt, Stacy, or Ezra: three of the better barkeeps this expert has met. The reason I pick Lucky's is that it's a ways away from the harbor, and I've got business to talk about . . . and I'd better do some biz as a beer is five or six bucks and a glass of vino more like twelve. Even at that, it's a man's kind of joint, with wood floors, wood stools and tables, white walls, and gentle Casablanca fans overhead. It has a good *Casablanca* touch to it . . . if only Bogie were here. As it is, the walls are covered with pictures of old movie stars, most of them dead . . . who had probably walked the palm-lined street outside Lucky's big many-paned windows at one time or another.

The price of the drinks is high even by Santa Barbara standards but worth it for many reasons . . . one is it keeps out the riffraff. Almost taking a high-caliber slug to the noggin makes me reckless with my money.

Cedric tries to beg off, but I don't let him escape, as I need him.

My friend Cedric, a world traveler who's my age but

has seen the elephant, is my height but twenty-five pounds lighter. He's blond, what's left of it, and green-eyed. The eyes are normally watery enough to float a small boat, but fast moving and intense. If one didn't know Cedric and his abject hate for the stuff, you'd presume he was on some high-powered dope. His complexion is sallow, particularly for a guy who's an expert skin diver. Cedric has dived shipwrecks and the barrier reef and sinkholes for Mayan antiquities and on and on. He claims to have studied to be a Buddhist monk, and I believe him. His vocabulary is unsurpassed, but irritating as he enjoys using it as a weapon against those of us less endowed with instant recall, or have little to recall at all.

He's not what you'd call handsome; in fact he's got a receding chin and a prominent if thin proboscis, to go with bad skin and crooked teeth. But if I were a woman, I'd love to sit and talk with him. The guy is fascinating and worldly. And a good friend, in spite of his constant vocabulary attacks. And as I discovered in a way I welcomed, he's more than a fair to middling martial artist.

After digging in my closet for my best jeans, topping them with a Jose Cuervo–emblazoned T-shirt and then a black goatskin leather jacket that looks like a grand—and probably cost that as I stripped it off an escaping smack dealer, watching him hotfoot it away coatless. Pulling on a pair of cowboy boots, I unlock my mountain bike from the deck box and peddle the Schwinn over to the boatyard and fire up my Harley Sportster. I have little choice in transportation—the FBI has impounded what's left of my van and my damaged but relatively intact oatmeal Chevy.

As I reach the gate of the boatyard, I'm flagged down by a lady in a rumpled suit and porkpie hat. I get stopped before I remember Alice Townsend, *Santa Barbara News-Press* reporter.

"How you doing?" she asks.

I turn off the bike. "Great."

"No, seriously, how's the old body doing?"

"Fine, thanks, most the tape's off."

"You didn't mention before that someone's been trying to blow your head off with a rifle as well as a bomb."

I shrug. "Goes with the territory."

"Remind me to stay out of your territory." She laughs. She's got a great laugh.

"You seem to explore my territory often."

Her smile fades. "You figured out who's trying to send you to bounty hunter heaven? Presuming there is such a place."

"Doubtful. But no, I'm still on the hunt."

"I've been doing a little background on you. When you get settled down, I'd like to do a feature article on you. You're an interesting guy."

"Interesting job, maybe. I'm just a guy trying to make the boat payment."

She fishes in her bag and brings out the trusty Nikon. Steps back a couple of steps and takes a shot. I give her my best scowl until the flash goes off, then shake my head, a little disgustedly, and laugh. "That for the paper? Bounty hunters need to stay out of the limelight."

"I hear you don't work in Santa Barbara County."

"True. It's not good to mess your own nest."

She smiles again. "You mind if I talk with your dad?"

It's my turn to laugh. "Since when do reporters ask who they can or can't talk with?"

And it's her turn to shrug. "He's a cutie."

I've heard my old man called a lot of things, but never a "cutie." Then I wonder if it's me she's interested in, or Pug. "I got to haul."

"Be careful, Dev."

I nod, smile, and fire up the bike.

As I'm pulling away, I hear her yell, "When are you gonna have some time?" But act as if I don't hear. I wave over my shoulder as I crank up the Harley.

The sun has done a hell of a job painting the western sky by the time I park the Harley and elbow my way into the crowded upscale saloon. The dinner crowd has begun to arrive, replacing the Friday-off-work-for-the-weekend crowd—not that half this crowd actually has to work for a living. Many of them will disburse to other places up and down the few blocks of Montecito's main drag to eat, as Lucky's has a limited number of tables and such superior food it's always packed. Then many will return to cap off the night with fifty-buck-a-shot brandy . . . and enhanced by Eric, the manager, with endless style, grace, and polished humor.

I scan the crowd, the pretty people. There must be a hundred thousand dollars' worth of beauty shop and gym time in the place, not to speak of the diamonds and Rolexes, yet the substance is of real people, successful and accomplished, as well as graced with old Montecito charm. Of course, flakes filter through.

I'm probably the only warm body in the place clothed with designer Kirkland—Costco's brand name—with Tony Lama for manly footwear. The rest of the patrons are pure Armani, Gucci, Cline, and Karin.

I get a few stares as I'm still gauzed and taped: the backs of my hands, the back of my neck, and unseen spots on my chest. The explosion was on Tuesday, and it's Friday. I've removed the stuff from my face, as it was just a little much. But I'm blotched and have tiny scrapes and cuts covering cheeks and forehead. I'm not a pretty sight, even in my Costco best.

I usurp a table in a far corner just as a couple leave, and by the time I have a twelve-dollar glass of house red in front of me, Cedric wanders in. He's in designer Salvation Army. He does not receive appreciative knowing glances of approval except from the truly high class, who know that looks deceive.

I order him a beer as he approaches, knowing he favors Amstel Light, then fill him in on the potential ass-chewing by SBPD. In moments, I've reiterated my need to locate the eighty-eight-foot Benetti, and am beginning to fill him in on Orozco's escape from prison and where I've heard our old friend Dr. Hashim now resides, when our conversation is interrupted.

Butch Bohannan is one of the many trust fund babies who call Montecito home, although you wouldn't know it by appearance. He looks like he's competing with Cedric for worst dressed, but in fact it's designer grunge. He's stylishly semishaven with the appropriate two-day shadow. His faux-faded jeans are torn at the knees. The shirt is Hawaiian, with a bold flower print. Without being asked he grabs an empty chair from a nearby table and pulls it up to ours, and between us. He doesn't offer a hand in greeting, but it's just as well, as a hardy handshake is all I need with the backs of my hands still sore as a boil.

"What's up, mates?" he asks, with a phony Australian accent, giving us both a capped-tooth grin. "I heard you had a little trouble, Dev, ol' buddy. You look like hell in a handbasket. You guys come up to God's country to check out the upper crust?"

Cedric gives him a crooked smile. "If you've been to the sewer farm, you'll notice an 'upper crust' on the ponds."

"Unh . . ." he manages.

Cedric slaps him on the back and gives him a sincere, if sympathetic, smile. "Butch, your hebetude never fails to impart a lachrymose warmth to my innermost soul."

He eyes Cedric suspiciously. "I warm your soul?"

"After a fashion. A bilious warmth, a little like gastroenteritis . . . nonetheless a warmth."

"I'm getting a beer," Butch announces, thinking he's been insulted, but not sure, and rises and moves to the bar, probably trying to avoid tipping the cocktail waitress, and willing to stiff the bartender.

While he's gone, my cell phone rings. It's Pug, who informs me that he's talked to Andrew Bartlett, and there's a graveside service for Sandy at ten A.M. on Monday, near San Francisco. He's going, and I assure him I'm going too and that I'll have Cedric make the arrangements for both of us to fly up.

"So," Cedric asks, "what do you want me to do with the good doctor?"

"Get in his head, via his computer, of course . . . but let's talk later. More pressing, the old man and I need to be in San Francisco Monday in time for a ten A.M. service."

Butch is nearby, and I'm paranoid as he is one of the harbor bums, albiet a rich one, and I don't want talk going around about the fact I've learned that Toke Butterworth and the Benetti have gone missing at the same time . . . until I'm ready.

"You know I'm tied up tomorrow?" Cedric mentions.

"I also know how you like to work in the wee witching hours. You've got all night. Call me before you leave if you have anything . . . and with our flight time."

Ced and I sip our drinks, hoping Butch will move on, but he returns, beer in hand. He's a big guy, my height, but heavier. Of course, his heavy is beer, booze, and high living and a bunch of it's in gut and cow butt. He looks even taller than me, but it's the current style of moosed spikes in his dirty-blond-colored surfer hair that makes him appear so.

"So," he says, giving me his best lecher look, "did you check out the chicks at the end of the bar?"

Since I came in a pair of ladies on the shady side of forty have entered. By the looks of them—tight sweaters, tight Lycra pants, Botox-smooth brows, and enough silicon to seal the leaks in the *Titanic*—my bet is they're on the prowl for a guy with a fat wallet. There's a blonde with highlights of pure white in long straight hair and with boobs like volley balls, and a brunette with enough curls to make Janet Jackson jealous. The brunette is well endowed, the blonde doubly so.

"Didn't notice," I reply to Butch's inane question. The bad news is we have to put up with him in this great bar, the good news is he's on my interview list. I'm actually interested in picking Butch's pea brain regarding Toke Butterworth, who I think is the most likely candidate to have taken the Benetti for a joyride, now that Skip Hanson's been eliminated. Toke went missing about the same time as the Benetti. I know Butch hung out with him at one time, and I also know that Terry, Toke's real name, knocked Butch into next week a year or so ago, causing him to have a couple of his shiny white caps recapped. Butch is carrying a grudge, which normally makes for an eager informant. The only thing better is an angry ex-wife.

"You're getting old, Shannon," Butch says. "Of course, your looking like you've been dragged up here from L.A. behind a locomotive keeps you out of the running. I'm going to grab those chairs over there and invite them over."

He's an interloper at our table already, and now he wants to add to the insult. But that's okay, as they'll be much better company than Butch.

But I can't help but get in a dig. "Butch, I've seen your act. You couldn't pick up a bitch dog if you had a medium-rare T-bone in hand. I've seen your 'how about you and I' lousy line. You'll tell them how great you are, and they'll puke and be on the run trying to recover their seats at the bar."

He reddens. "Okay, smart-ass, I'll bet you fifty bucks I can walk out of here with one of them in thirty minutes."

"Save your breath," Cedric advises. "You'll need it to blow up your date when you get home."

That gives me a good laugh, and makes Butch redden even more.

Chapter Eight

Cedric grabs his wallet and checks his resources before answering, as I make up my mind if I want to take pennies from a mentally dead man's eyes. "I'll take twenty of that," Ced says.

I might as well get my share. "And I'll take the other thirty. But no bull, Butch. You walk out of here with one of them who's *agreed* to head up to your place, not just walking her to her car." Butch's place is a ten-million-dollar-plus pad left to him by his folks, so that would seem to be giving him quite an edge. But then, I know Butch, and he needs all the edge he can get.

He sticks out a big, if soft, paw, and shakes with both of us.

I check my watch. "It's seven-eighteen. You've got until twelve minutes to eight."

He nods, then he moves away to where the two girls are talking, between eyeing the crowd of men as if looking for an insurance policy for their old age. I'm surprised to see him head back to the table with them.

"Grab some chairs, Cedric," he commands. Cedric narrows his eyes, but rises.

"Ladies," he says, giving them a welcoming smile, "take my seat."

I jump up. "And mine. We'll find some more."

We manage to cajole a couple from tables with four chairs and only three patrons. Then reclaim our spots at the table. Cedric, who has a polite streak lurking somewhere deep in his psyche under all that smart-ass, asks their names, then makes the introductions. Janet and Penny.

"So," Penny, the blonde, asks, "you're the famous bounty hunter Butch was telling us about?"

"Bail enforcement . . . but it's much the same thing."

"You been in a car wreck?"

"Yeah, I guess you could say that."

She's had work that must have cost a month's gross for some high-income type, and has had enough time under the knife that she's beginning to look a little plastic—a Barbie doll with a few years on her. But under it all, she's got a nice smile and a sincere manner.

I have to laugh. Butch got them to the table on my credentials, not his own. Fairly clever.

"So, bail enforcement agent?"

"Yes, ma'am. I'm a bail enforcement agent. Some folks call us bounty hunters. We go after skips . . . those who don't make their court date, and are out with OPM."

"Other people's money, right?"

"Yes, ma'am."

"Ma'am . . . folks," the brunette, Janet, says. "That's cute. You from the South?"

Janet's a pretty woman, shopworn, but pretty. She has a knowing way of right looking into you. "South Santa Barbara," I say. "But I hang out in some strange places with some strange *folks,* all in the job." I emphasize the folks this time. "And you pick up phrases and ways of enunciating. Besides, my mama taught me good manners."

Butch laughs, but it's at me, not with me. "You've been around Cedric too long . . . enunciating. Jesus, you two are a case."

We make small talk for a while, until Butch realizes he's being left out of the conversation. I'm still on bounty hunting with Janet, and Cedric is extolling the virtues of Buddhism with Penny.

To verify that what he's about to say is true, Butch pulls out his wallet and removes a pair of business cards, each of them imprinted with a full-color photo of his house with the sea in the distance. He sets them on the table in front of each of the girls. "Hey, ladies, I've got six thousand feet overlooking the ocean, and I'll bet you like to party."

The girls basically ignore him, after a quick glance.

He can't leave well enough alone. "Full bar, Jacuzzi, some great porn movies."

The blonde, Penny, snaps her head around and eyes him. I can't help but get the impression she may have starred in a couple of blue flicks. "What's that supposed to mean?" she asks, and she's not smiling.

He shrugs and grins. "That means let's party."

She turns back to me, ignoring Butch. "So, how does one get in the manhunting business? Not that I'm bad at it myself, but so far there's no bounty on the ones I corner."

I smile, then try and regale her for a while longer, at least enough so that she won't be tempted by the six thousand feet overlooking the ocean.

"Hey," Butch says, slapping the table to try and get some attention, beginning to see his fifty flying away. "We're all big kids." He smiles, but only one side of his mouth turns up, as he pokes the blonde in the ribs. "How about you and me going to my place and screwing our brains out?"

She acts as if she hasn't heard him.

"Hey," he repeats, leaning closer to her, "I'd sure like to get in your pants."

She snaps her head back to meet his waiting gaze, her reply cool and calm. "There's already one asshole there."

Cedric and I laugh so hard we're red in the face. I'd normally defend a lady from such a crass approach, but this one has a rapier wit and needs no help.

Butch chokes, trying to get something out, then reddens,

but to prove he's an asshole through and through, doesn't weaken. He turns to Janet, the brunette. "How about you? You look like the smart one. Smarter than any phony fucking dumb blonde. . . ." He laughs, but no one laughs with him. I feel like clocking him one, but I still need his goodwill to get some answers. Besides, the girls seem well armed. He eyes Janet with a sincerity I'm surprised he can muster, and says, "I'd sure like a little pussy."

It's barely out when she retorts, "I would too, mine's as big as this tabletop." She flashes him an irritated tight-lipped smile.

Again, Cedric and I almost go to the floor. This is not these ladies' first time at bat, not that I thought it was. But those are home-run classic replies to crass comments. I'm proud to know the girls, and Cedric can't wipe the smile off his face.

They turn back to us, and Butch rises quickly, stammering, "F . . . F . . . Fuck all of you."

And just as quickly, Janet comes back. "Sorry, I don't date outside my species."

I think my buddy Butch is going to have apoplexy.

Cedric speaks to him as he rises, "Now, Butch, you're a man who really knows how to tank an assignation."

He looks both confused and angry, but turns to walk away. He's at the back of the table and has to pass. I stop him with a hard grasp on his wrist. "You owe me a few bucks, Butchy boy. How 'bout we meet for breakfast and I'll buy, and even at that, I'll call the bet even . . . if you answer a few questions?"

He tries to pull away, but I have an iron grip, even though it pains my burned hand. He relents, relaxes, then looks down at me, as if bored. "What questions?"

"Tomorrow."

"Where?"

"Sambo's, seven o'clock."

"Too early. Tomorrow's Saturday. Make it eleven."

"Fine, then lunch, at . . ." I start to say Brophy's, but I don't want to contaminate one of my joints with this dipshit, but I do want to pick his pea brain. "At Joe's, State Street."

"Noon."

"A few minutes before, to beat the rush."

"See you there." He gives me his back the instant I release his wrist.

"Very generous of you," Cedric says, glowering at me as Butch clomps away. "That was partly my remuneration you gave away."

"Yeah, yeah, I'm buying dinner at Café del Sol, okay?"

"Good enough. For all of us, right?"

"Sure. If the ladies would care to join us, it would be my pleasure."

As you enter Café del Sol, located across from the bird refuge, halfway between the harbor and Lucky's, you pass the bar. Seated there, her back to me, is a lady I'd recognize from any angle. Cynthia Proffer.

"Can I buy you a drink, or dinner?" I ask, leaning over her shoulder. She smells of Michael, a perfume I know she favors. I like it.

"Working," she says, hardly acknowledging my presence. Then she turns slightly and gives the ladies a cursory glance. "Besides, it looks as if you're well accompanied."

"Casually, nothing serious."

"Nothing serious, hell. That's a serious set if I ever saw one." Her tone is less than pleased, which pleases me. "I'm working, Shannon." She gives me the cold shoulder. I guess the cold shoulder, in some instances, is a good sign. She could easily have given me an elbow to the ribs. Or worse, not given a damn enough to do either.

I decide to let her work without further attempts at having her join us. She and I both work the nighthawk shift far too often. Cynthia leaves in a few minutes, I'm sure tailing a guy in a fifteen-hundred-dollar suit who's left just ahead of her, probably an errant husband about to get his comeuppance.

The evening is pleasant, but I'm in no mood or physical condition to carry it over until the morning. After a great dinner, I chide Cedric about the work I need him to do, thank the ladies for their great company, and haul out of there for the boat.

Sandy again visits me in the night, hobbling in my nightmare up on one leg, and I again am able to get to sleep after promising her that I'll find and do more than merely punish the bomber . . . that I'll make him hurt. Futa knows I'm not sleeping well, as he curls up against the small of my back and purrs me back into, thank God, dreamless-land.

Maybe I should have invited the brunette over for a tour of the boat and a nightcap. A good friend would have, as I stuck Cedric in the position of having two lovely ladies to deal with. I've found a plethora of that commodity usually results in a dearth, to put it as Cedric might.

My phone shakes both Futa and me out of deep sleep. He stretches while I answer the cordless, which I've had the forethought to let reside on the bunk-side bureau. As I reach, I glance at the clock, it's six A.M. It's Cedric, himself.

"You are a true friend," he says, and I think he's being facetious.

"Hey, I wasn't up to it."

"And it's a good thing. I ended up with a superfluity of pulchritude at my disposal."

I sigh. I'm not awake enough for this. "And that means?"

"Women everywhere. All over me. Blonde and brunette. They just left."

"I'm happy for you. But then you didn't get anything done?"

"They left an hour ago. I haven't got anything new on the Benetti, but I'm on to the lady in Coeur d' Alene. She's an early riser, already on her computer buying via the Web from Neiman Marcus . . . at least someone is. Whoever it is, they're on her computer and using her credit card. A lady of good taste, and unlimited budget. She blew a grand before seven A.M."

"So, did you get Pug and me a flight to San Francisco on Monday?"

"Alaska Airlines, and you're going on to Spokane if you want."

"I want. Perfect. I owe you big time."

"Now for the bad news."

"And that is?"

"The good doctor in San Francisco is getting smart. He's got a hell of a firewall on his computer, and so far I can't break through."

"You've been at it what, an hour?"

"Fifteen minutes on that problem."

"Give it some more time, Cedric. You can do it."

"I'll call you after I get back from retreat . . . and I need it. The ladies hurt me bad."

"Hurt you good, you mean. You're going to the Buddhist thing?"

"It's not a thing, it's a retreat."

"Okay, okay, but get back on the computer as soon as you can. I need to know if that son of a bitch has been anywhere near Santa Barbara in the last month."

"You got it. I probably don't need to get into his system to find that out. Airline records—"

"What if he drove?"

"Credit card records—"

"Unless he paid cash." I'm always thinking "street" and Cedric thinks Google. We make a good team.

Cedric shrugs. "I'll get on it tomorrow night. The other good news is he's wireless."

"Wireless?"

"Yeah, wireless. He has a transmitter in his house, part of his router, his connection to his computer is wireless, which means if I can get within a hundred feet or so from his place, I can pick up everything he's doing on the Web."

"No kidding?"

I never should have acted interested.

"Kismet. I found it just as we might need it. The program turns my handheld into a scanner and I can pick up his waves. I got a new toy."

"I knew you would have. Legal?"

"So long as I don't record it. But when did that start worrying you?"

I ignore the question. "Call me later with an update."

I think about trying to sleep some more, but know myself well enough to know that the mind is now racing, and sleep is out of the question.

In the small head off my stateroom, I decide I'm sick of bandages, and work the tape on my chest loose, trying to keep from denuding myself of chest hair. I find that there are only three cuts that have taken stitches, and one with six is the largest, and the rest are mostly bruises and abrasions.

I doubt if running water will hurt the cuts, and I'm nuts for a shower, so take one, but don't scrub the cuts. The good news is by the time I'm drying off, I'm not bleeding anywhere. I take my time, making a cup of tea in the microwave, then returning to the main stateroom and cleaning up. I strip the bunk so I can hit the laundromat, then use a little cleanser on the head and pile the towels with the sheets. It takes me a couple of hours to get everything shipshape.

The bad news is I feel someone board and I'm still stark naked. I grab some trunks and pull them on and head aft, passing my bureau and snatching up my Smith and Wesson as I do. I make the main salon just in time to see the hatchway fill with a large body in a cheap suit.

I don't know the guy, but he has his hands on the rails, and I have mine on the weapon, so I'm not worried.

"What's up?" I ask, my tone less than welcoming.

His eyes must be having trouble adjusting to the dim light in the salon—I haven't opened the curtains yet—and he seems surprised that I'm standing there, automatic hanging loosely at my side.

"Shannon," a voice calls out from behind him. I recognize Babs Benson's voice.

"He's got a gun," the guy says, his voice a little shaky and his eyes a tad wide. He's got a thick face to match the shoulders and gut, and a nose like a lumpy red potato. I'm surprised I don't know him if he's a cop, and I presume he is as he's with Babs.

"He's home, and licensed to carry," she says from behind him. "Dev, this is Detective Victor Ambrose. Put up the piece."

I eye him like a bull at a bastard calf, but turn back and flip the automatic through the passage to my stateroom and onto the bed.

"I don't have the coffee on yet," I say, "but then I don't remember inviting you." As I speak, he arrives at the salon floor and Babs fills the hatchway behind.

"We're not here for coffee," the big guy, Victor, says, pulling his cuffs from a leather case on his belt. "Turn around and give me the wrists. You know the drill."

"What?" I'm sure I haven't heard him correctly.

He pulls his coat back, exposing a tidy little police special in a belt holster. "The wrists, asshole."

"You got a warrant?" I demand, then ignore him, looking up over his shoulder. "What's up, Detective Benson?" I ask Babs, deferring to the fact she has an office compatriot with her and is obviously here on business.

"You've got to come in for some questions," she says, with a shrug.

The big dick steps forward and tries to shove me around, pushing on my already sore chest. Then he gets insistent, trying to slip an arm under mine to put me in a wrist-bar come-along. Mistake. I don't know what his problem is, so I shake him, step backward, then using the extra leverage he's given me by making me plant a foot, bring one up from low and bury the short right into his solar plexus. He oofs like a walrus passing gas while his eyes go even wider and he doubles as he stumbles back.

I take pity on him and shove him back even harder, rather than bring up the left in an uppercut and smash that potato nose worse than it's already been spread over his ugly mug. This is not the boy's first time at bat, even though he's a .150 hitter.

But we must respect the law. "Like I asked, you got a warrant?"

"Dev," Babs yells. "He's a cop."

"He's an doofus pea-brained asshole," I say. He'd like to respond to that, but he hasn't caught his breath yet, and won't for a while. I think I felt the pleasant impression of his backbone on my knuckles as I drove that one home.

"Step back and let me handle this," Babs orders the guy, passing him and facing me square on. "He insists on us cuffing you. Turn around and give me your wrists. The FBI found a fingerprint on the second bomb. The one under your four-door Chevy . . . yours."

"My Chevy?"

"Your fingerprint, dummy. On the bomb. Under your Chevy."

Chapter Nine

I'm flabbergasted. My fingerprint on the bomb? "Can't be," I manage.

"Turn around," Babs says, "and come on downtown so we can get this straightened out."

I stand and digest that for a moment. "Keep the dickhead away from me."

"My word of honor," she says.

I turn and let her snap her cuffs on my wrists, which she does gently so the blood can still flow, then realize I'm still in my trunks. "How about letting me change?"

"No . . . fucking way. Read him . . . his rights." Doofus has almost caught his breath. He does, then clamps his jaw and lunges for me, but Babs, true to her word, steps in front of him and wards him off. Not bad for 110 pounds against 250.

She shoves a finger in his chest, getting her petite little nose right up in his face. "That was your fault, Ambrose. They didn't say anything about arresting him, just to bring him in for questioning. Go get him some clothes. We can take them with us."

He eyes me, then her, then me again. "That was a cheap shot. I'm gonna stomp your dumb ass into a grease spot, soon as I get you alone," he says, but merely shoves both of us aside and moves to my room, just as my phone rings.

I give him a nod and a hard smile. Then turn to the lady. "Please get that, Babs?" I ask.

Ambrose looks furiously at her, a real dagger glance. He snatches up my cordless and flings it against the bulkhead. It falls to the deck in pieces.

"Nice," I say, half amused. "I was going to replace that piece of junk anyway."

"Fuck you," he says, and continues toward my stateroom.

"Make sure everything matches," I call after him. "I'm a slave to fashion." I've been around Cedric too long, I'm getting as smart-ass as he is. The fact is I'm still a little astounded to spend much time trying to be clever. How could my fingerprint have been on the bomb? It has to be a forensic mistake of some kind. A glitch in the chain of evidence, or some damned thing. But I can understand why my presence might be demanded. In fact, I'm a little surprised there's not a fleet of squad cars.

"Let's get a head start," Babs says in a low voice, "so he doesn't kick you off the dock." She moves me toward the ladder.

"I can swim better with these cuffs on than that fat toad could with water wings," I say, loud enough so I know he can hear me. The bad news is he's rousting my stateroom, I can see clothes being flung out into the passageway, the stateroom I've just spent an hour putting perfect.

"Move it," Babs says, and I do.

As we're progressing up the dock, she explains as she reaches for her cell phone, "I'm calling your dad and will get him to meet us there. Don't rat me out on this. It would piss Ambrose worse than you already did."

"Thanks," I manage, but I'm lost in thought. Perplexed, in fact.

She does as she says, and luckily gets the old man, then hangs up and turns to me. "What the hell did you do to Vic? He was real anxious to come along."

"I've never seen the guy."

"Vic Ambrose."

"Ambrose. I hauled in a kid named Ambrose a few months ago . . . a twenty-five-year-old kid. Tony Ambrose, an FTA on a DUI and hit-and-run. His second failure to appear. Made three grand on that one."

"That's Vic's kid."

"Now I get it. I hauled him out of his grandmother's house in Ventura last Christmas. They always come home for Christmas. I put on a Santa Claus suit. The kid met me at the door with a big grin. His family doesn't believe in Santa anymore."

"And Vic wasn't there. He's divorced and I'll bet it was his ex-wife's folks' house."

"I would have cut him some slack . . . twenty-four hours' worth . . . had I known his old man was a cop. I had no idea, with the pickup thirty miles from Santa Barbara."

"Too late now. Vic's been gnashing his teeth to get at you."

"And that's exactly the reason I don't work in the county I live in. How was I to know he was hooked up with the PD?" She merely smiles and shakes her head.

Saturday's a busy time in the harbor, with hundreds of tourists. I'm the main attraction with pointed fingers and clicking cameras as I'm being led to the parking lot by a foxy female half my size.

Iver, my good friend and occasional employee, is heading out of the parking lot as we pass. He stops and places his hands on his hips and watches us approach.

"What's up?" he asks.

"Wanted for questioning," I offer as we pass. Babs nods, and being cop careful, watches him closely. She met Iver at Pop's birthday dinner, but doesn't know him that well.

"Anything I can do?" Iver asks.

"Make sure Futa's fed, in case this takes a while."

"No sweat," he calls out as we near the squad car.

She has me tucked into the rear of the patrol car by the time Ambrose gets there. He's carrying a T-shirt that I've worn to stain the taffrail, nicely stained itself, a pair of two-hundred-buck tan dress slacks that I have to have cleaned almost every time I wear them, and a pair of beach flip-flops. As head butler and valet, Ambrose leaves a little to be desired. I decide discretion is the better part of valor, and keep my mouth shut.

I'm lucky he didn't find the Santa suit to bring.

By the time we reach the quasi-Spanish-style police station, I'm thinking pure defendant. This time it isn't the conference room, but rather a small interview room with the not-so-innocuous mirror on the wall. I wave at whoever is lurking behind it as soon as Babs removes the cuffs.

Ambrose slings the clothes on the table and I suit up, pulling the slacks on over my trunks, then I take a seat.

"You want coffee?" Babs asks.

"Fuck him," Vic offers, but he's cooled, and it's with little enthusiasm.

"Please, hot and stupid, like I like my detectives," I say, giving him as hard a look as I can muster, then add, "Male detectives, that is."

"I'll have my day," he mumbles. I'm sure he's hoping the recording device that I know is covering the room does not pick it up.

"Are you guys going to keep up this good cop, bad cop routine?" I ask.

"I am bad, sonny boy," Vic says, leaning down on his knuckles on the tabletop, glaring at me.

"You want a cup, Vic?" Babs asks, seemingly trying to maintain the peace.

"Please," he says. The first civil thing he's said since he stumbled down my ladder. "Christmas Day . . . you frigging prick," he mumbles, and I shrug.

We sit in silence until she returns. She is followed into the room by Detective Paul Dowty, Pop's old partner, FBI Agent O'Mally, and SBPD Chief Hector Sandoval. As there are only four seats at the table, Vic Ambrose remains standing to the rear of me, I'm sure a tactic to make me nervous. Babs leans against the mirror.

There's an ominous, heavy feeling in the room, and I'm being drilled by five sets of eyes.

Nobody speaks for a moment, so I take a sip of my coffee, stretch and yawn, then jump right in. "So, I understand there's a print of mine somewhere it shouldn't be?"

O'Mally glares across the table at Babs, cutting his eyes from her to Ambrose. "I'd as soon do my own interrogating, ladies and gentlemen," he snaps.

"The print?" I ask.

He clears his throat and centers laser eyes back on me. "The print. Your right index finger, Mr. Shannon. A clear ten-point print found not on, but inside, the device recovered from under your Chevrolet four-door sedan—"

I clear my throat, somewhat mimicking him, and interrupt. Not a good way to make a friend, but he's being anything but friendly at the moment. "A device that my father and I sent you to search for. That you missed, when it was fairly obvious that there might be another device."

He reddens a little. What's obvious is that it's still a sore point with O'Mally. "That's not a mitigating factor, Shannon. The fact *is* your print was *in* the device." He speaks slowly and deliberately, as if to the village idiot, and continues in the same vein, "Only someone who worked on the device would have a print on the *inside*. We also found the controller, across the street in the flower bed. And your prints were on it, along with those of a still unidentified woman . . . judging by the size of the prints."

I decide it's time to get serious, but can't help but answer in the same pedantic manner. "That *couldn't* be, Agent O'Mally. I don't *build* bombs. I've never been around a place where *bombs* were built. Tell me *exactly* where the print was found."

He eyes me carefully. "This was a fairly sophisticated

device. Activated by a radio wave. Actually it's a small servo motor, such as is used on model airplanes. It was set up to close a circuit with the push of a button on a distant controller. A hundred and fifty yards distant, I'm told."

"A servo. From a model." Then it dawns on me. "Made in England?" I ask.

Again, he eyes me carefully. "How did you know that?"

"I had a model boat, a radio-controlled boat. A lovely Swedish lass sent it to me from England, in remembrance of a sail we took last year. It was a kit that I assembled myself. Just last week I gave it to twelve-year-old Johnny Roosevelt, whose father is a live-aboard at the harbor. Small prints, as you said. A twelve-year-old, and small for his age. He's right across the main channel from me on a sixty-foot catamaran. The damn model boat is four feet tall and I didn't have room for it, and"—I hesitate for effect—"I lost the controller early last week, and decided not to replace it, but rather to give the boat to Johnny, who helped me out by feeding my cat a couple of times. You can check with Bert . . . Bertram Roosevelt, Johnny's father."

There's a long silence in the room and all eyes are on me, then Sandoval turns and speaks to Ambrose. "Follow up on that, Vic."

Ambrose grumbles and leaves the room. I can feel the tension in the room lighten a little.

"So," O'Mally continues, "you contend that someone stole the boat you gave to this kid and used the servo out of it to make the device? And stole the controller from you prior to getting their hands on the boat?"

"That's all it could be."

"That's a stretch," O'Mally says, and everyone at the table seems to agree.

"Is it a stretch to think I'd build a device to bomb myself? Is it a stretch to think I'd kill a beautiful lady I barely knew? It's a hell of a stretch to think I'd leave prints on the activating controller and that I'd activate it and be able to throw it across four lanes of traffic before the bomb detonated. Yeah, that's a real stretch . . . from Ursa Minor a few thousand light-years away. . . ."

I get no answer, only blank stares.

Ambrose is back in the room, looking smug. "He doesn't answer his phone." He eyes me. "I guess we'll just have to keep Mr. Shannon over the weekend, until we can get him in front of a judge. You want me to read him his rights?" he asks the chief.

Before he can answer, I suggest, "Call Cynthia Proffer. She has Bert's cell phone . . . she did some work for the Roosevelts."

"Do it," Sandoval says, and Ambrose grumbles again, but leaves.

Sandoval and O'Mally chat about the Homeland Security Agency while we wait, then Ambrose, crestfallen, returns. "I got him. At Disneyland, of all places . . . with his kid. He confirms what Shannon said. Somebody stole the kid's boat over a week ago."

They spend another hour grilling me. Sandoval, a busy man, is called out of the room two or three times, and O'Mally takes at least three calls on his cell phone. Finally, they run out of steam.

O'Mally rises to his feet. "I still say it's too big a stretch to believe a guy who builds a bomb steals a victim's model boat to get the servo, and steals a controller and makes sure the vic's prints remain." He eyes me for a long while. "Everything I've ever learned says we should read Mr. Shannon his rights and book him for murder."

Chapter Ten

I'm sure the look on my face is incredulous, and I'm sure Agent O'Mally is enjoying it to his core.

His expression changes and he looks a little crestfallen as he continues, "However, I don't think we can hold him, under the circumstances."

I shake my head, knowing the prick went through that speech just to get my goat. He's on his feet so I follow suit and stand. "Then I'm out of here."

Sandoval rises also. "Shannon," he instructs, "I wouldn't be leaving town until we get this thing squared away."

"I'm going north on Monday, Chief." Then I tell him a small lie. "I'm taking the old man with me." I am taking him as far as San Francisco.

"How far north?"

"San Francisco," I say, looking him straight in the eye, "to Miss Sandy Bartlett's funeral."

"Okay. Particularly since one of us is going also."

"Good, then Pug and I'll have some company on the trip."

I don't mention that I'm going on to Idaho, which is a little close to the Canadian border. I don't want the chief getting nervous.

Vic Ambrose is so red in the face and his jaw is so tight I think he might pop a valve and fill the room with steam, but I give him a friendly nod as I leave. Babs follows me out.

"I knew there'd be some explanation," she says.

"Thank you for that," I say, and give her a sincere smile. "You're okay, Detective Benson."

"You had time to do anything on June's disappearance?"

"Not much, but I've got Cedric and some other folks working on it, and I'm beating the pavement myself. Nobody disappears, Babs. We'll find her, you and I if it comes to that." She lays a hand on my shoulder, but it's a very intimate gesture the way she does it.

As she walks me to the front door of the PD, her tone is more than just a little serious. "I think you better figure out who this guy is, Shannon. He's been very, very close to you, if he knows that model boat was yours, and if he stole the controller from you and the boat you built from a neighbor kid you'd given it to. He's watching everything you do. I get the feeling he's teasing you, wanting you to hurt, hurt bad, before he finishes the job. Making sure your prints were on the bomb was conscious and deliberate. He's a devious bastard."

"You think he might have missed me on purpose?"

"That's one scenario."

I shrug, then turn back to her. "Come see me sometime," I say, pushing my way through the door.

"I'll see you Monday. I'm covering the funeral. That person in the bushes, taking pictures, that'll be me."

"Early morning flight?" I ask.

"Real early."

"Come even earlier, I'll buy you breakfast at the airport."

"Ha, I'll barely make the plane. Underneath all this makeup is a gargoyle. It takes me an hour as it is."

"That I seriously doubt." I give her a wink. "But one of these days, I'd love to find out what you look like when you first wake up." I wave, she blushes, and I'm out of there, then realize I don't have wheels. Santa Barbara's police department is a pleasant two-story building near the downtown residential area; Figueroa is a great street with huge overhanging trees, making a tunnel of the lane. Not a bad place to walk, so I do, up to State Street, Santa Barbara's main drag. It's been a long time since I've taken a cab in Santa Barbara, but seeing a vacant one, I wave him down. As I'm riding to the harbor, I realize I don't have my cell phone and the old man was heading for the PD. I borrow the cabbie's and give him a call.

"I'm shooting the bull with Dowty," he tells me. "I understand you're a suspected bomb builder?"

"Come by Brophy's, sixish, and we'll play catch-up." We agree to meet.

I've got only a day and a half before I leave town, and I've got plenty to do. We're still not on to the *Orion*, the eighty-eight-foot Benetti I've agreed to locate—although we're sure she's moving south along the Mexican coast— nor do I have any idea what happened to my friend June Fredrich. I decide to do a little old-fashioned investigative work on those two items while I await the return of Cedric from his retreat, and his doing some more wizardry on the computer.

Able Stearns was one of the early founders of Santa Barbara. Stearn's Wharf, which forms the east side of the harbor, was originally developed by him. Parking on the wharf is restricted and a small parking-ticket booth rests where the wharf joins the land, at the terminus of State Street where it dies into Cabrillo Boulevard, which fronts on and parallels the beach and harbor. I have the cabbie drop me off and I hustle to the boat and change clothes. It's warm enough for shorts in beautiful Santa Barbara, and I don them and keep the stained tee on so I look like just another working stiff just off work. I want to casually interview everyone I wander across who's a local and who might know something about what goes on at the harbor. I wish I could ask about who might be shooting at me, and bombing me, but I don't even have the questions. What do you ask, "See anybody making a bomb lately?" Or, "See anyone firing a high-powered rifle at me lately?"

This will be the third time I've made the rounds, asking about Toke and about June Fredrich. But people have days off, and change shifts, and you've got to keep pounding away.

The parking ticket booth is manned during the daylight hours, so I stop in to say hello to the attendant.

My objective is to find out who, in addition to one I already know, Terry "Toke" Butterworth, has been missing since about the same time the Benetti disappeared. Part of the problem is that no one, including Darwin Winston-Gray, who owns the *Orion*, knows exactly when the *Orion* slipped away. Darwin was in Hawaii for two weeks, and reported her empty end tie to the cops and his insurance company three weeks ago. He called me in only last week, after deciding he would, in fact, take a substantial loss on the craft if she wasn't recovered. It seems Intercontinental Insurance had only insured the boat for her original purchase price, which did not reflect most of the million Darwin has sunk into her since and the appreciation in her value as a result.

I've learned that Toke Butterworth was permanent crew on the *Orion* for over a year, but was fired by Darwin during a shouting match only a week before Darwin left for Hawaii. Rumor has it, as has often happened with Darwin, they had a falling-out about what was owed to Toke. It doesn't take a Sherlock to deduct that Toke might be her new captain, somewhere far beyond the reach of U.S. law enforcement.

If I had hijacked her, I'd be headed for some place where I could sell her. There are only so many Benetti hulls in the world, and fewer eighty-eight-foot ones. No legitimate person would buy a boat he suspected was stolen, particularly one so easily identified. So that leaves the four *d*s: despots, dictators, dopes and dope dealers. If I had to guess I'd say the *Orion* was on her way to either South America or Indonesia. The problem with Indonesia would be getting her there without someone stealing the boat you done stole. The area is renowned for its pirates, and pirates not afraid to take on a massive oil tanker, much less a pleasure yacht. So, if I was to put my money on it, and I will before it's over, it's South America.

Toke is a big strapping redheaded kid, if a guy about my age, thirty-five, can be called a kid. But he's always doing kid things—surfing, sailing pumpkin-shell racers, skateboarding around the harbor—so he qualifies as a kid if anyone his age does. And he always has a kid smile on his freckled mug. He was, however, a fair hand on board, as Pug testified when I brought Toke's name up a couple of weeks or so ago. Toke has crewed on *Copper Glee*, Pug's boat, a time or two when Cedric or Iver was missing, and is as strong and willing as he is big. He's also deeper than he appears. I've often suspected that under the kid cover, he's a very smart and cunning guy, if any guy who habitually uses dope can be considered clever and cunning. That's yet to be proved.

The first thing I did a week ago was put Cedric to work on the keyboard to find out what he could about Terry Butterworth, but he turned up zero, zilch, nada. Terry, it seems, is as elusive as the twelve-year-old he portrays when it comes to background, credit cards, driver's license, bank accounts, and anything other than a birth certificate. He was born in Tracy, California, in the central valley. Then just disappeared, at least so far as record keeping is concerned.

Tracing the *Orion,* via Toke, is about as productive as toking one on a big bomber of a dooby just before you're going to take your SATs. Which is how Terry got his nickname, as he always reeked of toking Mary Jane. Probably among the reasons he has no driver's license.

Even as immature as Toke is in many ways, he's a good sailor, and wouldn't have taken the *Orion* out alone. Eighty-eight feet is not exactly a single-handed sail. So if Toke's not traceable, maybe one of his newly acquired deckhands is, and that's my mission today. Of course, I'm presuming he has newly acquired deckhands. He could have been pissed enough to take the *Orion* out to the trench and scuttle her. In that case I should be looking for the tender aboard which he came home.

But the first supposition is the best one. Who else is missing?

There's a cute little pug-nosed blonde in the parking booth, but she's new to the area and doesn't know Butterworth from baloney, so I wander on out on the wharf. The Harbor Restaurant is the halfway mark out on the boardwalk, and looks out over the harbor and marina. It's early, only ten-thirty, and the restaurant is between breakfast and lunch, a good time to shoot the bull with the employees. And I know that it was one of Toke's favorite hangouts; in fact I remember him running with one of the girls who worked there. I corner the upstairs bartender, whose face I recognize as he's an old-timer around the harbor, but I can't remember his name for the life of me. I do remember that not much goes on in the harbor that he doesn't know about. I relax and have a cup of coffee while I ease into the subject at hand. He's a Bill Gates look-alike, and an outsider type. Maybe that's what his life is, sitting back and watching the rest of the world go around.

"So, I got a good friend looking for a job," I say. "You guys doing any hiring here?"

He's shining glasses as we talk. "Lost a fry cook and a waitress in the last couple of weeks . . . but you know

Santa Barbara, there was a line out to the beach wanting those jobs."

"Who left?" I ask.

"Pancho Reyes, the fry cook. I think he's in the can for back child support. And Meegan."

"I remember her. Tall girl, long dark hair?"

He looks my way for the first time, looking a little like a dog begging for a handout. I expect him to drool on himself any moment. "Meegan Howard. The most striking blue eyes, almost turquoise, you've ever seen. And man, what a set of legs."

It dawns on me where I'd met her. At a beach party. "Didn't she date Toke?"

"The asshole with the skateboard? Yeah, I tried a hundred times to score with her, but she was hung up on that guy. Before him, she went with Skip Hanson, another dickhead as far as I'm concerned."

No wonder Skip was eager to give me a hand. Toke stole his girl. "She say where she was going?"

"Nope, just didn't show up for work one day."

"What day?"

This time he looks a little suspicious. "She in trouble?"

"No, hell no. Just curious."

But he still gives me the doubting look. "Betty the bookkeeper can tell you if you really want to know." He turns back to his glasses and I surmise that's all I'm going to get from him.

Then I have a second thought. "Hey, Fred, you know June Fredrich?"

He eyes me again. "What am I, Mr. Answer Man today?"

I laugh, then bore in. "You know she's missing?"

"Anyone who reads the papers knows that. She's been gone a long time. She used to hang out here once in a while. A good tipper."

"Any thoughts on her?"

"Maybe. What's it worth to her old man?"

That pisses me off. I stand from the bar stool and lean forward. I can feel the heat crawl up the back of my neck. "I don't know what it's worth to him. But it's a way to keep my goodwill. And you've got about a half minute to do so."

He curls his lip at me. "Do I want to?"

"Your nose does."

Chapter Eleven

He gets it. "Okay, okay. She was in here with some guy from Channel Islands Harbor a couple of times. A surfer dude. Usually at Sunday brunch."

"Just the two of them?"

"No. A bunch of those surfer types, but she was zeroed on this big sandy-haired kid. A spring/fall kind of thing . . . kind of romance, looked like to me. She picked up the tab for the lot of them."

I can't believe that June might have been straying, particularly with some kid. I never got any vibes from June that she was interested in any extracurricular activities. In fact, it was just the opposite. I don't believe the possibility, but I press nonetheless. "Did the cops get on to this guy?"

"I told them about it, but I heard the guy split for parts unknown."

"Name?"

"Don't know."

"Bullshit."

"No shit, Shannon. I don't know. Surfer dudes are a pain in the ass. I try and forget them."

It's more info than I've gotten in the last week out of this one guy, so I overtip—maybe it's a little guilt from laying the nose threat on him.

I do stop by and see Betty, in the little office off the main dining room. Middle-aged Betty with Coke-bottle-bottom-thick glasses appears to take full advantage of the feed-the-help-whatever-they-want policy at the Harbor Restaurant, as she fills the little desk chair to overflowing. But she's got a nice smile even if over multiple chins—a smile she promptly loses when I ask about Meegan.

"Who wants to know?" she asks. This may be an uphill battle. So I rely on possible parental concern, presuming she is a parent.

"Her mom and dad asked me to find out where she is. They're worried as hell." Works every time.

She melts, then quickly shuffles through some paperwork.

"She didn't show up a month or so ago. I still have a check for her if you find her. It would kill me if my daughter went missing."

"She left without picking up her check?"

"Yeah."

"How much?"

"Her parents need to know that, too?" She's eying me with bloodshot watery gray eyes over the top of her glasses. I've found that bookkeepers are always a suspicious lot.

I give her my most hangdog look, almost ready to break into tears over these poor distraught parents. "They need to know anything that will give them some peace of mind and let them sleep nights."

"Hmmph," she says, but again goes to the paperwork. "Three hundred forty-six bucks plus change."

"That's a strange one. It would sure as hell worry me if my kid didn't show up to collect that kind of dough."

"Me too," she says, again into helping the folks. "I thought about calling the cops, but her roommate came by and said Meegan had an emergency and had to fly somewhere, and tried to pick up the check. I wouldn't give it to her and told her to come back when Meegan had an address."

"So you could mail it to her?"

"Yep."

"But no address yet?"

"Nope. Or I would have told you so you could have told her mom and dad."

"Her roommate have a name?"

"Probably, but I didn't get it."

"I'll check back."

I'm back upstairs in a heartbeat, and picking the Bill Gates look-alike for info. "Meegan has a roommate?"

"Silly Swanson."

"Silly?"

"That's a nickname. Don't know her real name." He holds up a glass, looking for spots, then turns to me. "You sure she's not in trouble? Meegan, I mean."

"Not that I know of. Fact is, she's missing, and her folks are worried about her."

"She lives in Goleta, in Silly's house with two or three other girls. Silly has the master lease on the place. One of those ticky-tacky tract houses that's now worth about a mil."

"You're a good man, Charlie Brown."

"It's Fred."

"Fred?" I ask, figuring he didn't get my quote.

"Freddy Brown," he says, looking a little disgusted.

I cover. I didn't remember that his name was Brown. "Yeah, Fred, I know. I was being funny."

"I get that Charlie crap a lot," he says, and I disappear while he's racking the glass he's just despotted.

I wander the wharf over, hitting the tourist spots, then work the regulars along the winding walkway along the beach. On weekends there's an artist fair along the beach, at least a half mile of booths: wind chimes and pottery and artwork and all the rest. It's not the best time to interview the locals, as the tourists are overrunning them. I move on to the landing and wander from Brophy's to the nautical museum to the boat brokers, and wind up at Howard's Boatyard and crank up my Harley. By now I have a half dozen names of boys and girls who haven't been seen around the harbor for the last month. Harbor types come and go, so it's not unusual. I do have a good lead in Silly Swanson. Maybe Meegan met with foul play, but far more likely she met with a boyfriend who wanted to take her away on a South Seas cruise on an eighty-eight-foot yacht. So I mean to follow up on Silly, but first I have a lunch appointment.

I've got to meet Butch Bohannan, who had the hell kicked out of him by Toke Butterworth. Nothing like a man with an ax to grind when you want info.

Joe's is an institution in Santa Barbara. The south end of State Street was skid row at one time, but now it's stylish shops and restaurants. Joe's, which at one time was next to the Salvation Army, has moved a half block from City Center. But it still has style, with sculptured tin ceilings, a rock front on the bar, and period décor illustrative of its past. The best news is the food has always been plain but exceptional fare; that hasn't changed.

Before we're through the soup I've confirmed most of what Fred "Charlie" Brown told me, plus learned the name of the surfer from Channel Island's Harbor. Ventura is the first harbor south of Santa Barbara, then Channel Islands. It's larger than either of the first two, but a surfer dude with a handle like Slider Dunbury, real first name Phillip, shouldn't be hard to locate.

Particularly one who is a champion sail-surfer. I have to listen to the intricacies of parasurfing, or sail-surfing, through half my lunch—it seems Butch has been in some competitions himself, never winning or even placing, of course—until I get back to the subject, Slider, who knew June.

Slider, who won a major West Coast event in parasurfing, a sport made famous in the James Bond flick *Die*

Another Day, or something like that. Parasurfing, where one is pulled on a surfboard by a parasail tethered by a 50-to-150-foot line, and one can do acrobatics over the waves. Also known as sail-surfing. I've watched it, and have to admit it's a cool sport.

Slider won't be hard to find, as the sport is still a small community. Butch continues to regale me with his exploits as a parasurfer, and why one small mistake has always kept him out of the medals even though his performance was otherwise superior.

Dessert couldn't come any too soon.

I've got one more piece of business to take care of this afternoon. Dr. Antonio Scanoletti, the angry owner of the bichon frise who's been dognapped. He's sworn he'll have a copy of the divorce decree and a letter authorizing me to serve as his agent in the doggy recovery. I'm to meet him at his golf club at four P.M. for a cocktail, and final instructions, as if I need them to recover a puffball pooch. But I do need the paperwork.

As soon as I get back out on the street, I call Babs. "Hey, I need a list of everyone you dicks have interviewed on your sister's disappearance."

"Jesus, Dev, you're asking a lot. I told you I wasn't assigned to that case and in fact have been told to stay away from it."

"Then I'll be covering the same ground that's already been plowed. I need a list."

"I'll see what I can do."

"Did your guys interview a Slider Dunbury, from Channel Islands?"

"Oxnard actually, if my memory serves me right. No, we could never locate the guy. He was some kind of surfer prince, but he's riding a wave somewhere else."

"I want to talk to him."

"So did the department, but he was nowhere to be found."

"Get me his last address."

"That I can probably do."

"See you on the plane."

She's quiet for a long moment. "Pug said you guys were meeting at Brophy's later. Would I be sticking my—"

"Hell no. You're invited. I'll buy dinner rather than breakfast."

"See you around six."

She clicks off without a good-bye, before I can ask if she's Pug's date or mine.

I've got to hustle back to the boat and change. Can't wear a stained T-shirt and flip-flops to La Cumbre Country Club. As I'm jogging along, my cell phone chatters again. It's my newfound friend, Skip Hanson.

"Hey, Dev. I think I'm closer to that grand."

"How so?"

"I ran into a friend of my old girlfriend, who told me that she split with Toke."

"Meegan?"

"Shit, you already knew."

"Old news, man, but keep trying."

"I get something else, I'll call."

La Cumbre Country Club rests serenely in Hope Ranch, between the city proper and the sea. It's in a series of low ravines without views of the ocean, but it's beautiful nonetheless, and manicured, and makes one wish one was a golfer. Of course belonging to a club like this in or around Santa Barbara is a six-figure investment. The clubhouse resides securely on a knoll surrounded by a parking lot on the north and a driving range on the south, but has views of the course and is stylish but in a conservative manner. I stop at a wall of pictures of past presidents and officers and am not surprised to recognize a couple of celebrities.

Scanoletti is in the bar when I arrive, and by his noise level it's apparent he's been there since lunch. He's loud and boisterous, at a table of six other laughing guys. He's easy to recognize as he's a rotund little fellow a half head shorter than me, with black curly hair, now beginning to go gray around the edges. Not the picture of a golfer that one might imagine, although he does have on the proper yellow-monogrammed bill cap, collared purple shirt, and by-God plaid—purple, yellow, and white—pants. I wonder where one finds plaid pants these days—particularly purple, yellow, and white—but then again I don't frequent golf specialty stores.

He smells of cigars and booze.

I'm in those same tan slacks jerked from their hanger by Vic Ambrose, tan boat shoes, and matching stretch belt, and a short-sleeve yellow polo shirt, my image of what a golfer should look like before he dons his spikes. I find Antonio, Tony to his friends, with a fat cigar between stubby fingers, regaling five other members.

"Bullcrap to getting married," he says as I walk up. "Just find a woman you don't like and give her a house." The rest of the guys break up at that one. Seems like he's getting plenty of empathy from this particular group.

He glances up and sees me, ignores me, and doesn't break his monologue. "Oscar Wilde said bigamy is having one wife too many, monogamy is the same." That brings a hardy chuckle, but doesn't rock the house like the last line. But he's not fazed. "Divorce, in case you haven't looked up the definition, is the Latin word for 'rip out a man's wallet through his genitals.'" A generous laugh again. He glances back at me, and gives me a perfunctory "Wait at the bar, will you?"

I nod and move away. I guess he doesn't want his buddies to know he's spending the price of a small new car to get his doggie back. As I move away, I hear another line. "Actually, my wife and I got along fine. We went to a nice restaurant twice a week. She went on Wednesday and I went on Friday." Another polite laugh. "She loved electric gadgets, mixer, toaster, bread-maker . . . so, being a dutiful anxious-to-please husband, I bought her an electric chair." The laughs are fading so he rises, mumbles he has some business to take care of, and comes to join me before the bartender has even noticed me.

"What's your pleasure?" he asks.

"A beer's fine."

"Bring us a couple of Bud Lights," he yells at the bartender, then turns to me. "Take them out on the patio. I've got to get the stuff out of my locker."

I do, take a seat where I can enjoy the view, and in moments he's there with a sheaf of papers.

He gives me a reassuring smile. "Letter of authorization, your agreement . . . signed . . . with a couple of changes by my attorney . . . and the divorce decree. It clearly states that the dog, Snarl, a bichon frise, white, weighing approximately four pounds, is awarded to me. She gets Fluffy."

"There're two dogs? How am I to tell the difference?" I ask.

He eyes me with some amusement in his eyes. "Fluffy's black and brown," he says. "You can figure that out, can't you?"

"That's not over my head," I say, a little sarcastically.

I've taken one sip of my beer and we're through, at least as far as he's concerned. He starts to rise.

"Let me see the changes?" I ask.

"Changes?" he asks innocently.

Chapter Twelve

Dr. Antonio Scanoletti is eyeballing me with the innocence of a child, but one who has his hand in the cookie jar.

"Changes to my agreement," I repeat. "That's the world's most simple document. What's to change?"

He digs through the sheaf of papers and hands it to me. It has the witness signature line and the date crossed out, and a paragraph added as to where the agreement is to be adjudicated. Fought over, is a better layman's phrase. This addition merely says it will be argued in California courts, which is fine with me. The good news is he has the thousand-dollar retainer check clipped to the top of the pile. At the worst, my expenses are covered.

He gives me an oily smile. "My attorney said you don't need a witness to an agreement like this."

It doesn't take a Rhodes scholar to figure out that if a guy doesn't want a witness to what he does, he's up to no good. If he's concerned about where a document is going to be reviewed by the court, he's presuming it probably will be. Now the question is: I intend to live up to my part of the agreement, does he?

So I decide to eliminate the possibility. "You want to pay me a hundred percent up front? Then I won't require an agreement," I ask, knowing the answer.

"Of course not."

I give him a tight smile. "Then I need a witness to your

signature. *My* attorney says I do." The fact is I drew this simple agreement myself.

He shrugs dismissively. "Mine says not."

"Are you the guy who has signed Dr. Antonio Scanoletti on the bottom of that simple one-page letter agreement?"

He hesitates, then has to answer in the affirmative, but he's looking off into the tall trees surrounding the clubhouse as if he's irritated at this small disruption.

But I'm relentless. "Then you should have no problem having a witness testify to that fact."

He snaps his gaze back and glares at me.

It's my turn to shrug. "You know, Dr. Scanoletti, you really don't need me, you can get some dipshit to do this dognapping for you—"

"No, no, I want you to do it. I want Snarly to get home safely. Come on back inside and I'll have the bartender witness it."

We do, he instructs the bartender that the signature is his, gets his signature on a new hand-drawn line as witness under the crossed-out one, then we return to the patio table. He sips his beer while I carefully go through the papers and make sure everything's in order. I look up and nod. He rises.

"Follow me out to my car. I've got Snarly's travel case."

As we walk, I can't help but ask with a laugh, "Snarly? I presume the little darling likes to growl and bite?"

He looks at me as if I were a little retarded. "That's irony, Shannon. You ever heard of irony? He's a lapdog, for Christ's sake."

"Yeah, I have heard of irony." In fact, I think it ironic that this sawed-off little shit has such a mouth on him. It seems my lot of late.

This guy is an orthopedic surgeon who makes three or four mil a year. He should know something about health. He's overweight, and he's smoking like the little-engine-that-could as he chugs out to the parking lot. He's out of breath by the time we reach a big black four-door Mercedes 500. I can't help but notice that there's a white plastic model of a little dog hanging from the mirror over the dash. He digs in the trunk and hands me a little hard suitcase, curved on the top, with black hardware wire on either end. One end is a door. The thing is crocodile or alligator hide patterned, the hinges and hardware look like pure silver, and I'm sure both are the real thing. It has a cushioned bottom. A grand's worth of dog transportation, I imagine. I bet he raised hell if his wife paid more than fifty bucks for a purse or a pair of shoes.

I get the strange impression that this guy is going to stiff me, but at least I have the grand retainer, and grounds to collect presuming I show back up with pooch. As I snug the doggy Samsonite onto the back of my Harley, I decide that he's not going to see the pooch until he has the dough in hand—not a check, but the cash. I learned a long time ago to abide by my instincts. It's kept me alive more than once, and out of the courtroom almost as often.

I just have time to shower and shave before my dinner with the old man and Babs at Brophy's.

I've been extra careful when approaching the boat of late, checking out all the lookyloos on the breakwater and the distant wharf and anywhere that might be a good spot to take a shot. It's an impossible task, however, as there are folks everywhere on a Saturday. I board and pull up short when I find an envelope taped to my main hatchway.

It has a simple hand-printed Shannon on the outside. I tear it open and read it with more than a little interest.

> *How can you be sure there's not a bomb in your bilge, Shannon? Are you a little nervous lately? Are you about ready to join your redheaded friend in heathen hell? Sleep well, wondering when? . . .*

I carefully handle the envelope and paper. The paper has a strange feel and texture. It's full of fiber. It's unusual. Some kind of reconstituted stuff. That's a good thing. I consider calling the FBI to see if they're interested in searching *Aces n' Eights*, but don't want the hassle. I do drop into the main salon long enough to grab up my binocs, then return to the dock. I step back twenty paces from the boat and carefully do a 360 looking for anyone paying undue attention to me and the boat, but again, it's an impossible task. I use my new cell phone to give Pug and Iver a call. And invite Iver to bring his tanks and Pop his good sense to help me do a quick search of the boat.

Iver suits up and checks the hull for strange explosive protuberances, and Pop and I go through compartments, engine room, and bilge from bow to stern. Nothing.

As soon as we're finished, we all walk the docks and talk with anyone who might have seen something, but get nowhere. I invite Iver to join us at Brophy's and call Cedric. As I suspected, he's not returned from his retreat yet, but I leave word on his machine where we are.

I send Pop and Iver on, as I still have to change. The two of them and Babs are into their second drink before I show.

"I thought you were going to welch on dinner," she says, flashing me a smile.

"Nope. A promise is a promise."

"I'll take that note to the FBI," she says, holding out her hand. "They've got some off-paper print-lifting techniques that are over the top."

"It's on the boat. After dinner."

"Good."

Cedric joins us by the time we've got our salad, and he, Iver, and the old man all leave early. I think Pug is plotting some alone time for Babs and me, as he knows we have to go back to the boat for the letter and he's almost dragged Iver and Ced away, and I don't argue. It seems that the old man has been playing Cupid.

I am able to put Ced on to Meegan, the waitress missing from the Harbor Restaurant, and onto Silly Swanson, suggesting he do his cyberspace magic on both of them.

When Babs and I get to the boat, there's a couple of calls on my machine. She mixes us a drink while I return the first one. It's Mason Fredrich. I put a finger to my lips at Babs, letting her know I don't want the party on the other end knowing there's anyone who might be overhearing the conversation.

"So, Dev, have you turned anything up?" he asks.

"Mason, do you know a guy named Slider Dunbury?" He answers a little too quickly.

"Dunbury. Never heard of him. Why?"

I take a deep breath as my next question is hard to ask of this guy. "Do you, or have you ever, had any suspicion that June might have been seeing someone else?"

"No." He almost yells it. It's denial and a seeming affront. Then he repeats, "No, no, no."

"I'm sorry I had to ask."

"Come on over here, Dev. I need to talk to you."

"I can't tonight," I say, eyeing Babs, who gives me what I take as an encouraging smile.

"Please?" he asks.

"Can't do it. Another commitment."

"When can you?"

"Tomorrow's Sunday. I'll drop over tomorrow."

He's silent again. "No, forget it. No, June was not . . . would never . . . see someone else. We loved each other very much, as anyone will tell you."

Not Fred "Charlie" Brown, I think, but don't say. *Fred thinks June and Slider might have been a thing.* Instead, I encourage, and lie, "There was never any question in my mind, Mason. But I had to ask."

"I may call you tomorrow," he says, and hangs up without a good-bye.

The other call is from Darwin Winston-Gray. I return it

and he's his usual charming self, beginning the conversation with a sarcastic question, "You haven't left yet?"

"I'm closer, Darwin. By the end of the week I may have something." I grab a file off my chart table and open it to some hen-scratch calculating I've done as he replies.

"The end of the week," he almost yells. "Hell, they could be in China by the end of the week."

"Not if my calculations are close to right. She carries five thousand gallons of fuel—and you said she was topped off—and cruises at just under fifteen knots if you press her, ten knots if you really want some range. She's been gone twenty to twenty-five days, depending on when she left. She could have traveled nine thousand miles running her twenty-four hours a day, but that's highly unlikely. You've got to stop for fuel once in a while, and maybe to provision up . . . or just to feel some solid ground underfoot.

"My guess is if they're pressing hard, they are still no more than four thousand miles out, and less is probably more likely. Relax for another week. I'll be on to her."

He sputtered a few times while I went through the numbers. But his tone is more mild now. "But I could be right, nine thousand miles . . . It's only 6,500 to China."

"If she had a tender loading fuel while she's under way, she could go around the world. If my aunt had six inches she'd be my uncle. Like I said, two to three thousand is more like it."

"A week, then. I'll give you another week. What do you know so far?"

"I know she stopped in Ensenada, but that was before you reported her missing."

"That's something, anyway. At least we know what direction—"

"Could be anywhere from there," I say, not wanting him to begin to get confident, or to send someone else on the hunt.

"So, when are you heading south?" His tone is a little on edge again.

"As soon as I get another report of her whereabouts. Within a few days, I'm sure."

I don't bother to mention that I plan to spend at least a couple of days up north.

"Keep me posted," he says, and hangs up. I don't know why it is that no one tells me good-bye lately.

But then, I couldn't care less. I have a beautiful woman looking at me over a glass of good wine. One of my favorite pastimes.

I no more than set the phone down when it rings again. Cedric doesn't bother with a hello. "I didn't find anything on Meegan here locally, but the Swanson girl is online, and guess who's just e-mailed her from the *Orion*?"

"Meegan Howard."

"How did you guess? The bad news is it's a satellite connection, and the *Orion* could be anywhere in a hundred thousand square miles of a particular bird's satellite coverage."

"And the good news?"

"They just cleared the Panama Canal and turned east-northeast. She said the 'captain' didn't tell them where he was going, but she knew it was northeasterly."

"The Cayman Islands?" I'm guessing.

"Don't know, but I'll stay on it. It could be any of a thousand places."

"Damned if they're not making time. That's a lot farther than I figured."

"I'll call back if I get anything else."

"Don't bother. I'm going to hit the sack." I wink at Babs, and I'm happy to say, she winks back. "If you still want to bang on the keyboard, look at flights to the Caymans. Nearest landfall, I think."

"Jamaica's the same general direction."

"Then Jamaica too."

It's quiet on the other end of the line for a moment. Then he tries to send me to the dictionary again. "I'll continue to concatenate these leads while you attempt to get the local police to truckle to your whims." But the dictionary's the last thing on my mind.

"I'll ask you what that means tomorrow, Ced. Good night."

At least I'm polite, although I don't wait for him to reply before disconnecting, and reconnecting my gaze to hers. It's interesting that a mere look like that coming from a beautiful woman makes the blood rush to one's loins.

"Have I shown you the rest of *Aces n' Eights*?" I ask, feigning innocence.

"No, you haven't. Is that one of those"—her tone lowers, and she's purring like a cat—"'do you want to see my etchings?' questions."

"Precisely," I say, my smile not so innocent this time.

"Can I fill my wineglass first?" she asks.

I guess she was my date, not Pugs's, but I know he'll be happy for the two of us.

There's always something exciting about making love to a woman for the first time. The fact there may be a bomb in the near vicinity that your search has missed adds a little extra spice to the mix. Although, in this case, no extra seasoning necessary.

It turns out that Babs is an old-fashioned girl. Even though we're both satiated, she's up, dressed, and leaves, at four-thirty A.M. Doesn't want the neighbors to see her depart after daylight, I'm sure.

This is a woman I could get used to having around. Beautiful, responsive, exciting, and knows how to treat a man as we men believe only an Oriental woman might.

I sleep in, indulging myself, then awake in the middle

of the morning to another beautiful day in paradise. I pull her pillow to my face and inhale deeply. Good odors, having a woman in bed. Honeysuckle, if I have my flowers correct. I smile and chuckle a little. I never expected a demure little lady—even a cop lady—to be such a wild ride. Leaving my completely destroyed bed unmade, it being Sunday, I leave the chores and take my coffee on the deck with good company, Futa. After a careful perusal of my surrounds, making sure no one in the vicinity is carrying a gun case, I relax on a deck chair. Again, a visual search is a fruitless effort as tourists are already infesting the harbor and art walk along Cabrillo, like termites.

After my coffee, I go to the chart table and fire up the computer for a little surfing of my own. Before I leave the country I always utilize the CIA's world fact book, and various National Security Agency public documents. It's amazing what one can find online. I spend the morning reading about the Cayman Islands and Jamaica.

Just before noon I get another call from Cedric, who's intercepted another message from Meegan to Silly. It seems Meegan wants Silly to get that last paycheck, and to cash it, and to apply it to one of her credit cards. She even gives Silly the credit card number. That brings me a smile. Something for Cedric to zero in on. Meegan cautions her not to tell anyone about the fact she's contacted her, and she mentions the name Rupert as being on board, and that Rupert knows a guy who's going to "set them free."

I've never heard of a guy named Rupert. But I intend to head back to the Harbor Restaurant and have another talk with Fred "Charlie" Brown. So I use the phone and invite Cedric to lunch. Cedric already has lunch scheduled with Iver, so I invite them both to join me.

But I have something to do first. I find a note on my chart table. *Call me sometime, for something besides cop stuff*. Nice, demure, small, perfect handwriting. She can be a real coquette. I'd have preferred hearing what a great lover I was, but this is second best. And a phone number is noted there. Maybe she really does want me to call. So I waste no time doing so. There are certain rules of etiquette in regards to mornings after, and I have hardly yet had the chance to follow them. One of them is to let the lady know she was cared for and appreciated and that this is not a one-night thing, even if you think it probably is. In this case, I hope it's definitely not. The other is flowers, but I'd much prefer sending them to her residence, and don't yet know her address. I get her on the phone and invite her to lunch, but she's working and is somewhere in the Santa Ynez Valley working an interdepartmental gig, and has to pass, but assures me that my call and invitation are welcome. I get a warm and cuddly feeling every time I'm around that woman, and more so now after a night of great sex and some actual cuddling, sex again, and more cuddling. So I invite her to dinner and imply a rematch, anxious and eager to see if our evening could possibly have been as good as remembered, and oftentimes the second meeting is even better. I'm disappointed that she's "tied up" for the evening. Maybe she wasn't as impressed as I was, nor as anxious for a second time at bat.

The best defense for a slightly wounded ego is to keep busy.

One of my few toys is an Atlantis Wav Kayak that I keep at Howard's Boatyard. It's small enough I could keep her on board, sixteen-plus feet long and twenty-two inches wide, but he offered and it does take up a lot of deck space. I've been remiss with my exercise regimen—staying away from my normal runs on the beach—but being a couple of hundred yards offshore will make me far more difficult to hit. I've got an hour before meeting the boys at the Harbor Restaurant, and that's time to really stretch the muscles with a paddle—and I can tie her alongside the wharf without even having to go out on the street.

I drag my little composite ship out to the beach and launch her into the surf, which is only a little nutty. I make it, but have to bail a little surf out as soon as I reach calm water, then set out westerly paralleling Ledbetter Beach, where I've been shot at twice. However, this time I'm two hundred yards offshore. I'm really getting into it after fifteen minutes and am halfway to Point Santa Barbara when I decide I have to turn around. The gulls are working a bait boil, the pelicans circling high overhead, the islands are clear in the distance, the clouds are billowy pillows overhead, and I'm covered in a sheen of perspiration from honest effort. It's a good thing, and I'm soon to be rewarded with lunch with friends and hopefully with some new information that will make me some money.

I love this boat. She skims over the water like a cormorant. She's a graceful sleek bird, barely dragging her toes in the water.

Life is good.

I'm halfway back to the breakwater, digging hard, probably making six or seven knots, when my eyes widen and I stare at the bow of the boat. My immediate reaction is she's breaking apart a couple of feet back from the bow, then I realize that something has cut a groove across her hull.

Life is in the crapper.

Damn if I'm not being shot at . . . again.

Chapter Thirteen

As quickly as I recognize what's happened, another shot strikes the bow with a crack that reverberates up my spine. It hits where the boat is semisolid, injected with nonsink urethane foam. It knocks the bow four feet to the starboard, and inertia leaves my shoulders in place but takes my legs and hips with the boat, and I go over, flung to the surface as if we'd been clipped by a fast-moving speedboat. The kayak rights itself, but I decide momentum is my friend and discretion is the better part of valor and swim down and under the boat to the other side, making sure I keep my head low enough that I'm hidden from shore behind the boat. I envision the way the boat looks through a powerful scope, and don't want to make any kind of a target. She remains dead in the water, and I'm ecstatic that I'm not. I've taken the double-ended paddle with me, and don't even try to slip it back in the little cockpit, even though it's clumsy to hang on to.

I stay there for a long time, kicking quietly in the water, keeping my head down so low my mouth is underwater and I have to blow lapping salt water out of my nose to catch the occasional breath, hanging on with only my fingertips showing over the hull.

Just out of curiosity, I inch forward to check the hull on my side. There's no chance of her sinking as she's polyurethane-filled both fore and aft, but that's not what I'm worried about. So far, we've had no evidence to follow up on the shooter, no proof that I've even been shot at, other than my statement so. But now I see we do. The shooter hit the boat on the shore side, the port side, and on my side, the starboard, there's no exit hole. Twenty-two inches of urethane would stop almost any expanding bullet and it has stopped this one. I'll have to tear into the hull, but I've got a bullet, with a chance for ballistics.

Now the only thing I have to do is get back to the harbor with the evidence, without my personal hull being blown all to hell. Unlike the Wav, I *will* sink.

I feel as if I wait forty-five minutes before I struggle back aboard, but the fact is it's probably fifteen. The boat is pierced from the second bullet, but it's done little harm and she functions fine. I function fine also, driven on by a good shot of adrenaline. Not wanting to present a slow target I give it hell all the way back to the wharf, tie her off at a ladder, check the hole in her hull, and determine that whatever this guy is shooting, it makes a hell of a hole, and waste no time getting up the twenty-five rungs of the ladder to car level and into the Harbor Restaurant. By the size of the hole, it's a .45/70-caliber slug, maybe larger. No wonder I felt as if a jumbo jet made a very close flyby when I was narrowly missed on the beach.

Iver and Cedric are sipping beers at the upstairs bar, and I'm happy to see Fred, behind the bar, busily serving the lunch crowd.

"You're late," Cedric says. "That cop business a little hard to leave?"

He's being a smart-ass, meaning Babs, as he knows she came back to the boat with me.

"I've got a fairly good reason for being late, nosy, as I'll share with you in a moment. But for your information, Detective Benson was at the boat last night, as you know, collecting evidence to take the FBI, namely the letter that was taped to the boat. That was all business. She left early."

"Yeah, monkey business. She left early all right, early this morning. Looked like an assignation in progress to me." He eyes me, waiting for a confession, but I'm stoic.

Iver jabs me in the ribs. "Let's get you a beer." He waves Fred over. "Get him an Amstel," then turns back to me. Iver is often serious, most times even reticent, but today his demeanor is downright maudlin. Unusual for him. "I've got some news too," he says quietly, as if his dog just died, but he doesn't have a dog. "You first, bro," he commands me. "Why were you late?"

I fill them in on the latest shooting, and the fact my boat is carrying the first tangible evidence of the attempts on my life other than the note I got, and the small fact my van was blown all to hell, and that I can use some help retrieving the shell. "Other than that," I say with a sarcastic laugh, "it's been a great morning. What's your news?" I ask Iver.

"The perils of being black," he says, frowning.

"What?" He has both Cedric's and my absolute attention. We've been working beside Iver so long that his being black never seems to enter the equation. He's a good friend, and a hell of an associate. The fact he's black is an aside.

He speaks without emotion. "I've got the black man's pariah . . . prostate cancer."

Cedric and I are both stunned to silence. My stomach knots, then I manage, "So, what's that mean?"

"That's where I was the other day when I took the day off, getting a biopsy. They jam this thing up your butt and shoot holes through your colon into your prostate with a little gizmo that feels like a Colt .45, but is actually only a little needle, taking samples. It's damn lousy fun, but not if it saves your life, I guess. Anyway, it means I have to take some treatments, or get sliced up, or some damn unpleasant thing. There's a good chance they'll change this old bull's interest from ass to grass."

I'm silent for a moment, weighing this lousy news. "How old are you, Iver?" I finally ask, knowing he's just past fifty as I remember us giving him a raucous party when he reached the half-century mark not so long ago.

"I'm fifty-two."

"Too damned young for this," Cedric says.

"My thought exactly," I say.

Iver gives us a tight smile. "A hundred and two would be too damned young."

"What made you go to the doc?"

"Went to a free clinic and checked my cholesterol, and when I was there they did this PSA thing. My PSA is twenty-three, which means something was going on in my prostate."

"So, what kind of treatments?" I ask.

"Not sure yet. I've got a meeting with the doc Monday morning and we're going to talk about my options."

"That's good," Cedric says. "Let the docs do what you think is right, but you and I are going to get you on a diet program right now. Starting with this lunch. Then I'm going to lay out my own treatment."

Iver smiles tightly. "You doctoring now, Ced?"

"Don't knock it, man. I've been lots of places and worked with lots of cats who cure things with what they have at hand. I've got a Chinese friend in San Francisco, an herbologist, and I'm going there tomorrow. Cancer is a result of your mistreating yourself. Believe it or not, your body's your friend. It wants to live too, along with your soul. You've been polluting the temple, man, even if you didn't mean to. My friend in San Fran will know what to do."

"A witch doctor?" Iver asks, smiling still, but tightly.

"He doesn't do bats' tongues and toads' eyes. He's a gentleman who practices the ancient art of healing . . . with herbs. Herbs that counteract the poisons you've let creep into the temple. Herbs that make your body not believe the lies the cancer is telling it. Herbs that kick your body in the butt and make it get to work on its own." He gets even more serious. "Whatever I bring back from Chang Soo won't hurt you, Iver. I don't have that many friends, man. I don't want to lose one. I want you to promise me you'll do one thing for me . . . for yourself?"

"What's that?"

"Two things really. One, keep a strong attitude, knowing you can beat this thing, which you can. The brain runs the railroad, and even if it let you get off on the wrong track, it can bring you back to the right one. It's a slight misstep your body has taken, and can be corrected. The other is to try some things that won't hurt you, but might . . . will . . . help you. Herbs that the Chinese have used for thousands and thousands of years. I've seen many instances where my friend has cured those folks the doctors are patting on the head and placating, and getting ready to send to a hospice. And done it with herbs the docs laugh at . . . but in fact don't understand."

Iver shrugs. "Can't hurt, I guess."

"Damn straight," Ced says. "Now, let's eat." They head for a table near the windows, but I hold up a minute, preferring to speak to Fred out of earshot, where he won't be reluctant to talk. I wait until the Bill Gates look-alike comes to my end of the bar, to use the blender, then ask him, "Hey, Fred, you know a guy named Rupert?"

"Sure, skinny black guy with a pearl eye who worked some of the boats around here. He drank rum and Coca-Cola, and ordered it with a Jimmy Buffet accent."

"A friend of Slider's?"

He shrugs. "Not that I know of. But I sure don't know all of Slider's friends, nor do I want to."

"Thanks." I head for the table.

Cedric is in the process of giving Iver a diet lesson. I get there in time to hear "No fats. Lots of grains and fruits and vegetables . . . particularly tomatoes. Lycopene's in tomatoes, not to speak of ten thousand other compounds we don't yet understand. In fact, all red fruits and vegetables are full of lycopene. Chow down on all the beets and strawberries and radishes and rhubarb you want."

Iver looks a little strained. He waits patiently until Cedric runs down. Then says, a little tentatively, as if trying to convince himself, "French fries are vegetables."

Cedric shakes his head vigorously, disgustedly. "French fries are fried. French fries are not your friend, Iver. No fat, remember? You can have all the potatoes you want, boiled, or baked, so long as you eat a lot of other good stuff. You can make French fries in the oven, roasted without grease, but go easy on the salt."

Iver knows he'll get no rest from Cedric, and I can see in his eyes that he's wishing he'd never told us.

"Hey, man," I say, laying a hand on his shoulder, giving him a light squeeze, "we're with you all the way."

He gives me a sad smile, a look I've seldom seen from this strong, virile man. "I know you are, but the hell of it is, this is a trip one can only take alone. I ain't ever been much scared of anything, but, fact is, this scares the hell out of me."

There's a long moment of silence at the table. Then I speak up. "Still, we're walking beside you, bro."

"I know that, and appreciate it," he says. "Let's eat."

Cedric changes almost everything Iver wants to order, until he ends up with a broiled chicken breast, a fruit bowl, and a salad with a dash of olive oil and vinegar.

In order to move the conversation to a lighter subject, I mention that Fred does know a Rupert and that the guy works in the harbor at times.

Iver glances up from his salad. "Rupert Beauchamp?"

"I don't know the guy's last name."

Cedric jumps into the conversation and fills Iver in on the e-mails he's intercepted. Iver, polite as always, waits until he's finished, then informs us that he knows Rupert Beauchamp pretty well, that Rupert once worked on the *Orion*, and that he hasn't seen him around for the past three weeks or more.

"Bingo," I say. "I'll bet Rupert is with them. And the e-mail said 'Rupert knows someone who is going to set us free.' The next question is, where are they heading?"

"Rupert's a Jamaican," Iver says, offhandedly.

"I'm feeling a little like I won the lottery," I say, with a broad smile. "Do you know from where in Jamaica?" I ask.

"Blue Mountains. He hung with the Maroons." A hint of pride creeps into his tone. "Black men who defeated the British in battle. They've lived free in the Blue Mountains for a century and a half."

"Maroons I read about this morning. They live off to themselves in the backcountry."

"They do. They've also got a couple of villages down on the water. The reason I know that Rupert hung with them was I spoke some patois to him—"

"A Jamaican dialect?" Cedric asks.

"You speak patois?" I ask.

First he answers Cedric. "It's a dialect made up mostly of English, but some French and Spanish. It jams the words together." Then he addresses me. "My grandmother was Jamaican. I understand it a lot better than I speak it, but I speak a little. Damn little. I do know a lot of sayings. Irie, mon."

"Irie?"

"Means good."

"Sayings . . . like what?" I ask, testing him.

He thinks for a moment, then smiles. It's obvious these are fond memories. "Whaajoketoyuadettomi."

He speaks so fast it's all gobbledygook. "Okay, what's that mean?"

"What is a joke to you is death to me. It means . . ." He

thinks a minute. "It means not all jokes are humorous to everyone."

"True. Another one? Slower this time."

He laughs, then thinks for a second. "Mi cum yah fi drink mile, mi nuh cum yah fi count cow."

Both Ced and I laugh at that one. He still speaks so quickly there's no way you can decipher what a single word might be.

"Okay, you got me again," I say, shaking my head.

"Yeah, mon. No problem, mon. That one is: I came here to drink milk, not to count cow . . . which means, I have come to reap benefits, not to work. That's patois, and that's standard Jamaican Rastafarian attitude. But there's some heavy peace and love thrown in as well, motivated mostly by fine-stemmed high Blue Mountain ganja. It's easy to dig love and peace when you're floating on a cloud of Mary Jane smoke."

"You're as handy as a pocket in a shirt," I say, giving him a plain old Americanism in return, and giving him a bigger smile than I feel. All I can think about is this good friend, a man's man, who always has a great sense of humor, a ready smile, and is one of the world's great listeners, withering away, succumbing to a gnawing monster in his gut.

"Anyway, Rupert's patois was mixed with Creole, hard to understand for me. That's a backcountry Blue Mountain thing . . . not a coast thing. My grandma talked a lot about the Maroons."

"Ced, start working on getting Iver and me to Jamaica, but don't book it until we're sure." Then I have second thoughts, and feel a little guilty. "You can go?" I ask Iver.

He shrugs. "Hope so. I'd like to . . . never been. I'll know more after I meet with the doc."

The rest of lunch we're lost in our own thoughts. We head out. I row over in my wounded bird and they walk back to Howard's Boatyard, where we're going to perform some surgery on the Wav.

In a short time, I'm holding a big shell in my hand. I'd guessed a .45 caliber by the size of the hole, but this chunk of lead is even bigger.

This guy has proved again that he doesn't only want to kill me, he wants to blow me apart, splatter me all over the ocean for the birds and fish to pick at.

Chapter Fourteen

Before I can call Babs to tell her about the bullet, my cell phone rings. It's her.

"You okay?" she asks.

"Peachy," I say, and laugh a little, if a little nervously.

"Great. I was scared to death."

"How did you know I was shot at again?"

"We got a 911 from an apartment building on the bluff. It made an old lady a little nervous to hear the muffled report of what sounded like a gunshot coming from the second-story deck next to hers. She peeked around the wall adjoining the decks, just in time to see a guy firing a very big rifle for the second time. We've had people out there for well over an hour, but I just heard about it. Unfortunately, the perp saw the old lady, Mrs. Rothstein, and split."

"Can you meet me there? If you can, I can give you a bullet, in pretty good shape, that I'm sure the old lady saw fired."

"I can. That's a break. I'm halfway in from Santa Ynez and can be there in twenty minutes."

She gives me the address. Two good breaks in one day, almost too much to stand.

I'm patiently waiting in front of a two-story apartment building on the bluff overlooking Ledbetter Beach and the channel, sitting astride my Harley, when she arrives. At first I think it's apartments, then decide it's a small condo complex, as there's a FOR SALE sign on one of the units. As it happens, that's the unit next door to the address Babs has given me. The forensics van is still parked in front of the for-sale condo. Together, we go in to speak with Mrs. Rothstein.

"Call me Gilda," she says, with a big smile.

"I know you went through this once," Babs says, "but we have just a few more questions."

Gilda's a Rubenesque woman, if as short as Babs. She weighs twice as much, but is twice as old, probably more. Late seventies, I'd guess. She has a smile that makes you think she came by the plumpness with a lot of good food, good cheer, and laughs. Her eyes crinkle as if she were smiling even when she's not. She's wearing stylish slacks and a lace blouse, and you'd think her younger than her years if it weren't for the wrinkles and a small lace ribbon in blue-gray hair.

We take a seat, and I notice a big tabby cat on the patio. "I've got a cat. Big, but not as big as yours."

"I love my Felix. He's a dear."

I can see I'm in good. Cat lovers are cat lovers, and give those who do the benefit of the doubt.

"I've got the water on for tea. I love my tea."

She brings out a tray with a pitcher, matching china cups, cream and sugar, and a little rosewood box, and rests it on a leather ottoman with an upholstered green and white sofa facing it against the wall, and two green upholstered chairs on either end. There's a Renoir reproduction in a gold frame on the wall over the sofa. The apartment is a little frilly for my taste, but nicely put together.

She opens the box with a liver-spotted but nicely manicured hand, and we get to select from over a dozen teas. I go for the Earl Gray, Babs the English Tea Time. Gilda pours daintily, and I try to use a teacup that will not accept my stubby finger.

"I haven't had so much company in one day in years," she says, obviously pleased, then her brow furrows. "Oh, my, my manners, would you like a bagel?"

Her smile is infectious, and we both laugh and shake our heads.

"So," I ask, "you saw this man with the rifle?"

"Oy vey, it looked more like a cannon."

"A big rifle?" I ask with a smile.

"The size of a German machine gun," she says.

I study her for a moment, wondering if she's old enough to have gone through the nightmare in Germany, but decide if she did, she was very young.

"How big?" I ask.

"He had it resting on a tripod, like you'd use for a camera. It was probably as long as I am tall. It had a barrel this round." She shows me the end of a fist.

"Fifty caliber," I say, almost to myself.

"I don't know from calibers, young man."

"Fifty caliber," I offer, this time aloud, "used for sniper work at times, with a homemade flash suppressor that doubles somewhat as a silencer . . . that's why the barrel looked so big."

"And what did this man look like?" Babs asks.

"He was inside the apartment with the sliding glass door open. I almost fainted when I looked around the wall." She blushes. "I'm a very private person, mind you, and don't spy on my neighbors—"

"We're very glad you were interested," I say. "Very glad. Neighborhood watch is an important part of law enforcement." Babs looks at me and rolls her eyes, like what do I know about *real* law enforcement? But I'm undaunted. "What did he look like . . . what you could see?"

"Dark. Mexican or Latin, I imagine. He was bent over, looking through the thing on top of the rifle. The sight, I think you call it."

"The scope?" I ask, trying to help her.

"Yes, yes, the scope. I really didn't get a good look at his face, and couldn't judge how tall he was. But fairly tall. Taller than Tobias . . . that's my dear late husband. He had a full head of black hair, the man, I mean." She laughs a little nervously. "All I could really see was that big gun, almost pointing at me."

"And he saw you?"

"He did, and pulled his face away from the thing, and yelled at me, but I was ducking out of the way at the same time."

"Yelled?" I ask. "What did he say?"

"I think he called me a name."

"What?" Babs asks. Her tone is gentle and soothing. She's done this a few times before with old people.

"Can I say it?"

"Of course," Babs says with a smile, and reaches over and pats Gilda on the hand.

"A nosy . . . a nosy old bitch. He had a little accent."

"What nationality?" I ask.

"Who knows? Just an accent."

"And you did what?" I ask.

"I grabbed Felix up, ran in, pulled my patio door shut, and locked it. Then as soon as I caught my breath, I called 911."

"Had you seen him before?" I ask.

"Not that I know of."

"Did you notice any strange cars outside?"

"No, but as you saw, each condo has its own garage. This is a very nice condo complex. I did hear one that sounded like it was spinning its wheels right after I saw the gun, but I didn't look out."

"It's a beautiful complex," I say, and Babs nods.

She smiles, proud of where she lives.

"I bought it after Tobias passed. He left me . . . comfortable. He was a good provider, my Tobias."

I rise before we get into the children and grandchildren. "You've been very helpful, Mrs. Rothstein."

"Gilda, please."

"Gilda then."

Babs stands also. "I might want you to look at some mug shots."

"How exciting. I'd love you to catch this . . ." She giggles. "This schmuck. He called me a name. You haven't finished your tea."

"It was wonderful, Gilda," Babs says. "But duty calls."

We're out of there and next door, where we run into Agent O'Mally coming out of the perp's apartment. There are tire marks in the driveway where the shooter spun his tires leaving.

"Well," he says, "if it isn't the big-time bounty hunter."

"And victim," I add, with only a touch of sarcasm.

"And victim," he agrees. "How are the cuts and scrapes?"

"I'm holding together."

"Did you find anything helpful in there?" Babs asks.

"It'll be in our report," he says. "Your guys had already tracked up the scene by the time we got here." He's condescending, as usual.

"Maybe this will help." Babs hands him a tissue, containing the bullet I've given her.

"Where the hell . . ." O'Mally says, staring at the chunk of lead and brass.

"Out of my kayak," I offer.

"This should have gone right through a kayak," he says, still a little perplexed.

"I figure that I was at least six hundred yards from here, a couple of hundred yards out in the bay. Past the swell. It hit the bow, where there's twenty-two inches of polyurethane."

"This is a break." Then he looks up, frowning, a little

fire in his eyes. "You should have let my people retrieve this."

I give him a tight smile. "I thought of it, but then you guys would have had a lot too much fun tearing up my Wav."

"Wave?" he asks.

"My kayak. As it is, it's going to take a little mending."

He sighs deeply, shaking his head in disgust. "You're a real asshole, Shannon. Are you sure you didn't mark this?" I shine that. "God punishes me with amateurs."

"And me with supercilious bureaucrats who think they are the only game in town."

"Watch yourself, Shannon."

"Jerk yourself, Agent." I haven't liked this guy from day one, and it's going downhill from there. I turn to Babs. "I'm going on inside."

O'Mally laughs sardonically, then scowls, stepping between me and the door. "No, you're not, Shannon. This is a crime scene and you've got no standing here. You go inside, and I'm arresting you for interfering with an officer in the performance."

I know my face reddens; he's gotten to me. And that irritates me even more than the fact he won't let me wander around. He's merely being his asshole self. I take a deep breath, then relax as I exhale. A yoga thing Cedric taught me, and it seems to work. "Good," I say with a smile. "I need to get my afternoon nap." I turn to Babs, just as Detective Vic Ambrose, the gruff cop whose kid was the FTA who fell for the Santa suit, lumbers out of the apartment. He eyes me up and down, then looks at Babs. "What's he doing here?"

"He brought us over a bullet. I imagine it's the one fired from this apartment."

"The hell you say?"

"One of the ones," I correct. "He lobbed two of those mortars at me."

O'Mally glances at the ball of lead and brass. "This fits with what the neighbor told us. Big bullet, .45 or .50 caliber. I'll have the lab tell us exactly what it is and probably the maker in a couple of days."

"Close?" Ambrose asks me, looking hopeful.

"Missed me by a mile."

"But screwed up his little boat," O'Mally says. He's also looking smug. I'm beginning to think these guys would be happier if they'd dug this pound of lead out of my liver, letting my supply of Jack Daniels dribble away. Then, I've done little to endear myself to either of them.

"I'm gonna go take a nap," I say, and head for the Harley. Then I turn back. "You might check the garage for tire tracks. Mrs. Rothstein said she didn't see any strange cars out here, but this guy didn't carry this .50 caliber over here in a backpack on his mountain bike."

Ambrose reddens. "Look, whiz kid, we'll do the crime scene. You just keep being a menace to the community."

I wave back over my shoulder, with the middle finger a little too prominent in hand configuration. "Only a menace to skips, Ambrose. Only to skips."

"Prick," I hear him say to Babs, but ignore it.

I actually could use a nap, so I head for the boat.

The boat, I'm happy to say, is still there—not blown out of the water. Futa is more than willing to join me in the rack, still unmade, still smelling of flowers, the scent of a beautiful half-Oriental lady.

We're asleep in a heartbeat. Not Babs and I, but Futa and I. I'm sure he had a night of chasing wharf rats, and I've had a day of dodging them, only mine were two-legged ones. That, and the bad news Iver had, has made me want to cover my head with a pillow. Luckily, one of mine smells like honeysuckle, so I use it.

Tomorrow, Pug, Cedric, and I, with Babs nearby, go north to pay our respects to a nice lady who didn't deserve to die. Then I'm off to Coeur d' Alene, to make an easy stack of Franklins that will finance my trip to Jamaica.

Yeah, mon.

Chapter Fifteen

Dressed in our best bib n' tucker funeral attire, we land at the San Francisco International Airport, south of the city, rent a car—Babs won't go with us but rents her own as she's working with a digital camera, recording who attends—and we head north. I secretly wish she was going on to beautiful Idaho with me, a working vacation, but haven't said anything. Cedric informs us that San Francisco has no cemeteries other than the Presidio, the now-closed army base. Years ago they decided land in the city was just too valuable to relinquish it to the dead for all eternity. Those already buried were disinterred and moved, mostly to the city of Colma, just south of San Francisco.

Colma, with well over a million residents, but with only fifteen hundred or so live ones. Sixteen cemeteries dot the landscape—some with ethnic or religious specialties, and one with species preference, a pet haven. Not a town in which I'd enjoy living. Besides the abundance of bodies, there's no sand, surf, or palm trees.

There are well over two hundred people at the graveside, enough cops to make one believe it would be a good time for a bank heist in San Fran. We pay our respects to Sandy. For the fifteenth time, as I pass and rest my hand on her coffin, with mouth dry, I promise on my very life to avenge her. Then, eyes averted, I shake hands with her father. This time he limply accepts the hand. I'm totally self-conscious, first because of the tie, suit, and wing-tip shoes that it seems I haven't worn in eons, and second because I feel dreadfully responsible for the beautiful lady who's the reason for this somber gathering of friends and family. Had she not met me . . .

I'm anxious to get on with the revenge part, and encourage Pug to hurry out of there. We wave casually to Babs, and Cedric drives us back to the airport. He drops us off and goes on to San Francisco to fulfill his mission—hopefully electronic eavesdropping on my old nemesis Dr. Mohammad Hashim and herbs for Iver.

I have to run to catch my flight to Spokane, where Renegade Pig member Jack Doolin, a retired ATF officer, known as Poker Jack to his friends, is picking me up.

Security is its normal hassle, but I've left my piece home, and don't have so much as a collapsible sap, as all I'm taking is a carry-on. This is only a dognapping, after all. . . .

The plane is not the smallest passenger jet I've ever been in, but it's close. As soon as I start down the narrow tunnel leading to the plane, I begin to feel the walls close in on me. It's the damned claustrophobia from being trapped two hundred feet deep while diving for Commercial Marine. I spent twenty minutes waiting to be rescued, and could never deep-dive again. Small places scare me worse than if I had a New York strip wrapped around my waist and was facing a family of starving grizzlies. I narrow my eyes and follow the Zen method Cedric has preached to me. I chant happily, breathe deeply, and stumble along until I'm seated.

A young girl in a tie-die blouse and well-pimpled cheeks is in the aisle seat, and I implore her with my most boyish grin to move to the window so I'm less constricted. She pops her gum at me and in a grating whine informs me she is afraid of heights and can't look down. I guess one phobia is as good as the next, so I stumble over her, take my seat, and continue my silent chant until we take off, then I bury my head in the in-flight magazine.

It's late afternoon when Poker Jack meets me at the Spokane International Airport, Alaska Airlines gate. He's a gnome of a man, as ugly as a balustrade gargoyle, who reminds me somewhat of one of my favorite now-departed actors, Charles Bronson. But Jack's complexion is even worse and I imagine Bronson is a lot bigger. Jack's bright orange T-shirt, stenciled with *Rock Creek Testicle Festival, Come Have a Ball*, and black leathers would be hard to miss. With long wispy gray-blond hair askew, I'm sure from wearing his motorcycle helmet, he sticks out his hand. I can see he's a guy who probably did well undercover, as he looks far more like a dope dealer or gun runner than an officer of the law, and certainly isn't dressed for court.

I told him over the phone he'd easily recognize me as I'd be the guy who looked completely out of place wearing a tie, imitating Tommy Lee Jones in *Men in Black*, sans hat.

"That's a new one," he says, glancing at my carry-on. I've packed a few things, including one of those fold-up vinyl bags that I can expand to pack and carry on after I check the pooch and this doggie tote on the way back. I packed my things in the alligator and brass doggy travel cage, garnering more than one odd glance from other travelers.

I presume they think I have a dupe kit, socks, shorts, polo shirt, down vest, low-cut hiking boots, and jeans as pets.

"That it?" he asks, his brows furrowed on the chance I have other luggage.

"That's it. Don't plan to be here long." We head out to the parking structure, and to my surprise, he has an old pea-green Harley with a side car. There aren't many firsts left for me in the world of motorcycles, but riding in a sidecar is one of them.

I had no idea a bike could rattle like a dump truck half-full of scrap metal, but this rig does. After a couple of backfires that make me squinch up a good portion of the sidecar's tattered upholstery—I'm a little loud-report shy of late—we're off in a cloud of black exhaust. I'm a little distracted by checking out the mountains in the distance, and when we get to the parking booth he doesn't reach for his wallet but merely eyes me. I finally get the hint and grab my wallet and pay the couple of bucks. And in minutes he's heading for I-90 and east to Coeur d'Alene.

Thank God we've only got a twenty-five- or thirty-mile trip, as it's overcast and cold. My tie's streaming out behind me like Isadora Duncan's scarf, so I manage to loosen it and get it off. By the time we've gone a mile, I'm wishing I'd have pulled the down vest out of the dog carry. I do manage to stuff the tie into the cage, but am afraid to fish out the contents to get to the vest, as I'd probably have underwear scattered all over the freeway. So I hunker down, and pray for it to be over.

The freeway is lined with new businesses, car dealers, light industry, etc., but beyond it's beautiful tree-covered hills and it gets prettier as we get closer to Coeur d' Alene.

By the time Poker Jack pulls off the freeway and up in front of a biker bar, just before we get into Coeur d' Alene, my teeth are chattering and my nose and ears have lost all feeling. The joint is painted bright red with black trim and neon beer signs punctuate windows that have gone unwashed since World War II, but it looks like a warm version of heaven at the moment.

"Thought I'd introduce you to some of the boys," he says, and heads to the door without waiting for my comment, not that I could reply as my teeth are clattering like the windup ones that dance across the table. There are three other Harleys parked in front. Unlike Poker Jack's sidecar rig, these are cherry polished chrome.

I do take the time to ditch the suit coat and don the black down vest before I follow him inside to the serenade of the crack of pool balls.

And the three Harley riders are the only ones in the place, and they're gathered around the fifty-cent green-felt-covered table. They barely glance up from the game as we wander over. All of them are smoking cigars as big as Barry Bond's bat, and the smoke hangs low in the place. A small herd of steers has been sacrificed for the amount of leather on these guys, and they're wearing T-shirts, which I scan as they approach: *Jesus Loves You, But I Think You're an Asshole*; *The Proctologist Called, They Found Your Head*; and last but not least, *Use Coke Around Me and It Had Better Be Brown, Wet, and Over Ice*. Merle Haggard, who was probably smoking a joint when he recorded it and consequently wouldn't be welcome in the third guy's house, is on the jukebox regaling being an Okie from Muskogee and how they don't smoke it there.

Jack introduces me to three of his cohorts: John "Tollbooth" Tollbee, retired LAPD; Willard "Jockstrap" Holstrep, retired fire chief of Redmond, a little town in Oregon; and Patrick "Greengords" O'Hanley, now known merely as Gords, retired U.S. Fish and Wildlife. I'm informed, with more info than I need to know, that Gords got his handle due to the color of his nads after he got a vasectomy a few years ago. Young wife, he brags. All good guys, and all graying, including the beards and mustaches that I'm sure they couldn't officially grow until retired. They made up for lost time, playing catch-up now that they're not subject to the whims of some bureaucracy. It's also obvious they no longer have to run some obstacle course to keep up with some physical job requirement, but have relaxed the regimen. They rack their sticks and move me to the bar, where Poker Jack immediately launches into a tale about a deal he worked with Pug years before.

"You're dressed pretty damn downtown to be going on a dog rescue," Gords says.

"Double-duty day," I answer. "Funeral this morning in San Francisco, work this evening in Coeur d' Alene. I've got some clothes with me." I turn to Jack. "In fact, I think I'll use the boys' room and change. I about froze my nads in that sidecar. . . ."

"And I guess that would be a real loss to womanhood," Jack say and laughs. "Knew you was cold. I'll order you a . . . ?"

"Jack Daniels, neat," I say, "but just one until the work's over."

He shrugs. When I come back, much more comfortable with my suit and white shirt stuffed in the critter cage—where the damn monkey suit belongs—the drink's waiting. I down it, and say, "Shall we do it?"

"When you see the scene of the crime, you'll know why, but these boys are gonna come along."

I eye them carefully. "This isn't a high-dollar deal." I haven't mentioned how high it really is.

Jack laughs. "Hell, I'm splitting the two hundred you promised with them . . . fifty apiece. All we want out of this is a little of the old times and a good meal. We'da' done it for Pug being one of us."

When I decided to come, I upped his pay to two hundred, providing he'd pick me up, transport me, and lend the local knowledge. But, being as how there's three of them, I sweeten the take. "Tell you what, we get the pooch and I'll pick up the dinner tab. Best steak in town." They toast each other, then upend their drinks, and we're out of there. Then I have a small stroke of genius and call the skinny beak-nosed barmaid over. "How much are your hamburgers?"

"Four bucks."

I peel a five out of my wallet and flop it on the bar. "Bring me a raw patty, in a little aluminum foil or sandwich bag, please."

"And the five's mine?" she asks. I love entrepreneurs.

"And the five is yours, beautiful." The beautiful part is another light-year stretch of the imagination, but she relishes the lie, smiles, flashing a missing tooth, and its neighbors who soon will be, and heads for the kitchen.

"Didn't feed you on the plane?" Jack asks.

"Nope, doggy mission, remember?"

He laughs as I stuff a ball of hamburger in a sandwich bag in my pocket.

I guess Poker Jack figured the parking fee was business, my business, as he has no trouble paying for the round of drinks, even though I throw a twenty out on the bar.

To my surprise, our first stop is a marina at the west end of the lake, a lake as beautiful as any in America, particularly in the setting sun. Jack informs me, "The boys are taking Tollbooth's boat. You'll see why when you reconnoiter the place."

And I do, as after a long winding road around the lake's shoreline, he stops at a spot where we can see across a small bay. I'm warmer than I was the first leg of the trip, but still shivering. It's almost dark, but I can still make out a log house on a point, dim lights under the eaves outside. The living room lights come on as we study the place, so obviously someone's home, unless it's a timer. It's two stories, fifty feet up off the water with a deck cantilevering twenty feet out over what looks to be nothing but cold deep dark blue below. There's a long stairway leading down to the water along the edge of the point that faces us, and a boathouse there.

"High dollar," I say.

"Everest high," Jack agrees. "Probably three or four mil. The old girl did right well for herself."

"I know her asshole old man well enough to hope she did," I say. "Is the water deep in this lake?"

"Where the house is, there's a trench along that sheer wall over a hundred feet deep. We fish this cove a lot."

He laughs, and I get the impression that fishing is a big part of his life. Then he cranks the bike up again and we go rattling off down the pine-lined road. In moments, we're at a tall wrought-iron gate wide enough to embrace a semi, flanked by eight-foot masonry walls, with a cobbled driveway behind that winds down to the house still high above the lake.

"There's a buzzer over on the wall," Poker Jack says, "unless you want to try doing it the easy way."

"I guess I might as well," I say, misunderstanding him, and climb out of the sidecar and walk toward the button.

"By the easy way," he explains, talking to my back, "I meant steal the damn mutt. This is a woman, a scorned woman, you're dealing with."

I sigh, but continue toward the buzzer, then lean over and poke the button. A bright mercury light, twenty feet above and off to the side, immediately illuminates my location, and in a few moments a sultry voice asks, "That you, Andrew?"

"No, ma'am." Then I hear the low hum of a servo motor and glance up to see a video camera mounted on the same pole that carries the mercury light. It reverses direction and zeros in on me. I can see its lens telescoping out for a close-up. "I'm Dev Shannon," I say, speaking into the grate over the buzzer but looking up at the camera, "and I'd like to come in and speak with you."

"About what?" The tone of voice has changed drastically.

I tell a small white lie, not much of a stretch under the

circumstance. "The Santa Barbara Judicial Department has sent me to have a talk with you."

"I don't live in Santa Barbara anymore." The tone is growing harder and colder.

"That's fine, Mrs. Scanoletti—"

"My name is Potter, not Scanoletti."

"Isn't this Margaret Scanoletti?"

"This is Marge Potter. I used to be Scanoletti, but no longer . . . thank God, it's such an ugly name." She sounds sincere.

I take a deep breath. "Okay, Mrs. Potter—"

"Miss Potter. I'm no longer married."

"Miss Potter. Could I come in and talk awhile?"

"I have nothing to say to you, to the Santa Barbara Judicial system, or to anyone from California. I've had all the fruits and nuts I can stand for one lifetime. Don't ring my bell ever again. I'll call the police if you do. The chief is a friend of mine. As you can see, this property is well protected. And you should know, I've got a big gun."

Chapter Sixteen

"Mrs. . . . Miss Potter, I'm here to talk to you about Snarl."

There's a long pause, then she says, "There's no one here by that name. Besides, no one from the Santa Barbara Judicial District would arrive in some side-thing contraption driven by a Hell's Angel."

That almost makes me laugh aloud. Not the Hell's Angel, but the *no one*. And she's right, seldom would an officer of the court arrive in a beat-up pea-green Harley driven by a gnome dressed like a Hell's Angel, with or without a sidecar. But I contain myself. "The bichon frise, Miss Potter. The one granted your husband in the divorce decree."

"I only have one dog."

"You're violating a court order, Miss Potter. Why don't you just—"

Suddenly I get a dial tone, and the bright mercury light goes black. It's now dark enough that I have to stand for a moment to let my eyes adjust. I surmise that she no longer wishes to discuss the matter. Poker Jack is chuckling.

"A woman scorned, remember?" he chides. "That woman is like my wife, she has a speech impediment. Every now and then she stops for a breath. Then she hangs up on you. You didn't have a prayer, boy."

"I guess I had a mental lapse." I lean against the sidecar for a moment, then look up to see the camera has tracked me. There's a small red light on the face of it, I presume indicating that it's still on, working fine, and keeping track of potential interlopers.

I climb into the sidecar, saying loudly, in case there's a mike that can pick it up, "Damn, I give up. Let's go home," then under my breath and close to Poker Jack's ear, "Drive me out of sight of that damn camera."

He fires it up, and we drive far enough that I can leap out and fade into the trees on the lake side of the road without being seen. "I'm gonna grab the mutt," I say. "I'd appreciate it if you'd wait close by. You got your cell phone?"

He nods. "Yep, and a Motorola radio to talk to the boys in the boat. Tollbooth and the boys should be just offshore . . . out there somewhere, at least in a few minutes if they came like hell, and Tollbooth don't know from slow . . . and I'll be cruising up and down the road. You want to take the cage?"

"Nope, I can handle the little mutt until I get back here, and I might have to jump the fence." Then it dawns on me, "She's expecting somebody named Andrew. I'm going to hustle back and see if I can get in the gate when she opens it for 'Andrew.'"

"Sounds right." He nods. "Good luck." He guns the bike and sidecar away.

I've noticed that the trees have been cut well back away from the wall, and the wall is constructed so the joints in the rock are almost full of mortar, leaving little toehold. Someone knew what they were doing, securitywise.

I get up against the wall and work my way back to the gate. The wind is coming up, and it's damned cold. November in northern Idaho, what did I expect? It's hard to remember the rest of the world is not Santa Barbara, when you're lulled by seventy-plus-degree days.

I find good cover where the camera can't detect me,

check my watch, and wait. Fifteen minutes pass, which seems like an hour, then I see headlights coming. I smile when the car wheels off the road and stops at the gate, and a tall guy with perfect Gumby-styled gray hair, who looks slick enough to be a used car salesman, climbs out of one of those sporty little bright red BMWs, and walks to the buzzer.

"Andrew?" I hear the sexy voice ask.

"In the flesh," he says. "Got a great bottle of Stag's Leap."

"And I've got the steaks. You're a darling dear. I can't wait to tell you what happened."

"What?"

"Get in here and get that wine open and I'll fill you up and fill you in."

The gates begin to part and he moves away to the car, fires it up, and spins the wheels going in.

I watch the doors swing fully open, the BMW pass through, then they begin to close before I sprint for the opening. I have to squeeze through, but make it, and again scramble for the trees lining the drive.

Then I pause a moment to study the gate mechanization. There's no box and buzzer inside, so I guess it's the weight of the vehicle on a pressure pad in the driveway that makes the gate open from this side, and probably an activator like one that opens an automatic garage door. That's the bad news; I may not be able to open the gate from the inside. I study the trees on the inside of the wall and note that they are not nearly as well trimmed back. I see a couple that I could probably climb and some limbs high enough and sturdy enough that will get me over the wall. Now I wish I'd brought the damn cage, as I try to picture me hanging on to the ball of fluff and climbing a tree at the same time. It's not a pretty picture.

Oh well, I'll face that farce when I come to it.

There are a few perimeter lights under the eaves of the

house, and another six-foot fence surrounding it, with another gate. The BMW is parked in front of a four-car garage. I make my way through underbrush to the rear of the house carefully, as I know there's a fifty-foot cliff falling away to water somewhere nearby. Why two fences? I ask myself, then, as I pull even with the back of the house, facing the water, my answer resonates through the slats in the form of a baritone bark, sending a chill up my back.

Sometimes I wonder why I didn't pay attention in class, at least in a doggy training class somewhere. I remember Scanoletti's purposefully innocuous words, "The other dog, Fluffy, is black and tan." Now I know why the fee is so high. The little dog, Snarl, is, of course, tiny. Irony, remember, so, stupid . . . the big dog, Fluffy, is anything but. The realm of doggydom rolls through my mind like a slide show: sloppy, happy, black, and tan hunting hound; springy little miniature Doberman, sharp teeth but weak jaws; sharp and large-toothed full Doberman known to rip out throats; and of course the large and lovable rottweiler, known to eat the ferocious Doberman for a snack with his large canines and alligator jaw.

Damn, I'm doggy dumb.

This would only happen to a cat lover. The dogs in the mind's-eye slide show keep getting bigger and more ferocious until the picture sticks on the Roman Legion war dog, the rott, as he's lovingly known to the prowler and burglar haters who own one, and here I am about to burgle a backyard. I press my eye to a slat in the fence, and can see across the lighted yard.

Ah, the good news. There's another cyclone-wire-enclosed kennel, and Fluffy is pacing back and forth inside, his eyes locked on mine, as if he can see me through the fence, and I wouldn't be surprised if he could. I know he can smell me as he's slathering like awaiting a prime rib roast. He's only barking every once in a while, but he's continually growling, and the low rumble seems to rattle the ground underfoot like an approaching train. The image is not one I savor.

Ah, the better news. Snarl, the bichon frise, the puffball, my target, my little fistful of Franklins, scampers out into the light, runs up to the cyclone kennel, and barks viciously at the bigger dog, if you can call a high-pitched yap a bark.

Fluff pauses, and looks at the ball of fur as if he'd like to snap its backbone—probably jealous of the little punk because he has the run of the place—but again turns his attention to me.

I take a long look at the house. I can see the living room clearly through large picture windows, and no one's near. They're probably in the kitchen working on those steaks she mentioned, sipping Stag's Leap. I wish I was with them, as I shiver in the cold.

But Snarl's not going to get home to Santa Barbara without me, so I vault the fence.

Fluff goes wild, leaping and snarling, gnashing the fence wire, and Snarl imitates him, staying as close to the cyclone and as far from me as possible upon seeing the intruder in his inner sanctum.

I sprint across the yard to the cacophony of barks, the timbre of which is now rattling the nearby evergreens.

I slow as I near the fence line, where Snarl seems to be confused . . . Does he want to climb into the cage with the rott, which he can't do, or face the intruder? I pause and fish the hamburger out of my pocket, open it, smile carefully, not showing my teeth—I guess I learned something about mutts—and offer up the treat.

Snarl is not impressed, and Fluffy goes even wilder.

"Come here, little Snarl," I say, in my most enticing voice.

He weakens. The aromatic, intoxicating essence of ground beef. He quiets, testing the air like a tiny stallion with a mare on the wind. He's now paying no attention to the rott, who's bouncing his 120 pounds-plus up against the fence, slathering and snarling—maybe easy for the bichon frise, but a little hard for me to ignore.

I'm amazed Miss Potter and her dinner date haven't appeared at the back door, wondering if a grizzly has intruded on her happy home, but not yet.

Snarl quiets even more, and takes a couple of tentative steps forward. I encourage him seductively. "You sweet little doggy. I have something good here."

Another step. He's only five feet away.

I dive for him, but the little puffball is fast and slithers away. I roll up against the cyclone, and insanity overcomes the rott. He manages to catch a tiny bit of the down vest that's intruded through the two-inch square of the cyclone fence, and as I scramble away it rips in his teeth.

I charge after the fleeing ball of fur and manage to corner him, just as the yard lights up like a football stadium. Hearing the panic-laced screams of Miss Potter, I ignore her and keep my eye on the ball. I fake one way and Snarl breaks the other, but I dive and am able to snatch a leg. He yelps, and the scream from his master goes up an octave.

I'm sixty feet from the fence where I came into the yard, and about to break for it, when I hear a loud, manly, "Don't move or I'll blow you all to hell."

My eyes focus on the car salesman with the Gumby hairdo, standing in an open sliding glass door. Miss Potter, beside him, has stopped screaming and stands with arms folded, looking smug, then she reaches for something on the doorjamb. She has good reason to look smug, as her paramour has a double-barreled shotgun aimed a little high, but in my general direction. Gumby has morphed into Genghis Kahn. It's amazing what a double will do for one's intimidation quotient.

At the same time, the gate to Fluff's cage springs open. Radio controlled, I'd guess. More motivation for her smugness. The barrel-chested behemoth has got to backtrack twenty feet to round the gate to get to me, but he's on his way. Luckily he's too eager to bloody his teeth with bounty hunter and his feet slip on the concrete kennel floor, and what I imagine he's deposited there. He's spinning in place.

Counting on the fact Gumby's not anxious to face a manslaughter charge over someone else's mutt, I turn and, with my one free hand, clutching Snarl tightly in the other, take two paces and, adrenaline-fueled, vault the much nearer and lower four-foot fence on the lakeside of the yard. Landing with a crash six feet below on a wood deck amongst deck chairs and tables, I sprint for its lakeside edge. Another low rail fence keeps one from stumbling off, and I'm surprised it's not higher as I stop and stare. This is the cantilevered part that I saw across the bay, fifty feet above the water. With the overcast it's black as the inside of a mausoleum. I'm fruitlessly trying to locate Tollbooth and the boat as I turn to check my rear and simultaneously I hear the blast of the shotgun, see the fire from the muzzle, and then see the backlighted silhouette of a massive snarling behemoth clear the fence separating backyard and deck.

Shot cuts the air over my head, sounding a little like a passing F-16. At the same instance, the bichon frise, who's known far and wide to be a pacifist—obviously a vicious prevarication—clamps needle teeth into the side of the hand not gripping him. The little bastard can bite.

Hoping against all hope that Poker Jack knows his lake, thinking of two hundred crisp uncrinkled Franklins awaiting, and having little choice—in fact none—just a step ahead of a lathering monster who wants my throat, I leap out into the darkness.

God, Poker Jack, be right.

Chapter Seventeen

Fifty feet is a long, long way, particularly when you imagine a rocky reception, and when a puffball with surprisingly strong jaws is using your hand for a chew toy. On the way down, it dawns on me, *Where exactly was that boathouse?*

I have the presence of mind to point my toes, protect my crotch with my free hand, and hold the hand holding the mutt over my eyes.

We hit the water with a numbing crash, not only from the fall but from the sudden permeating, bone-chilling cold. I'm surprised we didn't have to smash through surface ice. Not knowing the depth to expect, I've remembered the training I'd taken in the Marine Corps, and immediately angle my legs so my depth of penetration is minimum. Surprised I don't hit bottom and that I'm not trying to kick to the surface with shattered femurs, I stroke to the top, sputtering when I surface. The puffball has been shaken loose from his grip on my hand and has decided survival the better part of valor. We surface within four feet of each other. He's coughing and swimming, but in circles. I easily snatch him up by the nape of his fuzzy little neck and resist the urge to pop his sweet little head off. Counterproductive.

Even that far from Miss Potter's deck, I can discern the wail of "shoot him, shoot him." Thank God, Gumby is still weighing the consequence.

"I might hit the dog," Gumby yells in reply.

I strike out, stroking one-handed for the middle of the lake. After I figure I've swum fifty yards, I stop.

The yelling deck side has receded. In the darkness I'm sure I'm out of sight, but surprised they don't have a spotlight searching for the pooch and me.

I'm also sure that since my butt's not full of buckshot, Gumby has lost all claim to the medium-rare filet Miss Potter had awaiting him. Were we to run into him at the promised steak dinner for my chums, I'd include him for his restraint in not blowing away the friendly neighborhood dognapper.

The only thing now preemptive in my mind is the cold; arctic, glacial cold. To say it's merely cold would be one of the world's great understatements. It was cold in the sidecar, it's frigid in the water, about five-minute-survival frigid, I'd guess.

"Tollbooth?" I shout. It echoes across the water. The overcast keeps even starlight from penetrating the velvet blackness.

There's no answer.

I shout louder.

Nothing.

I consider swimming back toward the shore, then hear the sweet quiet rumble of an expensive, powerful outboard crank up. For only a moment, a spotlight sweeps the water from a hundred yards away, passing over me so I don't think I've been seen, but then it clicks off and I hear the motors rev. In moments, engine sounds are cut, and I hear a low voice from a drifting boat.

"Shannon?"

What a team these guys are. "Right here," I say, and a line bounces off my head, which I grab.

"You shot?"

"Nope."

"You bit? I heard what sounded like a pack of wolves."

"Only a puffball bite."

"You got the mutt," Tollbooth says, a smile on his bearded face.

"Your steak is assured," I reassure him. Then add, "If you get me out of this damn freezer."

"Steaks at my favorite place are thirty bucks," he cautions as he drags me around to the back and a swim-step flanking the big outboard. I hand him the mutt and he pulls me aboard.

"Cheap at twice the price," I reply, my teeth clattering, as he wraps a coat around me. He drops the dog in the bottom of the boat, and I'm happy to see that his little needle teeth are banging together as staccato as mine, and am confident that he's not anxious to leap back into the arctic sea.

He's obviously not as he finds a protected spot under the seat, curling up to shiver in silence. Tollbooth has a towel, and fishes him out and begins vigorously drying him. He gives the old boy a generous lick across a bearded cheek. Tollbooth looks up at me, grinning. "I'll keep him if you don't want to take him back."

"I gave my word of honor."

"I'll even pass on the steak. He's a cute little fella."

"Word of honor."

He laughs. "I already got a toy poodle."

"I'm happy for you," I chatter, but even with banging teeth the sarcasm rings through.

He eyes me skeptically, then asks, "You jump, or were you pushed?"

"Chased by a mastodon and an irate lover with a shotgun."

"Ballsy," he yells, shaking his head in some amazement, as Jockstrap fires up the boat and roars away. Gords is even more useful, as he opens a bottle of Wild Turkey, takes a long swig, and passes the fifth back to me.

"Ballsy? Stupid is more like it," I say, then take a long gullet-warming drag on the fifth, and in moments it's washed over me, heating my blood to the end of the smallest capillary. I backhand my mouth, then offer, "But it was jump or become kibbles and bits." I have to yell over the loud motor, but know he hears me as he laughs, then reaches for the Turkey.

A great steak, $250, deductible, added to the cost of the trip, but great company and a good night's sleep in Poker Jack's guest room, and an excellent free breakfast of biscuits, eggs, elk sausage, and home fries, thanks to Milly, his wife, helps offset the extra cost, and I'm winging my way back to Santa Barbara with Snarl safely tucked away in the luggage compartment.

Life is good.

At eleven-thirty A.M., as I step out of the plane in Santa Barbara and turn my cell phone back on, it beeps, informing me of one or more waiting calls. The first one is from Babs, seemingly social, so I'll return it later; the second is Pug, which I return. He's merely checking to see that I'm home in one piece, and if I need a ride, which I do. He's on his way. The third is Cynthia, who claims to have some new information but does not answer at either home, office, or cell. The forth is Cedric, who is still in San Francisco and does not answer his cell. The fifth is Mason, who leaves me a message that the continuation of his arraignment is scheduled for this coming Thursday, day after tomorrow, and would I please attend? I guess he needs his hand held. The sixth is from Skip Hanson. I return his, and he asks me, "Where can we meet? I have an *Orion* boat pirate crew roster for you. Bring money." So we schedule a drink at Café del Sol at six.

Six phone calls, and life is still good. An anomaly.

Snarl has survived the high altitude in good shape, but is more than a little eager to exit the doggie carry. As I have no leash, he's going to have to wait. Still, the little fur ball seems glad to see me. Maybe a hand-in-paw swim in the arctic has bonded us.

I call Dr. Scanoletti's office and am put on hold for twenty minutes until the receptionist finally comes back on and informs me that the doctor is in surgery and will return my call. I've gnawed on my last conversation with him for some time, and have decided that he'll get the pooch when I get the dough. I know, if instinct is working at all, that this guy is going to try to stiff me. I'll do what I can to upstage his larcenous urges.

Now I decide to make the tough call. Iver has had an appointment with his urologist this morning, and they're supposed to discuss treatment options.

I dial him up while I wait for the old man to appear in his Ford pickup. He answers on the first ring. "What's the game plan on the prostate thing?"

"Nothing. The doc agrees, reluctantly, to wait a couple of months, and see what Cedric's herbs do. He laughed at me for listening to Cedric, but said a couple of months probably wouldn't matter much. They graded this thing in some way and he says mine is a slow grower. I have another appointment just after New Year's."

"Are you gonna be able to go to Jamaica?" I ask.

"No reason not to and all the reason in the world to go. I may just be able to get some answers from those folks down there that you can't, white bread."

I laugh. "Right, mon. I'll get Cedric to make the reservations. Speaking of Cedric, have you heard from him?"

"Nope."

"Let me know if you do, or better yet make sure he calls me. He's not answering his cell phone."

"Will do."

Just as I hang up, my cell immediately rings. It's Cedric, and I accept a collect call.

"Where the hell are you?" I ask.

"Jail."

"Jail? What the hell for?"

"Seems Mohammad the madman made me, and called the cops and they busted me for burglary, but reduced it to trespass."

"Trespass? You told me you could make that thing work if you could get within a hundred feet."

"Yeah, but it worked a lot better from closer, so I jumped the fence last night and hid out in a small garden, hothouse actually, behind his town house. Nice place, by the way. He's a prodigious orchid grower. Some great specimens. I guess he had some kind of silent alarm system . . . even in the little garden, and in a few minutes there were cops coming out of the town house and in through the garage like the katzenjammer kids. Mean bastards. No respect at all. They couldn't get me for breaking and entering as it turns out the gate was left unlocked; at least they found it so, as was the greenhouse, so they changed it to simple trespass."

Which means Cedric picked the lock, as he's a master with a set of picks. "So, you got a bail hearing coming up?"

"The system here is deft and efficacious. Done done it. It's only a smidgen, a lousy grand. It seems trespass is not a capital crime. But my credit cards are maxed out and I've found bondsmen to be doubting Thomases who won't accept promises. You know anybody up here?"

"I'll have you out in time for an evening plane. But, Ced, you screwed up. No reason to get that close."

"Devlin, if I could press control, alternate, delete, and reset this past twenty-four hours, believe me, I would. You're closing the proverbial barn door after the Parahippus has fled, as evolution did to that particular progenitor of the horse. Please do get me out of here. There are some real temerarious, phrenetic, mendacious throwbacks in this lair of louse-ridden miscreants. My roomies, if I can refer to my three 250-pound ebony sons of Ethiopia, are absolutely misanthropic."

"Big, badass black guys." I can't help but laugh, even though he sounds deadly serious. "I would presume that's an undesirable circumstance."

"Opprobrious would be an understatement. By the way, as they were hauling me out of the doctor's garden, Hashim said to give you his regards, and inquired as to your health. He lacked sincerity. He then mentioned that he normally cures the mentally disturbed, but also knows how to create the problem. I think it was a threat. The guy can trace his linage directly to Bella Lugosi."

"What's the good news . . . did you get anything on your little computer snoop box?"

"They are suspicious and are holding my handheld for evidence, I'm sure suspicious as to what I was really doing, and think the handheld holds some mysterious answer. But what they don't know is I got a bunch of stuff and already uploaded it to my home computer, and I ejected the 256-meg memory chip that my next batch of info was begin recorded upon, and it's somewhere among the genus *Platanthera*."

"Which means?"

"Orchids. I buried it in the peat moss."

"Don't go back, Ced. Let's see what we get off the stuff you already uploaded." Then it dawns on me, "Are you on a safe line?"

"Jail pay phone."

"Then you've already said too much. We'll talk when you get home. By the way, Ced, try and not use words like opprobrious, whatever the hell that means, and you may live long enough so I can get your bail covered."

"My urges are purely recrudescent. Confucius said, 'With coarse rice to eat, with water to drink, and my bended arm for a pillow'—which is all *I* have, by the way—'I have still joy in the midst of these things. Riches and honors acquired by unrighteousness'—that would be the unsuccessful efforts of my roomies—'are to me as a floating cloud.'"

"Ced."

"Okay, okay, just get me out."

"Sit in the corner with your back to the wall. Chant quietly in Chinese. Look like you've got advanced AIDS so no one will risk getting splattered by your blood. Cross your eyes and roll them occasionally, and maybe they'll think you're crazy . . . which wouldn't be much of a stretch. Anybody in their right mind will leave you alone. I'll have you out in the shake of a Buddhist prayer rattle."

"It's prayer wheel."

"Whatever."

"I will chant a prayer composed by His Holiness Tenzin Gyatso, the fourteenth Dalai Lama of Tibet, honoring and invoking the great compassion of the Three Jewels, the Buddha, the Teachings, and the Spiritual Community."

"That'll work."

"May you live long and prosperously."

"May you live till I get you out."

Chapter Eighteen

Pug is blowing his horn at me, so I ring off and as we drive out of the airport and get right back on the contraption and call a bondsman I know in San Francisco, whose office is a half block from the jail. He assures me Ced will be out, as I promised, in time to catch his scheduled flight home.

"Have you eaten?" Pug asks.

"Nope. Let me call Babs and see if she can join us." I do, and she's working at her desk and says she wants to talk to me and will join us.

"We're eating with Pug . . . is that okay?" I ask. I don't know how personal she wants to get, now that we have some personal things we can talk about. Hopefully she wants to talk about getting back together, as nature made us.

"Of course," she says, and I try not to sound disappointed.

"Where?"

"Wine Cask?"

"High dollar," I say, then wish I hadn't as I now sound like a tightwad, as I presume I'm paying.

"Der Winersnitzle," she says, her tone a tad sarcastic.

"Wine Cask," I agree.

In less than twenty minutes we've left Snarl to have the run of the truck cab and we're seated in one of Santa Barbara's better eateries. Babs's mission seems to be to find out how I did in Idaho, and I hope, to reinforce our growing relationship. She has nothing of particular interest, workwise, except for the fact forensics has concluded that the bullet was .50 caliber, and barrel markings are distinct and it can be traced to a weapon, should one ever turn up.

"Well, bounty hunter, did you apprehend the errant pooch?" she asks.

"Save your leftovers," I say, with a grin. "The perp is already in-*car*-cerated . . . in Pop's car . . . which seems appropriate."

"Did he come up and jump in your lovable lap?" she asks.

I smile at the thought she might think my lap lovable. "More like a fifty-foot death-defying leap, into a not-so-lovable ice cold lake," I answer.

"Tell me about it?" she asks, seemingly fascinated.

I see my chance, and jump on it. "If you'll come to supper with me."

Pug smiles, and I know he's been eager to ask about what happened, in his prurient manner, after he left us on our way back to the boat. But he's a gentleman of the old school, and would never say anything, particularly in front of the lady. He eyes her expectantly, slightly nodding his head in encouragement.

Babs laughs, then suggests with sarcastic humor, "Der Winersnitzel?"

"Nope. The hot spot of your choice in the Channel Islands Harbor, if you have Slider Dunbury's last address like you promised."

She eyes me as if she's being used and abused. "Is that the only reason you want to have dinner with me, Mr. Shannon?"

"Hell no. I have devious plans involving ravishing the body and soul of a ravishing detective." The old man turns a little red, but Babs smiles.

"Ravish the body but nourish the soul, little cricket," she says in an inscrutable oriental manner, then laughs, then adds, "In that case, you're on." She glances sideways at Pug. "At least regarding the dinner part. I have Dunbury's last address on a pad on my desk. And in addition, and I'm risking a suspension, I have a list of interviewees, which I didn't promise."

"You're as intelligent and efficient as you are beautiful."

"Right. What time we leaving?"

"Meet me at Café Sol at six . . . if that's okay. I've got a little business there, then we'll head out. With luck, we can be at the Whale's Tail or some place of your choice, other than a wiener joint, by eight. We got to take your car, as I'm down to the Harley . . . unless you want the wind in your hair."

"And bugs on my teeth from smiling all the way to Oxnard. No, thanks, not my idea of a way to begin a date, at least not a nighttime date. My Acura will do, but you'll have to drive."

Babs has to exit early to a pile of paperwork, and leaves Pop and me sipping some great post-lunch coffee.

He finally gets around to asking, "You like her as much as I think you should?"

"Like her a lot, Pop." I shrug. "Don't know her all that well yet, but like what I do know a hell of a lot."

"Umm," he says, eyeing me over the top of his glasses. "Sounds like you know her pretty damn well."

"Twenty-first century, Pop, enlightened adults, remember?"

"Yeah, yeah, I know, I'm still in 1960 with the Platters."

"Not all bad."

He shrugs, then changes the subject. "Did Poker Jack and the Pigs help you out?"

"Saved my bacon, to use a bad pun. Good guys."

He laughs. "That Poker Jack is a great guy; dog-butt ugly, which served him well undercover, but a great guy."

It's my turn to laugh. And I can't help but add, "He's got a great little wife. Sweet as she is cute, too, and she'd have to be. Poker Jack is so ugly Snarl closed his eyes when he was humping Jack's leg."

"Bull," the old man says, and we both laugh. With the old man shaking his head and chuckling, I pick up the check and we head to the harbor. I left Iver in charge of feeding Futa, but wouldn't be surprised, with all Iver's had on his mind, if he forgot. If he did, *Aces n' Eights* will be littered with bird parts, or far worse, rat remains. I'm eager to get home before that happens; besides, it's going to be interesting to introduce our temporary houseguest, Snarl, to my gracious yowling roommate. Futa has, I've noticed, an aversion to the average canine. Let's hope the little bichon frise lives to get back to his master, and isn't in need of Dr. Scanoletti's orthopedic surgical skills when he does.

I board the boat with morbid anticipation, as I now always do when I'm away from her for hours. Thank God, there's no note posted over the hatchway. Then again, maybe no warning's a worse sign. As I'm carrying a doggy motel, Futa welcomes me with a yowl and standoffishness, but I can see that his bowl is half-full. Even with his own crushing problems, Iver's remembered to protect the harbor birds from Futa's ravenous wrath.

I set the dog carrier down, and with some trepidation, but hoping against hope there won't be a wall-to-wall dog-and-cat fight, open the door. Snarl is out in a flash, jumping and wiggling like the yap dog he is, then foolishly spots Futa, his back slightly up, standing in the passageway to the forward cabins. Futa looks more disgusted than frightened. Snarl charges, yapping at the top of his little lungs. To his surprise, this cat doesn't retreat, but meets him head-on with a pair of claw-laden slaps that turns him yelping and sends him back to the dog carrier.

I can't help but laugh and decide that they can work this out much better without two-legged interference.

There's a call on my machine, informing me that the PD is through with my Chevy and I can pick it up at the impound yard, which I immediately do, only to decide it has to go directly to the body shop. I pause only long enough to shower, shave, and slick up for my evening with beautiful Babs, then go to face this tangible reminder of Sandy.

Before I head out, I consider closing Snarl up in my cabin, but decide to let him take his chances with the limited freedom of a fifty-five-foot boat. I do put Futa's food and water up on a bookshelf that's one of his favorite perches, worrying that he'd shred the pooch if he decided to partake. I find a three-day-old pork chop in the fridge and take it out on the deck where I set it next to a water bowl, then have to hustle back down to answer the phone.

"Hold for Dr. Scanoletti," a female voice commands.

In a few moments, he's on the line. "You got Snarl?" he asks, in the same commanding tone.

"I do."

"Then bring him over to my office."

"You got nine thousand cash?"

There's a long silence, then in a very level, obviously strained tone, he says, "No, I don't keep that kind of cash around the office, and the banks are closed. Drop him by, send me an invoice, and I'll pay it like I do all my bills."

"No can do, Doc. Cash on delivery."

"Your agreement said nothing about cash." His tone is even more stressed.

"My agreement said ten grand, which you agreed to, so I guess we'll just have to wait until tomorrow, when it's cash for pup."

"He's my dog."

"It's my agreement, and now it's my money, per that agreement. Nine thousand balance, in cash."

There's another long pause and I can almost feel the grinding wheels of his greedy little brain. Finally, in a faux-happy tone, he says, "Fine. Bring him by tomorrow, about eleven. That'll give me time to get the cash from the bank."

"Perfect, see you—"

"Is he okay?"

"Peachy."

"Is he with you?"

"Did you want to speak to him?" I say, with a bit of a chuckle, then bite my tongue.

"I just want to know if he's safe."

Time for a small white lie. "I have a cat. I left him with a friend who loves dogs."

"Hmmph," he manages. "Tomorrow, Mr. Shannon."

"By the way, you didn't mention that the black and brown dog wasn't Snarl's brother."

Now it's his turn to laugh. "They are good buddies. You didn't ask, I didn't offer."

Worrying about getting my chores done, and being on time for my date, I hang up without further conversation.

I do pause long enough to clip my cuffs and holster with my small Police Special on the back of my belt, under the blue blazer I'm wearing in honor of my beautiful date. After all, I have a smidgen of work to do.

The side of the Chevy that had faced the van is beat all to hell and the windows must be in shards somewhere out at sea. It'll be more than the average ten-year-old four-door Chevy is worth to fix her up, but I have so much invested in the beautiful polished and balanced engine that it still seems a good investment.

Rosco Champness, the body man I use and whom I go see after viewing the mess that was my innocuous stakeout and chase car, has a better suggestion. "Let's find a newer Chevy with a good body and change out the engine." A stroke of brilliance, and a bottom line that doesn't dig nearly so deeply into my pockets. Having located Rosco's sixteen-year-old son, at no charge, when he ran away from home a couple of years ago, has paid off handsomely, in addition to the case of Jack Daniels he dropped off at the boat.

He says he'll handle the whole thing, and I'll only be out the cost of the new body, probably less than a grand, and parts, and he'll keep the new rig's old engine for his labor. We shake, and I'm back on the Harley and headed for Café del Sol and my meeting with Skip Hanson, smiling because I figured I'd be out five grand or more.

Skip is waiting outside for my arrival, and I don't see Babs's Acura yet, which is fine as Skippy might be reluctant to talk if he knows she's SBPD. Both of his stocky exposed shoulders are tattooed, one with a dragon riding a surfboard and one with a black panther, and show clearly as the sleeves of his T-shirt have been cut off. His tan legs are exposed from just below his knotty knees down to the Jesus sandals he wears, and the hair on them is bleached almost white. The shorts must have been stolen off some Crip or Blood, or more likely bought at goodwill after a gang member discarded them, and they're low enough on his waist that I wonder if he'll be able to hold them up. He's a walking testimony to the worst in fashion. I'm surprised as Paco, the bartender, lets him slither past to get to the patio, but he does, probably because he sees Skip's with me. Had I known the guy would be attired like an Oxnard cholo I would never have suggested meeting him here.

We move out to the patio where no one is seated yet, and as I don't want to foist him off on one of my favorite places. He's smiling as if he just hit the lottery, which means he must have something good . . . or thinks he does.

"Now, how much are you willing to fork over for a full list of passengers and crew on board the *Orion*?"

I shrug. "How about drinks and a pass-go-without-going-to-jail card?"

"I ain't done nothing to go to jail for," he says, with confidence, but he cuts his watery blues away. He's an adept liar, but not adept enough for a guy who's been lied to by the best. He looks back with schoolboy innocence.

The fact is I did my homework, or more accurately had Cedric do research, on Skip when I thought he might be the majordomo of the pilfered boat caper, and happily noted that he does have a warrant outstanding in Las Vegas. Seems he and a couple of buddies tore up a motel room a couple of years ago, and have an assault and battery charge after they dotted the eye of a manager who complained.

It's nice to possess negotiating power.

As I study him, trying to decide if it's time to use the hole card, he continues to blather, "How about ten thousand bucks?"

I laugh a little too enthusiastically, although it wouldn't be an unreasonable request if, and only if, it led me directly to the boat and was payable on my receipt of the bounty. "Skip, Skip, Skip," I say, still chuckling, "you are delusional. You tripping on acid?"

"Bullshit, Shannon. You said you'd pay—"

"And I will." Of course I was more enthusiastic before I found the wants and warrant on the old boy. "I'll give you a hundred bucks right now for a list of names." I reach behind my back and pop loose the cuff case from my belt and plop the cuffs on the table between us. "And I won't haul your sweet ass in."

He stands. "You've got nothing—"

"Las Vegas," I say, moving my chair back away from the table. He hesitates, then spins on his heel and breaks for the low fence between patio and parking.

Chapter Nineteen

He's quick, but not quick enough. He never should have cut his eyes to the fence, judging if he could make the jump.

I'm ready for him, and nail him with a flying tackle just as he's jumping. I imagine he outweighs me a little, but his athletic abilities are lacking, and his direction yields to mine. We're a foot deep, in posies and flower bed soil, me astride his chest, him sputtering, when I advise him, "Skip, I'm tougher than you, faster than you, and probably a hell of a lot smarter than you. And trust me, I've had a hell of a lot more experience than you, and if you keep dicking around, I'm going to tie you up like a macramé. Now, do you want me to feed you handfuls of this flower bed—and I know what they use for fertilizer and it's not chile verde—or do you want to get up and act like a gentleman?"

He struggles, a little wild-eyed, so I stuff a handful of flower bed dirt in his mouth. He's spitting and coughing, not much liking the flavor or the consistency.

Getting his airways and mouth clear, he glances over and glares at the waiter, who's standing in the doorway with a wide-eyed customer on either side. I've known Toby for a long time, and he's surprised at nothing.

"You ready to order, Dev?" Toby asks, as if nothing unusual were happening.

"Not quite," I say. "Skip here is still trying to make up his mind if he wants chicken droppings or the special."

"I'll stop back by in a few . . . . You want I should hand you your cuffs?"

I'm out of reach of them without letting Skip up. "Nope, we're coming to an understanding. Skip?"

"Okay, okay, okay, okay," Skip mumbles. I let him up and he brushes off, picks up his chair, and sits back down. "Twenty-five hundred," he mumbles, without much conviction.

"You're a good guy, Skip, and you do what you say you'll do. I like that, so I'm gonna cut you a break. I'm gonna forget you're wanted in Las Vegas. And I'll tell you what, I'll give you a hundred right now, or if you want to wait and if . . . and I say if . . . I recover the boat and collect the fee, I'll give you five hundred."

Again he hesitates. "How about a hundred now and a thousand if you get the dough for the boat?"

"Nope. Five hundred if I get the dough, or a hundred now . . . one or the other, not both."

"I'll take the hun."

His rent must be due. I peel it out of my money clip and lay it on the table. He reaches for it, but I catch his wrist. "The list?"

He pulls back, digs a crumpled paper out of his back pocket, throws it across the table, and snatches up the Franklin.

"You buying the drinks?" he asks with a crooked grin.

"You're pressing your luck," I say, wanting him gone when Babs arrives. "Besides, I got a date. Where'd you get the names?"

"You didn't pay for that info." He shrugs, rises, and jumps the low fence between the patio and the parking lot, and is gone. "They better be right," I yell after him. He waves over his shoulder at me, a gesture that looks remarkably like he's flipping me off. It's a good thing I'm not offended by such trivia.

Timing is good, as Babs has parked her Acura across the street in the Bird Refuge lot and is coming to join me. I enjoy watching her approach, the setting sun backlighting her and a flight of ducks behind landing among assorted seabirds on water gone golden with reflection. When she passes out of sight at the entrance, I take a second to glance at the list. Seven names, Meegan's included. It seems good old Skip doesn't mind if his ex-girlfriend goes to the slammer. True love. I think I recognize a couple of the others from the harbor, and I'm not at all surprised to see Terry Butterworth, a.k.a. Toke, at the top of the heap, nor Rupert Beauchamp, the Jamaican. The names will be good fodder for Cedric, after he arrives and has time to scrub the jail scum away in a hot shower.

I smile, a hundred well spent, presuming he didn't make up the whole damn list, other than Meegan.

The shapely half-Oriental Barbara A. Benson walks out onto the patio. "I caught your action as I drove up. You had me digging in my purse for my piece. You training a new recruit, or was that serious?"

"Not very. Small misunderstanding."

"Small misunderstanding that ended up with you standing on his chest. You look cute with a daisy in your hair," she says, and flashes me a devastating smile.

I reach up and pluck a flower and some foliage out of my hair, and we both laugh. Luckily, my clothes have fared well and I won't have to change, merely brush off.

In moments, Babs and I are inside enjoying a saltless margarita on the rocks, her choice and fine with me. Then it dawns on me that drinking straight bitters would be fine with her across the table. I don't know if I'm falling, but I'm certainly well smitten.

We finish one drink, then head out for the forty-five-minute-to-an-hour drive south along the coast to Oxnard, where I plan a quick stop to check out Slider Dunbury's last place of residence. The Acura boasts a sunroof, and she does end up with a limited amount of wind in her jet-black hair. It becomes her, then again damn near everything does.

I'm surprised when we find the address and pull up in front of a nice Mediterranean-style home near the River Ridge Golf Course. Babs chooses to wait in her Acura, when I go up to ring the bell.

An elderly gentleman with an oxygen bottle strapped on his waist and a small pencil-size clear plastic tube leading from it to an ear-to-ear harness, with an outlet in front of his nostrils, answers after the third or fourth ring.

"You're a little impatient," he says, wheezing slightly, breathing deeply.

"Sorry, sir, I didn't mean to be."

"What are . . . you selling?" he asks, a little impatient himself.

I flash the brass, and he studies it a moment. "What's Bail Enforcement?"

"Hunting down the bad guys."

I get a slight grin reflecting his wicked smile. Then he says, "I wish I could still be one."

I laugh, and like the old guy. I introduce myself.

"I'm M. Harden Brown."

"You got a minute?"

"Sure, come on in."

I follow him into a living room where the TV blares loudly. *Jeopardy* is on the tube. He carefully lowers himself into a Lazy Boy, picks up a tuner, and mutes the sound. There's a larger tank beside the chair, and he sits aside the plastic tube wrapping from ear to ear and picks up an apparatus from the larger tank and resets a small mask in place over his nose.

"Damn emphysema," he mutters. Then waves me to another chair nearby. "What's up?"

"Slider Dunbury?"

"Phil? Did he show up?"

"Is he missing?"

"A few months now."

"Your stepson, or grandson?" I ask, noting his last name is not the same, while trying to judge his age.

"Hell no. Tenant. Rented the . . . the mother-in-law quarters around back."

"Did he skip out on the rent?" I ask.

"Well, he did owe some rent . . . but he left . . . all his things."

I can see he gets short of breath as wheezing breaks his conversation on regular intervals.

He continues, after wheezing, then taking a deep draw on the oxygen. "I'll bet the sound system alone was . . . worth a grand or more. I personally think . . . something happened to him. I had to get a court order . . . to clean out his stuff. Goddamn . . . California courts anyway."

"Any idea what might have happened?"

"I kind of liked . . . the kid. He actually . . . helped out . . . once in a while." The old man actually manages a wink. "He brought around . . . some cute chicks." Then he coughs. "I stored his stuff in . . . a ministorage where I . . . I got some things."

I'm wishing I had the picture of June I'd gotten from Mason, so I can see if she was one of the cute chicks, but don't. I rise, worried that the old man might croak any time. "Thank you, sir. I've taken up too much of your time."

"Right. Hate to miss . . . the ten thousandth . . . *Jeopardy* I've watched." He laughs, then goes into a fit of coughing.

"I'll let myself out." I head for the door.

He calls after me. "Hey." And I stop and wait for him to catch his breath. "You don't smoke . . . do you?"

"No, sir."

He, mumbles, "Good," waves, and I head out, hearing *Jeopardy* fire back up on the tube, glad to be in the fresh air.

I fill her in on the ride to the harbor, but she doesn't seem surprised about any of what little I'd gleaned.

I have to ask one question. "You don't suppose they split . . . ran off together?"

The glance I get is a transference from coquette to cold. "No way."

We get a prime table at the Whale's Tail, overlooking the harbor. Over a pair of plates full of king crab, she expounds on the forensics report regarding the slug. "I was specifically told to keep you out of the loop, but do you know anything about long-range .50-caliber sniper rifles?"

"I know that while I was in Desert Storm a Marine Corps sniper took out an Iraqis personnel carrier with a Barrett Light Fifty, as we called them, an M82 something or other . . . firing a single armor-piercing bullet, and two other vehicles surrendered to him as a result. Made the corps believe in the Barrett."

"Well, that's what was buzzing around you. I'm surprised you didn't die from the shock wave as it passed."

I laugh. "Good for a thousand yards, three-fifths of a mile, in the right hands and with the right conditions."

"So, all you've got to do is find a guy with a Barrett."

I dig out a little more crab, dip it in hot butter, relish it with a slow chew, and watch her eat. There's something sensual about a woman who truly enjoys eating.

"What?" she says, glancing up from picking the last morsel from a shell.

"What what? I was just enjoying watching you enjoy."

She changes the subject back to the sniper, whom I'd

rather forget at the moment. "So, who among your many admirers owns a Barrett?"

"I don't know, but I'll put Cedric on it. There can't be too many sold. The hell of it is, now Sig Sauer, Steyr, Amarlite, and Colt make one as well, and God knows who else. The Russians, I'm sure. So it's no longer quite that easy."

"Well, let's find out." She winks at me while daintily dabbing a little stray butter from her chin. I'm happy that the coquette has returned. "I'm starting to be able to barely stand you," she says, in mock seriousness, "and I'd like to have you around for a while to see where it goes. Besides, I like your father."

"I'll grow on you," I say, with more confidence than I feel.

We get back to Café del Sol, where I've left the Harley, and she stays in the car when dropping me off.

"You are coming over to the boat." A salesman's closing question, framed as a statement of fact. I don't get a reply. "For a little after-dinner . . . whatever?" I ask. First one to speak after a closing question loses . . . I know that, but blathered nonetheless.

"Can't do it. It's a habit I think might be hard to break."

"And there are some good habits, you know. Besides, one time is hardly forming a habit."

"Yeah, but two times might."

"You know I have to leave the country for a while, venturing into the deep dark jungle, possibly never to return."

"Where?" She actually looks concerned.

"Jamaica."

"Ha. Deep dark beautiful women, you mean. White sand beaches and fabulous resorts. Cheap rum, steel drum bands, Bob Marley reggae music. How dangerous and foreboding."

"You like reggae?"

"I like Marley, he was a poet."

*Men see their dreams and aspirations
Crumble in front of their face
And all their wicked intentions to
Destroy the human race.*

How can you not like a poet?"

"Great," I say, with another wild try. "Then come on over and I'll read some Robert Service to you."

"I've heard 'Dangerous Dan McGrew.' He's not Elizabeth Barrett Browning, but I'm glad you like him. It's a start. Got to head home, bounty hunter."

That didn't work. It's time for emergency tactics. I study her for a moment, then walk around to the driver's side and lean in and lay a deep wet one on her, dropping a hand to brush a hard nipple as I do. It's to no avail. She takes a deep breath as I back out and lean on the door. I'm gazing at her as if she's about to miss the ride of her life.

"Got to head home," she finally says, and starts the Acura.

"You're killing me here," I say, as it purrs to life, my lip almost in a pout.

"Like I said, stay around awhile. I've got to work this out in my head. A guy who likes poetry other than Playboy lymrics can't be all bad."

"I could help influence your decision. If you'll come . . ."

"If candy and nuts were ifs and buts." She laughs, but I don't, I'm still pouting. She shakes her head. "I'm just afraid you could." She waves with one hand while hitting the window button with the other, and survival reflex causes me to jerk my hands away. She laughs at the hurt look on my face, and is gone with a squeal of the tires.

Jesus, I think, what a waste of good blood transference. I stand for a while, enjoying the Santa Barbara night, then when my attitude and interest in the gorgeous departing lady is less obvious, decide to go into the bar for a nightcap. I need one.

The place is packed. Paco is still working and pours me a generous three-finger Jack, neat. But I'm not in the mood for the bar BS, down it in a hurry, and head back to make sure Snarl is not stripped of all his fuzzy white hide by his feline roommate, Futa the Terrible.

I've been in the habit of leaving the deck lights on, including the mast floodlights, while I'm gone, hopefully dissuading potential bombers from boarding, but left in such a hurry I forgot. So it's dark as hell on my end of the long dock.

I'm carrying the blue blazer over my left arm, and reach to the back with my right, enjoying the cool grip of the .38 as I board. I stand studying the deck. Nothing amiss, until I walk to the hatchway and see that the brass hasp that normally carries a small padlock has been ripped away. Now the .38 comes out of its cozy little holster.

I've had a visitor.

Chapter Twenty

Carefully turning the knob, I shove the main hatchway door open, but step back up and away from being silhouetted for a moment. I hear something and brace myself, but then Futa, calm and serene, pitter-patters up onto the deck, stretches and yawns, and heads for the break in the railing that leads to the two-step portable stairway on the dock. Watch out, wharf rats.

"A fine watch cat you are," I chastise under my breath.

He wouldn't have been anywhere nearly so calm had there been a stranger on board. I make my way down to the salon deck and switch on the light, police special still in hand. I'm not completely satisfied and switch on lights as I make my way forward to my stateroom in the bow, then back again to the main salon. Whoever was aboard is no longer in residence. Now, if they just didn't leave a present for me: two or three pounds of C5 wrapped in a pretty bow.

I'm halfway through searching the main salon when I notice Futa's food and water bowls on the bookshelf and remember why they're there.

The damn pooch is missing.

Son of a bitch.

Scanoletti, the rotten low-life lying son of a bitch.

I start to call him, then realize I don't have his home phone, nor do I have a cell phone number.

Just as a precaution I go ahead and search the boat

from stem to stern, including the lockers, engine room, and bilge. It takes well over an hour.

No dog, no surprise packages that I can find.

Tomorrow I'll have a chat with the low-life doctor and try to restrain myself from making him his own broken-bone patient.

Between beautiful Babs and Scanoletti, I can't sleep. So I get back up and call Cedric to make sure he's home safe.

"What's up?" I ask when he answers his home phone.

"Computer stuff."

"As usual. How'd you make out with your recent roommates?"

He laughs. "I took your advice and started chanting. Hell, those guys treated me like a long-lost brother. I wouldn't have been surprised if they'd been Moslem, but you can't imagine how my jaw dropped when they turned out to be Buddhists. Black Buddhists. We're bosom buddies. I figured they were in the can for a break-and-enter or a dope deal. They were in for civil disobedience, a protest sit-in over the occupation of Tibet at the Chinese Trade Consulate."

"It's a strange world. Did you get anything from the experience . . . from the doc's computer, I mean?"

"Working on it now. A good part of it is encrypted, and it'll take some time."

"Keep on it." I go on to put him on the list of names I've acquired, and the fact whoever shot at me was the proud owner of a .50-caliber sniper rifle.

"I'll be up all night," he says, but sounds as if it's a happy thing. He's a night person, and loves the excuse. "Two more things: I've found no indication that Dr. Hashim has been out of San Francisco in the last couple of months by plane. I've found no credit card charges that indicate he's driven here. By the way, I have tickets for you and Iver to Jamaica."

"When?"

"Tomorrow."

"Crap," I can't help but say. I'm not prepared.

"You said when you get back from Idaho. I got them cheap because of the Saturday layover. Pretty good connections, too. L.A. to Phoenix to Houston to Miami to Jamaica, back in a week. You're on the red-eye leaving at ten P.M. tomorrow from LAX."

"Jesus Christ, Cedric, you think that's good? That's four legs. I won't have time to line up a foreign cell phone. Hell, I could do better than that. Futa could do better. . . ."

His tone grows chilly. "Be my guest."

"Jesus, that's a crock," I sputter.

"Dev, it's seldom you're an ignore-anus."

"You mean ignoramus," I say, and immediately regret it as I should know better than to attempt to correct Cedric's vocabulary.

"No, I mean ignore-anus. That's a person who's ignorant *and* an asshole."

There's a long silence, then he continues. "One should keep one's words tender, for tomorrow one may have to eat them. The Internet is a democratic institution, available to all those who wish to avail themselves of it. You're the guy who said 'cheap.' Cheap is usually not an airline option on short notice. If you'd care to give it a try, possibly you can come up with a first-class, direct-to-Mo-Bay, round-trip for ninety-nine ninety-five. . . ."

He's right, and I eat my own words, even though they're not so tender. It's time to salt and pepper the crow. "I'm sorry. You're right. I'm sure you did your best. Nobody can do better than you." I sigh deeply, reconciling my smart mouth to the fact I have neither the nine-thousand-dollar dog nor a beautiful woman to consol me, and decide to hit the hay and keep my eyes and mouth shut until sleep works.

I wake up pissed, work out with free weights on the deck—to hell with the sniper—then dress in my leathers and boots and head out to find the illustrious deadbeat Dr. Antonio Scanoletti. I can't give a lot of time to the effort as I have some preparatory work to do before heading south to LAX and winging away to Jamaica. I give Iver a call on my cell as I'm walking up to the boatyard and the Harley.

"How you feeling?" I ask when he snaps up the phone on the first ring.

"Hey, man, I don't feel a damn bit different. Cedric brought me back half a bale of damned Chinese herbs, and not a collard green among them."

I laugh. "Maybe we can get you a plateful in Jamaica. You ready to go?"

"I've got a duffel bag packed and will be waiting by the front door."

"All I got is my Harley, so can we take your pickup?"

"It's gassed."

"I'll leave my bike in Mrs. Olsen's backyard if she doesn't mind."

He laughs. "I weeded all her flower beds yesterday and wouldn't take nothing other than a ham sandwich. We got major pull around here."

"See you there about four. That'll give us time to stop at Duke's in Malibu and have a drink and some chow and still get to the airport two hours ahead of the flight."

He confirms the time. "Four."

As soon as I hang up, Cedric calls. And I say, "Hey, man, I was a real butt last night—"

"The art of conversation is to leave unsaid the wrong thing, at the tempting moment. I too have sinned in that regard, as you well know. Not to worry. Let's get together. There're some things I dug up that could be interesting. We need to talk."

"Lunch?"

"If that's as soon as you can."

"I got a busy morning."

"Lunch at Brophy's, and to atone for your sins you're buying."

"Deal. Of course I would be buying anyway, unless you came into an inheritance. But you can feel guilty for taking advantage and feed Futa while I'm gone."

"He's better company than you. Brophy's, a little before noon to beat the rush."

In thirty minutes, I'm killing the bike outside Dr. Scanoletti's office building. There are a number of offices in the big Mediterranean-style three-story structure, but Dr. Scanoletti and Dr. Robinson share half of the first floor. I check my watch as I dismount. It's a few minutes after nine. Even a big-time orthopod should be in the office by nine.

The receptionist looks overworked and harried. The room already has a half dozen patients waiting.

"Doc in?" I ask, and actually muster a smile.

She eyes me up and down, and gives me a tight smile. She's a good-looking lady, about my age, but wearing a wedding ring. "Do you have an appointment?"

"Social call."

"Your name?"

"Shannon."

Her eyes widen just a tad, and I know she's been warned that I may come calling. You've got to be a World Cup pro liar to fool me.

"The doctor is operating this morning, then he's off to a conference on Maui."

"Tough life," I say, still smiling. The number of patients in the waiting room don't tell me much, as, with the way doctors overload themselves needing to make the Porsche payment, that many could be waiting for the other doc, Robinson, but then again . . . I survey the waiting room, and one little old lady has overheard the Maui thing, and is looking very concerned. I'll just bet she has an appointment with Dr. Scanoletti.

"I'll tell him you called," the tidy-looking receptionist says, dismissing me. "Try back in ten days or two—"

"No problem," I say, and turn as if I'm heading out the door, but make a quick right to an inner door that I presume leads to exam rooms.

"Mr. Shannon," she yells behind me, a bit of panic in her voice. As I pass through the door I hear a buzzer ringing in the back of a long line of exam rooms. I move along the hall, checking each room as I pass. In one, a pair of nurses are layering a fiberglass cast on the thigh of a teenage boy. The next four have patients reading magazines, waiting patiently for the docs, which, I presume, is why they're called patients.

At the end of the hall are two walnut doors, on each side, each with a high-dollar brass nameplate. Scanoletti is engraved on the right, and I open it, needless to say without knocking.

I would have thought she was honest about the operating room and that he wasn't in, had the speakerphone not been rattling away as some nurse, I presume in some hospital or lab, reads the results of lab tests to an empty, still vibrating desk chair.

There's another doorway, and I move right on through it and find myself in a rear parking lot. A big black Mercedes is blowing me off with its exhaust, disappearing out into the Patterson Avenue traffic as I stand, disgustedly, with hands on hips.

There will be another day, and I'm the dog who'll have it.

To add insult to injury, the door has closed and locked behind me. I hoof it back around to the front and reenter Scanoletti's reception area and walk over and belly up to the counter.

"You got a home phone or cell phone for Dr. Scanoletti?"

"Of course, but you're not getting it, Mr. Shannon. No one barges in on my doctors."

I glance around at all the patients, then turn back to her. "He's not in now, you might as well send his patients home." I'm tempted to tell the roomful of folks what an asshole their revered doctor is, but then they are all in some kind of physical trouble, and hurting them more wouldn't be right. I bite my tongue.

"I've called the police," the lady says, eyes a little wide.

"Because I took the wrong door?" I ask, my smile just a tad insincere.

"Because Dr. Scanoletti told me to call the police, should you come in here bothering us. You wait right—"

"I mean to bother only the doc. Tell the doctor that he would be wise to honor his agreements," I lie, just to harass him, "and that I have a police forensics unit at my boat, checking for fingerprints, and that it's five to fifteen for breaking and entering . . . even a boat. And please, please, tell him this verbatim: he doesn't want me taking his ex-wife's side in the matter at hand." Her eyes grow wider and wider as I speak. "It's been nice, Miss . . . ?"

"It's Mrs. . . . Mrs. Rodriquez."

"Please advise the doctor to sit light in his chair, in his Mercedes, at home, and at the club." Then I chuckle. "Come to think of it, the fat little bastard couldn't sit light on a bet." I give a poor imitation of Schwarzenegger, "I'll be back," then add, "In fact, I'll be everywhere." She gets an over-the-shoulder wave as I leave.

Before I reach the Harley, my cell phone rings. It's Dr. Scanoletti himself.

Chapter Twenty-one

The doctor sounds like he believes he's the original Italian stallion. "You've been beaten, Shannon. You've got a thousand, why not give it up?"

"Give up is not in my bag of tricks, Doc. I'll tell you what, you fork over the nine thousand you owe me, and I'll forget the insult of your breaking into my boat."

"You don't think I would be stupid enough to do something like that . . . myself. I've got friends, Shannon. Good friends who belong to an old Italian group. Sicilian friends."

I laugh. "Why is it every Wop thinks he has friends?" He has no way of knowing that I'm one-fourth Italian, and can speak with some authority.

His tone is as if I'd slapped him, and as if he's jumping up and down having a tantrum. "You'll see, you'll see."

"No, Doc, you'll see, hear, and not like what you feel." I see a black-and-white coming down Patterson, so I have to hang up. "Doc, I've got to run, and I can't hear you over the Harley, which I'm going to use to run your fat ass down on the golf course. You were a real jokester, the laugh of the place, when I came to pick up the paperwork. You'll be the laugh . . . laughingstock . . . of the place the next time you see me at La Cumbre. Bye now."

This time when I hang up, I hit the caller ID and check the last number. The overeducated bastard has called me on his own cell phone without blocking caller ID. When

I get back from my trip, I'm going to make his life miserable. And, come to think of it, I'll have Cedric pick up that mantle while I'm gone.

Nobody can screw up your life like my friend Cedric. Now I'm extra glad I've promised to buy his lunch.

Putting a new hasp on the boat takes a portion of the rest of the morning. Getting on the Internet and finding a contact in Jamaica takes the rest. I e-mail my list of bail agents in the Southeast, then I call my old buddy, Scott Olson, the president of the National Institute of Bail Enforcement, and pick his experienced brain about who might know the ins and outs of Jamaica, and he reminds me of a mutual friend, Walter Fernandez, a kick-ass take-no-prisoners bail enforcement agent on the East Coast, who is the recognized expert in matters Caribbean. So I tell Scott I owe him another bottle of good scotch. He reminds me that I have yet to send him the last promised bottle, so I up it to a case for the insult. Forgetting a fellow bail enforcement officer is not like me—it's an information business, and good sources are almost as important as good friends. Maybe I can get a case cheap in ex-British Jamaica. Walter is at the top of his form and it takes him five seconds flat to dig up a name and address, including the e-mail address. Bobby Bainbridge comes well recommended. A bottle of good Jamaican rum, Walter informs me, will settle the bill. I pick his brain for a while specifically regarding Jamaica, and he fills me in, particularly on the number of private security firms who work as consultants for the many resorts and hotels. It turns out they even have a number of private quick-response teams who show up on short notice with sophisticated weaponry, SWAT teams to coin an Americanism. It seems the local police are undermanned, underarmed, and not particularly responsive.

Walter has been worth his weight in rum.

By the time I'm ready to head to Brophy's, I have two

dozen replies to my e-mails, but most of them are social how-the-hell-are-you messages. Two of them refer me to the same name, B. Bainbridge, Jamaican private detective, and one of them has an e-mail address—not that I need a backup to Walter's referral. I'd trust him or Scott with my life.

I shoot off an inquiry to Bobby before I leave for lunch. I need a car, driver, and local knowledge, and offer to pay a hundred a day, plus fuel. I've taken the time to check stats on Jamaica and found that the average income is around twenty bucks a day, so this should be more than fair for a professional person.

It's a Valhalla day overlooking the harbor, not a cloud in the sky and in the seventies, as we find a seat on the upstairs patio at Brophy's. Cedric is in a rare mood as we each await a salad and bowl of their great clam chowder.

First Ced hands me a sheaf of papers. "Jamaica stuff," he says, and I know he's done some research for me. He starts replaying his night as we sip ice tea. "There's a hell of a lot of those .50 calibers sold around the country these days."

"So, no luck?" I ask.

"Maybe. I got into the records of a number of companies, not only manufacturers, but I had to check out distributors and dealers. I started geographically, in northern California, thinking that Hashim is our main man, even though I was beginning to think he had nothing to do with it as he hadn't traveled to Santa Barbara in the last few months."

"So, you've changed your mind?"

"Not completely. . . there's a dead skunk in the middle of the road, stinking to high heaven."

"And that means?"

"I found a guy in Richmond, across the bay from the city, who has sold a half dozen fifties this year. Big Gun

Gus, he calls himself. He specializes in fifties, and is a dealer for the Windrunner, a very high end firearm."

I shrug. "So, that doesn't tell us much."

"And he didn't sell one to anyone named Hashim."

I throw up my hands. "Hell, there's a lot of them sold, that doesn't make our man a buyer."

"The guys name is Gus Pritchard. He sold one to a guy named Jamal Mahmoud—that's an Arab name in case you thought it was Norwegian—and guess what?"

Even being a smart-ass, as usual, he's got my full attention. "What?"

"There's an e-mail to Jamal1956 at aol dot com on Hashim's computer. Nineteen fifty-six is the year of Moroccan independence. Isn't Hashim Moroccan?"

A slowly growing smile crosses my face. "As always, you're brilliant, Ced. Keep after it."

"Big Gun Gus sold this guy a .50-cal BMG Windrunner SS-99 single-shot about five months ago."

"What a coincidence."

"That's not all. I followed up on the crew names you gave me on the *Orion*."

"And?"

"And one of them, Raymond Cox, is a skip from Fresno on a spousal battery. He was a carpenter, and decided to use his hammer for his avocation as well . . . beating women. Hurt his wife real bad, left her for dead. A hundred-grand bail. His mother put her little house up to guarantee some of the bond, but the bondsman is out on a limb for the majority of it."

My favorite kind of skip. I can nail him and feeling I'm not only doing my job, but I'm helping a little old lady who he's shafted. What kind of a prick would leave his own mother hanging like that? "Sounds like the best part of Ray ran down his father's leg. So, we might pick up a few scheckles in addition to the boat recovery, or as a consolation prize if we lose out."

"Right. I've already contacted the bondsman, Andy Mikhalranian, who says he's heard of you, informed him that you're having to leave the country to do the job, that it's a thirty percent fee of the fifty grand that's at risk, and he's sending the paperwork. He's forfeiting one hundred percent in forty-five days, then has to evict the poor old lady to recover even half of that back, so I had a big hammer. Unlike most of you Neanderthals, he's a twenty-first-century guy and I should have the info among my e-mails when I get home, and I'll forward you what you might need."

"Get me what you can on the rest of them. You know I've got to leave town in a couple of hours?"

"I made the inept reservation, remember?" He's still rubbing it in. "But print out what I send you just before you leave the boat. I'll work on it as soon as I can finish this."

The waitress, Betty, whom we both know, has arrived with salads and chowders at the same time, as we've requested.

While we eat, I fill him in on Dr. Scanoletti and close with a caution, "I don't want to injure him financially or physically, no lawsuit, please. I just want him eager and anxious to pay when I get back. So anxious he's jumping up and down."

Cedric is looking at me as if he's about to have way too much fun, and I know that Doc Scanoletti's life is going to be Keystone Cops meet Abbot and Costello who meet Frankenstein while I'm gone. I suspect Scanoletti will come to Jesus when I return.

When I get back to the boat, I have an e-mail waiting from Bobby Bainbridge: *can help you for a hundred a day, no problem. Send flight number and arrival time and I'll pick you up. MoBay or Kingston? B. Bainbridge.*

I do as requested, informing Bobby that we're arriving at Montego Bay at nine-twenty A.M. on Air Jamaica, which we'll connect with in Miami, and that we're looking for an eighty-eight-foot Benetti, the *Orion*, and that it's all right if he does some preliminary work on the problem. I attach a picture of the *Orion* to the e-mail. Now all I have to do is pack.

The boat rocks and I hear the old man yell out, "Permission to board?"

"You bet."

"I hear from Iver you're taking off to some enchanted island?"

"Close."

"You won't be here for Thanksgiving?"

For the first time I realize that we'll be gone over the holiday. "I guess not, Pop. I'll cook up a turkey when I get back."

"First time since your mom died we haven't had Thanksgiving together."

"I wish I could."

"I know you do. Come home with the bacon . . . the boat . . . so to speak, and we'll have prime rib for a change . . . on you."

I thought for a few minutes the old man was going to pout because I'd be gone. But it looks like he's toughened up.

"Besides," he says, "I've been invited to Thanksgiving dinner." He's got a twinkle in his eye.

"Babs?"

"Nope."

"Come on, who?"

"Alice Townsend."

"The reporter?"

"One and the same. Seems your old man hasn't lost the old blarney yet."

I laugh. "I like her. She said something about you being cute, and I didn't tell her the truth. Decided to let her live out her fantasies. Have a good time."

Iver is pacing the floor when I get there, the trip down the coast is easy and scenic, the early dinner and drinks at Duke's in Malibu is great, and the well-intentioned boys and girls in security at LAX search diligently but do not find the few tricks I've packed just in case we get a little trouble . . . which seems to follow me like a flea-bitten mongrel after a bitch in heat.

It's a bit of a grueling flight, with three of the four legs so short we didn't get much sleep, but we arrive in Montego Bay on time. The airport is on a flat near the water, and the approach is over the bay, which is beautiful from the air. A pair of huge cruise ships are docked there, disgorging thousands of tourists, who, from my perspective, look the size of ants. The town will soon be infested. A few freighters and a plethora of smaller fishing boats dot the harbor, but mostly it's yachts and pleasure craft. The shore is lined with hotels and resorts, but beyond are the things you don't see in the travel brochures, hillsides packed with shanties and shacks. It's obviously a poor country.

I'm surprised that the air terminal itself is modern and nice by small-city American standards. There are over a dozen embarkation gates and it seems to be served by at least four or five airlines.

There's a tall black lady, five-ten at least, well dressed in a flowered blouse and tailored slacks. Her medium heels bring her to six feet. She's holding a hand-lettered sign: BOBBI BAINBRIDGE FOR MR. SHANNON.

With Iver on my heels, both of us toting carry-on duffel bags, I walk over and acknowledge that I'm the guy she's looking for. She sticks out a well-manicured hand. "Welcome home to Jamaica, mon. I be Bobbi Bainbridge."

I guess I look surprised, as she laughs. "De didn't tell you I was a lady-type detective, I be guessin'."

"Works fine for me," I say, returning her smile. In fact,

I've found having a woman on the team to have its advantages, which makes me think of Sandy Bartlett, and wish I was working on that particular problem. But the well-oiled vengeance machine doesn't work so well without the oil, and the lubricant too often is money. I do take a moment to consider that women are winning the discrimination battle, when a couple of hard cases like Walter and I don't bother to discuss the fact Bobbi's a she.

I introduce Iver, who's looking at her as if his prostate is just fine; he obviously agrees with my observation that she's a fine example of "she," if his look is any indication. Iver is even taller than my six-two, so he can look down on her.

Bobbi, in turn, eyes him up and down with appreciation. "You be a pretty one, Mr. Iver," she says, and flashes him an even bigger smile. She points from one of us to the other. "Ebony and Ivory."

"We ready?" I ask.

"All fruits ripe . . . no problem, let's flex, mon."

Iver says in a low tone as we move away, "It means everything is okay and let's go."

In moments we're out of there, through a busy parking lot full of cars and buses, onto a modern two-lane highway. Bobbi is driving a recent-model Toyota Corolla, four-door, white, and unobtrusive, and sitting to my right as Jamaica observes the British tradition of right-hand drive. The attitude of drivers is anything but "no problem, mon" as they swerve in and out of lanes, but there's little in the way of horn honking or obscene gestures.

Bobbi is carrying a cell phone, and is on and off it at least three times before we've traveled from the airline gate to the car. I can understand enough of her conversation to know she's working on the location of the boat.

She informs me that she hasn't located any boat named the *Orion*, but she has feelers out for both the name and the type of boat. I, too, presume she would have been renamed.

"So," I ask, "would you know if she's moored somewhere around the island?"

"I'd know soon, unless she's in a maroon town. The maroons keep to them own selves, and don't let their business be known."

We only travel a few hundred yards east on the highway when she ducks between a car and a bus that would squash us like a bug, and pulls off into another parking area, this one with only a couple of cars and trucks. "What's up?" I ask.

"I got us scheduled to take a little ride."

"Okay, on what?"

"A Cessna, mon. A 210 Cessna. For three hundred, we can circle the island and check out all the moorages and harbors. Fastest way, mon. Be savin' us days. You got the three hundred?"

"I do, and it's a great idea. Let's hit it."

Iver hates to fly, particularly in small planes. And I'm claustrophobic as hell in any small spaces. He doesn't think it's anywhere nearly as good an idea as I've forced myself to say, but his attention is on Bobbi, and I know he's going. Alvin Tobrey is a small wiry guy who looks like anything but a pilot. His white shirt, made to look as if it were made from flour sacks, has *British East India Flour Mill* printed on it and hangs unbuttoned. He's wearing sandals. With me in the front and Iver happily in the back with Bobbi, we're in the air in a few minutes. But not until Alvin's done a thorough preflight of the airplane. I know enough to know if a pilot's careful, and I'm comfortable with this no-nonsense guy, no matter how sloppily he dresses.

He's only a dozen feet in the air when he sucks up the gear and is turning back to MoBay as soon as he clears the palm trees.

I notice him cross himself, and under his breath, say, "*Pras ja,*" and put my seat back so I can speak to Bobbi.

"He said *pras ja*. What?"

She laughs. "Praise Jah, praise de Lord, mon."

In MoBay we take a closer look at everything that's near the size of the *Orion*, but nothing matches the picture I have. He does a 180, recrosses the bay, then heads east along the island's north shore.

Jamaica's two and a half million people are multiracial and live on over four thousand square miles of mountainous to flat terrain on an island 146 miles long and fifty-one miles wide, at its widest. Most of the island is covered in forest or farms. Fine coral sand blankets her beaches. Blue Mountain, on the easterly end, at almost 7,500 feet reigns over all.

Theirs is a typical Caribbean story. The Spaniards killed off the native Taino population with overwork and European disease, then imported slaves from Africa. They lost the island to the British, then regained it, then lost it again. Slavery was abolished, mostly due to rebellion, in 1834. Bauxite and aluminum exports ruled the economy for years, but now tourism is her mainstay. With over 350 miles of coastline, I know we're in for a long eye-tiring day . . . unless we get lucky.

We don't.

I've spotted and noted a dozen boats in the length range of the *Orion*. White with a blue waterline stripe, she's not unusual; of course if I were to steal a boat, I'd paint her first thing, particularly painting out her name. I'd also fly the flag of a different country of registry. And the hell of it is with Meegan's e-mailed guess at a heading, and the fact there's a guy of Jamaican descent aboard, those things alone certainly don't mean the island is the *Orion*'s destination. Hell, they could be headed for Portugal, if someone aboard has the dough to keep her tanks full.

But I'm a long ways from giving up.

I've seen one boat that could be her at the far end of the island on the south shore, near a place called Morant Bay, almost to the eastern tip. She's painted dark blue, and her superstructure is not right, but that, too, could have been altered—a welder or even a carpenter could easily change the profile of a boat. We could have flown to Kingston, which would have been much closer to Morant Bay, only twenty-five miles, but that's twenty/twenty hindsight.

Had we not had the whole south side of the island still to cover, I'd have had Alvin drop Iver and me off in Kingston. But as it was, we find ourselves back in Montego Bay with a five-hour-or-more drive in front of us.

What the hell, it's a good way to see the island.

As we move east the road gets worse, and the shanties more prevalent. The occasional old plantation house or new mansion punctuates the countryside, but they stand out like polished diamonds in a pile of gravel. I learn that hundreds of plantation houses were burned in the slave revolutions of the early 1800s, and only a dozen or so remain. Fields that I presume were onetime sugarcane now are grazed by livestock or gone fallow, and now are spotted with royal palms that host climbing vines. Bony cows are staked out mowing the grass, and goats and roosters run free under the palms, some of their tall slender trunks being climbed by vines with leaves the size of elephant ears. Under the humanity and their intrusion, as in most places, the flora and fauna are beautiful.

Bobbi keeps the radio tuned to reggae music, and seems to know the lyrics of half the songs. I study her as she studies the road, but sings along with:

"Them crazy, them crazy,
We gonna chase those crazy
Baldheads out of town,

Chase those crazy baldheads
Out of town. . . ."

The lyrics swing in content from love your neighbor to revolt and lynch the baldhead, which is fairly explicit as there are only a few of us on the island with short hair.

Many rivers and streams are bridged by the road, and the occasional swampy area is bisected by a raised roadbed. Bobbi informs me that swimming in the swamps is not advised, as Jamaica has its own variety of alligator.

I pick Bobbi's brain as we travel. "So, I guess you're carrying?"

"In the purse, mon."

"I read that guns are outlawed in Jamaica."

She laughs. "Yeah, mon."

"But?"

"But it's bad. It's worse in an election year."

"Why's that?"

"The bakra man, the politician, he give guns away to be gettin' the vote."

"Bakra is a politician?"

"Bakra is any man who lords over you, mon."

"Oh."

She laughs again. "It come from the old times, when the overseer man, the bossman on de plantation, use de whip. He make your back raw, mon. He be de bakra man."

"Makes sense."

Her look is not quite so jovial as she glances at me. "But we kill mos' those bandooloos and hang dem from a high flame-de-forest tree."

I ponder that awhile, then ask, "So there are quite a few guns around?"

"Everybody got a gun, mon."

Chapter Twenty-two

She laughs that hardy laugh. "Half the Jamdung man have de piece, mon. But not to worry, I be more than a fair shot."

"How good?"

"I be hittin' a yellowfly on the wing, mon. You want me shoot off left wing or right?"

I laugh, then ask only half in jest, "You think getting this boat is a shooting thing?"

This time there's no hint of a smile. "Mus' be a million U.S. dollar for a boat like dat?"

"More, maybe."

"Den it be a shootin' ting, mon. My price go to two hundred a day, if the shootin' or de bat work starts."

"Mine too," Iver says from the back, then laughs deeply.

"I don't want you to jeopardize your license, but if it comes to that, can you get us each a piece, or tell us where to go to get one?"

"Anything you want, mon."

She swings off the main road time and time again to check moorages that can't be seen from the main highway—there's a slight chance the boat couldn't be seen from the air—or to talk with someone she knows. We're gone from the airport a couple of hours, and have stopped five times or more when she pulls into an open-air bar next to a take-out stand. I take a deep breath, as they're working on the highway and we've been dodging construction equipment, and forced into narrow lanes that result in six-inch clearance of passing tourist busses and dump trucks. So far, it's not the most relaxing sightseeing trip I've ever taken.

What the residents lack in fine structures and architecture, they make up for in color. The bar is painted blue and yellow, and the take-out stand red and orange.

"Time for a Red Stripe and de jerked chicken, mon," she says. The weather is warm and the bar looks cool and inviting, but the odors of meat grilling waft from the stand and turn us before we seek the shade of the bar.

"Red Stripe?" I ask Iver and we pile out behind her.

"Local beer."

While we're eating, Bobbi is questioning a bartender she seems to know. This woman doesn't have any stop in her, and I'm liking her better all the time. When she says "no problem, mon," she means it.

We've stopped a dozen times before we reach Ocho Rios, one of the primary hotel areas on the north coast, where I'm told we're spending the night as we can see nothing after dark and the sun's fading behind us.

Bobbi turns to Iver in the backseat. "Mr. Shannon a hitey titey mon, or will me cousins place be irie?"

"The baldhead will be fine wherever," he says, and laughs in his deep baritone.

"Baldhead?" I ask, a natural question as I have a full head of black Irish hair, and I've heard the term several times on the radio.

"Anybody who doesn't have dreadlocks, mon," Iver says, picking up the dialect. "You mostly, but me too. Anyone who tows the line and doesn't revolt and grow his dreadlocks."

I'm beginning to understand that patois is merely a jamming together of English words, but has been done for so long that they've taken on a compressed state that now barely resembles the original. Dweet, I'm told, means do it, and on and on.

Still, there's no understanding when a pair of Jamaicans launch into patois.

She stops at a market, buys two six-packs of Red Stripe and an overflowing bag full of groceries, then works her way off the main road onto a dirt road up the mountain, finally stopping in front of a small but well-tended house painted bright pink. The front and side yards are dirt, but there are well-tended flower beds lining the house and an immaculate fenced garden in a side yard. Bougainvillea, covered with light yellow blossoms, embraces the west end of the house.

"My cousin, mon," she says with a smile.

We have a great evening with Bobbi's cousin Sarah and her five kids, none of whom is over ten years old, drinking Red Stripe for us and Kool-Aid for the kids, eating rundown, a stew made with salted mackerel; johnnycakes, patties of fried bread; sweet dumplings; and a variety of fruit right out of what they call the forest, but I'd call a jungle.

I get Bobbi off to one side and ask about Sarah's husband, and she laughs and explains, "In Jamaica there be more women than men, by many, many."

"Why's that?" I ask.

"Well, mon. Mon a no-good, a booguyaga, who drowns in de rum or Red Stripe, and woman take a boyfriend. Husband kill the boyfriend, husband go to de jailhouse. Just like that, not enough men."

"That happen a lot?" I ask.

"Lots of guns in Jamdung, mon."

Her children have given up one of the two bedrooms and their flat hard beds for Iver and me. I leave him and Bobbi drinking Red Stripe, talking, and laughing, and I go to bed . . . wishing I had my piece, and a cell phone.

Tomorrow and the days following might not be so sociable.

We're up and gone with the sun. A couple of fried plantains and coffee will hold us until lunch, which we hope to have in Morant Bay. Bobbi has changed into a bright yellow blouse and wears a wide-brimmed hat with a matching yellow hatband. The lady has some style. Iver and I are both in khaki cargo pants, black T-shirts, and hiking boots. I'm wearing a Raider's bill cap, silver on black, but Iver has gone native and bought a wide-brimmed Panama with a flowered band. It becomes him.

The fastest way to the blue boat near Morant Bay is over the mountain to Kingston, only sixty miles on a good road. Lunch is another roadside stand after we pass through the capital city, a much bigger and much rougher place than Montego Bay, and it's one o'clock by the time we reach the point where I think the boat was moored. The road has pulled up and away from the coast, now steeper and far more rugged on the slope of tall Blue Mountain. The seaside is now two or more miles down the mountain through a palm forest with thick clinging undergrowth.

We can't very well walk the coast to locate the boat, so Bobbi makes a turnoff where a sign points to Port Morant, a few miles past the town of Morant Bay.

Her plan is to hire a boat to cruise the coastline, and I agree. Bobbi locates a man in a bar near the little harbor who owns a diesel fishing boat, and in less than a half hour we're rounding a low point on the east side of the deep indentation in the coastline that shelters Port Morant, and in fifteen more minutes we've entered a sheltered, much smaller harbor where the sleek blue yacht is anchored fifty yards offshore. A white two-story house with a bright teal-blue roof perches on a promontory to the east, commanding a view of the Caribbean unequaled by most of the other fine houses I've noticed.

At least a dozen servants move about, tending the grounds, caring for the structure. The main house must be five thousand square feet, and on either flank smaller single-story houses of a couple of thousand square feet are connected to the main by covered walkways. A shuttered hexagonal gazebo is cantilevered off the very point, commanding a 270-degree overlook.

We cruise up close to the blue boat, but before we're within a hundred feet we're being motioned away by two gorillas carrying what appear to be AK-47s.

The boat has no tender, which rested on the rear deck of the *Orion* near a pair of davits. But the davits are there. I grab a pair of the fisherman's binoculars and study the superstructure. From this close, it's apparent that she has been crudely added to in order to change her appearance.

The stern carries the name *Corazón de Jamaica* in white letters on the blue background, but it's clear that it's been roughly painted. The painter was no artist.

"Well, mon?" Bobbi asks.

"I think we've got our boat," I say, then caution her to stay silent, as I've already said too much in front of the fisherman. She nods, then turns and tells him to head home.

We grab a six-pack of Red Stripe and Iver and I walk out and sit on a rock on the beach overlooking the harbor while Bobbi wanders around town doing her thing.

I'm worried about Iver; he's looking a little hollow around the eyes. "Hey, man, you feeling okay?"

"Don't be asking me how I'm feeling all the time. It makes me remember that I could be feeling lousy. I feel great."

"Did you bring your herbs?"

"I was afraid the customs was going to lock us both up. I got a couple of old one-a-day vitamin bottles stuffed with the crap. They didn't open them."

I laugh. "Well, I guess we'll test the Homeland Security boys on the way back in."

The sun is low in the west and our beer is long gone by the time Bobbi returns.

"Well?" I ask.

"I need a beer, mon. Let's go to Billabong's down de beach. We can eat there when you be gettin' hungry. Best rice and beans and ackee and salt fish on de south shore."

We're up and off, and I realize my stomach is growling.

Billabong's is a white clapboard place, but nicely painted and trimmed in gray. Even the metal roof is painted to match. Palms, with a natural fence of undergrowth, flank the place, but behind them is a patio that looks out onto the beach.

As we're sitting on the Billabong's patio, sipping a tall rum punch, we have to spend a while chatting with the owner, an expatriate Australian, before we talk business.

Finally, his black Jamaican wife calls him to the kitchen, and we can get on with it.

"Well, what's the scoop?"

"Scoop?" she asks.

"The story. Who's in the big house looking down on the boat?"

She shakes her head, deadly serious. "De price jus went up, mon."

"Let's talk price later. Who is the guy with the big house and the goons with the automatics?"

"Sylvester Gunn, a maroon natty dread dundus, married to an obeah woman. Everyone fears them."

I sigh deeply, and glance at Iver. It's obvious even he's stumped by this one.

"Okay," I say patiently to Bobbi, "now, please, in plain English so this baldhead can understand."

"He's a maroon, a dreadlock man, but whiter than you, mon. He's a dundus. How you say . . . a man with no color in de skin or eyes? His eyes be pink, his skin pale, his natty hair be dirty white."

"An albino?"

"Yeah, mon. He looks like he crawled up out of the swamp, or bloody hell."

"And you said something about his wife?"

"An obeah woman. A witch, mon. Everyone on dis end of Jamdung be fearin' her."

"Pretty damn nice house?"

"He de main man for ganja on dis side of de mountain, and de word now he de main man for de meth and coke."

"That makes sense."

"But dat not all."

"So?"

"He want to buy de big house from Mr. Grayson, but Mr. Grayson not sell to the ganja man. Two year ago, Mr. Grayson drowned dead on his own beach, and Mr. Sylvester buy de house from de estate at auction. Some way cheaper, some say."

"So the word is . . . ?"

"Nothing stand in de way of Mr. Sylvester. He a true dog-heart man. Got no feelings for nutin' don't feed him."

"Maybe something stand in his way," Iver says, and laughs.

"Dawg ave shine teet laaf affa butcha," she says, falling back into total patois.

"A dog with shiny teeth laughs at the butcher," Iver repeats in clear English.

"Okay, so?"

"So," he says, thinking as if he's still trying to decipher, "you should know when things are in your favor, which means in broad terms that we should go home and leave well enough alone."

"F.F.C.," I say, and Iver knows I mean fat fucking chance. This time it's her turn to look confused.

Iver laughs, but I don't follow suit. Loud music suddenly blares out the window of the bar, and Jimmy Buffet is regaling Margaretaville. My eyes are glued to the inside bar where I see some shiny long black hair falling across fair-freckled Irish shoulders, reaching to the middle of the girl's bare back, across a very tight bikini string. Then I shift my gaze to the guy returning across the bar from the jukebox, the blond thick-shouldered guy clambers onto the stool next to her.

"Iver, you remember Meegan from the Harbor Restaurant?"

He shrugs. "The one supposed to be on the *Orion*?"

"One and the same. Take a peek over your shoulder. That's her, and I'll bet the old boy next her is our old buddy, Toke Butterworth. The face and those Schwarzenegger seventeen-inch-arms are very familiar."

"Things be lookin' up, baldhead," Iver says, and now it's my turn to laugh.

In moments we're up and entering the bar from either end.

Chapter Twenty-three

I measure him as I approach. He's broad-backed and fills the T-shirt with knotted muscle. He looks as if Gold's Gym may have been his second home. Strong, but probably slow and pea-nutted from too many steroid shots.

I have to give it to Toke, he is calm and collected when I mount the bar stool beside him, on his right I'm sorry to say as I'm right-handed, and would have to backhand him to use my strongest arm. Meegan, however, goes pure ivory white, then reddens.

There's a six-foot-six hogshead-barrel-big bartender mopping the bar with a soiled towel, but he ignores us. He's obviously a Rastaman, with thick dusky dreadlocks hanging to the center of his wide back.

"What's up, Butterworth?" I ask.

Toke glances casually my way, Orphan Annie eyed, then his eyes focus. He's been hitting the ganja hard, if the pupil dilation means anything. "As I live and breathe, if it ain't a boy from back home. Shannon, ain't it?"

"Sure is. Dev Shannon, employed by an old buddy of yours, Darwin Winston-Gray. You remember Darwin?"

"I do, and that prick ain't never been no friend of mine."

The way he's fingering his tall rum drink, I have a feeling I'm about to get it in the face, so I stand and back away a step. Iver is stationed by the doorway out to the parking area, just in case Toke thinks he can make a break for it.

But he doesn't throw the drink, or break for the door. In fact, he breaks out laughing as he spins on the bar stool to face me. "It's too late, Shannon. The friggin' *Orion,* like the *Titanic,* is long gone."

"No problem, mon," I say, in my best Jamaican. "She didn't go too far; in fact, I see she's moored only a few miles east."

Toke's smile is far too superior for my taste, considering how nice I'm being, and how much trouble he's in. "So, you found the *Corazón de Jamaica*?"

"I did, or I should say, we did. I brought some help from home."

"You're gonna need it, if you think you're going to get that boat back from Cool White."

"Who?"

He smiles a lazy smile at me before he answers, "Sly Gunn. Cold White if he has one of those big white hands squeezing your windpipe; Cool White to his dear friends . . . but I don't suggest you call him either."

I look past him at the girl, who's watching this exchange with wide eyes. "Meegan, you're looking good. Tropical cruising becomes you."

"Thanks," she manages with a squeak.

"How about you . . . you think I can get the boat back?"

She shrugs.

"Then how about I have Toke here get it back?" I return the lazy smile to him.

But it's Meegan who speaks. "I don't . . . think . . . anyone could get it back. Not even the army."

"Jamaican army? How about the U.S. Marines?" I ask.

"Well . . . maybe the marines."

I have my cuffs stuffed in my back pocket, and pull

them out and dangle them from a finger. "How much did you get, Toke?"

The big bartender has stopped his mopping and walked back up the bar to stand across from us. He's eyeing the cuffs as if he's had some experience. "Hey, mon, we don't be havin' no trouble in here."

"For the friggin' boat?" Toke asks me, ignoring the big man.

"No, fool, for your dog and pony act. Of course for the boat."

"I done spent it," he says, his eyes following the swinging cuffs as if I'm hypnotizing him.

"Then, old buddy, if you're all that's left, you're going to jail, along with little Miss Meegan here. I shouldn't say along with, 'cause there ain't gonna be no sweet meat where you're going. I suggest you come up with the proceeds of sale, so you can negotiate with this Mr. Cool White in good faith."

Now the drink comes, glass and all, but I duck to the side to keep him from driving the glass into my eyes, and as he's trying to get around Meegan, catch him on the back of the head—which is the only target I have—with a hard right.

He goes hard down on his face, but spins to his back before I can nail him to the floor.

I dive for him but, on his back with his legs up, he gets a hard kick in that takes me on the collarbone and knocks me off to the side, stunning that arm and driving me into Meegan, who's trying to get away from the bar and run the other direction.

As I'm recovering from the hard blow, Toke spins and gets his legs under him, and is about to break for the front door when Iver surprises him with a smashing right uppercut to the forehead, followed by a straight left that breaks his nose. I can hear the telltale crunch, and it spins him around facing me. He comes up with a pistol that was shoved in his belt under the loose shirt, but I'm close and committed to the punch.

This pile-driving right takes him between the eyes, which roll up in his head and the gun clatters away before he can level it. I snatch him behind the neck with my left hand and bring his already smashed face into one, two, three quick rights. He sags to the floor like the sack of crap he is, spewing blood from broken nose, smashed lip, and crushed ear . . . and I let him slump.

When I was knocked into the brunette she careened back to her knees between the bar stools, but now she's up and breaking for the back door. I dive and slap a heel, which tangles her up and she goes on her face. I'm up off my belly and onto her with a knee in the small of her back before she can recover, and glance back to see Iver hooking a still unconscious Toke up tightly with his cuffs. He's got the pistol shoved in his belt.

I should have let her go as I could then have seen Bobbi in action, as she's positioned at the door, waiting and seemingly ready.

And it's a good thing, as I look up to see the big black bartender rounding the end of the bar, a long flat cricket bat in hand.

"Hey, mon!" Bobbi screams, loud enough to stop a cab in uptown New York. The bartender slides to a halt and turns to see her holding a little Beretta automatic, and it's competently zeroed in right between his eyes. Then her voice quiets and in a soothing tone, advises, "Sorry, mon, no wickets for you dis day."

Just as he relaxes, the Australian crashes through a pair of swinging doors that I presume lead to the kitchen, as he's apron adorned and carrying a meat cleaver.

"Easy, mon," the big bartender says to his boss, holding a palm out flat toward Bobbi as if stopping the bullet, and he slowly lowers the bat in the other big hand.

The proprietor, seeing the pistol, does likewise, but looks very concerned.

"No, mon, no trouble, easy now," Bobbi says to the boss, in an even more calming voice. "We not be dissin' you, mon, or your fine establishment. Dis be all business. You go back to de ackee and salt fish. We got dis ting handled. No need for de law here. He be de law," she says, motioning to me. I dig my wallet out and flash the brass at each of them in turn.

The bartender nods, drops the bat on the bar, and returns to the other end and picks up the towel, but he doesn't take his eyes off the lady with the automatic.

Smart man.

The Australian, with his wife peeking out of the kitchen behind him, shrugs, and with the cleaver hanging at his side, returns to his kitchen.

Iver and I catch Toke under each arm and drag him out behind the bar to the garbage area. Bobbi follows along behind with a very frightened Meegan.

I motioned to a palm tree and Iver and I drag him over and lift him to a standing position. Iver pops off the cuffs, wraps Toke's arms around the tree, and recuffs him, his back tight against the rough palm—he's stretched tight. It can't be comfortable, but then that's the idea. He's coming around, and finds himself half collapsed down the tree, and has to fight to get his legs under him. But he does, and straightens up. He glares at me.

"You prick, I'm gonna—"

"You're gonna stand there like a good boy, all week if necessary, until you tell me, number one, where the booty is that you got for the boat, and two, everything you know about Mr. Cool White and his friends . . . particularly the ones with the AK-47s."

"Fuck you."

"Iver," I ask politely, "would you give Mr. Butterworth's arms a little hoist? I think he might be uncomfortable."

Iver slips to the back of the tree and lifts Butterworth's cuffed wrists—against the shoulder joints. He fights against Iver, but Iver has long, lean, honestly earned muscles that won't be denied. The arms don't naturally bend that way, and Toke bends as far forward as room allows and winces in pain.

"Jesus Christ," he yells.

"Jesus isn't going to help you, Toke, me lad."

Iver hoists them again, and Toke cries out this time.

"Is that better, Toke, or would you like them a little higher?" I ask in a pleasant tone and with a smile.

"Please, please don't," Meegan begs.

"You're upsetting your shipmate," I say to him, smiling. "Now let's not upset her anymore. The booty?"

"It's in the back of the car," Meegan screams out as Iver begins to run his arms up again.

"What car?" I ask.

"The Rover. We traded a kilo for a used Land Rover."

"Out front?" I ask.

She nods, tears flowing down her cheeks. I nod also, but at Bobbi, who walks over and fishes the keys out of Toke's shorts and disappears around the building.

"Now, Toke, it's about that grand theft charge back in California."

"Come on, man, you got what you want."

"The hell I do, if I had my way I'd flush that crap down the nearest crapper. I want the boat, and you're gonna make a little trade with Mr. Cool White for the *Orion*."

"He ain't no fool, Shannon. He ain't gonna trade no million-dollar boat for no nineteen keys. He's got hundreds more."

I smile as Bobbi arrives from the front, driving the Land Rover cross-country and over some of the underbrush, to the back of the bar. She parks it and climbs out.

"I checked under a false floorboard in the back, mon. He got nineteen kilos of pure Colombian snow-white."

Reaching out, I pinch Toke's cheek as if he were a child. "I'll tell you what, little man, we're gonna go back inside and finish our drinks while you give it some thought." Actually, I'm worried about what the bartender and Australian are up to, and I want to get Meegan alone, since she's so anxious to spill her guts.

He puffs his barrel chest out and I think he's gonna try and kick me, but then he reconsiders as I continue. "You're gonna figure out how we're going to get the boat back, using those nineteen bags of dirt you've still got. That, or it's back to California and a lot of years cooling your heels."

"I can't—"

"You'd better. 'Cause if you don't, your life is pure shit from here on out; if you do, I'm gonna turn you out. Not that I can free you from the wanted charge, that's gonna follow you . . . but I can give you some time in the sun. It's not *you* I want, it's the boat, or it's the jailhouse for Mr. Butterworth. You're a big boy, but not so big a half dozen brothers can't hold you down and have their way. You'll soon be known as butter-butt."

"Fuck," he says, but I get the feeling he means, "I'm fucked."

I lead the way back inside and motion the big bartender over.

"We cool here?" I ask.

"You got de badge, mon," he says.

"Then set us up with three Red Stripes and whatever the lady was drinking." I pat the stool next to me and motion Meegan over. "You sit between Iver and me. We need to talk."

She nervously sits, and Iver flanks her. She's silent until the drinks are served, then turns to me. "Am I going to jail?"

"You could, unless you take my advice."

"Anything," she says quickly.

"You look like a girl who might have believed a guy if he said he owned an eighty-eight-foot boat."

I can see the light come on. "I did. I did. Phil told me he owned the boat."

"Good. Now, I need to know exactly how you came to find Mr. Cool White, what transpired, how many people Mr. Cool has around that big house, and where the rest of your crew is."

"What crew?" she asks so innocently you almost believe that she doesn't know what I'm talking about.

"Meegan, think a long time in a cold cell. Think bad food and big ugly women with hairy warts on their face who want your flawless face buried in their smelly crotch. The big bull-dike bitches in the state pen will *love* you. I don't have time for any more bullshit, understand?"

"I'm sorry. They are my friends."

"They *were* your friends. Right now, the next twenty years of your life depends on your fessing up. Whole truth, nothing but the truth . . . you know the drill. Now, save your sweet young ass and talk."

The first thing out of her lips sort of screws up my plan.

"Well, it wasn't twenty kilos, it was forty."

"Where's the other twenty?"

"Ray Cox and Rupert, Marge and Penny, they just drove off when we walked in here."

"And they've got the other twenty?"

"You can probably catch them before they get back to Kingston . . . if you hurry. Ray plans to sell his share there . . . or maybe trade for a boat to take it home."

"What are they driving?"

"A pickup thingy."

"A pickup thingy? What color thingy?

"Blue. Pretty sky-blue."

"A big thingy, or a small thingy?"

"Small."

"How many doors?"

"Two, but it's got those little doors behind the big ones for the tiny backseat."

"Extended cab?"

"I guess. Your legs get all crampy in the backseat."

"They carrying?"

"Carrying?"

"Guns, do they have firearms?"

"Yes, they got them from some creepy guys in Kingston before they went to see Cool White. Man, you talk about creepy . . ."

I don't know Ray, but I know Rupert by sight. And it shouldn't be hard to spot four in a sky-blue compact pickup.

I hate to split my forces, old Marine Corps training, but I'm in a quandary. I might cut a deal with Mr. Cool White with nineteen instead of twenty, and no law involved, but not with nineteen instead of forty. He didn't get to be the head snowman from dealing away twenty-one kilos for zero zot.

"Hey, boss man," I yell to the Australian in the kitchen.

He appears, a mango in one hand, a paring knife in the other. "I need to leave the lady cop here watching these two while I chase some more bad guys."

He shrugs. "I got a storeroom you can lock them up in, but cuff them . . . I don't want them in my stuff."

"Great. We'll post the lady outside the door, if that's okay with you."

He nods.

We gather Meegan and Toke, leave him cuffed, and lock them in the storeroom. I caution her, "Don't touch the man's stuff." Then turn to Iver.

"Iver, let's hit it." Bobbi tosses me her keys but I toss

them back. "We'll take the Land Rover. In case we need the four-wheel drive," I say, but really mean that I don't want to leave the nose candy, even with Bobbi. It's a lot of dough, probably a minimum of three hundred grand stateside, and a lot of temptation. And I don't know her all *that* well.

"Can I borrow your piece?"

"The price is up, mon. Two hundred a day from here on out. And I don't loan you no pistol. You be borrowin' it wid out me knowing."

"No problem, mon."

She flips the Beretta to me. I pop the clip and see it's full: Beretta Cheetah auto, .380, ten shots. "One in the chamber?"

"No, mon."

In seconds I'm behind the wheel of the right-hand-drive Land Rover, figure out the gears, spin the wheel, throwing gravel out in a spray, then crash through the underbrush and am out on the narrow two-lane road, gunning it for all it's worth.

The chase is on.

Chapter Twenty-four

They've got maybe a fifteen- or twenty-minute head start, or a little more. And it's only twenty-five miles or so, but it's a windy twenty-five, and there are plenty of distractions along the way, not to speak of traffic.

And they don't know they're being chased.

The road to Kingston winds along the mountain side, two lane, rutted, and rough with potholes big enough to eat a bus. And there are plenty of buses and trucks dodging and bobbing and weaving. Luckily, Iver trusts my driving as I do his, and he hangs on without comment as I weave in and out, passing on the right as I should and when possible and necessary on the left soft shoulder. Jamaicans have proved to be a tolerant bunch, used to close, fast driving, but I reduce them to horn honking and lewd gestures.

The good news is construction slowdowns, where my soft-shoulder tactics gain me ten to twenty cars, buses, and trucks at a time.

We've gone ten or more miles, driving like madmen, when I spot the blue pickup a few cars ahead, a Nissan, fairly new and probably faster than the Land Rover. I duck in and out and around the last of the vehicles separating us, find an opening, and pull up in the opposite lane alongside the pickup. Rupert, the black guy of Jamaican descent, is driving. He glances over and focuses his one good eye on us, and his eyes widen, even the pearlescent one. The carpenter, Ray, the wife beater, is in the passenger seat. He seems to be a tall guy, a head taller than Rupert. Iver waves them over, a big smile on his face, his hand in his lap gripping the snub-nosed .38 he filched from Toke. "Hey, Rupert, pull over, man. Let's bullshit."

I have to drop back, as a dump truck is bearing down on me. The girls, whom I don't remember ever seeing, are peering out the back window. I can see the rapid animated conversation going on in the front seat. It's obvious they're not interested in seeing anyone from good old Santa Barbara. Then Rupert puts the pedal to the metal and the pickup shoots ahead.

With the traffic slowing him, and with me willing to take the soft shoulder, I catch up with him again as he's hemmed in behind a tourist bus and oncoming traffic. The road makes a hard left, and I'm able to get up beside him on the left on the soft shoulder, and this time it's me who yells at Rupert. "Hey, man, it's Dev from Santa Barbara. Pull over."

He flips me off, only lifting his hand off the wheel momentarily. Then he guns the Nissan and it shoots around the bus, leaving me. There's a long stretch of open road ahead of him, and he's Wile E. Coyote, leaving me in the dust.

"I could shoot out a tire next time we catch up," Iver suggests.

"Maybe, but we're already testing our luck, should the local cops show up."

I think back, remembering the highway, and a very steep stretch that oxbows down the mountain just before you reach the outskirts of Kingston. It's a long series of switchbacks on a steep mountainside dotted with a few palms, but mostly covered with underbrush.

"Let me try and catch him one more time," I suggest, before wanting to try the bold plan I'm formulating.

"Give it hell," Iver says, tightening up his seat belt.

We weave in and out crazily, but Rupert seems highly motivated, and he's doing the same. It doesn't take him long to catch on to the soft-shoulder trick. I can't get within a half dozen cars from him when a wide vista and the city of a million stretches out far below, just as we reach the first of the switchbacks.

We take it, and I see that he's still a quarter mile ahead of me. Each switchback, east, then west again, is at the end of a half a mile or so. As we pass the halfway mark, a quarter of a mile to the next switchback, I yell at Iver, "You up for a little boonies bounce?"

He shrugs. "Do what you gotta do."

I pick a spot, then whip the wheel to the right, over the edge. It's only 150 yards to the road, when you point your nose down. We crash through the underbrush—if there's a bolder hidden in the tangle, we're mush—me on the brakes rather than the gas, and I have to veer sharply to avoid the occasional palm, but we bounce out onto the road just as the Nissan roars past.

"One more time!" I yell, and we charge straight across and get air under all four as we leave the highway.

"You crazy sumbitch," Iver yells, but he's grinning broadly. The Land Rover is a little top-heavy, and as we lurch around palm trees, I'm afraid we're going to roll her, but she hangs on. We get air under all fours again, and I hold my breath as there's a high berm where we're landing, and I don't know if we can clear it.

The front bumper of the Rover buries itself in the berm, snapping our heads and bruising our chests and bellies with the seat belt, flinging soil and greenery in a shower—but she gets her rubber under her and flies on over, landing twenty feet above the road.

"Oh, hell," Iver yells, as we realize there's a six-foot dropoff, a cut in the hillside, where the road is.

The bad news is, due to the berm slowing us, we're not

going fast enough to make the leap. We nose down sickeningly and she flips and lands hard in the center of the road on her top, which is shattered into a thousand pieces. The good news is our belts hold and there's a three-inch roll bar that keeps our no-longer-smiling faces from being ripped from our shoulders by grinding pavement.

We're both shocked with the impact, and the belt impressions in our chest and gut.

"You okay?" Iver manages, upside down. Both of us hanging like sides of beef in a cold house, we eye each other.

I have to wait a second to get my breath back, but after a laugh of relief, finally answer. "Where's the Nissan?" I hope we didn't go through this for nothing.

A squealing of tires occurs as we're desperately trying to free ourselves with our full body weight against the seat belts. I pop free first, and clamber out the space my driver's-side window once occupied. I start to move around to help Iver out, and realize the brake squeal was from the Nissan, and there are black rubber marks where he almost collided with our wreck.

He's backing up, making almost fifty feet before an oncoming truck makes him brake it and change his mind. He has plenty of room to go around on either side. Slapping it back in a forward gear, he guns it, heading for the backside of the Rover. Luckily, the Beretta has managed to stay in my belt, and I charge to the back of the Rover, jerking it and jacking in a shell.

I put two quick ones in the Nisson's radiator before I have to dive to the side, roll, and come up on one knee in time to pull off two more at the driver's-side rear tire.

Then I run around to the passenger side of the Rover to make sure Iver's getting out okay. He has, but is disappeared halfway back inside the Rover, looking for the

.38. He comes up with it, and we both stand and look over the bottom of the vehicle, its wheels still spinning.

I glance over my shoulder, and see the traffic piling up behind us, then look down the road and see it stopping in the other direction.

The Nisson has swerved out of control as the tire flattened, and gone off the road, bouncing over a pile of rocks that luckily blows out a front tire. He makes it another fifty yards, barely able to steer, before slamming on the brakes.

Rupert Beauchamp piles out of the driver's right-hand side, and Ray Cox is out of the passenger's. I think they're headed into the brush, but to my great surprise, they're charging us. I guess brother Ray has a little bit of a temper, as he's leading like the alpha wolf, slavering, wanting blood. Both of them are carrying.

The Jamaicans have good eyes and ears, and see that all hell is about to break loose. Wheels are spinning as cars are backing up then shooting forward, trying to turn around before the shooting continues.

"Here comes Custer," Iver says with a wicked grin. "I'll take the front."

In the cover of the overturned Land Rover, with Iver at the front and me at the rear, we wait until they're at fifty feet, running at full tilt, then expose ourselves just enough to get a shot off.

Ray's on my side, and I'm not preoccupied with killing him, but a man charging you with fire in his eyes and a semi- or possibly full-automatic weapon in his hands is not to be coddled. My first shot, just as his weapon begins to chatter, stitching the pavement beside me, is benevolent, taking him high in the left thigh. He spins completely around, which means I got bone, then pitches forward on his face.

He's better with a framing hammer than he is with an automatic pistol, thank God.

Rupert Beauchamp is no street hood, and throws his hands in the air before Iver gets off a shot, at the same time flinging the weapon away. With arms stretched straight up, he's backing away, the whites of his eyes visible around the pupils. I guess he thought he'd find us in a heap still inside the car.

Ray, unfortunately for him, is not finished. He's on his belly, and extends the weapon out in front in both hands, trying to get a bead on me. This time, benevolence expended, I aim for his forehead and fire. I hear his scream, which probably means I missed the forehead—the perils of a borrowed weapon.

But the Uzi he was carrying and firing, which I now recognize, is flung aside and he's rolling around in pain. Both Iver and I charge forward and I give the Uzi a kick, spinning it across the lane into the soft shoulder.

Ray's shoulder as well as his thigh is bloodied.

I stand over Ray as Iver spins Rupert around and frisks him.

"You're not too quick, Ray," I suggest to him.

"Fuck you," he manages through gritted teeth.

"No, thanks. You want some advice?"

"Fuck you," he repeats, this time with more fervor.

I step forward, and place a foot on his shoulder and grind a little, enjoying the wife beater's scream. He, too, can reach a woman's pitch.

I ease up, enjoying his sobs. "Now, Ray, I'll ask again. You want some advice?"

"Yes. Yes. What? Oh, shit, that hurts."

"Iver and I could haul you and Rupert back to the States and you'd do a lot of time in a very bad place, or you can stay here and wait for the ambulance, after I tourniquet your leg and pack that shoulder wound. You don't have long to decide, as you're bleeding out quick."

"I'll wait here, man. This hurts like hell."

"Yeah, I know, and your wife and I and maybe even

your mother are glad it does. However, there's a little trade-off."

"What. Man, I'm bleeding to death here. How about some help?"

"The trade-off, Ray."

"What?"

"I'm unloading your truck and taking your loot back where it came from, but I've got a problem."

"What? Bandage me up, man."

"The problem, Ray."

"What?"

"You got to tell the Jamaican cops that you and Rupert got into a little argument, and shot it out. My name is not to come up."

"Okay, okay, man."

I yell at Iver to strip Rupert's T-shirt off, and he does and brings it to me while I'm jerking Ray's belt off. He borrows my cuffs, as his were left on Toke, and hooks Rupert up. I tourniquet Ray's thigh, slowing the blood to a trickle, then rip off a piece of the T-shirt and pack his shoulder wound, then tie it in place as best I can with the rest of the shirt. All to the sounds of his racking sobs.

"Get his buddy over here," I yell at Iver, who shoves Rupert over.

"Rupert, you're going to hold this in place until the ambulance comes, understand?"

Then I explain to Rupert that if he doesn't want to go back to a California jailhouse, he's to tell the cops that he and Ray shot it out.

With luck, before the cops sort it out, we'll be out of the country.

Ray is worth some money to me, and for his wife's and mother's sake, I'd like to haul him back. I will rat him out to the U.S. embassy, as he's going to spend a little time in a Jamaican hospital and won't be hard to find, and maybe they can get him home to face justice. I've already given him my own brand. Right now, he's a risk; he could blow our entire op, and I can't chance that. Hauling a wounded man around might just attract a little unwanted attention, and he would likely die on me. Under the current circumstance, it could be Iver and me in a Jamaican jail alongside Rupert and Ray, and I can't imagine that a Jamaican prison is any kind of a good time.

Now we have another problem, one fairly well disabled and one wrecked vehicle. I see that there's a truck a couple of hundred yards away, blocking the escape of a couple of vehicles.

"You go have a chat with the girls and make sure the goods are in the Nissan; I'll arrange for some transportation."

"If we can get the Land Rover turned over, it'll probably run. They're pretty damned tough."

"Okay, I'll get some help."

While Iver walks downhill to where some very frightened ladies are waiting by the Nissan, I run up the road to the traffic jam, where a crowd is berating each other over their quandary in trying to get the hell away.

I flash the badge—completely worthless in a foreign country—at the crowd. But it seems to relax them.

"Anybody got a heavy rope or chain and want to earn a hundred bucks, U.S.?"

The guy who's trying to turn the flatbed around steps forward. "I got a chain, mon."

"You get your truck down to the Jeep and bring the chain."

In moments, we have the Rover back on her feet, and have only to repack the cocaine, which is well wrapped but scattered all over the road, and reseat the battery, which has flopped out of its frame. She fires right up. Iver quickly loads a pair of suitcases that he's retrieved from the Nissan in the back of the Rover, and another prize he found behind the seat, an old Model-70 30.06

Winchester bolt action with a new three-to-twelve variable scope; and in moments we're in four-wheel working our way up the hillside and around the traffic.

"You square the ladies away?" I ask, as I'm finally able to pick up some speed.

"You bet. We may have bought a little time at least."

We're on the last of the switchbacks, when far below I see the flashing lights of cop cars and an ambulance.

But we've got a hell of a head start, particularly if the boys and girls we've left behind take threats seriously.

Iver digs in a pocket and flashes a cell phone at me. "Rupert had this," he says.

"Hell, give it a try. See if you can raise Cedric."

It takes him a while to figure out the country codes, but in a few minutes he hands me the phone. "It's ringing."

"Hey," I say when he answers.

"You're missing the fun," Cedric says, and I can hear the laugh in his voice.

"Oh yeah. We're having a little ourselves."

"Ol' Doc Scanoletti is a real kick in the butt."

"How so?"

"Seems he took a new lady out to dinner at the Sage and Onion the other night, and all his credit cards were canceled . . . very embarrassing for a pompous prick like Scanoletti. She took a cab home, without the little fat man."

"The hell you say, and he was a little embarrassed?"

"You bet. But yesterday was the highlight."

"And?"

"And, our boy recently bought himself a Bentley convertible."

"Really? And he couldn't afford to pay me a lousy nine grand."

"But it's a real mess."

I get a bad feeling. "You didn't do anything to get us sued?"

"Hardly. He took his shiny new wheels down to the

beach, parking it away from the other cars, I presume so he wouldn't get any parking lot dings in the beauty."

"So?"

"So, it turns out seagulls love Bentleys."

"What?"

"For the price of a lousy loaf of day-old bread, he's a very frustrated and angry man."

"Come on, Ced, what happened?"

"It seems he left the top down, and somebody spread bread crumbs all over the car, even inside on the beautiful lambskin upholstery."

"And the gulls . . . ?"

"Boys will be boys and gulls will be gulls. They left about eight pounds—that's an estimate only—eight pounds of processed fish all over that Bentley, inside and out. I also stopped the power, water, cable TV, DSL line, and newspaper at his house."

I have to laugh aloud.

"And the hell of it is his checks are bouncing."

"You didn't clean out his accounts?" Again, I get a little tightness in my gut.

He sounds offended. "That would be illegal, Devlin. Of course not. I did, however, move his money out of his checking account into his payroll tax account, and cancel his automatic transfer, which would have had one account cover the other in case of an overdraft. He bounced about a hundred checks, including his payroll. And one of his girls quit, a Mrs. Rodriquez. They got an e-mail on the office computers from a kiddy porn site, with explicit pictures, thanking the good doc for subscribing. Scanoletti's life is a little frustrating, flat-out topsy-turvy, at the moment."

"Maybe he'll be a little more willing to pay up when I get back."

"Hey, where's Pug?" Cedric asks.

Chapter Twenty-five

"I dunno. He's not around?"

"Nope. I thought we were gonna fish today, but he didn't show up at the boat."

"You call the house?"

"No answer."

"Maybe he had a dentist appointment or something and couldn't get a hold of you."

"I've had my cell all the time."

"What's up with Hashim and your work on the stuff you got off his computer?"

"I'm getting there. It was really well encrypted."

"And the arraignment?" I'd asked Ced to attend Mason Fredrich's arraignment, to see if we could learn anything.

"Looks like they've got some evidence. Mason's boat was spotted in the channel the day she went missing, and, of course, there was some blood found in the gunnels. His attorney laughed it off, as you're always skinning yourself on a damn fishing boat, as you well know. Mason said he was out by himself when he was first interviewed. But that's not the worst part."

"And what is?"

"Some guys claim the *June Blue Moon*, the Fredrichs' boat, was on the backside of Anacapa, and that they'd seen his wife there earlier in the day with some guy trying to learn to surf sail."

"So, why would he ask me to help find her, if he was

the bad guy? Which I can't believe. Sounds pretty flimsy to me."

"Appearances, or so the DA said. His attorney mentioned he'd hired someone. They OR'd Fredrich at the original arraignment, but the new judge laid a million bucks' bail on him at the second hearing. Seems they came up with the eyewitnesses after the original hearing."

We're nearing Port Morant and the bar, so I reluctantly hang up. Funny, Pop didn't mention going away, and it's not like him not to show up at the boat when he's got someone scheduled to go out with him.

Hell, maybe he's getting a little long in the tooth and forgetting things.

Just on a lark, as Iver is fetching Bobbi, Meegan, and Toke, I call Babs on the cell. "Hey, beautiful."

"I figured you'd forgotten all about me, with all those beautiful native girls batting eyes at you."

"Impossible. Hey, have you seen my old man around?"

"Had lunch with him day before yesterday. What's up?"

"Cedric said he didn't show up at the boat today. That's not like him."

"Not at all. He's rock steady. If you don't mind, I'll check out his house and see if I can run him down."

"Please. I'll owe you one. There's a key under the flowerpot on the outside plant shelf in front of the kitchen window."

"One may not be enough."

"Pardon me?"

"You said you'd owe me one . . . one may not be enough."

That makes me smile. "You make me want to fly home on the next ride."

"Hurry."

"I'd give you a cell number, but I don't know the number of this damn thing. I'll call you back, in the morning at the latest."

"Dev, I miss you."

"Be there as quick as I can."

"Stay safe."

"Jesus Christ," Toke whines as I hang up and they approach. "What the hell did you pricks do to my car?"

I have to admit that it's hardly the Land Rover that left. Its top is smashed and virtually gone, its hood and fenders on the passenger side are smashed in, we had to pull the front one out to get it off the tire. It's a bloody mess, to coin an appropriate Britishism.

"It's got some character now," I say, then add, "Besides, it's not your car, it's Cool White's if I have anything to say about it. And I do."

We cuff Toke in the backseat of the Land Rover, and give Bobbi one of my little Motorola radios and a quick lesson in its use. She'll follow a quarter mile behind and park somewhere where she can't be seen. While we're on our way to the turnoff to Cool White's place, I make a phony call. I've seen a number of billboards, advertising security companies and one who seems to pride itself on its quick-response team, and I use that name. "Is this Blanton Protection and Security?" I ask, speaking to the bell tone.

I carry on a one-way conversation. "Are your people in place?"

Pause.

"Good. Do we need that many?"

Pause.

"Okay. If I'm not out in thirty minutes, or you hear any shots, call the local cops, but don't wait on them. Storm the place."

Pause.

"Okay, mon," I say, and hang up. I turn to Iver. "Those guys are a badass bunch. I'd hate to be up against them."

"You're gonna get us all killed," Toke says, and Meegan begins to sob in the backseat.

"You two just do exactly as I say, and we'll get out of there with our skins."

Iver glances over. "We probably should just steal the damn boat."

"Iver, there are probably a half dozen guys with AK-47s on board the *Orion*. They won't let her go softly into the night."

He shrugs. "I'll back you up . . . all the way to the morgue."

"Jesus, I don't need that from you."

He shrugs again. "Hell, I'm probably going there anyway."

That shuts me up. Nothing like a morbid vote of confidence from one of your most trusted friends. I've noticed that he hasn't been quite himself lately, and can understand why. Even the suggestion of cancer gives me a chill. As does any foe I can't see.

When we reach a locked and guarded wrought-iron gate, flanked by eight-foot rock walls, I swing in and stop with my nose to the iron and look over at Iver. "You can get out and wait here," I offer.

"Shannon," he says, disgustedly, "who the hell do you think you're talking to?"

"Sorry. Thought you might be feeling bad."

"Get off the 'you feeling bad' bullshit. Let's go."

He waits in the car, his hand on the .38, while I approach the gate. The guard does not appear to be armed, but he's wearing an unmarked khaki uniform with a belted coat—under a black John Brown belt but without the holster—an officer's visored cap, and could have a hideout gun in a pocket or on the ankle. He'd look pretty respectable, if it weren't for the knappy dreadlocks hanging to his shoulder.

"Sylvester Gunn?" I inquire, using his boss's legal name.

"An' who you be, mon?" he asks, looking with disdain at the beat-up ride we're in.

"My name is Dev Shannon, and he's going to want to talk to me."

"Wait."

He walks away, disappearing behind the wall to what I imagine is a wall phone.

In moments, he returns. "He don't be knowin' you, man, and he busy."

"Tell Mr. Gunn that I've got Mr. Butterworth with me, and I've got his dope, and that I have to talk a deal with him."

He shrugs, but walks back behind the wall.

In a few seconds, he's back. "You wait de minute, mon," he says. In a few more seconds, a big black Toyota Land Cruiser arrives, with four gorillas toting AK-47s. They climb out and three of them take up positions behind the SUV. All of them are stylish in dreadlocks, from shoulder length to reaching to the waist on one of them.

The fourth one is a fine-looking full-sized fellow, were it not for the fact he is missing an ear, and has a puckered scar in the temple just in front of the stump.

He motions to the guard, who again disappears, and the gate opens, but just enough so he can pass through.

"I be Herman," he says as he comes close. "You be turnin' around so I can pat you down."

I've returned Bobbi's Beretta to her. "I'm not carrying, but my friend in the front seat has a piece. You guys aren't afraid of a guy with a little ol' pistol, are you?"

He laughs, sets the AK aside, and pats me down to make sure. He comes up with the little Motorola. "What be dis?"

Since he doesn't know, I take a chance. "My music, mon. You want, I get some Marley."

He returns the radio, laughing, then walks over and visually checks out Iver and the two in the back. He notes that Toke's hands are cuffed behind him, then gives me a hard look. "You be some kinda cop?"

"Nope. Not here. Besides, I imagine you guys own all the cops in Kingston and sure as hell in Port Morant."

He laughs again. "Not be ownin' all, just the captains and commissioner. Still, I got to be holdin' your iron, or you not be goin' in to see Mr. Cool."

I shrug, then yell at Iver, "He says we don't take the iron inside."

Iver climbs out of the car and eyes the situation carefully, then surprises me a little. "Then I'm waiting here. You go do your thing. I'll be out here with our friends."

I give him a barely perceptible nod and climb in under the wheel.

"Out," Herman commands. "You be riding in the black car, I'll be driving dis one down."

I do as directed and Iver backs away from the Land Rover. Meegan starts to climb out, but I reprimand her and she stays, but doesn't like it.

We wind down a long lane to the house, which rests in a final level spot in the floor of the canyon on a five-acre flat, but still high on top of a cliff overlooking the bay and open sea beyond. The foliage- and palm-covered hills rise up on either side. The rock wall must enclose forty acres, and runs to the very edge of the cliff about a hundred yards on either side of the building complex. I know, from seeing the place from the sea side, that stone steps lead down to a generous-sized boathouse that probably houses a pair of smaller boats. The house is flanked by two smaller structures, but they're each the size of a comfortable American mid-income home. They're connected to the main house with covered walkways. Servants and caretakers move about, ignoring me and the guys with the guns as if it's standard operating procedure.

With two armed thugs in front and two in back, Meegan, Toke, and I are escorted into the main house. The front door is four feet wide and nine feet tall, carved with a pair of frolicking dolphins. The entryway is tiled, the walls stark-white and covered with wild native paintings, and the great room beyond boasts twenty-foot ceilings. We move through the great room and out onto a covered patio, overlooking the sea, and the *Orion*, moored about three hundred yards out.

Sylvester Gunn is not hard to recognize. He reclines in a deck chair, a *Playboy* magazine in one hand, a tall fruit-laden drink in the other. Dark sunglasses are a stark contrast to dusky white skin and light eyes. He momentarily removes the glasses, shading his eyes with a hand. I'm wondering if he's a true albino, as his eyes are more yellow green than pink. I'd laugh, as he reminds me of a lizard or snake I saw at the Santa Barbara Zoo, but it probably would be injurious to my health to do so . . . besides, it would be impolite.

He does not stand, does not offer a hand. And he sure as hell doesn't smile. The guy with no ear has set aside his weapon, and walks over and takes a seat in a chair near Gunn. I presume he's a number-two man.

"Why de cuffs on dat man?" Gunn asks, with a head motion toward Toke.

"He broke the law, as did you," I say, not being smart-ass, merely stating a fact.

"Dat's what we do 'roun here," he says, and Herman guffaws.

"You're Sylvester Gunn?" I ask, as if there was any doubt.

This time I get a hint of a smile. "Who de hell you tink I am, Bob Marley?" This brings a laugh from his goons. There's Bob Marley music echoing from the patio speakers.

"So, you're Gunn?"

He eyes me coldly. I'm not trying to intimidate him, but am trying to stay on an equal footing, as hard as that might be, surrounded by his weaponry.

"What happen him?" he asks, motioning to Toke, whose eyes are both blackened and whose nose is swollen to double size and as black as one of Gunn's goons.

"He broke the law."

"What you want, mon?"

"The boat. It belongs to a client of mine."

This time the smile is genuine, if a little reptilian. "De boat be mine, mon. I trade like a gentleman with Mr. Butterworth here."

"Mr. Butterworth is going to jail, and I've got your coke and a car to give you."

"Maybe he go to jail, maybe no. Maybe we trade, maybe no," Gunn says, then motions to one of the other goons. "Get de cuffs off dat man." He turns to me. "You got de key?"

I dig them out of a pocket and hand them to the goon. He pops the cuffs off Butterworth, who stands rubbing his wrists and limbering up his shoulders.

He looks at Gunn, and there's fire in his eyes. "You mind if I knock Dilbert's dick in the dirt?"

Chapter Twenty-six

"No, mon, good to see de baldhead's do de knuckle dance."

Toke charges me, swinging with a sucker's sweeping overhand right. Now is not the time to be demure, and I sidestep and clip him with a hard-driving right under the ear as his exuberance takes him by, spinning him around and rolling his eyes up in his head as he goes flat on his back, flattening a small table next to Gunn and spilling his drink and shattering the glass.

Gunn snatches up the *Playboy*, which he'd laid on the small table. Toke is not out, but close. He is trying to get his bearings. He lies there, finally testing his jaw to make sure it's not as broken as his nose. I'm sorry to note, I don't think it is.

Gunn rises and motions to a goon. "Get Marta to bring me anudder drink. And get one for Mr. . . . what you say you name be, mon?"

"Shannon. Dev Shannon."

"For Mr. Shannon."

"Thanks," I say. Toke struggles to his feet, eying me, but not making a move.

"You take de seat." Gunn motions to a deck chair fifteen feet from his, and Toke minds.

Gunn zeros those greens on me. I'm glad he's put the shades back on, as those eyes are disconcerting at the least.

"So, mon, why I be trading?"

"Because I can put you back whole. I've got thirty-nine keys and a beat-up Land Rover. Runs good though."

"I don't be wantin' no coke, mon. I got coke. In fact . . ." He glances over where two other goons have exited the house carrying the two suitcases and a large box, I presume all are loaded with the thirty-nine kilos. "In fact, mon, I done got all de coke, and de car, and you in de bottom of de bay, I say so."

I shrug, then zero my baby blues on him. "And you got a hell of a lot of trouble. I got twenty of Blanton's boys outside your walls right now, and they don't much like you and are looking for any excuse . . ."

He's deadly serious. "You make a threat at me, mon?"

"I think it was you doing the threatening, Mr. Gunn."

He studies me for a moment, then smiles. He's got a gold front tooth with a half-carat or so diamond centered in it. He's a bling-bling man. "You got de big *cajones*, mon."

"Nice rock," I say, trying to lighten the moment.

"So, tell me again why I be taken' my goods back?"

"Because it's the smart thing to do. No loss, and no big-time trouble."

"No loss hell, I got de boat. What kind of law you be, mon?"

I pull out my wallet and flip it over to him with it folded back so the badge shows, then tell one of the biggest lies I've ever risked. "Bail enforcement officer, Mr. Gunn. We're a small division of the Drug Enforcement Agency. The DEA . . . we've known about you for a long time. The boat belongs to a friend of the president of the United States, or we wouldn't be messing with it."

For the first time, we hear from Toke. "That's a crock of bullshit."

I turn casually to him. "You remember the deal I cut

with you? Boat, no jail. No boat, your butt gets reamed by a gaggle of old boys as attractive as Mr. Gunn's goons."

And we hear from Meegan for the first time. "Phil, please, please. I want to go home."

He calms down, then offers with a shrug, "He does have a bunch of guys out in the bush, Cool. I heard him talking to them on the phone. Some quick-response team thing."

Gunn almost growls at him. "You be callin' me mister. You salt me, mon. Cold White don't take to be tricked."

I'll have to remember to ask Iver or Bobby what it means to be salted.

I think it's going my way, when a woman walks out onto the patio. Her floor-length gown is some kind of wraparound with a print of dancing skeletons, and she's got a bone necklace hanging around her neck that reaches to her waist. As she gets closer, I realize it's made from the heads of small animals and rodents. Now, that's a fashion statement if I ever saw one. She's a head or two shorter than Gunn, Toke, or me, and is not what you call pretty, but she emanates power. Her eyes are so deep-set I don't at first see the fire in them, then they light up, and they seem to be stoked with the fires of perdition. I presume this is Mrs. Gunn, the obeah woman.

For the first time, Gunn rises. "Mr. Shannon, dis be my woman, Leah Miranda Gunn."

"I be his wife," she corrects. She walks over and extends a hand, holding mine for a long time, looking deeply into my eyes, maybe into my soul, seeming to get vibrations through her grasp.

"Nice to meet you," I say with a smile, and wonder if I mean it.

Then she turns to Gunn. "Dis mon skin teet plenty. What dis I hear 'bout me boat?"

He shrugs, looking sheepish, and I know I'm in deep ka-ka. I'll also have to ask what "skin teet" means.

She turns back to me. "You tink you be takin' my *Corazón*, Mr. Shannon?"

My Santa Barbara Spanish is good enough that I know that *Corazón* means heart, and if this woman is referring to her own heart, I sincerely wonder if she has one. But I smile. "Trying to make things right, Mrs. Gunn," I say as sincerely as I can. "I'm not looking for trouble, just trying to right some things."

"I be tinkin' not," she says, losing the smile. "It be my boat, and she not goin' nowhere wit no baldhead." She moves up beside Slyvester, humming as she does, then sings in a low voice:

*"Here comes the con man,
Coming with his con plan.
We won't take no bribe.
We got to stay alive,
Chase those crazy baldheads
Out of town...."*

She moves over closer to the sea side of the patio, singing in reggae cadence as she goes. She's got a great voice, but I'm not sure I like the words.

*"The truth is an offense but not a sin!
Is he who laugh last, children! Is he who win.
Is a foolish dog bark at a flying bird!
One sheep must learn, children! to respect the word."*

This is getting a little weird, even for me. I expect her to whip out a dead chicken and to ask me for some nail trimmings and a lock of hair so she can make a doll to stick with pins.

"Then, if we're through here, I'll be going," I say. "Nice to meet you, Mrs. Gunn." One of the great all-time lies I've told in a sorted life. "Sorry we couldn't come to terms, Mr. Gunn," I say, which is the truth, then I turn and head for the door, knowing when it's time to leave, but a couple of the goons step in front of me, AK-47s at easy rest.

"We talk a bit more," Gunn says, and I turn back to see he's now seated with Leah Miranda at his side.

I can feel the little Motorola vibrate in my pocket. I reach in and fish it out; the act causes two of the goons to come very close, shoving the muzzles into my side and back.

Even with the discouragement, I bring it up to my ear. "Yeah?"

"Tell Cool White not to reach for his drink."

It's Iver. "What?"

He's emphatic. "Tell Cool White not to reach for his drink."

I trust Iver with my life, which I'm doing again at the moment, and lower the radio to my side. "Mr. Gunn, I see you've got your drink back. Please don't reach for the glass."

"What, mon?" he says, looking a little confused.

The glass explodes, and the crack of a rifle shot reverberates in the canyon. The goons dive for cover, then are up with their muzzles panning the hillside where the report of the rifle originated.

To both the Gunns' credit, neither of them panic. I get the impression that Leah Miranda thinks some evil demon protects her, and she can't be killed. I now know why Cool White got his nickname. He is deadly cool, under the circumstance. I don't think the guy even flinched when the glass exploded in a million shards and his fruit drink mushroomed up in the air.

The radio vibrates again.

"Tell Cool he's to go with you to the boat, if he wants his woman around, and he's to tell the wife not to move as I can put the next one in her ear, so get her a magazine and tell her to relax."

"My associates say to tell your lady not to move, but to relax with a magazine."

"Why dat?" he says, but he hands her the *Playboy*.

"Because they want you to take me to the boat, or you won't have an obeah woman to help you out."

I swear he goes even whiter than normal. I know Bobbi is with Iver, as he has the radio, and she's probably filled him in on who is the true power in the odd couple. Gunn rises and walks over and whispers in her ear, then moves over to me and says in a low voice. "You kill my woman, I feed you *cojones* to de fishes, den take you 'part piece by piece."

"Not for a while, you won't," I say, actually managing a smile.

We start to turn, but are stopped my Leah Miranda's lyrical voice. "Mr. Shannon, mon."

"Yes, ma'am?" I say politely.

"You know de mon's curse, mon?"

"No, ma'am."

"Dat's when you lay wid a beautiful woman, and it don't get hard, mon. You be cursed, mon. Forever, mon. You never satisfy no woman again. And you a young man. Pity, pity, pity." Her smile is absolutely reptilian, making Cold White's look like an altar boy's.

I swear, I feel the color flowing out of my face, and I must be as white as Gunn. "I don't believe in that voodoo crap," I manage.

"You be belivin' soon, baldhead, you be soon."

She says it with such conviction that my smile rings phony, and rings true, as I'm not happy.

"Tol you, Sly, dis man skin teet too much."

Now I know what "skin teet" means, to skin teeth, to smile.

"Let's go, mon," Cool White says in the low voice, "before she put de curse on me, too."

That's comforting. Even her husband thinks she's got the power. Why do I have this limp feeling between my legs?

But I turn and stride for the door, grabbing one of the AK-47s out of a goon's hands as I pass. He resists, but Gunn snaps at him, and suddenly I'm well armed.

"Please." It's Meegan, her tone pitiful.

"What?" I ask.

"Take me with you. Take Phil. They'll kill him."

I shrug. We'll need someone to do the grunt work on the boat until we get to the nearest port that we can hire on a couple of guys. Besides, he's worked her before and knows her idiosyncrasies, which all boats, like all women, have in abundance.

I motion them to come along.

We circle the house and find the head of the stone stairway, and descend through five landings at least a hundred steps to the boathouse. As suspected, there's a thirty-foot fishing boat and a beautiful old wooden Chris Craft speedboat inside.

I'm a fan of old wooden boats, and love this particular model. She's a Chris Craft Racer, built in the late forties. "Great boat," I say, just as if I weren't commanding him with an AK-47.

"We be gettin' dis done," he says.

In moments, we're heading for the Benetti, are alongside, and climbing the portable side stairway.

As Iver suggested, we're met by five goons, each of them carrying an AK.

But I've got the advantage, as the muzzle of mine is buried in the side of their boss.

"Put down the weapons, and step to the rear of the boat," I command.

They stare at their boss as if they can't believe what's happening.

"Do like de mon says," he orders.

I can see the reluctance with which they abandon their weapons, but each of them does so.

As soon as we're aboard and things are in order, the radio vibrates again.

"How about telling those old boys to take a swim, then send Cool over to that rock outcropping to pick us up?"

"Sounds good to me," I say.

Gunn has overheard the exchange. "Two of my boys don't be swimmin', mon," he says.

There are life rings hanging from the sides of the superstructure. I motion to them. "They can paddle. Give them a life preserver."

He gathers up two of the rings and, after I take the precaution of cuffing Toke to a handrail, I follow him aft.

"You boys be going for de swim," he says, and his men look at him in disbelief. One of them has absolute fear in his eyes.

But one by one, they leap over the side, until the last one, the one with wide eyes, rebels.

He turns back from the side rails, shaking his head.

"Throw him over," I command. Gunn is a big man, even larger than the goon, but it's a struggle for him. Finally, the man is headfirst over the side, and safely in the water with his life ring and two of his buddies calming him down.

"Tell them to swim home."

I wait until they're seventy-five yards out, a quarter of the way back to the boat dock, then I say, "You ready to pick up a couple of my partners?"

"Why not, mon?" he says, but he lacks enthusiasm.

"Then take the boat to that rock outcropping, and remember, the guy who blew that glass all to hell from four hundred yards . . ." I exaggerate, as Iver could have been as close as 150. "Remember, he's got you covered from one side, and I've got you from here with this automatic." The outcropping is two hundred yards the opposite way from the house, too close for him to risk the AK-47. A few bursts could cut the wooden boat in half, with concentrated fire.

"No problem, mon."

There are a line of armed men, over a dozen, standing on a rock quay near the boathouse, watching as we hoist anchor, fire up the diesels, and drag the Chris Craft out to sea. As we move away, I pick up the binocs and see that his men are loading up in the thirty-foot fishing boat, which I'm sure is much faster than the Benetti.

When Iver came aboard, he was alone, and I'm concerned about Bobbi.

"Where's all your buddies?" I ask, still keeping up the scam.

"They gonna wait in the weeds awhile, then head back to the home base. They got vehicles, mon," he says, reminding me that Bobbi had her car somewhere up on the road.

Gunn takes the chair next to me, with Iver casually leaning on the bulkhead behind us, the AK comfortably in his arms, as I pilot her out. Toke is still cuffed to the rail outside enjoying the ocean breeze, and Meegan is below in the galley trying to whip us up a sandwich.

"What you gonna do wid me, baldhead?" Gunn asks.

"You're gonna ride with us a little while, then you're gonna climb back in the little boat and go home to your sweet wife"—I almost choke on that one—"and you're gonna come to your senses and realize you're even. You've lost no face with your men—"

"De hell you say. My people . . . de see you be draggin' me 'roun."

"Still, you're economically even. You can square away the rest. You didn't get where you are being a pussy."

"No, mon." He laughs. "Dat true. But I not be trading no key for no beat-up Rover."

"That's for the insult, mon. You can't be slappin' no friend of the U.S. president in the face."

Iver gives me a strange look, but says nothing, and I continue, "Can any of those apes of yours use the radio on the other boat?"

"Yeah, mon. Herman be my first mate."

I study the angle of the sun, and judge it's only an hour to sundown. Unless they've got some great radar on that fishing boat, there's no way they can follow after dark, and I'm going to make a 180 as soon as Gunn's out of sight. "There's the VHF. Give old Herman a call and tell him I'm cutting you loose, but if I can see anything on the horizon that looks like a boat, you're going all the way to Florida with me"—a lie as I'm heading for Panama—"and then I'm turning you over to the DEA."

He gets on the radio and raises Herman with the first try. He starts to talk, rattling away in patois, and I reach over and jerk the mike out of his hand.

"You speak clear English. No Jamaican."

In clear concise English with a touch of a Brit accent, he repeats what I told him, and does so convincingly.

I realize what life must be like for him, when he asks to have a long-sleeve shirt, pair of gloves, and wide-brimmed hat. "The sun, he kill me, mon," he explains.

I cruise five miles or a little more out to sea, hove to, pull the Chris Craft around to the ladder, and he descends.

I can't help but yell at him before he steps on the bow of the smaller boat. "Hey, Cool White?"

He looks up. "Yeah, mon?"

"Since I cut you loose, get your lady to take the curse off me."

He laughs, and it's not an encouraging one. "She her own woman, mon. I be lucky I don't be havin' one on me when I get 'ome."

Oh well. I guess I take my chances.

Chapter Twenty-seven

It's well after dark by the time I do another 180 and run west, then turn north into Kingston Harbor. I've given Toke the impression that I'm going back to Florida, and he'll have to take his chances with the law there, and he's begged me to put him ashore in Jamaica, which I'd hoped he'd do. I've decided I don't want to risk his sabotage, and we're too few to watch him as I'm afraid is necessary. We've picked his brain about the boat, and discovered that he's traded the main twenty-thousand-KW generator off in Costa Rica on the way down for provisions, enough money to get through the canal, and topping off the tanks—a piss-poor trade. We'll have no problem with the eight-KW auxiliary. I idle up to a petroleum company dock and let him jump for it, hoping he'll break an ankle, then head out to sea.

Meegan stands listlessly and watches the lights of the pier disappear, then I notice tears rolling down her cheek.

"You okay?" I ask.

"He said he loved me. He didn't even say good-bye."

This beautiful girl is naïve, at best, stupid at worst. But it's not nice to be anything other than kind. "Meegan, he's running for his freedom. And you're better off. A guy who'd put you at risk along with himself doesn't know the meaning of love."

"You think so?"

"I know so. You're a beautiful girl, and there's about a

million guys out there waiting for you. Nice clean handsome guys with steady jobs, who want to hold and protect and provide for you."

Now she begins to cry with deep racking, body-shaking sobs. Good job, Shannon.

The good news is we're well provisioned, as Cool White's had time to stock her up. She's a mess, but it's mostly cosmetic.

As we're heading west along Jamaica's south shore, I get on the cell phone again and call the old man, both on his cell phone and at home. He doesn't answer, which worries the hell out of me. Then I dial Babs.

"Hey, I'm glad you called," she says. "I wasn't going to bother you quite yet, but I've put out a limited all-points on Pug. You know, spot and report kind of thing. Of course I've checked all the hospitals and our records."

"Why the APB?" Now I'm really worried.

"I went by the house, he wasn't there and his truck is in the garage and I didn't need the key, the front door was ajar."

"Pop's a nut for keeping the house locked up. The neighborhood is not what it once was."

"There was an electric teapot on the kitchen counter, still on, with the water boiled out."

"He's also a nut about turning off anything electrical. He used to raise hell with me if I left a light on. Anything disturbed, like there was a fight of some kind?"

"Nope. Lights were on all through the house, the door open, and the teapot. I checked his closets and he's a real neat-nic. I'd guess all his luggage is there, as there's a full set, and his closet is full of clothes, each shirt, pant, and suit nicely spaced, and his dupe kit is in the bathroom cabinet. The bed was unmade, which doesn't figure as the rest of the place is shipshape. I talked with all the neighbors and got nothing."

"You do good work."

"Thanks. But I haven't found him, and I don't like that part."

"I'm not going to panic. He's getting a little forgetful. Things change when people get older—"

"Pug's in his early sixties. That's not old."

"We've got the *Orion* and are on our way home. It'll be a couple of days before I get to some place with an airport. I'm coming home first chance, unless you turn him up soon. And I mean real soon."

"Congratulations on the boat. . . . You're really worried?"

"I know my old man, and, yeah, I'm really worried."

"I'll keep on top of it."

I call Cedric as soon as she's off. It won't be long before we're out of range of the cell phone, and I'll have to figure out what the electronics of the *Orion* offers in the way of communication. I'm hoping there's a working satellite phone aboard, otherwise I'm sure I'll be trying to figure out a single sideband.

"Blessings," he answers.

"Blessings yourself."

"Hey, how's it going?" He still sounds jovial, which means Scanoletti is still miserable.

"Great. We have the *Orion* and are heading home. Ced, the old man is still missing." I fill him in on Babs's efforts.

"Yeah, that worries me, too," he says. "I'll get with Babs and see what I can do."

"Tell me some good news."

"Scanoletti is about ready to check himself into the looney bin. Another of his girls quit, and his partner is questioning his sanity and his morals. There was an ad in the *News-Press* where he said he wouldn't be responsible for any of his partners' debts." He pauses to laugh. "Seems also that it showed up that he hadn't paid his bill at La Cumbre and the manager jumped him." He laughs again, then in broken speech interspersed with laughter, manages, "But this is the best part. The goats he ordered were delivered to his house and placed in the backyard when he wasn't home, and I guess he was a little disturbed when he found all his landscaping reduced to piles of small pellets."

"Okay, enough already. I'll be home in a couple of days. Lay off him before he does end up a couple of cards short of a deck and I never can collect."

There's a long silence. "You're ruining all my fun. I was just getting started."

"Promise me . . . ."

"Okay, okay. I'll help Babs."

"And the San Francisco connection?"

His tone changes. "I was keeping that for last. You said you wanted some good news."

"And . . . ?"

"And guess who Jamal Mahmoud is."

"Please, no guessing games."

"Mahmoud is a phony name, his real last name is . . . Hashim. I got a driver's license picture of him and did a little computer comparison of a guy who's wanted in France, Germany, and badly wanted in Israel. A guy who has some terrorist ties. And that's our boy. Dr. Mohammad Hashim's own little brother, fifteen years younger. He trained in Yemen, but didn't want to traipse off to Afganistan with his jihad buddies when he had a chance to come to the good old U.S.A."

I let out a deep sigh. One mystery solved, now to solve the threat by taking them out, or distant second best, getting them put away.

"Have you told anyone? Babs, the FBI, anyone?"

"Nope. I thought you might want to handle this one yourself. As I recall, we tried to let the law handle our last problem with Hashim the Hannibal imposter."

"Okay, good work. See you in a couple of days. And, Ced, find the old man, I'm really worried now."

"We'll find him. You get home safe."

It's 550 miles to Cristobal, Panama, the mouth of the Panama Canal, or Colon as the Panamanian city that borders the canal is called. And there's only two of us whom I trust to take the helm. As is common, we take four-hour watches. Meegan, to her credit, tries to stay near the helm to keep us awake, and supplied with coffee and grub. She's a fair hand and a damn good cook.

I manage to wait five hours before I call on the satellite phone I find on board. No news is the bad news, and there's no good news, and won't be until we locate Pug.

Normally I would cruise a diesel boat like the *Orion* at sixteen hundred RPM making ten knots, which is ideal for fuel consumption, but under the circumstances I push her at 2,400, and am averaging fourteen knots, or just a little over sixteen miles per hour.

That means it's a day and a half to Colon and an airport.

It's the longest day and a half I've ever spent.

Luckily, I arrive in time to catch a midnight flight to Mexico City, then only a short layover and on to LAX.

It's still a hell of a trip, and I'm beat up when I finally land. Of course, customs gives me hell as I look like hell, and as one of the cute little beagle dope dogs thinks he's found the honey hole. I guess I got some of the stuff on my clothes when was helping Iver load it into the Land Rover. I've called Cedric, and he's waiting at the baggage pickup, but he has a long but not boring wait as they keep me for over three hours, and subject me to X-rays and a cavity search.

I think they've been polite when they ask if someone is meeting me, then learn that they've paged and pulled Cedric into an interview room, and do a good cop, bad cop with him for almost the same amount of time.

Not my finest hour.

I am, as Sandy Bartlett's dad, Andy, once suggested, hammered dog shit, by the time I'm back in beautiful Santa Barbara a little after noon on a gorgeous Sunday.

But not so tired that I don't head straight for my childhood abode, Pug's house.

But Babs has done a great job, and I learn nothing. I'm sick at heart when I have Cedric drop me off at the dock and drag my way on the two-hundred-yard walk down the main and offshoot dock that takes me home to *Aces n' Eights*.

I stop short when I reach the hatchway to the main salon. Damned if somebody hasn't used chain cutters on my new lock. At least this time they didn't rip the hasp out of the teak. I merely slip the remnants of the lock, which has been kindly replaced, open the teak door, and shove the top back, and am so tired I almost hope someone's waiting to blow me away as I descend the four stairs to the salon deck.

The only killer awaiting me is Futa, who welcomes me with an ankle rub. His water and food bowls are full, so Cedric deserves a pat on the head, but Futa's closer, and I bend down.

But no one gets the pat, as I notice a nicely lettered note on my chart table. The bottom falls out of my stomach as I read.

> *Shannon: I have your obnoxious father. You should have listened when I told your associate that I knew how to hurt someone. You will hurt because I have him. He will hurt more if you do not do exactly what I say. Drive to San Luis Obispo, take your cell phone, and you will get additional instructions. He will hurt so badly you will live in agony the rest of your days, not sleeping, awakening in a sweat because of your dreams of what you*

did to your father. You will hurt so badly, you will want to hurt yourself. I'm thinking of beginning with a drop of muric acid in each ear and each eye, and so on. Drive your motorcycle, not a car.

If you tell anyone about this, he will die.

If you have anyone with you, he will die.

If you do not do exactly what you are told, he will die.

If I do not like the expression on your face, he will die.

Now do so.

Chapter Twenty-eight

I realize with a sick feeling that I haven't had my cell phone for days. With great trepidation, I reach over and grab it out of its charger. There are a half dozen calls, the last one only an hour old, the first is from Sol Goldman, who wants me to go after a bad guy FTA; the second is from Cynthia, who has broken up with her boyfriend and wants to commiserate; the third is from Dowty, Pug's ex-partner at SBPD, who's worried about the old man; and the last three are a voice I don't recognize, but he has an Arabic accent and a nasty attitude. He's getting more and more frustrated with each call, wanting to know if I'm in San Luis Obispo yet.

God, I hope I haven't killed my old man with a sin of omission. Of all the times not to have my cell phone with me.

I call Cedric and tell him to haul ass to the dock and give me a ride the few blocks to Mrs. Olsen's, where Iver lives and where I've left the Harley. I pack a few things that will go in my saddle bags, and wear my goodie belt under my black leather jacket. My brand-new S&W Model 625-10 ACP .45 revolver is in a holster at the small of my back, my .38 police special is in my ankle holster, and a small can of mace and a pair of opera-size-small but powerful ten-by-twenty-five Nikon binocs are cradled on my goodie belt. I also grab up my Mosberg twelve-gauge riot gun, which I've made a special sheath for on the rear of the bike, a sheath that looks nothing like a gun scabbard.

While we're on our way there to Mrs. Olsen's, I give Ced explicit instructions about what I want him to do, as I know he won't be able to keep up with me in his old van, even though I know he loves the old man almost as much as I do. In addition to mine, I take his cell phone, and tell him to borrow another one and call me on his when he has a number.

And not to tell anyone else what's transpiring. I fear police or FBI involvement, knowing that these guys want me, and the best way for me to end this quickly, and have any chance of saving Pug, is to offer myself up and take my chances. The FBI would not go along with that approach. Pug is in trouble because of me, and there in my place. This I have to rectify.

I'm on the highway, heading north, the Harley roaring and throbbing between my legs, a pair of headphones on so I can hear the cell phone if it rings.

Normally the drive north along the California coast is one to be savored: along the ocean for thirty miles until you reach historic Gaviota Pass, then through a tunnel into the lush valleys of the Santa Barbara wine country just after you turn off to the quaint Danish village of Solvang, then across rolling oak-covered hills to the verdant and fertile Santa Maria Valley, then the Nipomo Plateau, then along the ocean again after passing through the clustered five cities—Arroyo Grande, Shell Beach, Pismo Beach, Oceano, and Grover Beach, sister cities enjoying ocean views—then inland toward the lovely old mission town and current university city of San Luis Obispo. A drive to be taken leisurely, good restaurants, white sand beaches, sunsets shining across the Pacific.

My tired burning eyes are glued to the pavement, and the broken white lines flicker past at eighty to ninety miles per hour, all the while praying I won't be slowed by some CHP officer who takes unknowing umbrage at my crisis. It would take some time to explain why I'm armed like a SWAT team.

I make it to Pismo before the phone chatters again, and almost wreck myself getting off the highway and getting it answered.

It's Babs. "Can't talk," I say abruptly. "Going to San Luis. An emergency. Please don't call back, I'll call you." I haven't let her say two words before I've hung up and done a wheelie getting back on the freeway.

I'm at the Avila Beach turnoff only a few miles from San Luis Obispo when the ringer blasts my ears again. I slide to a stop on the Avila off-ramp, throwing up gravel, and have it by the fourth or fifth ring.

"I have a very large firearm cocked and pressed to your father's forehead."

"I'm here, I'm here," I say.

"You are in San Luis Obispo?"

"Almost, only a half dozen miles or so. I didn't have my cell—"

"Your carelessness very nearly was the end of your worthless father, which would be my pleasure as he is not a pleasant guest to accommodate."

"He's harmless," I say, but know better. I'm sure he's pressing them to a rabid frothing anger at every opportunity.

"I . . . think . . . not," he says, stressing each word individually.

"Let me talk to him . . . please."

"I think not. Take Highway 1 west, then north from Morro Bay. We are watching you and if you have anyone with you, your father will die, slowly and painfully. Do not pass Cambria Pines without hearing from me. You will be out of cell phone range after that city, and will need final instructions to get to us."

"Then what?"

"Then you die, of course. Or your father dies now and you die later. It is your choice."

"Don't come," I hear the old man shout in the background.

At least he's alive.

I can hear the beep signaling another call before I hang up, and switch over to find Cedric. He gives me another cell number, which I memorize. The prefix is easy, it's the most common cell phone prefix in Santa Barbara, and the rest of the number is 1066, also easy, as I remember it as the year of the Battle of Hastings. Another trick Pug has taught me, association.

He's too young and vital to die, I have to get there and save him, even if I take a bullet.

I make the turn north at Morro Bay and am running along the ocean again, then move slightly inland away from the ocean until Cambria. I know this country well as I used to come up here to hunt. It seems ridiculous but the song "The Phantom of the Opera" keeps running through my head. When I pull up just short of Cambria at the intersection of Highways 1 and 46, I realize why. Cedric's cell phone is in my shirt pocket, and ringing with the first couple of bars of that music. At least I'm not going nuts. I grab it.

"Where the hell you been?" he asks.

"Couldn't hear the serenade. Where are you?"

"Babs came by just after you left and I borrowed her cell phone, but she insisted she come along. We're in San Luis Opispo."

"She hasn't reported this?" I can feel the heat rise in the back of my neck.

"No. Hell no. I made her promise before I agreed to bring her along."

"Okay. I'm waiting for a call from our friends, then I'll call and fill you in. Right now, keep coming to Morro

Bay, then north to Cambria, but if you see me still waiting here at Highway 46, for God's sake ignore me."

There are rolling hills on both sides of the highway, and fog is rolling over those to the west, between my location and the ocean. And it's no low bank, but a couple of thousand feet high. A herd of big charolet or limousine cattle, almost white in color, graze the hillside to the west. It's a pastoral scene that I wish I could enjoy. I hope I'm near where these assholes await, as once this fog reaches the highway it will really slow me down.

Not so patiently I pop my knuckles, sitting on the roadside on the bike, realizing it will be dark in a little over an hour. That could work to my advantage, as could the fog.

A black Ford Mustang has passed me twice while I'm waiting, but the windows are tinted so dark I can't see the occupant. It could be something, or it could be a sightseer. The second time it passes I bring the phone up as if I'm talking, but snap a digital picture with my cell, then wait until the Mustang goes out of sight and note the license number, in case the picture didn't pick it up.

My wait's not long, as my cell phone rings.

"Who were you talking to on your cell phone?" the voice asks. The Mustang was one of them.

"I received a call from someone I do business with. I'll turn it off if you like."

"No, I need to reach you. You know your father will die if you are not alone?"

"You've made that very clear."

"Proceed up Highway 46 4.1 miles and you'll find a dirt road leading north. There are three mailboxes and a sign pointing to the QS Mine. Go exactly 3.7 miles up that road, then pull over and wait."

I dial Cedric using his cell phone, and fill him in, but tell him not to make the turn off Highway 46 until he hears from me. I plan to have them call in the troops, but not until I know I'm where the bad guys are and have a chance to rectify the situation. If they dust me, then maybe someone will bust them. I know it will take the FBI and local law at least an hour to get moving, and that should be plenty of time.

I'll be dead, or the bad guys will.

In just this short time, the fog has crept down the hillside, obliterating my view of the cattle. It's thick, and rolling in fast, but I'll be moving away from it, back inland, and it probably won't be a factor.

I fire up the bike, clear the trip portion of the odometer, and follow the long straight stretch of two-lane highway until it begins to wind up the coast range, and quickly I come upon my turn.

This road is single-car wide and dirt. It winds steeply up the oak-covered mountain, passing three small ranches.

I cleared the odometer again when I stopped to make the turn, and reached into the saddle bags and activated a device I brought from *Aces n' Eights*.

As tired as I am, I hope I'm not missing something, but can't imagine I am as I'm running on pure adrenaline, and I've found it a good substitute for sleep. The road flattens and I pass through an open gate, a two-by-three-foot sign to my right. It's been shot full of holes and has been there for many years, but I can still make out the letters. There's a small creek to the left of the road, coming out of a long gentle canyon behind the mine site. The creek is lined with California sycamores, now almost devoid of leaves, and below the big branches of the mottled sycamores, thick river willows. I'm very close to where I'm supposed to stop, but I slow so I can read. QS MINE, CONSOLIDATED OIL AND MINING CORP. NO TRESPASSING.

I almost idle forward until the odometer hits the mark. Ahead of me, painted gold by the late sun, I can see an old mine site. At a hundred or so yards from my parking spot, a two-story corrugated metal building rests at the base of a mountain that's been surface-mined. A cut is a hundred yards deep into the mountain beyond the building, but the interesting thing is the large metal structure directly behind the building. It has a silolike structure with a walkway that once held a belt delivering ore to its top, and a large trapdoor to expel spent ore at the bottom. Below the trapdoor is a spot where a large dump truck could park to be loaded and haul away the now worthless material. This silo has legs, holding it ten feet above the surface.

Scanning the country around me, looking for any movement, I remember back to a fishing trip Pug and I took when I was very young, maybe twelve. He stopped by the side of a dirt road to take a leak, and explained the old mine site next to which we'd parked. It, too, was a mercury mine, and it, too, had a tall metal structure that Pug explained was a retort, where mercury was literally cooked out of the ore.

He knew how it operated as he'd taken a tour of a mine like it when employees were hoping to bring criminal charges against management because two of their workmates had died from mercury poisoning, as a result of leaks in the containment apparatus. It ended up being a civil suit, and Pug was not involved.

It's still light enough that I can see traces of red mineral in the ugly cut in the mountain side. Cinnabar, a red ore that contains quicksilver—mercury—and is heated in the retort gasifying the mercury, which is cooled and collected in an intricate containment system of piping that flows, in this instance, into the two-story building.

The windows are all knocked out of the building, and the retort itself, three stories high and at least twenty feet in diameter, has been scraped to some extent. The upper sections of the retort have been removed, leaving windowlike voids. I would guess the scrapers found it more trouble than the rusted tank metal was worth, and abandoned the project. Off to one side, four propane tanks rest, each at least twenty thousand gallons. It takes a lot of heat to run a retort.

I scan the scene, then notice only six inches of a vehicle nosing out from behind the metal building, then hear a vehicle running, the low rumble of a powerful engine, and glance over my shoulder. The black Mustang has topped a small rise behind me on the road I entered upon. He stops, and sits quietly, watching, I'm sure with the intent of blocking my escape.

Glancing back, I catch the golden reflection of the sun on either a pair of binocs, or a rifle scope, and don't wait, but dive off the bike into the underbrush at my right just as a shot shatters the silence.

Chapter Twenty-nine

A big slug strikes the left handgrip, blowing the headlight and turn indicator switches into a million pieces, bending the heavy bar, and folding and knocking the bike to the ground. The sound of the shot reverberates through the canyon, causing dust motes and leaves to float eerily down from the sycamores and willows. It was a tremendous roar, which means if it was the Windrunner, they have the flash suppressor and makeshift silencer removed—maybe they blamed it for their lack of success to date. With any luck they think I'm hit and my mangled body has merely been blown down the slope into the thick brush.

I scramble into the creek, and on my belly in the six-inch-deep freezing water, slosh upstream a dozen yards before I kneel, knowing I'm out of sight.

These boys have proved before to be far too anxious. Why they didn't just invite me inside, I don't know. I guess they figured they had me hemmed in, and from what little I know of my tormentor, he wants to do just that, physically and mentally hem and torture and antagonize.

I'm absolutely sure I'll find my old nemesis Mohammad Hashim either behind the rifle or nearby and his brother Jamal at his shoulder, or maybe that's Jamal back in the Mustang? Then again, they could have a third party with them.

I move forward a few more yards, then belly my way under the willows up the hill to my right where I might have a good line of sight at the retort. They certainly have the elevation and angle of fire—as my old marine gunny would say, they're looking so far down your throat they can see your asshole—but I need to know exactly what I'm facing. I'm happy to note that there's a little trickle of water flowing down the steep hillside, joining the creek, and it, too, is lined with willows. I'm able to stay out of sight until I get twenty feet higher, and can see through the thick copse of willow branches.

I loosen the Nikon and focus on the missing panels of rounded metal, forming a makeshift window in the metal wall where the shot originated from. Sure as hell, there's the shadowy profile of a shooter with a big rifle, probably the .50 Windrunner. Beyond him and across the retort, which must still be three-quarters filled with ore, I can see a pair of thick arms extended up, and just the top of Pug's head between them. He's handcuffed to one of the gas lines that circle down the retort, which fuel the burners at intervals all around the walls.

I have only a moment to study the scene, when my cell rings again. Before I answer, I switch it to vibrate so it doesn't give my location away.

Not that it matters, as it's the Arabic voice. "Mr. Shannon, I presume you know who this is?"

"My . . . favorite . . . shrink?" I decide to sound as if I'm hit, near my last breath, as it may give me some advantage.

"I certainly hope I am not your favorite anything. But, yes, it is Mohammad Hashim."

"You . . . carry a . . . grudge, Mohammad."

"You have no idea, Mr. Shannon, and please call me Dr. Hashim."

"Sure. Let my . . . old man go and . . . I'll walk right over to say hello . . . if I can walk."

He laughs. "I think you are faking being wounded and will run over, when you hear his screams. I hate this big rifle. I wished only to wound you so I could enjoy your pain, but again we have missed."

"No, you got . . . lucky . . . I think . . . I'm . . . losing . . . it," I say, and let the phone drop to the ground, so I won't be tempted to answer it again.

I need to buy time, as I'm trying to move back to the streambed and get closer to the retort. While I do, I call Cedric and Babs on Ced's phone. "Ced, have Babs call in the FBI, the marines, the coast guard . . . I'm serious about that one . . . and whoever else she thinks will help. I've activated the EPIRB off the boat, the emergency locator beacon, it's in the bags on the bike, and coast guard choppers can find me ASAP."

"You got it. We're at the turn and will be there in a few minutes."

"Ced, tell the FBI that we've got Jamal here. You said he's wanted in Europe and that may encourage them. But you hold back. Just don't let anyone out of here, in case I don't stop them. I think we're dealing with two vehicles, one a black Mustang, and two or three perps."

"Be careful. Have you found Pug?"

"I know where he is, if I can get to him in time."

I can hear the sounds of an argument emanating from up in the retort. I can imagine that Mohammad is berating his brother, but it's in Arabic and I can't understand a word.

As I begin to work my way around closer to the retort, I hear the sound of the Mustang idling closer, and move to where I can see it roll up and stop next to the Harley.

This guy is dark and swarthy, but looks nothing like Mohammad. So it's the brother up in the retort, and this is a third party. I drop to my belly and scramble back down the creek in the slimy moss-filled water until I'm only ten feet upstream from where the bike rests up on top of the bank. The undergrowth is heavy, and he'd have to be within a few feet to see me.

He, too, has a cell phone, and is talking in Arabic, I presume to the boys high in the retort.

Still talking, he begins to move down the small slope. It's just after sundown, and there are no longer shadows. In fifteen minutes, it'll be dark, but I can't wait. Opportunity knocks.

I hunker up in the willows, trying to make myself invisible, which is easier than normal as I'm wet and plastered with leaves and mud and moss. He is panning the undergrowth with an automatic. I'd like to keep up the ruse of being badly wounded, and don't want to fire a shot, so I wait until he's a half dozen steps from me, wading in the creek, and looking the other way. I slip the mace out of its holster and, with it in one hand and the .45 in the other, spring.

He hears me and turns, panning the weapon as he does, but is not fast enough. I bring the .45 down hard on his gun-hand forearm, at the same time spraying the toxic substance directly into his face. The automatic leaves his hand and plunges deep into the mossy creek, as he stumbles back, but I'm on him and pistol-whip him until he goes down unmoving.

He's face-first in the water, but I don't have time to worry about that, not that I am worrying. I hope the prick drowns.

I run upstream, bent low so I can't be seen from the high position in the retort and reach a spot that I think can't be seen from the opening. Working my way up through the willows, I note that I can't be seen, and run at the spot where I see there's a welded ladder that goes all the way to the top of the tanklike structure.

It's cold as hell, as I'm wet to the bone from the creek, and the fog is beginning to peek over the hillside.

Making it only a couple of rungs up, I see something

that hasn't caught my eye yet. There's a lever that works the hopper door, which is ten feet long and three feet wide. Were it open, the material in the hopper would come out in a hurry. There are piles of spent ore along the road, and some of it's in large pieces, the size of a human head or larger.

I hesitate only a moment, remembering that Pug is handcuffed to a gas line, and wondering if they are all standing on the ore material.

Is this a way to make this end in a hurry?

I'll have to run out where I can be seen from the opening high above in order to work the lever, but it's worth the risk.

I holster the weapon and charge the lever, hitting it hard, but it's rusted and barely moves. In desperation, I hit it again, then look up to see Mohammed staring down, then bringing a handgun over the edge and taking a bead on me.

I shift back and forth, trying to screw up his aim, all the time banging away on the lever, making headway, but only a little at a time. He's no marksman, and his first two shots kick up dust at my feet, but the third one makes fire shoot through my body, and I gasp for breath. My right arm, my strongest, is immobile, and I can't move it, and my chest is suddenly covered with blood. I manage to dive and roll back under the retort, then look up to see material begin to fall from a small opening in the hopper door, ten feet above me.

I scramble out of the way, not wanting to be buried by my own doing. But the material stops, as large pieces are quickly jammed in the small opening.

I feel for the wound, wondering if I'm about to meet my maker, but find it entered in the top of my shoulder, passed under my collarbone, and out my chest. I'm hurt, but I won't die in the next few minutes; it's clean through and through.

Risking trying to work the lever again with one arm useless would be a fool's errand. And the next shot could end it and I'd sure as hell be no good to Pug dead. Desperately, I scan the ground and piles of junk for some way to trip the hopper the rest of the way.

Then it dawns on me, thousands of foot-pounds of energy are resting in the small of my back. I've never shot left-handed, but I have a leg of the retort to steady myself. I cock the S&W and fire, missing the first shot. Five left. Carefully, I aim, and the slug ricochets away from the lever, singing as it flies across the mine area, and the lever gives a couple of inches of the foot I need. Again, and it moves three, the weight of the material above seems to be helping as it gets a bigger and bigger opening.

My fourth shot moves it again, and my fifth, and I can't see the lever for the suddenly cascading rock.

I have to stumble back to keep from being covered as the pile grows. I hear screams and see legs, then a body, which is slammed to the pile of rocks and partially covered.

The rifle falls into the debris, then another man tumbles out. A third one has not fallen, which I hope means Pug is hanging like a side of beef from the gas line. There's so much dust I can't make out who is who, but a man stumbles out of the cloud, coughing and rubbing his eyes with both hands, one of them holding a revolver. I don't recognize him. He must be Mohammad's brother.

"I'm here," I say coldly.

He turns one way, then the other, and finally zeros his vision on me.

He tries to swing the weapon, but the slug from my big .45 slams into his chest, and blood and flesh explode out of his back and disappear into the dust cloud. His arms are flung into the air and the firearm goes flying behind him into the pile.

I know that Mohammad must be the one who was partially buried, so while the dust cloud is settling, I dig my ankle gun out of the hideout holster, having to do so with my left hand. It's clumsy, but I make it.

Carefully I move forward, but caution doesn't seem to be needed as he has what appears to be a half ton of rock on his legs, and he's cut and bleeding on face, neck, and hands, and writhing in pain.

Glancing up through the hopper, I see that Pug, now twenty-five feet above solid ground, is looking a little disgruntled, but has managed to find a foothold on the two-inch perpendicular seam, where the plates are bolted together. It's only a toehold, but the interior ladder is only six feet from him. He's working his way over to the ladder, inches at a time, scooting the cuff chain along.

"Does that hurt?" I ask Mohammed, enjoying the question and knowing the answer.

"May you rot in hell, infidel," he manages.

I kneel down beside him. "You're a persistent prick. What brought on this sudden interest in killing me? Hell, you were home free in the city of nuts. You could have built a hell of a practice."

He's having a hard time talking, but I don't mind. I hope every word hurts like hell. He actually smiles. "I had only . . . a short time . . . to live, Shannon. Cancer is eating . . . my brain. My brother, who . . . I sponsored to . . . enter this country . . . is faithful to his . . . family. He asked me if . . . I had a final wish, . . . a last wish, and . . . that wish was to see my . . . most hated enemy . . . dead. He has been . . . very good at . . . making people dead."

He closes his eyes, and I surmise he doesn't have long. My conversation is interrupted by the old man.

"Jesus, Devlin. Do you think you might climb up here and undo these damn cuffs so I can get up this ladder and out of this rat trap?"

"You are one big complainer," I say, but head for the

outside welded stairway, which means I'll have to climb up the outside, go through an access hole, and down the inside. And it's getting dark. Tight places are not my forte, but I keep single-minded.

It takes me at least twenty minutes to get up, in, and release Pop, then another ten to get up, out, and down.

It's dark by the time the rescue operation is complete. He's bruised and swollen in the face, I'm sure from getting cracked because he wouldn't keep his mouth shut, and his wrists are solid blue and bleeding from hanging like a ham in a butcher shop. But he's still full of sass.

"You got a light?" I ask the old man.

"Oh, sure, those assholes let me keep my Boy Scout flashlight."

"Sorry. I guess not."

"You're hit. Let me work on that" he says, pulling out his shirt and tearing off a shirttail.

"Later. It's only seeping," I say, hoping I'm right and it's not bleeding internally.

I work my way around the rock pile, expecting to stumble on Mohammad's body, but don't find him, then circle it again.

I can see where some of the rocks have been rolled aside.

The son of a bitch is gone.

Chapter Thirty

As I'm searching in disbelief, I hear the *wop-wop-wop* of a helicopter, and conclude that the coast guard has found the locator beacon. A powerful searchlight suddenly penetrates the thickening fog, and the chopper's location, a couple of hundred yards in the air, is clarified. But he's not landing, not in this soup.

In the distance, I see the headlights of a car top the rise to the mine, and suddenly those lights silhouette a man, stumbling along in the road.

"The son of a bitch won't die," I say, then fish my .38 out of my belt and begin to run. Each footfall is a shooting pain through my whole body, as if a hot knife were being plunged again and again into my chest. The old man is limping along behind, not doing much better. We're a pair. . . .

The car, which I presume is Ced and Babs, stops, its lights on the staggering man.

I run fifty yards, then am surprised to hear another car on my right, and slide to a stop, searching the darkness. I'm suddenly flooded in powerful headlights charging down on me, and am about to be a hood ornament. I dive to the side and roll, and a Lincoln SUV roars by, fishtailing—the car behind the building. It bears down on the oncoming vehicle, ignoring the man in the road until it clips him solidly at forty or so miles per hour, flinging his body off to the side. It sideswipes what I can now see in its headlights is Ced's van, and disappears over the rise.

I lie for a long moment, up on one elbow, trying to catch my breath, trying to let the pain dissipate. Then I stagger to my feet and collect myself as the old man limps up.

"That was close," he manages, gasping for breath. It seems his ordeal has taken a lot out of him.

I again run like hell, ignoring the pain, to the man who's been knocked off the road, and am met by Babs and Ced, each carrying a flashlight.

"Jesus," Babs says, "you're hurt." She grabs her phone from Ced and dials 911, looking for an ambulance full of EMTs.

We find the crumpled body of the stocky Arab whom I maced. He's not breathing and has no pulse. Somewhere in the great beyond he's very disappointed to discover there are not seventy-two virgins awaiting, only the seventy-two angry Virginians.

"Damn it," I manage, "Mohammad must be in the Lincoln."

I grab the phone out of her hands as she's trying to give a location to the 911 operator. "Call the coast guard, they'll fill you in," I say, then hit the button hanging it up, and dial information and get the coast guard's number, and it automatically puts me through. I quickly explain that I need to talk to the chopper, lie about being an officer in distress knowing that'll get fast action, and they patch me through.

"There's a dark blue Lincoln SUV proceeding south, and it's our bad guy. Can you follow him?"

"Roger that, but there's an FBI chopper three minutes out. We'll put him on it. He's better equipped. We're setting down on top of the hill to assist you. It's clear on top, about two hundred yards up the hill, if you can make the climb."

I check my watch and see it's be a little more than an hour since I had Babs go to work on getting help.

"Point Mugu. The FBI chopper is from Fresno."

"You must have already been in the air?"

"Nope, but if we're not in the air within five minutes of a call, our ass is grass."

"Give me ten minutes," I say. But it won't take that as Cedric is motioning me into the van. The old man, Babs, and I load up. Ced's van is a beat-up pile of crap but it's four-wheel drive, and in moments we've worked our way between the oaks and are at the top of the hill, where the chopper is idling, its blades turning slowly. It's a good thing they got down when they did, as the fog is overcoming their location. Two helmeted guys in bright orange rescue overalls are standing near the wide sliding door of a Jayhawk rescue chopper. They're a pretty sight at the moment.

I flip the phone to Ced. "You and Babs take the van and get Pug whatever he wants. I'll be in a chopper full of radio gear. Wait at Cambria."

I jump out, and am surprised that Babs is following me and that the old man isn't. He must be out of it, as it's not like him not to be in the middle of the action. Babs catches up with me when I reach the chopper.

"You've got to get some medical help," she commands, having to shout over the jet blast.

"These guys are pros," I yell, and climb into the chopper, followed by the two coast guard guys. Babs climbs in right behind them. I'm barely seated, when one of them is stripping my coat off and using scissors to cut my shirt away.

"Entered from the top?" he observes as he works. "Nine millimeter, or so. I don't think your collarbone is broken, but it may have been nicked."

But I'm more concerned about my fleeing perp. "In a

minute. Can you get the pilot to try and follow the blue Lincoln?"

One of the other guardsmen sticks his head in between the pilot and copilot and taps him on the shoulder, the pilot hits a switch, and they trade comments via some mike and earphone system built into the helmets, and in seconds, as the first one works on my wound, we're airborn.

"He's in touch with the FBI rig. They've got the latest bird, an MH-68A, with infrared, night vision, and thermal gear on board, and think they're on to the Lincoln. He's already back at Cambria and turned north on Highway 1. He's in the fog, and they don't have a visual on him, but they're tracking him. He'd have to go underground to get away from that baby. We'll vector northwest and catch up. We've also got the CHP coming in from the north. We'll get him."

In a few minutes, we've broken out of the fog and can see the FBI chopper ahead of us, now low over the highway, and the lights of a vehicle below, moving fast. We pass over San Simion, and I glance inland and see the lights of historic Hearst Castle. I know that from here on, the highway climbs the mountainside high above the ocean. The Big Sur area hosts one of the most spectacular highways in the world, with magnificent vistas of the rugged Pacific coastline, but no highway on which to try and outrun authority. One miss and it could be a thousand feet before you stop suddenly on the rocks or in churning seawater.

The pilot and the FBI chopper are keeping in touch, and I'm being kept up to speed by the guardsman who bandaged me up.

"We're going to shoot on ahead of him, and try to come back in his face with our spotlights. That's worked before to encourage drug runners to give up."

"How fast are we?" I ask.

"We're 120 knots or so . . . maybe 135 miles per hour, but the FBI Shark is 140 knots. He's not getting away. The FBI reports that he's weaving badly, even on the straightaways. The dumb bastard has turned his headlights off, thinking that's going to help."

"He's hurt. Had a bad fall," I say, without explaining.

We shoot ahead until the pilot locates a straightaway. He lines up, drops low, with the mountain side too damn close on our left, and directs powerful multimillion-candlepower spots at a ten-degree down angle. We close on the oncoming Lincoln SUV. I'm on my feet between the pilot and copilot, and can clearly see Hashim shade his eyes as we close on him, but he doesn't slow at all. He is weaving.

This can't last long, him without lights, trying to negotiate a dangerous curving road by moonlight.

The guardsman taps me on the shoulder and I lean close. "The LT knows this coastline well and says there's a high bridge ahead, Bixby Bridge. He wants to drop low, then come up in his face as he nears."

"Whatever works," I say.

We shoot ahead. I, too, know the Big Sur coastline, and there're five bridges. The Bixby is almost twenty five stories above Russian Cove, a beautiful rocky cove with crashing surf.

And that's the spot the LT, the pilot of the chopper, has chosen to try and convince Hashim to give it up.

The pilot drops low in the canyon below the bridge, but not so low he can't be seen from the approaching road. I can see he's going to try and time it so he's up at road level and hits Hashim in the eyes with the powerful lights just as he reaches the bridge.

He's patient, then I realize maybe too patient. He flares upward and I can see he's going to be late, maybe fifty feet in elevation short.

Hashim and the big Lincoln are bearing down fast, and

we're climbing fast. He's onto the bridge before we're up where we can hit him with the lights, when we're all shocked by Hashim wrenching the wheel to the left, and crashing through the bridge guardrail.

The crazy shrink is trying to launch the Lincoln out into the air to bring us down.

"Jesus," I hear the guardsman yell, and see his eyes go wide. I'm flung to the side, smashing into the sliding door of the chopper as he makes a violent maneuver to avoid the plummeting SUV.

He swings out to sea and we can see the car arcing out and down, and down, and down, until it crashes on the rocks far below, and a ball of flame roars upward.

"No trial," Babs yells in my ear.

I smile. "Jesus, the old boy gave it a hell of a last try."

"Let's go home," she says, wrapping an arm around me.

But it's not to be, not for a while, as the chopper finds a small stretch of beach that it can set down on, and the FBI chopper follows suit. The two guardsmen in the orange jumpsuits and an FBI agent make their way to the charred remains of the Lincoln, having to wade a small canyon bottom creek to get there.

I'm beat up, and wait in the chopper, my head in Babs's lap. Another agent, his white shirt and tie showing beneath his green jumpsuit, comes over and interviews us. With a beautiful moon shining over the Pacific, and my head in the lap of a gorgeous woman, I don't mind. Particularly when he mentions that there's a large reward posted by some European family for the capture dead or alive of Jamal Hashim, a.k.a. a half dozen other names.

Now, that makes me smile.

It's noon, post medical exam, X-ray, and a very painful through-and-through swabbing with some heinous device covered with antibiotic, before we're back aboard *Aces n' Eights*, and I'm, hurt, wounded, and dead tired. I feel like

I might be able to sleep a week. If I can sleep at all, as they've got my arm in a sling, even though they found the bone intact . . . maybe a tiny chip, but no break.

Ced drops Babs and me off at the dock, but double-parks near the yacht club and escorts us most the way to make sure I get safely to the boat, then Babs follows me in and tucks me in my queen-size bunk.

"You got to work?" I ask her.

"I know what you're thinking, and don't even think about it, buddy. You're beat to hell and haven't slept in far too long."

I laugh quietly. "Yeah, but I could use the company."

"Futa's ready to cuddle up."

"How about Futa on one side and you on the other?"

She sighs deeply, then relents. "Okay, but no funny stuff."

"Maybe in a week, when I wake up."

There's something truly exotic about watching a woman who knows how to undress, do so. I fear I've lied through my teeth, or teet, as they'd say in Jamaica. I'm happy to note that the obeah woman is an abject failure at spell casting, as it's up and angry and roaring to be sheathed and relieved by the time Babs, naked as God made her lovely body, crawls in beside me.

"What a liar you are," she says, but she's laughing.

"Not on purpose. The big head can't always speak for the little head."

As I'm a poor wounded soul, with my arm in a sling, she straddles me, and I let myself enjoy the ultimate pampering. I'll pay her back, in spades, when I'm myself again.

I sleep until noon, and awake to the smell of bacon frying.

That's the good news. She waits until I finish a beautiful omlette, bacon, and homemade biscuits, before she tells me the bad.

"They found what's left of Slider. Phil Dunbury. The sharks had a go at him before he drifted up on the rocks on the windward side of Anacapa."

"And June?"

I can see a tear begin to form in her dark, pretty eye. "Not found yet." Then she tries to sound encouraged. "There's still nothing to really tie them together . . . except at the Harbor Restaurant, and that doesn't really mean anything. The eyewitnesses are weak, as usual, saying they saw Slider with an older blond woman . . . not able to make a positive ID of June. And there's nothing to tie Slider to Mason, but I know he's the bad guy here, no matter how faithful you are to your friends."

"So, do they think Slider got hit by a shark when he fell while sail-surfing?"

"The sharks didn't get so much of Slider that they couldn't identify the cause of death . . . a nice .357 slug almost passed through his chest, but a fragment was nestled in the sixth vertebra, found when his upper torso was X-rayed."

I'm in my shorts but now decide it's time to get dressed.

"Something's been bothering me since before I left for Jamaica. How about taking a ride down the coast?"

Chapter Thirty-one

Mr. M. Harden Brown is still in front of the TV, still plugged into the oxygen, only he's watching golf this Sunday morning.

After he inquires about my sling, and I tell a fib about falling on the boat, he continues chattering as well as possible, gasping every other word, motioning at the television. "I used to be . . . a hell of a golfer," he says, obviously lonely and wanting to make conversation, but I'm sore as hell, eager as hell to make this end, and in no mood.

"I'll bet you were. You know, you mentioned that you put all of Slider's stuff in a ministorage. Would you mind if we took a look?"

He eyes me carefully. I've introduced Babs to him as a detective, so he's a little more comfortable. But not quite comfortable enough.

"I think that . . . should come . . . from Slider."

"Sorry to tell you this, Mr. Brown, but Slider was found dead on Anacapa Island."

"Oh no. Did he . . . fall from that . . . damn kite thing?"

"We're trying to find out just what happened. You can read about it in the papers the next couple of days."

"So I guess . . . you can't get . . . permission . . . from Phil." He cogitates a moment. "Yeah, I guess . . . you can . . . have it." He manages to work his way to an entry table near the front door and pulls open a small drawer. It's littered with keys.

He fumbles through them, then holds out a key and a plastic card. "The card's for . . . the gate, and the . . . key's to the lock . . . on the unit. It's B-60. My stuff . . . is in the back . . . and on the east wall. . . . Phil's stuff is . . . in about a five . . . five-foot square . . . in boxes up against . . . the door. You can't . . . miss it. Bring back . . . my key."

"Yes, sir."

He describes the way to the ministorage, and we're out of there.

In fifteen minutes I'm sliding up the door to a ten-by-twenty-foot ministorage unit. Like all storage rooms, the stuff is covered with dust. Mr. Brown's stuff is stacked to the ceiling in the rear and to one side. But a separate pile is just where he described. We each take a box at a time and dig in. I'm thinking I might find some pictures of Slider and June together, something that would tie her and him. And who knows what else might turn up?

The old man has packed everything in Slider's apartment, including the canned goods. I'm surprised I don't turn up a loaf of bread and maybe a dozen eggs out of the fridge.

It's not with the food, but rather in a box of pictures packed with washcloths and towels, that a small white box catches my eye.

"What's this?" I say, picking it up, knowing full well what it is.

"I didn't feed you enough this morning?" Babs asks.

I'm opening the box of See's chocolates, just to make sure that's what it contains; and as one might surmise, it contains chocolates, if only half of them remaining . . . when something I see rings my chimes.

"Babs, how good are your fingerprint people?"

"Damn good, why?"

I carefully dig out two of the little paper containers, each of them holding the remnants of half a chocolate.

Turning one over in my hand, I study the sides and back. "I think there's a print here."

"So? People pick candy up when they eat it."

"But most are polite enough to eat the one they grab. How many people do you know who take a bite out of one to see if they like the filling, then put it back in the box if they don't like it? And you know you just might remove a glove, if you were wearing one, as it would be hard to pluck a chocolate out of the box with a glove on."

"No one I know would do a thing like that; I'd kick their butt if they did that to my box of truffles."

I laugh. "Well, these aren't truffles, thank God, they're hard-sided chocolates . . . at least relatively hard, but soft enough to hold an impression." I hold one up in the light so she can see its bottom, where there's the perfect impression of a fingerprint.

"That looks like a print." I have mixed emotions, as I want to solve this thing, but hate to do so if it proves Mason is the culprit.

"It is a print. And the insides of these half-eaten ones are white."

"And that's a surprise?"

"Nope. But it is a clue, and potentially a hell of a good one."

"A clue?"

"So, Sherlock, do you know who bites candy in half and puts it back?"

"Is this twenty questions?"

"Okay, twenty questions . . . guess who hates coconut?"

"You're a coconut, or maybe a plain nut."

I hate to say it, but I do. "Mason Fredrich, that's who."

"You don't suppose . . ." Now she takes a closer, far

more serious look. "Let's take them in. I'll see what the lab can do."

"And Mason claimed he didn't know Slider, but if his prints are on this box or the candy, he at least knew of him and was in his apartment."

"Or June brought him the candy from home, and Mason's print was already on it?"

"Maybe . . . you sound like a defense attorney . . . but at least it ties one or the other of them to Slider."

"True."

When we return the key to Mr. Brown, I ask him if he knows anything about the box of See's, and he tells me he gave it to Slider, as someone gave it to him and he hates chocolate.

So, Mason was in Slider's apartment, maybe looking for June, maybe wanting to do harm to her boyfriend?

All the way home I'm pensive, and don't say a word. When we roll into Montecito, she finally asks, "You feeling bad?"

"No. I feel fine physically, I feel bad as hell thinking that Mason might actually have done something to June. And I've been thinking about Anacapa. You think you can find out exactly *where* Slider was found?"

"As you well know, it's not my case, but I'm sure that's easy enough."

"Then do so, please."

"You gonna go play detective again?"

"Hey, your guys dug through Slider's stuff while it was still in his apartment. Did they find the suspicious half-eaten coconut-filled clue?"

"So, what do you think you're gonna find out there, besides sharks and seals and whales?"

"Nothing. I just want to take a cruise. Hey, you wanna go out there tomorrow?" If you really don't want a woman to go along, the best thing to do is invite her enthusiastically.

"I'm behind on my caseload, and tomorrow's a workday."

I almost say *shucks,* but that would be a little obvious. I'm sure I don't want her on this mission, just in case . . .

But I do talk her into spending one more night on board *Aces n' Eights*. I'm wounded, you know, and need constant attentive care.

She agrees, but only after she takes the suspicious Sees to the lab, and goes by her place to pick up some things, including what she's wearing to work tomorrow.

She's off to work, after I feed her on paper plates at the little stand near Brophy's as I can't cook with one arm and as she cooked last, and besides, she says she's not a breakfast person. Her English muffin and coffee confirm the fact.

As we agreed earlier on the phone, Pug and Cedric show up shortly afterward, and we're off to take a tour of the north of Anacapa. We're halfway across the channel, when my cell phone buzzes. It's Babs.

"You miss me already?" I ask.

"Thought you'd want to know. We got a seven-point match off one print, and five points off the other, and three of them were different points, so that's a ten altogether. There's no question, the print is Mason's."

"I wish I could say I was happy," I manage.

"I am," she says. "Now the prick can fry, or at least spend the rest of his life in the shit house."

She doesn't usually use that kind of language, but it seems appropriate at the moment. If Babs knew what I was really up to she would have raised all kinds of hell with me and would never have believed me again that I needed comfort and tender loving care.

I'm going skin-diving and spelunking, and not looking forward to it. And now I'm doing it with a vengeance, thanks to the fact we've put Mason on to Slider, the fox in the proverbial henhouse.

When I was a kid, the Channel Islands were owned by a combination of private and government entities. There was some cattle ranching, and the navy had a small installation on one of them, and outside the base—a communications affair—was the only place where fishing was limited. Now the five islands—San Miguel, Santa Rosa, Santa Cruz, Anacapa, and Santa Barbara—that make up the small chain are all part of Channel Island National Park. And a good portion of the offshore surrounding them is a marine preserve. We no longer frequent the islands, and in many ways, I'm glad they're protected.

Santa Barbara Island is far to the south of the rest of them, and of the four close together, Anacapa is the smallest and most easterly. It's actually three small rocky volcanic islets—East, Middle, and West Anacapa—of vertical balsamic cliffs that have taken more than their share of shipwrecks over the last couple of centuries, as they're relatively low to the water and hard to see, particularly in the fog. Peppered with wind- and water-carved and earthquake-fractured caves—135 of them large enough to be named—they're scenic and spectacular. The windward side, facing the channel, although facing almost due north, is lashed with heavy surf in these fall and winter months and the wind and water has sculpted some interesting formations. And I suspect it's rough enough that things will be a little on the topsy-turvy side today.

Pug, against his better judgment, has agreed to take us out on the *Copper Glee*, as she has equipment to refill tanks and is built for this sort of thing. He only did so after I threatened to take *Aces n' Eights*, and he knows that *Copper Glee* is far better suited, with four anchors with a hundred feet of chain and four hundred feet of heavy rope on each, to safely set up near the surf. She's a dive boat, and that's s.o.p. for her.

The good news is the fog is kind to us and the sun

shines and dances off the water, which is occasionally broken by porpoises or a seal or a flying fish. We see a whale blow in the distance, probably either a late blue or humpback, or an early gray.

As I suspected, it's rough as hell on the windward side. We idle along, Ced and I using Pop's powerful binoculars to search every foot of the shoreline, and the more shallow caves, little more than indentations, looking for anything out of order. That consumes two hours, and with the time it took to get here, it's late morning. Pug picks a spot two hundred yards from shore to anchor *Copper Glee*, while I shed the sling, and Cedric and I suit up in wet suits. I learn quickly that I can't use the tanks, as the harness falls directly over the wound, and the pain would probably knock me out. But I don't have to, where I'm going. Most of what I'm up to can be done wading and one-armed, and I've got Cedric suited and tanked up and the old man running the rubber boat, so my part of the deal is mostly eyes and suspicions. Without the weight of the tanks or a weight belt, the wet suit acts somewhat as a flotation device, but the old man makes me wear an inflatable vest nonetheless in case I get in trouble. With the pull of a small chain, I'll blow up like a puffer fish.

I plan to search the whole north shore of the Anacapas, if it takes days, which it shouldn't if we get lucky, including taking a hard look inside the deeper caves. We can cover some of the shoreline afoot, but most of it will have to be investigated from afloat on the Avon, merely getting as close as possible.

We'll be inspecting such colorful caves as Impalement, Cave, Crack of Doom, Sucking Slot, and Club Foot. With names like that, you just know this is going to be a real pleasure. In addition to our other equipment, we're all wearing helmets, as a surge can crash you into the low roof or jagged hanging formation of a cave in a heartbeat.

The caves range from only a few feet deep, to nearly a

thousand feet with branches and offshoots. And I hate enclosed places—actually hate is not the word, even fear and despise don't touch it. I go catatonic if I think about it, which I don't let myself.

But I'm driven to do this, as I know no one else would. Eyewitnesses saw Slider with a blond woman, an older blond woman, and his body—what there was left of it—and shredded parasail was found here. Mason's boat, the *June Moon*, was seen near here. And even though it could have been any of a million or so California blond women, that all speaks reams to me, under the circumstance. June Fredrich's blood was found in the *June Moon*, although that also could be easily explained away. And, of course, her car was found parked in the marina's public parking.

The fact is, it's overwhelming, presuming there's a body of flesh and blood to go with the body of evidence.

And last, but certainly not least, Mason told me the sidearm he "used to own" was a .357, and it was a .357 bullet recovered from Slider's chewed and shredded remains. It seems everyone who uses a firearm in the commission of a crime claims to have had it stolen "years ago." I had Babs call and have a friend check the SBPD records, and was not surprised when we discovered that Mason has never reported a stolen weapon of any kind. I truly hope I'm wrong about all this, and very well could be.

But I need to satisfy myself that I've done all I could do. Mason asked me to help him prove his innocence, and so far I'm proving his guilt. I want to do one or the other, and do it soon as it's been preying on me.

Most of the backside of the Anacapas is steep rocky face with little vegetation, ideal rookeries for gulls and terns, interspersed with the occasional rocky beach, usually where there's a fissure in the face of the low escarpment. We begin at the east end of East Island, below Anacapa's historic lighthouse, as that's where

Slider and the blonde were last seen, and near where the *June Moon* was spotted. Some of the caves are walkable, some we have to use the Avon in, but it's difficult and dangerous in the surge. We could have picked a better season, had this time not picked us.

We're carrying two powerful torches off the *Copper Glee*, and occasionally we have to use them, and for sure will have to use them soon, as the next two caves, Starfish and Cathedral, are very deep, very dark, and not for the timid. I'm doing my very, very best to remain calm and not let the continual claustro-fucking-phobia overwhelm me. My mouth is dry and my stomach knotted, but I'm ignoring it. I've found if I give the task at hand utter concentration, it helps. It also helps that I stay connected to the Avon, wherever we leave it, with Pug as commander and chief as he's still sore and beat up from his run in with the Moslem hoards. The Avon has an eight-horse outboard that is sufficient in most instances, but he still has occasion to have to use the oars, and has picked a tough job. At Pug's insistence, I have a one-eighth-inch nylon line, a spool of a thousand feet, tied to my waist and feeding out from the Avon. Ced and I are dropping crumbs, in a sense.

Starfish cave is over four-hundred-plus feet deep with three entrances, and harbors a huge tide pool. I was in it one summer many years ago, as an explorative youth, as I was in most the caves on the islands, and remember it as a deep dark, if interesting, monster, with bottomless pools fed by very high tides. The search of Starfish, as did East of West, Dinky, Big Cobble, proves fruitless.

Cathedral Cave, just to keep things confusing, has five entrances. All but two of them are submerged except at low tide. Just to keep one on one's toes, submerged rocks, almost impossible to see unless the torch is on the spot, appear from the cave floor as the surge recedes. The interior of the cave is a large L-shaped chamber, with cobblestone beaches. The whole structure is within a couple of protrusions, or points, that reach out from the mainland, and one of the points is completely broached by a cave, forming what's known as Cathedral Arch.

At one point, halfway back in one of the deepest sections of the cave, light filters down from above. The good news is it's fifty feet or more wide for a good part of the way. To make things as eerie as possible, light from subtidal cave entrances allow light to filter into the tide pools from below. God's swimming pool lighting . . . or the devil's.

We take the Avon in about forty yards until we're grounded on a gravel and cobblestone bar, and Cedric and I have to unload.

"I think we have to swim about twenty yards," Cedric cautions, "through one of the pools. You can wait and I'll go on back to the back and check it out."

"I'm okay. This suit is warm enough but cold enough that the pain seems to be dissipated. It'll probably hurt like hell when I do warm up."

Cedric leads the way, panning the beam from one cave wall to the other. A horrid odor takes the place of the fresh clean sea air, and the unspoken fears of both of us are placated when we come upon a dead sea lion on a rock ledge. The wind is singing in from the mouth of the cave, and turns upward through the vent, or blowhole, so most of the odor is dissipated by the time we're a hundred feet past the rotting carcass.

We cross a bar of clean white sand and come to the pool.

"You want to wait?" Ced asks.

"Hell no. Let's get this done. We've got most of a mile of coastline and another hundred or so caves. We could be here a month at this rate."

It's a good thing the torch is watertight, as I can't hold it up out of the water and stroke at the same time. Pop has tied it to my belt with a lanyard, so I just let it hang as I kick and paddle with one arm, across the pool. Cedric lights the way in front of me.

It's so dark there's little sensation of being closed in. I keep telling myself it's just like walking outside on a dark night, which doesn't bother me, and concentrate on moving forward.

But the fact is, I have the continual urge to break and run, or swim, for the outside.

We pass a small offshoot branch, but are able to search it fifty or sixty feet to its termination with the torches, and don't bother doing so by foot.

Our footing now is round pebbles, easy to walk on, then it becomes a small stretch of white sand. I can see the next hundred feet or so with the torch, and am tired and sore and about to suggest that we turn around, when my torch catches a reflection on a ledge near the end of the cave.

It's almost a pleasant spot, high ceiling and clean walls, with white sand and a couple of boulders that would make fine seats if you wanted to come into the bowel of hell for a barbecue. Not my idea of fun, but it might have been when I was an adventurous youth.

"Did you see that?" I ask Ced.

"What?" he asks. His beam had been focused on the opposite wall.

"Something shiny, more than a wet-rock reflection." I again find the spot with the beam, and it's definitely something metal.

We move forward, with easy walking on the packed sand. The ledge is six feet off the cave floor, and almost table flat.

Ced gets there first, and stops dead still, up on his tiptoes, sweeping his light back and forth in the indentation.

He turns to me as I near. "As God is my witness, you're not going to believe this."

I get close and step up on one of the seatlike boulders so I will have a clear view of the ledge, then when I've got solid footing, swing the light over.

Candles line the outside edge of the ledge, and again are in a well-spaced line behind the body that rests there. Her head is propped up on a pillow and her face covered with a fine lace that's been weighted down with rounded stones, I presume so the crabs can't get to her. Her body's covered with a comforter that's stuffed into a counterpane that looks to be fine Irish lace, and it too is weighted down with a solid line of round stones.

Her blond hair is splayed out behind her, and her look peaceful. The metal reflection comes from some of the shiny metal parts of the clarinet that rests on its stand. The stand that I saw in Mason's house, long after she was reported missing.

That means he's come back here, I guess to visit this deep hellish shrine he's built, appropriately enough, in Cathedral Cave.

There's no apparent cause of death, but I'd bet my safety line that she has a nice, round .357 hole in her chest. I won't bother to look, as I'd hate to have to, and the crime scene investigation boys and girls would much prefer I didn't.

A few of her favorite things, including pictures of her and Mason and relatives, line the rock shelf behind her. I cannot help but note that a picture of Babs is not among them.

It's cold in the cave, a constant temperature that is very near sea temp, so it's never a degree or two above sixty out here, and this time of year can drop to the high forties. Except for the fact her cheeks are sunken and her eyes seem to be recessed, she's remarkably well preserved. It's been months since she went missing.

In a low respectful voice, Cedric asks, "You think he

killed the sea lion and left it rotting there in order to discourage visitors?"

"I wouldn't doubt it. At the moment, I would believe anything about the crazy bastard. Let's get the hell out of here, this place is closing in on me like a mausoleum."

It's not a bad description of what I've seen, and it doesn't take me nearly as long to get out of the cave as it did to get in.

We radio the coast guard and the park service so one of them might get a boat here quickly, and so we don't have to wait longer than absolutely necessary, and one of the two armed rangers assigned to the park arrives in less than a half hour.

When we get back to the harbor, I borrow the old man's pickup and go straight to the police station, where Babs is working at her desk.

She looks up as I enter her squad room, and I can see she's already heard. I take a seat across the desk from her, even though she doesn't suggest it.

"Hi," she finally says, and I can see she's trying not to cry.

"What can I do?" I ask.

"Nothing. I'll be okay, in a year or two. They picked up Mason a few minutes ago. I guess he's crazy to the nth degree. He began blabbering as soon as they told him she'd been found, and was more worried about them bringing in her stuff than he was about his future."

"You want to come over for dinner when you get off?"

"I've got arrangements to make, and family coming in. Besides, you're a damn poor judge of character, which doesn't say much for your seeming to like me. Hell, you'd like John Wayne Gacy."

"I doubt it, but I can't deny being a poor judge in this instance. It appears Mason was so crazy he could even fool his old friends, not that I'm proud of being one."

"I'll pass on dinner." She cuts her eyes down at her paperwork. "And on seeing you for a while. I've got to forget that you were an old friend of that bastard before we try it again."

"Then I hope you've got a short memory," I say, but don't get the glimmer of a smile or her glance.

I rise and head for the door, but stop and turn back. "Remember, anything I can do, just give me a call."

She nods, and I make the door before she yells after me, "Dev!"

I turn back.

"Hey, thanks for finding her. That couldn't have been easy."

"I've had worse times, but I can't remember when."

"And buy Pug and Cedric a drink for me, will you?"

"I think I'll wait until you decide to come back around and can do it yourself."

She waves and lowers her face to the pile of paperwork on her desk. I stand in the doorway for a minute, hoping she'll look up and say, yes, she's coming over for dinner, but she doesn't.

When I get back to the marina, Ced is gone but Pug is awaiting me. He climbs off the *Copper Glee* and meets me on the dock.

"I'll buy you a drink," he says.

"I feel like I've been hit by a train, Pop, and I look like hell. Let's not."

"Tomorrow's another day," he says, a sad smile crossing his face.

"Yep, thank God."

When I get to the boat, I listen to my machine. The first message is from Iver, who has hired two good hands, is through the canal, and is heading upstream at a steady twelve knots. He knows to moor the boat out at the islands, just south of the U.S.-Mexican border in Mexican waters, while I make sure Mr. Darwin Winston-Gray has the money in an escrow account, an independent escrow holder who'll hand the dough over when the boat enters the Santa Barbara Channel. I don't trust the prick, and he doesn't get the boat until I'm sure of getting the money.

The second call is from my old buddy Dr. Antonio Scanoletti, who has heard I'm back in town, and tells me through what sounds like clenched teeth that he's anxious to meet with me and hand me a check for nine thousand dollars.

That'll pay a little rent, and makes me smile.

The third call makes me smile even more. "Hey, mon, it's Bobbi. I be tryin' to reach that lovely Iver, but I guess he still be at sea. Tell him I got de ticket he sent, and will be der at de Christmastime." What a kick, maybe old Iver's prostate is working better than I thought. Whatever he's doing, it's working better than whatever I'm doing. It appears I'm back to sleeping alone.

The fourth call is from my old buddy Sol Goldman, the Santa Monica bail bondsman, and my friend and best client. He's got a very large one for me, and even knows where the guy is hiding, so just about the time I think I'm fresh out of work, I'm back in business. The good news he's hiding on the headwaters of the beautiful Suwannee River, like the song. The bad news is the song doesn't mention that the headwaters are in the snake-and-gator-infested Okifeenoki Swamp in Georgia, nor that this guy is a former Green Beret who was born and raised in Waycross, Georgia, and knows the swamp like he knows fifty ways to kill a man with his bare hands, so it will be no lark. But it's a job.

The last of the five calls is the kicker. It's from FBI agent O'Mally, who also sounds as if he's talking while grinding his choppers. He speaks in a monotone. "Shannon, I'm instructed to inform you that you need to file a claim at our office for a hundred-thousand-dollar reward offered by the Von Stratten family of Bad Homberg, Germany. It seems their son was killed a few years ago in the bombing of a beer garden near Ramstein, the home of the 435th Air Base Wing. . . a U.S. Air Force base. A bombing meant for U.S. airmen that has been credited to one Jamal Hashim, a.k.a. Jamal Mahmoud, whose body was found under a pile of rocks near Cambria. A pile that we understand was of your making. If you get time, drop down. It's like you to fall in a pile of crap and come up smelling like a rose. I've got some paperwork for you."

I laugh. I'll believe it when I see it, as I've found these rewards usually are fleeting when the party who is wanted dead or alive is actually dead. Motivation to pay seems to float away with the soul of the bad guy, when the crying need for vengeance is fulfilled. But I guarantee I'll find time to fill out the paperwork. Sounds too good to be true, which means it probably is.

As I stand at the chart table listening to my calls, Futa gives me a purring ankle rub.

Somebody loves me, without equivocation.

More Books From Your Favorite Thriller Authors

Necessary Evil by David Dun	0-7860-1398-2	$6.99US/$8.99CAN
The Hanged Man by T.J. MacGregor	0-7860-0646-3	$5.99US/$7.50CAN
The Seventh Sense by T.J. MacGregor	0-7860-1083-5	$6.99US/$8.99CAN
Vanished by T.J. MacGregor	0-7860-1162-9	$6.99US/$8.99CAN
The Other Extreme by T.J. MacGregor	0-7860-1322-2	$6.99US/$8.99CAN
Dark of the Moon by P.J. Parrish	0-7860-1054-1	$6.99US/$8.99CAN
Dead of Winter by P.J. Parrish	0-7860-1189-0	$6.99US/$8.99CAN
All the Way Home by Wendy Corsi Staub	0-7860-1092-4	$6.99US/$8.99CAN
Fade to Black by Wendy Corsi Staub	0-7860-1488-1	$6.99US/$9.99CAN
The Last to Know by Wendy Corsi Staub	0-7860-1196-3	$6.99US/$8.99CAN

Available Wherever Books Are Sold!

Visit our website at **www.kensingtonbooks.com**

More Thrilling Suspense From Your Favorite Thriller Authors

If Angels Fall　　　　0-7860-1061-4　　　　$6.99US/$8.99CAN
by Rick Mofina

Cold Fear　　　　　　0-7860-1266-8　　　　$6.99US/$8.99CAN
by Rick Mofina

Blood of Others　　　　0-7860-1267-6　　　　$6.99US/$9.99CAN
by Rick Mofina

No Way Back　　　　　0-7860-1525-X　　　　$6.99US/$9.99CAN
by Rick Mofina

Dark of the Moon　　　0-7860-1054-1　　　　$6.99US/$8.99CAN
by P.J. Parrish

Dead of Winter　　　　0-7860-1189-0　　　　$6.99US/$8.99CAN
by P.J. Parrish

Paint It Black　　　　　0-7860-1419-9　　　　$6.99US/$9.99CAN
by P.J. Parrish

Thick Than Water　　　0-7860-1420-2　　　　$6.99US/$9.99CAN
by P.J. Parrish

Available Wherever Books Are Sold!

Visit our website at **www.kensingtonbooks.com**